"I'm sorry I dumped oatmeal all over you," Charley said, "but it's dangerous to make me angry. Besides, if all I've got to fear as reprisal is hearing a lot of silly Shakespeare spouted at me—"

"Don't count on that." Sir Antony waited until she looked at him before he added, "Use your head, angel. Think what more you risk if you infuriate me."

"What would you do?"

"Whatever I please," he said.

"I doubt that you would beat me," she said. "It is not in your nature to hurt someone smaller than yourself."

"You know nothing about my nature," he said. Slipping an arm around her shoulders, he tilted her face up with the other hand and kissed her, hard.

Never had a man dared to take such a liberty with her, but she felt her lips soften against his before she stiffened in outrage. Her hand flew up to strike him.

"Don't," he warned, stopping her with the single word. "You do not know what the consequences will be."

"We have a bargain!"

"Make no mistake," he said sternly enough to send shivers up her spine. "I'll do what I must to secure Wellington's safety, and yours. And before you decide that running back to Alfred looks better than staying here, let me point out one fact you have overlooked."

"What fact?" Between fury that he had dared speak to her so, and fear that he meant every word, her tongue seemed to have tied itself in knots.

"Just this," he said, grasping her chin again and forcing her to meet his gaze. "If you run away, and if my claim to the St. Merryn estates should prevail, it won't be Cousin Alfred upon whom you depend for your bed and board. It will be me."

Everybody loves Amanda Scott!

"Amanda Scott writes an exciting Regency romance filled with two great lead characters, a tremendous support cast, and a brilliant story line."
—Harriet Klausner on *Dangerous Angels*

"Amanda Scott is a master!"
—Mary Jayne Farpella for *Affaire de Coeur*

"Amanda Scott captures the Regency with a sharp pen and her dry wit, portraying the glamorous appeal and the sorrow of the era to a tee. Readers will be enchanted."
—*Rendezvous*

"A most gifted storyteller!"
—Joan Hammond

"Amanda Scott has earned her place among the select few."
—*I'll Take Romance*

DANGEROUS
ANGELS

Amanda Scott

Pinnacle Books
Kensington Publishing Corp.

http://www.pinnaclebooks.com

PINNACLE BOOKS are published by

Kensington Publishing Corp.
850 Third Avenue
New York, NY 10022

Pinnacle and the P logo Reg. U.S. Pat. & TM Off.

First Printing: January, 1997

Printed in the United States of America
10 9 8 7 6 5 4 3 2 1

To Denise Little

With gratitude, memories of pictures on goblets,

and a great deal of affection

Prologue

London, March 31, 1829

"Fox Cub? Thank God you're here! There is no time to lose."

The tall dark-haired gentleman standing on the single step outside Number Ten Downing Street smiled at the fair-haired man who had opened the door, and with a slight inclination of his head, replied, *"Le Renardeau, il est tout à vous, mon ami."*

"Good God, Tony, don't tell me you've forgotten your English!"

His light blue eyes glinting sardonically, Antony St. John Foxearth said, "Would it be surprising if I had, Harry? Must be ten years since I last set foot in England, and nearly as long since I clapped eyes on you." He glanced back toward Whitehall and the narrow entrance to the cul-de-sac that was Downing Street, then added gently, "I do understand your desire to prevent the scaff and raff from encroaching upon His Grace, but do you mean to keep me standing long on the doorstep? It's damned cold out here."

Stepping back, Harry Livingston said with a shake of his head, "You haven't changed a whit, Tony. Come in. He's waiting for you in his office." He put out his hand, and Antony gripped it firmly.

"It's good to see you, Harry. Have you, too, been cast off by your family, that you must needs play porter now for Wellington?"

Livingston grimaced. "More secretary than porter, but no. My father's got better sense than yours ever did, if you'll forgive me for saying so."

"Willingly. What's amiss now, Harry?"

"He wants to tell you himself. I'm playing porter this afternoon because he's cleared the house in order to meet with you alone. A damned foolish thing to do under the circumstances, but I daresay he knows what he's about. He generally does. He doesn't want your presence here widely known, you see."

"Was he worried that I'd take a stroll through Brooks's before coming here?"

Livingston flushed. "No, he wasn't, damn your eyes, and if you take that tone with him, Tony, you'll soon wish you hadn't. *He* hasn't changed."

Antony made a graceful little bow. "Lead on, Macduff."

Eyeing him suspiciously, Harry said, "That's Shakespeare."

"Just wanted to show you I haven't forgotten my English, dear fellow."

"Damn it, Tony, at school you used to start spouting Shakespeare whenever someone annoyed you. What the devil have I done—?"

"You are keeping me waiting, Harry."

"*I* am?" Indignantly, Livingston paused with his mouth open, then snapped it shut again and turned, muttering, "It's this way, damn you." Leading the way from the entrance hall upstairs, Harry said, "Very grand, ain't it? Soane, the architect, spent three years refurbishing this place before the Duke took office. He's only staying here till they've finished doing the same at Apsley House." Approaching a carved walnut door, he reached for the latch.

"Why you, Harry? As porter, I mean."

Pausing with his hand on the latch, Livingston looked over his shoulder. "Because he thought I'd be likely to recognize you after all these years. You haven't exactly mixed with the *beau monde* in France, Tony, or in Verona, for all he said we would have been at a disadvantage there without you after Castlereagh put a period to his existence. You will recall that I was with the Duke in Verona, I expect.''

"I don't associate with your world anymore, Harry. I've been made to feel most unwelcome in it.''

"Tony, that was years ago, and some of us, including the Duke, tried to change things. Why, I even—''

"Not many were like you.''

"Look, your father's been in his grave these three years and more,'' Harry said sternly. "You didn't even attend his funeral.''

"A little difficult, my friend. Word of his demise did not reach me for four months. By then I could see no reason to come back.''

"But—''

"We are keeping him waiting, Harry.''

Grimacing, Livingston pushed open the door and said brusquely, "He's here, sir, but what you can want with such a damned uncivil fellow, I can't imagine.''

The Duke of Wellington, now Prime Minister of England, got to his feet. Though approaching his sixtieth birthday, he had retained his wavy brown hair and his slender five-foot-nine-inch physique, and was still accounted a handsome man despite his large, bony nose. His bearing was stiff and aristocratic, but his bright blue eyes were twinkling when he stepped around his desk to shake hands with Antony.

"Sent for him because he's the one man I know I can trust to get to the bottom of things in Cornwall before they blow up in our faces,'' he said, speaking in his rapid, clipped way. "Well met, Tony. I need you. Some damned unfeeling Cornishmen want to assassinate me, so *Le Renardeau* had better go down there and put a stop to it.''

Antony smiled at the man who had had so much influence— both good and bad—on his life. "Must I, sir? I should think it would be a deal more sensible to avoid venturing into Cornwall until they've found something more interesting to do.''

The Duke gestured toward a chair. "Can't do that. I promised to attend the consecration of the new cathedral in Truro on the fourteenth of June. The nation is contributing a set of famous sacramental vessels removed from an abbey on the Tamar that was shut up during the Reformation and eventually destroyed under Cromwell. I don't dare even let the threat be known. We've got a new police bill before the Commons, and Robbie Peel believes that with luck he can push this one through.''

''I did hear rumors that he's trying again to organize a civilian police force.''

''We must succeed this time, Tony,'' the Duke said earnestly. ''I know the military too well to believe in soldiers as peacekeepers, I assure you. Any country that relies on its army to keep order in peacetime invites dire peril. Since Peel returned from Ireland ten years ago, he's tried to form a police force here like the force he created there, but Englishmen persist in thinking police of any sort mean tyranny.''

''Englishmen still value liberty above order,'' Antony said. ''As Fox once said, most of them would prefer to be ruled by a mob than by a standing army of police.''

''Our police will not be an army,'' the Duke said. ''Disciplined constables armed only with truncheons can master mobs, Tony. But we need time to push the bill through Parliament and time to set the scheme into motion. The last thing we need is a threat to assassinate me. Public knowledge of it would stir a general outcry. My opponents would demand either that I remain safely in London and break my word to the people of Cornwall, or that the military be sent in to keep peace while I'm there. The latter choice could lead to another Peterloo. And that, I need hardly say, would frighten off a lot of our support. Wavering members could easily decide that *any* police force is bound to develop into an ever-present army of violent men, and vote against us.''

Antony frowned. ''Forgive me, sir, but the reference to Peterloo escapes me. I've heard the name, certainly, but—''

Harry Livingston said, ''It began as a political meeting in St. Peter's Fields in Manchester, Tony, four years after Waterloo. Men militating for economic relief and parliamentary reform were united by the damned Methodists—''

''Don't blame the Methodists,'' the Duke said, smiling tolerantly. "England probably owes it to them that she's one of few countries not to suffer a revolution in the past fifty years. In any case, Tony, the gathering began peacefully. Women and children present—about sixty thousand people in all."

"That many?" Antony was surprised.

Wellington nodded. "Magistrates on the scene decided that if the leaders were arrested, the meeting would disperse. They called in the military to arrest them, and a troop of yeoman cavalry rode into the crowd." He sighed. "Their first victim was a two-year-old child, crushed in the onrush."

"But how would a civilian police force have behaved differently?"

"Those soldiers had been carousing. They were poorly disciplined, and their mounts untrained. They lost formation, Tony, foundering in the press of people. When they made their arrests, they lost their heads completely, smashing the dais and dragging down the banners. A contingent of regular cavalry, thinking the crowd had attacked the yeomanry, charged in to disperse them. In the resulting panic, people fled as best they could, leaving sabered and trampled babies on the ground. Fifteen died. Hundreds more were wounded or injured."

Livingston said, "The worst was that afterward Parliament passed all sorts of repressive laws. They sent troops in wherever the least hint of unrest stirred. Meanwhile, in Ireland, Peel successfully organized a civil police force. He wants to do the same here, but it will take months to get it through both houses, so we can't afford a flare-up in Cornwall. Half the nation believes Cornwall is a wilderness nearly as unpredictable as Scotland. Trouble there could ruin everything and set Peel's plan back ten years or more."

"That," said Wellington, "is where you come in. I want you to find out who the plotters are and stop them before I get there. You've no reason to love me, Tony, but you've served me well in the past. Can you bring yourself to do so again?"

"With all my heart, sir."

"Excellent, but you'll have to mind your manners. The most likely source of the trouble is a gang of smugglers and wreckers operating along the south coast. Our informant says they're in league with French smugglers who still think of me as the man who ended their emperor's reign, and the most lucrative period in their careers, as well. But though Cornwall is, as Harry said, thought by many to be foreign territory, remember that it's still England. Anything that even looks like the employment of spies is as unacceptable to the public now as it's ever been, and still believed by most to be alien to the British belief in fair play.''

"Plus ça change; plus c'est la même chose," Antony said bitterly. ''Who is our informant?''

''Alas, he signs himself only as *one who cares.* He does not even say whether he cares about me or about something else altogether.''

''So what would you have me do, my lord duke?''

''What you do best, of course, but don't break any laws, because if you do, you will be exceeding official instruction. I won't be able to help you.''

Antony grinned, understanding him perfectly. ''Perhaps I'd best pose as a lord then, rather than a smuggler.''

Wellington chuckled. ''I leave that to you to decide. Just keep this from blowing up in the public eye, Tony.'' He paused with a speculative look, then added, ''Speaking of lords, it occurs to me that you've a relative or two in Cornwall, lad. Might that pose a problem?''

''None whatsoever,'' Antony responded confidently. ''I've never met a single one of them, and I can't think of a single reason to alter that fact.''

Chapter One

Cornwall, April 18, 1829

When the large traveling coach suddenly increased its speed on the narrow cliff road, the monkey was the first of its dozing passengers to waken. His bristly round head popped out of his small mistress's large fur muff. Round, inquisitive shoe-button eyes glinted alertly in light from the gibbous moon hovering over the British Channel and the perilous south coast of Cornwall. The monkey cocked its head, listening.

Lady Letitia Ophelia Deverill, a child with nine whole summers behind her, was the next to stir. Her eyes slitted, blinked sleepily, then opened wide. When the monkey began to chatter nervously, she held it closer, murmuring, "Hush, Jeremiah, it's all right." Looking out the nearby coach window, however, she gasped and added less confidently, "I think it's all right."

Beside her, twenty-four-year-old Miss Charlotte Tarrant shifted, trying to find a more comfortable position, which was no easy task after days of lurching travel with three other persons and a monkey in the close, albeit luxurious, confines of the coach. Inadvertently, she stepped on her father's foot.

Charles Tarrant muttered, moved his foot, and opened one eye to glare at her.

The carriage rounded a slight bend, and moonlight streamed inside, so that when Charlotte opened her eyes, she saw his expression clearly. Smiling ruefully, she said, "Sorry, Papa. Letty," she added when Charles shut his eyes again, "whatever is the matter with Jeremiah?"

"I-I don't know, Cousin Charley, but are we not going rather fast? I just looked out the window, and all I can see is the sea, very far down."

Charley leaned across the child to look out the window. She and Letty occupied the forward seat, facing Charley's parents. Her mother, Davina, wakened, frowning.

"Gracious me, Charles," she said, "this carriage is swaying like the Royal Mail! Do tell John Coachman to slow down before he has us over the cliff!"

As Charles reached forward to knock on the ceiling of the coach, a shot rang out, followed by others. The coach moved even faster.

"Highwaymen," Davina screamed. "Robbers! Oh, Charles, where is your pistol? Why did we not go through Launceston? Oh, why did we not hire a guard?"

Charles snapped, "We didn't go by way of Launceston, my dear, because you insisted that we take a look at the Plymouth house, that's why. And we did not stay the night in Looe, which would have been the sensible course, because you don't like to travel on Sunday and thought we could reach Tuscombe Park tonight. Why anyone of sense would want to drive the Polperro Road, ever, let alone in the dark of night—"

Searching through her satchel, Charley interjected calmly, "But we *are* here. Ah, here it is. I've got my pistol, Mama, and the big one is in the holster by Papa's door, where it is always kept. John Coachman must have seen them following us, which is why he increased his pace. But with only two horses, and on this of all roads, it is a stupid thing to do. Shout at him to pull up, Papa. We can deal with highwaymen, but if we should go off the road or lose a wheel—"

As if thought had given birth to reality, the coach bounced

heavily over a rock, and with a screeching crack, the left hind wheel broke off its axle. Had it happened scant moments before, the carriage would have plunged a hundred feet to jagged, surf-frothed rocks below. But they had reached the rugged, unfriendly slope of Seacourt Head, a jutting triangular headland that formed the east boundary of St. Merryn's Bay.

When the wheel broke, the coachman did his best, but the coach was traveling too fast. Swerving, it lurched off the road, and he could not regain control. After a few awkward bumps, forward action ceased and the heavily laden coach began to roll ominously backward down the steep slope of the headland.

The horses strained, but the coach was too heavy. It dragged them backward, faster and faster, inexorably nearer the edge, until it caught on boulders and toppled over sideways, skidding briefly, then rolling. The horses screamed in panic.

In the tangle of bodies inside, Charley dropped the pistol she had snatched from her satchel and clung tightly to her small cousin. Windows broke, and dust and glass rained over them when first one side, then the other, hit the rocky ground. The nearside door flew open, and when the vehicle hit the ground again, Charley and Letty shot out.

Landing hard on her back against a steep slope of loose scree, with Letty on top of her, Charley felt herself sliding. She heard a sickening scrape of coach against rocks, her father's panicked shouts and her mother's screams, echoed by those of the horses. The sounds faded until she heard a distant, crunching thud, then, except for the sound of the surf far below, there was silence. Still sliding toward the brink over which the coach had plunged, she tried to dig her heels into the loose scree.

Letty struggled to free herself. Tightening her grip, Charley muttered, "Be still." She scrabbled wildly with her free hand, desperately seeking a handhold, anything to stop their fatal slide toward the precipice.

The surf rolled out again, providing a few seconds of near silence. From his lookout position, crouched in a cluster of boulders just above the tidemark on the beach they called

Devil's Sand, Antony heard a coach above him on the cliff road, then gunshots. Raising his eyes heavenward, he blessed the cliff overhang—the same steep overhang he had cursed an hour earlier when he feared he had misjudged the tide and might be trapped by the unpredictable waves. Several times he had reminded himself that the caves just up the beach were dry enough to store smuggled goods. But as the water inched nearer, and the moon finally slipped behind clouds that his comrades had expected to hide it much earlier, darkness and the noise of the surf stirred a primordial fear that had taken much of his overtaxed resolution to defeat. Now, with the moon's reappearance, he had new worries. Smugglers did not welcome moonlight.

At the same time that he blessed the overhang that would protect him if the fast-moving coach plunged off the road, he spared a thought for the passengers and horses. He had not spent so much time alone that he did not still think of others, although he doubted he would ever again feel the same magnitude of caring and compassion he had felt for family and friends in long-ago days, before his emotions withered and died. When they cast him off for disgracing them with his "unsportsmanlike activities" during the unpleasantness with Bonaparte, the break had devastated him. He grieved for them then as if they all had died. Memory of the expression on Harry Livingston's face three weeks before, when Harry rebuked him for missing his father's funeral, brought only a sigh of depression now. He had felt nothing at learning of his father's death, all bereavement spent long before, after his father gave him the cut direct in front of everyone at Brooks's Club in London. The wrenching pain of that moment stirred again, then vanished instantly amid panicked screams of horses and humans. The noise of the surf had muffled sound from above, but he heard the screech of coachwork on rocks somewhere near the headland at the west end of Devil's Sand. Then more horrible screams, a muffled crash on the beach, and silence.

* * *

Charley's skirt and cloak were caught up around her, pinning her legs together, making it nearly impossible to dig the heels of her half boots into the unstable mass beneath her. When she banged the back of her hand against a boulder, she managed to catch hold of the rock, breaking fingernails and crying out at the pain when one ripped below the quick. Feeling the wriggling body atop hers lurch awkwardly forward, almost making her lose her tenuous hold, she nearly snapped at the child to be still before she realized they had stopped sliding.

"I haven't got a good hold," Letty said matter-of-factly, "but I think it would be wise to wait till the moon comes out again before I try to gain better purchase."

Aware that her own grip on the rough boulder was not reliable, Charley realized that until that moment she had not missed the moonlight. It was much darker than it had been before. She wondered if that was why she had not actually seen the coach topple over the edge, or if she had simply been too concerned about herself and Letty to notice. Knowing the two of them were far from being safe, she thrust aside all thought of the horror that had overtaken them. Whatever had happened below, she could do nothing about it now. She was not even certain she would be able to do much about her own predicament, but at least she and Letty were still alive. If they slid over the edge, their chances of remaining in that condition were small. The worst of it was that she did not know how near they were to the precipice.

Letty stirred uncomfortably. "Cousin Charley—"

"Hush," Charley said, for another sound had reached her sharp ears from above. She nearly called out before she realized that the most likely persons to be at the cliff's edge were the highwaymen. Giving thanks for the clouds that hid the moon, she wondered how long they would do so. Already, she could see silver ribbons of moonlight edging them. The cloak she wore was her favorite dark sapphire blue, to match her eyes, and she knew that the nearby rocks and slope were dark in more places than they were light, so she had reason to hope the men would not see them.

Close to her ear, Letty murmured, "Won't they help us?"

Deciding that if the child had not given way to hysterics yet, she would not do so, Charley did not mince words. "No, darling, they won't. They caused the accident, and we could speak against them to the authorities, so they dare not let us see their faces. We must keep very still and hope they don't see us."

"My cloak is gray," Letty whispered, "but they might see my hair when the moon peeks out again."

"Pull your cloak up," Charley whispered back, realizing that the child's bright carrot-colored mop of curls might well gleam like a beacon. "Move slowly, and don't let go of that boulder if you can help it. I think if I don't move, we won't slide any more, but it's best to be careful until we can be certain. Curl up so your cloak covers all of you. And keep very still."

"I don't think they can hear us," Letty muttered. "I can barely hear their voices, or their horses."

"No, but sound travels up better than down, I think, and the more quiet we are the less likely we are to draw their notice."

Letty was silent. Moving slowly and cautiously, she curled into a ball with her cloak covering her. Just before she grew still again and silver moonlight touched the rocks around them, a piece of wool flopped over Charley's face.

She heard the men's voices again. Her hearing was acute, but she could not make out their words, nor did she think she would know the voices if she heard them again. The light faded, but Charley and Letty kept perfectly still.

Charley was astonished by her small cousin's presence of mind. She did not know Letty well, for the child had spent her entire life on the Continent. Though only nine, she was an expert horsewoman and more accustomed than most children her age to conversing with adults. Her parents, unlike most, had not relegated their children to the care of nurses and governesses, but spent a good deal of time with them, and enjoyed their company. Lord Abreston, heir to the Marquessate of Jervaulx, having served with distinction as a brigade major in Wellington's Army, presently held a diplomatic position with the British Embassy in Paris, a fact that both amused and astonished those well acquainted with Daintry, his outspoken wife. The couple had retained close ties to their home, however, and their two sons—both younger than Letty—would soon return to England for school. Letty herself was in England now to begin a six-months' visit to her mama's family at Tuscombe Park, but this, Charley told herself grimly, was not the introduction to Cornwall that her Aunt Daintry had intended the child to enjoy.

Antony hesitated only long enough after hearing the crash to peer through the darkness toward the sea. Still no signal, but he dared not leave lantern or tinderbox behind. Snatching them both up, he raced along the shingle to the broken carriage. Both horses were clearly dead, which was just as well, he thought. He could not bear to see animals suffer, but he could not have risked a gunshot down here and the mere thought of using his knife to put them out of their misery made him feel ill.

A moan from the carriage snapped his head around. He had not thought anyone could live through such an accident. The moon peeked out again, and he went still, knowing he might be seen from above. Slowly he tilted his head up, keeping one gloved hand over his face so the moon could not reveal it. Whoever had fired the shots he had heard earlier might well be peering down at him.

He realized quickly that even if they were up there, they would not see him unless they climbed out onto the headland, and the portion that overlooked his position was exceedingly treacherous. On the far side, facing St. Merryn's Bay, the slope was less precipitous. There was even a road leading to the point, where a lovely big house perched, enjoying a broad, sweeping view of St. Merryn's Bay and the Channel.

Even as these thoughts flew through his mind he stooped over the wreckage, trying to see past broken bits of coach to what lay within. He dared not risk a light, and the fickle moon had slipped behind another cloud. The moan came again, faintly. He moved a piece of the wreckage and found a man's crushed and broken body. The moans were not coming from him.

Moving with more care than ever, Antony shifted another piece of the carriage, and pale silvery light revealed a woman. She was badly injured, and he saw at once that there was nothing he could do to help her. She opened her eyes.

"Charley?" The word was clear but faint. When she tried to speak again, she could not.

Antony took her hand, wanting only to give her comfort. "I'm here," he said gently. "I won't leave you."

"Thank you." Her eyes closed. A moment later, the hand in his went limp. She was gone.

A hail of pebbles from above startled him and reminded him that men had been chasing the coach. He did not think they had started the pebbles falling, however. Far more likely, the careening coach had dislodged them and perhaps had loosened much bigger rocks. If he were wise, he would move before one of those fell on him. He would do the Duke no good if he were found smashed flat on a Cornish beach.

Briefly he wondered if the men would try to ride down to the beach. Having thought the coach worth robbing in the first place, they might believe it worth searching now. A path of sorts wound down the cliffside, one that a good horse could follow in daylight, but he had not attempted to bring Annabelle down it in the dark, and she was as surefooted as an army mule. He did not think anyone would come.

He had been keeping an eye on the sea and at last he saw what he had been waiting for. Light flashed from a covered lantern. Two more flashes followed. Swiftly, he opened his tinderbox and lit a sulfur match. Seconds later his lantern was lit. As he moved away from the wreckage, he saw yet another flash of light at the eastern end of the beach. So Michael had not trusted him to meet the Frenchmen alone. Not surprising. Since the man had known him less than a fortnight, he had been more surprised at being ordered to go without a second. A test, no doubt. He wondered if the other watcher had seen the coach plunge over the cliff. He did not remember seeing carriage lanterns. No doubt they had been broken and their lights extinguished soon after the coach left the road. It had probably rolled several times. He would have to consider carefully what he was going to do about it.

"Cousin Charley, I think they've gone."

"Keep still a few minutes longer, Letty." But Charley, too, had heard sounds of departing horses above them. She could feel the chill of the rock beneath her, and she could feel the child trembling.

"I-I lost my muff," Letty said in a small voice.

Charley knew she was concerned about much more than a fur muff, and she thought a moment before she said, "We cannot think just now about what we have lost, Letty. We must think about getting ourselves out of this predicament. That is the only thing, right now, that we can do anything about."

"It . . . it is very far down to the beach, is it not?"

"Very far," Charley agreed, "but if we keep our wits about us, we won't fall." She hoped she sounded more confident than she felt. To the best of her knowledge they were some twenty or thirty feet below the road, not far from where the slope of the headland met the side of the cliff, and perilously near the edge of that slope. It was, after all, little more than the point at which two cliff faces came together at slightly more than a right angle. In daylight a man in buckskins and wearing gloves might be able to climb back to the road easily. At night, with an unknown enemy nearby, two females in long skirts and heavy cloaks would not have an easy time, even though one of them wore stout half boots.

"Were you injured, darling?"

"I don't think so," Letty said. "I hit my head on the carriage door, but it was only a bump, and then I fell on you. Oh, and my hand is scraped, I think, where I first grabbed the rock. What about you?"

"I don't want to think about it," Charley said. "I don't think I broke any bones, but I am beginning to feel a few aches and pains, and I am quite sure I bounced against a few rather pointed rocks. My cloak protected me from the worst, although I did bang the back of my head when we landed, hard enough to make me see more stars than are showing above us tonight. I think your head must have hit my chin at the same time.''

''The moon is— Listen!''

A rattle of loose stones and pebbles startled both of them, but a moment later a chirping sound made Letty stiffen, then call out in a low, excited voice, ''Jeremiah!''

More chattering accompanied another rattle of stones. Then four small paws touched Charley's shoulder before the little monkey dove under Letty's cloak.

''Oh, Jeremiah, I was so worried about you! I thought you must have been killed. Oh, Cousin Charley, do you think Uncle Charles and Aunt Davina might have been thrown clear, too?''

Tempted though she was to say that anything was possible, Charley was a firm believer in honesty. She had loathed being lied to as a child, especially by grown-ups who insisted later that they had done so for her own good. Her Aunt Daintry had always been honest with her. She owed that same honesty to Daintry's daughter. ''No,'' she said with a sick feeling in the pit of her stomach and a shiver of horror as she remembered her mother's screams, ''I do not think they were thrown clear. They were still in the coach when it went over the edge.''

Letty was silent. Then she said, ''Those men on the road are gone. I think we had better see what we can do about finding a safer place for ourselves. I do not think we should try to climb back to the road till we can see what we are doing, do you?''

''No, and you make a sensible suggestion. I confess, I am afraid to shift my position. The rocks under me are very loose and I fear the slightest movement might start us sliding again.''

''Well, I think I can get behind this boulder I've been clinging to,'' Letty said. ''If I can, then I can brace my feet against it, and if you hold my hand, I think you can inch up behind it, too.''

Charley's first, terrified impulse was to tell the child not to move a muscle, but she was getting cold, and knew that eventually one of them would have to try. Better to do so, she decided, while they both still had some control over their limbs, and better that Letty try. The child would have no chance of holding her if she slipped, but she might hold the child.

Letty said, "I can get between you and the boulder, I think, but my cloak and skirt are dreadfully in my way, and these slippers I'm wearing do nothing to protect my feet or give me traction."

Charley felt her wriggle some more and did not speak, focusing all her attention on keeping her own body flat and perfectly still against the loose scree. She heard Jeremiah protest when Letty removed him from beneath her cloak. When the child shifted her weight off Charley, Charley felt as if she were beginning to slide again, but the sensation soon passed.

"I've got my feet against your side," Letty said. "This boulder seems stable. I am going to stand up."

Charley held her breath. A moment later, Letty dropped her cloak over her. Odd noises and movements followed, and even in the dim light, Charley could see the child doing something to her clothing. "What are you doing?"

"Tucking up my skirt," Letty said. "If I slip, I don't want it getting tangled round my legs again. It's all right," she added, with amusement in her voice. "I've got on my dimity pantalets with the Swiss lace that Mama bought me just before we left Paris, so if anyone should chance to see me—"

"You'll shock them witless," Charley murmured. "I brought a pair, myself, but I am not wearing them because my mama thinks—" She broke off, realizing the tense of the verb was probably wrong, then added with forced calm, "She thinks only men should wear pantaloons of any kind, but that's only because of Lady Charlotte Lindsey's having lost one leg of hers as she walked down Piccadilly, and causing such a stir. Mine are fashioned in such a way that one side cannot fall off by itself."

"Mine, too." Letty fell silent for a long moment, then said on a note of satisfaction, "There. Now I'm holding the boulder with both hands, and it is as steady as can be. Just one more moment."

Charley felt loose pebbles sliding past her with each step Letty took, and kept tight hold of the base of the boulder with her left hand. Her arm was stretched to its full reach, however, and she knew that if she trusted her weight to that slight hand-hold, or tried to pull herself toward the boulder, she would lose her tenuous grip. Difficult as it was for a woman of her active nature, she knew she had to keep still until the child was as safe as she could make herself.

Without warning, Letty's cloak was whisked off her. "Now, Cousin Charley," the child said. "I am sitting on my cloak, and my feet are pushing hard against the boulder. It hasn't twitched. If I hold your hand with both of mine—"

"No," Charley said firmly. "You must hold the boulder or some other solid object with your right hand. If both of your hands are holding mine and I begin to slip, my weight could yank you right out of there. Reach out your left hand from near the base of the boulder. When you find my hand, grasp my wrist as tightly as you can. Then I'll hold your wrist. Your mother taught—"

"Oh, I know," Letty exclaimed. "It's the way she swings me up to ride pillion with her."

"Right," Charley agreed.

The little girl's hand seemed very small, her wrist far too slender and fragile for the purpose, but her grip was tight and the slender arm steady when Charley grasped it. Charley's legs were still tangled in her skirts, so she spent several long moments moving slowly and carefully, using her free hand to twitch them free. When she could use her heels to dig into the scree, she inched her way up, but a few moments later when she tried to sit, the unstable surface beneath her shifted. Only Letty's tight grip kept her from sliding.

"Cousin Charley, are you sure sound travels up more easily than down?"

"I think so," Charley said, willing her heart to stop pounding and forcing her breathing to slow down. "Why do you ask, darling?"

"Because there are men and lights on the beach," Letty said. "I don't think they can see us, but a lot of loose rocks went over the edge just then."

"Do you think they can be the highwaymen?"

"I don't know. Most of them came in a boat, I think. I can just barely see a dark shape farther out on the water that might be a ship. The little boat is leaving again, but there are at least two men still on the beach!"

"Hold tight, Letty. I'm going to try again."

As Antony helped carry cargo from the longboat to the cave where it would be stored till the ponies collected it for transport, he thought about Wellington's warning against involving himself in criminal activities. If revenuers surprised them, they would have nowhere but the caves to hide. Michael had assured him that folks in south Cornwall were friendly to the free traders, but he was risking a lot on Michael's word, and he had little reason to trust the man—no more, in fact, than Michael had to trust him. The man had taken him on faith—that, and reference to a mutual acquaintance in France who would (if he knew what was good for him) vouch for Antony's "good" character. As yet Antony had heard nothing about an assassination plot, but he knew the locals would continue to test him for some time.

The only person in Cornwall who knew him for a government man was the agent for Lloyd's of London in St. Austell. Antony had paid Mr. Francis Oakley a visit, liked the cut of his jib, and told him he meant to do a little investigating of the coastal gangs for His Majesty's government. He had confided only so much to Mr. Oakley. The Fox Cub had learned long since to trust no one but himself with all the facts.

While he hauled kegs, he was constantly aware of the wrecked carriage at the west end of the beach. The moon had moved west of the headland, and the wreck lay in shadow. Unless someone decided to stroll to that end of the beach for some reason that Antony could not presently imagine, it would draw no one else's interest tonight.

Daylight was another matter. He did not know the victims. He had seen no crest on the door, and doubted that he would have recognized it if he had seen one. He had found no coachman either, he realized. Perhaps the man had jumped clear and gone for help. In any case, he would be wiser not to return by daylight, lest his villainous compatriots believe he was after their booty. But neither could he reconcile it with his conscience to leave that poor woman and her husband to rot on the beach if the coachman had not survived. Somehow, he must learn if anyone had, and if not, get word to the authorities about the accident.

Tucked between two boulders, with a third below them on the slope, Charley and Letty were as safe as they could make themselves. Huddled inside Charley's thick cloak with Letty's smaller one over them and Jeremiah snuggled between them, they soon grew tired of watching the activity below them on the beach, and fell asleep.

When Charley awoke, it was because Letty had moved away from her and was anxiously calling Jeremiah.

"Keep your voice down," Charley whispered. "Someone might hear you."

"The smugglers are gone," Letty said, "but so is Jeremiah. I've got to find him! What if he fell over the edge?"

"If he didn't go over with the carriage, you may be sure he did not fall later," Charley said, hoping she was right. "He is very agile, you know, so he has probably only gone exploring. He will be back soon. Maybe he will find some food."

Letty giggled. "Are you hungry, too? I did not like to say anything, but I am starving. There were apples in Aunt Davina's basket, too." The silence that followed was awkward, but for once in her life Charley could think of nothing to say. At last, in a small voice, Letty said, "I'm awfully sorry, Cousin Charley. I-I know that most likely they are dead. At least, don't you think they are?"

"Yes," Charley said. The alternative—that her parents could be lying in dreadful agony at the base of the cliff, while she sat doing nothing to help them—was too horrible to contemplate.

"Well, I am sure they must be, and perhaps it is only that

they are not my own parents, but should I not feel like crying, even so? Because I know I keep saying things I ought not to say—like about the apples—and . . . and . . .''

Charley reached for Letty's hand and gave it a squeeze, saying, ''I am very glad you are not weeping and wailing, darling, because that would only make matters much worse than they are.''

''Yes, but ought I not to *feel* like doing so? You are grown up, so I don't expect you to fall into flat despair, even though they are your parents, but I don't want to cry. I don't feel anything at all—except cold and a little tired.''

''I think we have both had a lot to think about just to stay alive,'' Charley said quietly. ''Moreover, I have heard that it is not unusual to feel numb at first. It is a great shock, after all, and everything happened very fast, so perhaps our sensibilities have not quite caught up with the reality of it all.''

''I don't seem to have much sensibility at the best of times,'' Letty said thoughtfully. ''Young Gideon has much more than I do. He cries if a bug gets squashed. I just think what a good thing it is to have one less bug to crawl on me.''

Charley chuckled and gave her a hug. ''Young Gideon is only five.''

''Yes, I know, but I didn't have much sensibility even then. Papa frequently says I've got more sense than sensibility. Mama said he had that from a book.''

''A fine book,'' Charley said. ''I have a copy at home. Do you like to read?''

They talked in this manner for some time, until Charley began to notice that the eastern sky was growing light. It would soon be dawn. She wondered if they would be able to reach the road. She wondered, too, if they would have to walk to Tuscombe Park, and if she could do so without first making her way down to the beach to be sure that what she knew in her heart was really so.

''Cousin Charley, listen! I think it's Jeremiah!''

''*Mon Dieu,* can there really be someone down there?'' The

voice from above them was masculine and deep. It sounded much closer than twenty or thirty feet away.

Charley and Letty kept still, and when Jeremiah leapt to Letty's shoulder and began to chatter excitedly, she grabbed him, shoved him under her cloak, and clapped a hand over his little mouth.

Chapter Two

"Nom d'un nom," the low, melodious voice went on, adding in heavily accented English, "first I am attacked by *le petit singe* in the night. Then I hear an angel's voice floating in the dawn *sans* an angel's body. Am I going mad, or what?"

Letty stifled a giggle.

"Alors, an angel with a sense of humor. Come, *ma petite,* where are you? *Je suis un ami.* I am a friend. I will not harm you."

Charley could see Letty more clearly. Dawn was coming. They would have to make up their minds quickly whether to trust this Frenchman.

"I like his voice," Letty whispered.

" 'Tis a fine voice, *mon ange,"* the Frenchman said. "How did you get down there? Were you in the carriage that so unfortunately plunged from the road. Do you always whisper to monkeys?"

Letty gasped, but Charley sighed and said, "I told you sound travels more easily than one might think. I certainly hope," she added, raising her voice so the Frenchman would hear clearly, "that you are not one of the villains who fired upon us."

"Nom d'un nom d'un nom! Deux anges!"

"Yes, there are two of us," Charley said crisply. "And we shall be very much obliged to you if you can get us out of here. I must warn you, however, that most of this slope appears to be covered with loose pebbles and gravel that want to shoot one right over the edge when one tries to walk."

"One moment then. I must consult with Annabelle."

"You have a companion?"

"A most excellent one. Annabelle is the prettiest little buttermilk mare one could ever hope to see, and the wisest."

"We are very cold, so could you please be so kind as to confer quickly?"

"Mais un petit moment, ma petite."

They heard a scrabbling sound, then silence. Letty said, "Do you think he is one of the smugglers, Cousin Charley?"

"At this point, darling, I do not much care who he is, so long as he can get us out of here and doesn't murder us."

"Papa said the citizens of Cornwall liked and protected the free traders when he was a boy. Do they still?"

"To an extent, I suppose. We hear many tales about whole gangs caught and sent for trial, only to have the jury or magistrate declare them innocent. Grandpapa was not so tolerant of their activities, however. He made it clear long ago that he would not allow such goings-on in St. Merryn's Bay."

"I am looking forward to seeing Grandpapa and Grandmama again," Letty said. "I have seen them only twice, you know, and one of those times I was a baby. Still, it is sad that we shall take them such dreadful news."

Charley did not want to think about that.

"That man mentioned the carriage," Letty said in a small voice. "Do you think he saw it?"

From above, the Frenchman's voice interrupted her. "If I throw a rope down, can you tie it round one of you, do you think?"

"Of course, we can," Charley responded, "if you manage to throw it far enough and if we don't have to scramble around to find the end."

"It is only about twenty-five feet long," he said.

"My goodness," Letty exclaimed, "how do you come to have such a long one with you?"

"That, *ma petite,* is my business," he said. "And I advise you to keep your voice down. I think we are alone, but it is possible that others linger in the neighborhood. Can you perhaps wave something so that I can see exactly where you are?"

"Wait," Letty said, "I have a better notion. Jeremiah can fetch the rope end."

"Jeremiah?"

"My monkey. He led you to us, after all."

"Will he obey instructions?"

"I think so, though it's a pity you have not got a bag of nuts to rattle. Call him."

To Charley's surprise, Jeremiah scampered off at the first call. Moments later, at Letty's command, he returned with the end of a twisted rope. Charley could just reach it to take it from him, but there was no slack when she did so.

"Can you let us have a bit more?"

"That is all there is, I'm afraid. Will it not reach?"

"Barely, but I think we can manage. Look here, Letty," she added, "you are going up first. I think if I brace myself against our boulder, I can help you move uphill until we can tie the rope around your waist."

"But Jeremiah might not carry it back again to you. He'll always come to me."

"Nevertheless, you will go first."

Letty did not argue with that tone of voice, and soon was on her way up the slope. Charley sat back down to await events. When Letty called down that she was safe, Charley called Jeremiah, but it was not the monkey who brought her the rope.

She knew the man was coming by the sounds of his descent on the loose scree, but even so, she was not prepared when he loomed over her in the semi-darkness. He seemed larger than his voice had led her to expect, very large. But since she was slight of build and only an inch above five feet, and he was uphill, she knew he did not have to be a giant to tower over her.

It occurred to her briefly that he might have come for her

to pitch her right over the edge, but her voice was steady when she said, "Why did you not send Jeremiah back?"

"*La petite* said the rope end barely reached you," he said, his voice still low, his tone even. "She also said the footing here was particularly treacherous. I have tied the rope around my waist, so I cannot come closer, but I believe that if you stretch out one hand to me, while keeping the other on your boulder for balance, I can reach you. Annabelle will do the rest."

"Annabelle?"

"Yes, Annabelle. Having no idea how large either of you was, and not being certain I could hold you if you lost your footing, I took the precaution of tying the rope to her saddle. It is specially designed to allow any number of things to be tied to it."

"Which is how you came to have the rope," Charley said, nearly certain now that her rescuer was one of the free traders. "Would I perhaps be more accurate in referring to that rope as a tub line?"

He chuckled, apparently undisturbed by her knowledge of smuggling equipment, and she found the sound infectious. It made her smile despite the horrid events of the night. He said calmly, "Give me your hand, *mon ange.*"

"What is your name?"

"They call me Jean Matois. *Now* will you give me your hand? Annabelle is bound to be growing deucedly impatient. Not to mention *la petite,* though she seems remarkably level-headed."

Reminded that Letty was alone on the road with only a buttermilk mare to protect her, Charley stood again, bracing herself against the boulder, and reached her hand out as far as she could. The stranger grabbed her wrist in a firm, warm grasp, and automatically she caught his wrist with her hand. He did not wear gloves.

Her feet slid, but the stranger steadied her, and she soon stood beside him with one of his muscular arms tight around her. He made a clicking sound with his tongue that seemed as if it could not possibly be audible more than a few feet away, but Charley was close enough to him to feel the warmth of his body enveloping her, and to feel the rope grow taut around his waist.

"Annabelle is very well trained," he said, his voice still low but reassuring. "Do not be frightened."

"I'm not frightened," she said. "In fact, I'm pretty well numbed by all of this. I expect it will overwhelm me tomorrow."

"Tragedy affects some people that way," he murmured. "I only wanted to reassure you about Annabelle's ability to help us up the slope."

"Oh, I can tell that she knows what she is doing," Charley said. "I have trained horses since I was a child, and in my experience they are generally more to be relied upon than men are. I do not deny that I'd have managed all this better if I were not encumbered with skirts, of course, but in any event I am most grateful to have your support now. I think my hands would have been too numb to hold onto the rope. I had all I could do to knot it around Letty."

He was silent, helping her work her way around a jagged outcropping.

She said, "I'm glad I didn't hit this when we were flung out. At least, I don't think I can have done so, although I don't know what I did hit. I only know that I came down flat on my back with Letty on top of me."

"You were fortunate," he said.

"We certainly were." She hesitated. Their progress was reasonably steady now. His grip was firm, and she could easily picture the mare backing away, pace by pace. Finally, gathering resolution, she said, "You mentioned the carriage, Monsieur Matois. If you were not one of the highwaymen, is it possible that you . . . that you were . . ." She could not finish.

"I was on the beach," he said gently. His arm tightened around her when he said the words, as if he expected some sort of impulsive reaction, but Charley was made of sterner stuff than that.

She drew a long breath, then said, "So you saw the carriage

after it fell from the cliff. Were . . . Did anyone . . . ? That is to say . . .'' Again, words failed her.

"They are dead," he said in that same gentle tone. "A man and a woman in the carriage and a second man some distance away. I did not see the second man at first, but when I went back—"

"You left them?"

For the first time, he hesitated. They were nearing the top of the slope, and even in her anxiety over what he might say, Charley became aware that Letty was not peering down, encouraging their progress.

Finally, her companion said, "I had to leave them for a time. There were others coming, you see, and—"

"I do see," she said, "or rather, Letty did. I know if you were on that beach, you are either a free trader or a riding officer, though I must say that, frankly, you don't sound much like either one. You need not worry that I will give you away. Folks hereabouts are generally friendly toward the lads, but if you mean to be so kind as to see us home, I advise you to say nothing to my grandfather about your activities. He is a justice of the peace, and he takes his position seriously."

"As well he should," her companion said, helping her onto the roadbed at last and making another odd clicking sound with his tongue as he climbed up after her. Then he whistled two notes, and Charley heard the quick clip-clop of a horse's hooves on the road. A moment later Letty and the mare emerged from the gloom.

The child was grinning from ear to ear. "Cousin Charley," she exclaimed, "isn't Annabelle clever? Jeremiah and I were just telling her some of the things you've taught your horses to do, and we've become good friends."

"Charley?"

There was an odd note in her rescuer's voice when he said her name, and she looked up at him in puzzlement. "Close friends and some members of my family call me so, monsieur. I am Charlotte Tarrant. Letty," she added, "our rescuer is Monsieur Matois. This is my cousin, monsieur, Lady Letitia Deverill."

"Letitia *Ophelia* Deverill," that damsel interjected. "Everyone calls me Letty. Why did you react like that to Charley's name? Like you'd heard it before."

Off to the east, Charley could see a golden-red thread widening on the horizon. She could see his face more clearly, too. He was not as large as she had thought him, but he was of greater than medium height, perhaps six feet tall. Although his shoulders were broad, encouraging one to think him very large, his figure was slender. The only memorable features of his face were light eyes set deep beneath a jutting brow and a square, stubborn-looking chin. His nose was straight but ordinary. He had a two-day growth of beard, and thick brown hair hung untidily over his forehead to his eyebrows. In back it touched the collar of the drab frieze coat he wore. His expression was wide-eyed, nearly simple-minded. Altogether an unremarkable specimen, she thought.

He did not answer Letty's question, busying himself instead in coiling up his rope and fastening it to one of several rings stitched right onto his saddle. When Letty repeated the question in fluent French, he grinned at her. Charley found herself rapidly revising her first opinion of his looks. His eyes crinkled at the corners, as if he smiled frequently. A dimple danced high on his left cheek.

He said, "Charley is a strange name for a female, is it not, *ma petite?* Even in England. One merely remarked upon that fact. How much farther must we go to reach your home from here, mademoiselle?"

"About five miles inland from the next bay," Charley said. "My grandfather owns most of the land this side of the River Fowey, from the bay to Bodmin Moor."

"The Earl of St. Merryn is your grandfather then," he said evenly.

"If you know of him, you must also know his reputation, monsieur."

"I do," he agreed. "A right stiff-rumped old reprobate, by what I've been told. Fires up like a Guy Fawkes rocket, they say, when anyone crosses his will. Never crossed paths with him myself, though."

"Temper runs red in our family, I fear," Charley said.

The corners of his eyes crinkled again, and as light from the east touched them, she saw to her astonishment that they were as blue as the sea on a sunny April morning. He said lightly, "Surely, *mon ange,* you do not have a fiery temperament. You are far too small."

"She's little, but she's mighty," Letty said. "That's what my papa says of her, at all events."

"Your papa reads Shakespeare," Matois said.

"Is that from Shakespeare?" Letty asked.

"Oui, ma petite, though you've got it wrong. It's from *A Midsummer Night's Dream,* and the right way is, 'though she be but little, she is fierce.' "

Charley eyed him curiously. "How is it that a free trader comes to know Shakespeare, monsieur?"

He shrugged. "One learns English from the curé, the—how do you say it?—the parish priest. He had only the Bible and a set of Shakespeare's plays from which to teach." He shrugged, then added glibly, "Annabelle is well trained and has excellent manners, but I have never asked her to carry a lady. A sad oversight in view of the present circumstance, you will say, but it cannot be helped. We shall have to walk."

Letty's face fell, and although she did not utter a word of complaint, Charley knew the thought of walking such a distance dismayed the child as much as it did herself. She said tartly, "My good man, it is all of six or seven miles from here. I've got half boots on, but you must see that Letty is wearing very thin slippers."

"Perhaps if I were to ride and hold the child before me, Annabelle will not complain," he suggested.

"And you expect me to trail along meekly behind you, I suppose." She had an odd notion that he was baiting her, but she dismissed it as being too ludicrous to contemplate. "I have a better notion," she said.

"What is that, mademoiselle?"

"I will ride Annabelle with Letty, and you may walk."

He scratched his head. "Do you think you can ride her,

mon ange? She will object, I assure you, and we have no sidesaddle.''

"Stand aside," Charley said curtly. Her manner swiftly calmed, however, when she approached the mare and began speaking to her. "You will let me ride you, Annabelle," she said. "I have no sugar to give you, nor carrots, but—''

A lump of sugar was pressed into her right hand from behind. Glancing back, she smiled uncertainly and thanked him. Stroking the mare, she gave it the sugar, waited until Annabelle nuzzled her for more, then said to Jean Matois, "If you will give me a leg up, I believe I can manage her now. She should not object to my skirts any more than she objects to all the items you dangle from her saddle, after all."

"Perhaps we ought to move farther from the edge of the road," he murmured. "If she should pitch you over the cliff, all our effort will have gone for naught."

Still speaking in the caressing tone she used with the mare, Charley said, "Don't be stupid. She won't pitch me off, whatever else she does. Give me a leg up. Letty, hold Annabelle's bridle."

Obediently, he formed a stirrup for her with his hands, and she put her left foot into it, being careful not to startle Annabelle. Holding her skirt away from the mare's side with her left hand instead of resting it on his shoulder, she put her right lightly on the pommel to steady herself and allowed him to lift her. Once she was balanced on the saddle—a smaller one than her sidesaddle—she took a moment to steady the mare before arranging her skirt.

"Shorten the left stirrup, please," she said quietly, "and tuck up the right one so it won't hit Annabelle's side when we begin to move."

"Will one stirrup be enough to steady you on that saddle?'' he asked.

"Good mercy, I don't use the stirrups to steady myself any more than I'll wager you do. As a child, I learned to ride without using either stirrups or reins."

"Riding astride, perhaps, but—''

"No such thing!'' The mare side-stepped, and Charley steadied it without pausing. ''I'll have you know that at ten I could ride a sidesaddle at a gallop, sitting on a handkerchief with a piece of paper between my lower leg and the saddle. I could do it without using reins or stirrups, and never lose paper or handkerchief.''

''Whoever allowed you to try such stunts wants flogging,'' he said in a tone more grim than any she had yet heard him use.

''That was my mama,'' Letty said matter-of-factly. ''She taught Cousin Charley to ride, and me, too. And also our cousin Melissa, who lives in Hampshire now. All of us can ride without—''

''Melissa!'' Charley exclaimed. ''Good mercy, what a ninny I am not to have thought of that before. We are much closer to Seacourt Head than to Tuscombe Park.''

Matois said, *''Bien sûr, mademoiselle.* This headland which saved your life is called Seacourt Head. It is no distance at all.''

''Don't be absurd. I mean the house, of course. There is a road along the west face of the headland that leads to a house on the point.''

''Mais, oui, and a fine house it is,'' he agreed. ''But it lies empty, does it not?''

''Not empty, merely staffed by very few servants. That is my cousin's house. She inherited it when her father died, but visits only for short periods and brings a host of servants with her. There must be horses we can borrow. From here to the road cannot be more than a quarter mile and from there, it's less than a mile to the house. We'll take the cliff path to Tuscombe Park House. This road curves east toward Duloe before it heads west again, so it would take much longer.''

''You might discover an aversion to any cliff path just now,'' he said quietly.

''Nonsense. I'm not afraid of anything when I've got a good horse under me.''

''And the child? Do you speak for her, as well?''

Charley glanced at Letty, who was frowning slightly. ''Will you be frightened to ride along the cliff, darling?''

"Oh, no. I told you, I have not got a smidgen of sensibility. If it is the shortest route, I vote that we take it. I was just wondering if it would not be better if I were to ride astride, since that saddle has not got a leaping horn. I've got my pantalets on, you know, so if monsieur will not be dreadfully shocked . . ." She looked at him.

"Monsieur will not be shocked at all," he said. "Shall I put you up?"

"Yes, please, but I think you had better carry Jeremiah until Annabelle becomes more accustomed to him, don't you?"

"Most assuredly." He lifted her up behind Charley, and although the mare skittered nervously, it soon settled down. Fifteen minutes later, when they found the road to Seacourt House, Jean Matois said, "I am glad you believe we shall find horses. Otherwise I should insist that we trade places halfway. I know that walking is excellent exercise, but I got practically no sleep last night."

Charley was about to tell him what she thought of trading places, but catching his gaze and observing a decided twinkle in his eyes, she thought better of the notion. Monsieur Matois possessed an impudence quite out of character in a man of his class. Apparently, Frenchmen of that class differed from their English counterparts.

They reached Seacourt House a short time later, and Sam and Aggie Corlan, the man and woman in charge there, were kind enough to provide them with not only a pair of horses and sidesaddles but breakfast of a sort, as well.

Charley noted that, in the presence of Sam and Aggie, Monsieur Matois behaved like any other member of his class, staying with Annabelle and generally effacing himself until Sam requested help saddling the other horses.

Since Charley had known the Corlans all her life, she told them what had happened, but asked them to tell no one else for the present. "I don't want Grandpapa to learn of the accident before I can tell him myself," she explained. "We mean to ride straight to Tuscombe Park from here, but I know how swiftly bad news can spread."

"Land sakes, Miss Charley, I don't know who we'd be

telling. There's only Sam and me, for our Todd's gone off to Hampshire. But here they be wi' the horses.''

Still munching one of Aggie's saffron buns, Charley let Matois assist her to mount. When he helped Letty, the little girl gave him an apple. Grinning at her, he polished it on his sleeve and took a bite. Charley knew Aggie had given him food, so she was not much surprised when he ate only half and gave the rest to Annabelle.

The gesture pleased Letty, for she told him so, in French, as they made their way around the large horse pond in the stable yard, past tall hedges protecting the garden, and back to the road. Once Matois ascertained that Charley also spoke French, their conversation continued in that language, dominated by Letty's eager questions about life in the French countryside, and his answers. Charley rode quietly, content to listen to them, having no desire to be alone with her thoughts. She spoke French well enough, but Letty was much more fluent, and much more eager to converse.

Frequently, children of English diplomats living abroad never knew they had lived in a foreign country. They spoke only English, were surrounded by English servants, and were never allowed to mix with the native population. Lord and Lady Abreston, however, had decided with his first diplomatic post that their children would benefit more by learning firsthand about other cultures than by ignoring them.

As son and heir of the Marquess of Jervaulx, Gideon Deverill, now styled Earl of Abreston, had enjoyed some choice positions. People who feared that his outspoken wife might ruin his diplomatic career had quickly learned their error. Daintry, Countess of Abreston, made friends wherever she went. Not only was she well read and well educated but she was an excellent horsewoman, as much at home on a hunting field as in a stately drawing room. That she was exceptionally forthright proved to be a refreshing change in a world where many searched and analyzed every statement for hidden meaning. That she chose to introduce her children to state visitors some people accounted an eccentricity, but when the children proved to have excellent manners, and poise and charm beyond their years, they too were soon accepted.

As a result of this unusual upbringing, Letty spoke some German and Italian, as well as excellent French, but Charley, listening to her converse with Matois, soon realized that the child's fluency might astonish even her fond mama. Trying to follow the conversation, Charley found that they had gone beyond her depth. She could pick up an occasional word or phrase, but their language now was extremely idiomatic and, she suspected, the sort of French one heard more in sordid streets and alleyways than in polite drawing rooms.

They were enjoying themselves, however, and she did not mind being left out. She watched Jean Matois, amused by the various expressions that crossed his face as he talked with Letty. Once he addressed a remark to Charley, as if he feared they had been rude, but when she answered in an offhand way, he seemed to know she was content to be silent, and returned to his conversation with Letty.

Jeremiah rode in a pouch Letty had fashioned from a shawl of Aggie Corlan's. The way the little monkey poked his bristly round head out now and again, as if checking their progress before snuggling back in the shawl, made Charley smile.

More than once her thoughts drifted to the carriage at the bottom of the cliff, but she wrenched them back to the present each time. She wondered if she had been wrong not to insist on going down to the beach herself. She was, after all, taking the word of a stranger that her parents were dead. Though she tried to think of other things, it was like having a sore tooth. Her thoughts kept drifting back to touch the pain.

When the main drive to Tuscombe Park House came into sight, Matois reined in and said, "That is where you go, *n'est-ce pas?*"

"*Oui,*" she replied automatically, halting her own mount when she realized he did not mean to ride farther. "You must let us make you known to our grandfather, monsieur. He will want to see you suitably rewarded."

His flashing grin brought a responding smile to her lips, but it faded when he said, "*Mais non, mon ange.* I require no reward beyond knowing you are safe. I will leave you now. Your people will find the wreckage easily, and they will look after you and *la petite,* as well. *Adieu.*''

Letty waved, calling good-bye to Annabelle. But the moment Matois had ridden beyond earshot, she said matter-of-factly, "He is English by birth, not French, I think."

"Good mercy, how can you imagine that? I heard the pair of you prattling away and using words, *ma petite,* that I expect your mama would blush to hear you utter."

Letty chuckled. "That is perfectly true. Papa was most displeased the first, and only, time he heard me speak so. But that was only because Grandpapa Jervaulx was there at the time and turned instantly into an iceberg. You know his way. At least, I daresay you don't, but although he can be as kind as anyone I know, it does not do to arouse his displeasure. Not only does he turn positively glacial but I have observed that nothing sends Papa into alt quicker than when one displeases Grandpapa."

"Letty."

The child looked at her. "Why do I think he's English?"

Charley nodded.

"Well, for one thing, although his vocabulary is quite extensive, he betrays an odd accent with some words. At first he spoke a lower-class patois, so I began doing the same. Then I slipped in some rather horrid idioms, and he did not seem to notice. Next I began changing from patois back to drawing room French, and he did the same quite easily, without seeming to notice. And," she added, "he spoke like a gentleman at times, even in English. That's what first made me wonder about him."

"I noticed that, too, now that you mention it," Charley said thoughtfully. "Perhaps he just attempts to ape his betters, but I think for the present we will say as little about Monsieur Matois as possible."

"That was another thing that made me pay heed to him," Letty said.

"What was?"

"Matois. It means cunning, like a fox."

"Does it indeed?"

Antony exerted himself not to look back, much as he wanted to enjoy one more view of the red-headed moppet and her beautiful cousin. Charley, indeed, he thought. Ridiculous to attach a boyish name to a woman with the glossiest black hair and the most kissable red lips he had ever seen. He felt sure that Jean Matois would not look back, but if Jean Matois were long in the presence of those two, he would soon lose his identity altogether. Playing a role was proving to be more difficult in England than in France. All too easily had he heard himself slip into the old speech patterns he had known from birth. Even in French—Lord, what a vocabulary the child had. But he was safer in French. He doubted that Letty was old enough to heed the way he spoke.

He would not see them again, which was a pity. He liked them both, and the ridiculous monkey, too. When the creature had first shrieked at him out of the darkness, he nearly jumped out of his skin. It had not once occurred to him what he might find if he followed it. He had done so only out of curiosity.

Hoping none of his comrades had seen him with the young ladies, he wondered if he ought to have warned them not to speak of meeting him. They could increase his danger considerably if they were to tell anyone that from time to time he spoke like an English gentleman. Better not to have made a point of it by requesting their silence, he decided. They would have more important matters to divert their attention from him.

For years he had blessed his ear for accents, his ability to mimic, almost unconsciously, both the cadence and pronunciation of whatever he heard. That gift had let him merge into many a group, regardless of class. It had also plunged him into trouble as a boy more than once, both with his stern father and with certain masters at school. Now, if he were not careful, it could land him in the suds again.

* * *

The front door stood open. Seeing her grandfather's butler on the threshold, peering toward them, Charley urged her mount to a canter. Letty followed.

When they dismounted, others appeared in the doorway. Most were servants, but Charley saw her grandfather hurrying toward them, his expression first delighted and surprised, then worried. Handing her reins to a lackey, she hurried to meet him.

"Upon my word, Charlotte," St. Merryn exclaimed, holding out his plump hands to her, "where did you spring from? This can't be little Letitia! My, my how you've grown, child. But what's the meaning of this? Surely, Charles has not so lost his senses as to allow the pair of you to ride ahead, and looking like a couple of shag bags at that. What can he have been thinking? Where the devil is he? And Davina?"

Seeing with alarm that he had worked himself into a state, Charley glanced beyond him at the butler, Medrose, who was hurrying in his wake.

Red-faced, St. Merryn snapped, "Cat got your tongue, girl? Where are they?"

"Grandpapa, maybe we should go into the house," she said gently.

"Nonsense, spit it out! Your baggage and servants arrived yesterday, but they said only that you'd gone to have a look at the Plymouth house. We heard a carriage went over a cliff last night, and I own, I worried till I realized you would have stayed the night. Now you're here all right and tight, but where the devil are your parents?"

"I don't know how you heard so soon about the accident," she said, "but I'm afraid that it was our—"

"No!" His complexion went from red to white in the blink of an eye, and he seemed to have difficulty breathing. "Not Charles. Please, child, not my son!"

"Oh, Grandpapa." Tears welled into her eyes. "There were highwaymen, and the coachman drove faster to get away, but—"

Breaking off when she realized he was not heeding her, she reached out a hand to touch his arm.

He snatched it away. "Not Charles," he cried. "Not my son!" He staggered.

The butler and a footman leapt to steady him, but he clapped a hand to his chest and collapsed.

Chapter Three

"Is he dead?" Letty asked.

"Letty, please!"

"I only asked because I saw an Italian ambassador collapse just that way once, and later Papa said that he had died. Is there anything we can do, Cousin Charley? Should they not put him to bed if he is not dead, and send for a doctor?"

Charley looked helplessly at Medrose, who nodded and called for another footman.

St. Merryn lingered three days but spoke not another word, and Charley felt as if from the moment of his collapse he had thrust on her the whole burden of looking after his estates. Her grandmother, a frail lady who had enjoyed poor health for years, collapsed on her sofa at learning of the deaths of her son and his wife, and her husband's subsequent seizure. Though Charley could leave Lady St. Merryn to the tender mercies of Miss Ethelinda Davies, the poor relation who looked after her, other important matters required her immediate attention.

Thanks to Medrose and Mrs. Medrose, the housekeeper, the household was running smoothly, but she knew better than to leave all direction to the servants. There would be many decisions to make. On the other hand, her grandfather's excellent land steward, Petrok Caltor, was quite capable of keeping the estates going with no more than a command to do so. It was he to whom she turned that first day for help.

"You'll be wanting to fetch home the bodies," he said practically when she met with him in his tidy office. "I'll arrange for all that. And," he added, bluntly broaching a subject she had not cared to mention, "we'll be putting them in coffins straightaway, miss, and shutting the lids tight. His lordship won't want no one gaping at Mr. Charles or Miss Davina in the condition they're like to be in. I'd not be putting the funerals off, neither, Miss Charley. Unseasonable warm it be for the middle of April."

"We'll see how Grandpapa does, Mr. Caltor, but we must send someone to tell the vicar. I think we'd best send for Grandpapa's man of affairs, as well."

"That would be Mr. Stephen Kenhorn of Bodmin, miss. If you will be so kind as to write him a letter, I'll have one of my lads take it to him straightaway, though it do be a Sunday."

The doctor arrived that afternoon. After he had examined St. Merryn, he joined Charley in the downstairs parlor where she had been conferring with the housekeeper. Shaking his head gravely, the doctor said he feared that the earl was failing rapidly.

"Your father's death was a great blow to him, my dear," he said. "I think he cared more for Charles than for anyone. Such a tragedy. You have my condolences."

"Thank you," Charley said. Dismissing the housekeeper, she added, "Will you look in on her ladyship before you go, please, sir?"

The genial doctor smiled his understanding. "To be sure, I will. I daresay she's taking all this very hard. Even were she not, she'd be sure to take a pet did I come by Tuscombe Park and leave again without paying my respects. You've enough on your plate, I'm thinking, without adding a bout of her megrims to the mixture."

She was tempted to ask him for some liniment for her bruises, but she did not, believing that, although painful, they were not serious. He had been gone long enough for her to make a list of things to do when Letty came into the room.

Taking a seat near the table where Charley was working, the child said with a sigh, "I have been reading to Grandmama so Cousin Ethelinda could go for her walk, but she hurried back when she saw the doctor's carriage. She asked him to look at the bump on my head, and he told her it's not broken, which I already knew." She paused, then added, "Is Grandmama really very sick, Cousin Charley?"

"Not really, darling, though she is certainly distressed just now. Generally, she enjoys the attention she receives on account of her ills. And, in truth, her frailty allows Cousin Ethelinda to feel useful. When I was a child, I was unfeeling enough to think her a mere barnacle who cosseted Grandmama so as to seem needed, but our cousin is very kind. I have long since come to appreciate her many good qualities."

"I should think you must," Letty said. "I was never more glad to see anyone in my life. Grandmama is upset, certainly, but she seems to believe Aunt Davina and Uncle Charles died merely to provoke her, and that Grandpapa is putting on airs to be interesting. She says she is the only one who truly suffers from their loss."

"I know, darling. Twice she has pointed out to me that, because my papa died before Grandpapa, I shall never be *Lady* Charlotte. As if I cared for such stuff."

"I know," Letty said with a wry smile. "She warned me not to puff off my being a ladyship because it might distress you. And when I told her I would never do such a thing, she looked wise and said I was only a child and might not know how words can hurt people. Really, she said that, as if her own words were of no moment whatever."

Charley leaned over and gave her a hug. "I am so glad you are here, Letty. I begin to think you are the wisest, most sensible person in the house. Where is Jeremiah, by the bye?"

"In my bedchamber. Grandmama is not fond of him, and Cousin Ethelinda is so restive that she makes him nervous. He's made friends with the maid who looks after my room, so he will be content for a while, I expect. Can I do anything to help you?''

"You may tell someone—Jago, I expect—that I shall want a horse saddled first thing in the morning. I must ride to Lostwithiel to have some proper mourning clothes made up. You had better come, too, I suppose. Grandmama and Cousin Ethelinda have proper things to wear, but I do not. My riding habit is the only black garment I own. Kerra is presently removing all the trimming, so I can show myself abroad. In the meantime, I intend to write letters to inform people of the accident. You should write to your parents. You may use some of my paper if you like.''

Charley decided not to seal her letters, knowing she might well have to add the news of her grandfather's death. Only Letty's and one other, to their great-grandaunt Lady Ophelia Balterley, in London, went post haste.

Letty left the room soon after her letter was finished. When Charley finished hers, she resumed her discussion with the housekeeper about necessary arrangements for the forthcoming funeral, then took supper with Letty and found other small tasks to occupy her until bedtime. By the time she retired, she was exhausted, and fell asleep at once, just as she had hoped she would. She did not want to lie awake with only memories for company.

The following morning, when she went downstairs to break her fast, she found Letty before her, chatting happily with the two footmen who were serving her. Charley joined the conversation, but ate less than usual, and was soon ready to depart.

As they left the stable yard, followed by Teddy, the groom who had served Charley since her childhood, Letty said, "I like Jago and Pedrick. They told me about when Papa came here the first time, and how Mama always wore a bright red cloak then. I'd adore to wear a red cloak, but with my hair, I simply cannot do so.''

"Certainly not with two recent deaths in the family,'' Charley agreed. "What else did you talk to Jago and Pedrick about?''

Letty eyed her uncertainly. "I hope you are not vexed with

me for talking with servants. Aunt Davina said I consort far too much with the lower classes, but I like people who will talk to me. Here in England, even more than in France, I have observed that grown-ups frequently do not talk to children. Or, if they do, they talk to me as if I were a baby with no understanding whatsoever.''

"I will tell you what Great-Aunt Ophelia said to me about that when I was your age,'' Charley said. '' 'I don't care who you count as your friends,' she said, 'because every friend is more valuable to you than an enemy or a stranger.' She did insist that I consider other people's sensibilities, however, and take care not to offend them.''

"Great-Aunt Ophelia is very old,'' Letty said. "When we stayed with her at St. Merryn London House, Aunt Davina told me she is in her ninetieth year.''

"She is elderly,'' Charley agreed, "but she is no less formidable for being past the age mark.'' She had a great fondness for Lady Ophelia Balterley, and wished very much that that staunch supporter of the female sex were at hand to advise her now. "You are very observant, Letty, and wise beyond your years. Moreover, I don't mind confessing that you are much more of a lady than I was at your age.''

"Ah, yes, but then I was *born* a lady,'' Letty said, shooting her a mischievous look from under her auburn eyebrows.

"Minx. I hope you don't become saucy while you're here with me. I know very well where your papa would lay the blame for that, and I'd prefer that you not give him my head for washing. He's the only man I've ever known whom I could not wrap round my thumb.''

Letty chuckled. "Mama says the same thing.''

They were riding along the River Fowey now, their way shaded by overhanging willows and alder trees. They chatted in a friendly way about family matters until they reached the cobbled streets of Lostwithiel and drew rein before the dressmaker's shop in the High Street. As they dismounted, Letty said with a twinkle, "Will she be offended that we came to her on horseback? Mama always visits her Parisian modiste in very grand style. She says Cerisette would be distressed if she did not."

"Today my need to ride was greater than my need to help Angelique impress her neighbors," Charley said frankly. "I've ridden here decorously enough to avoid looking like a wild woman, but on the way home I mean to gallop away my fidgets. I'm still feeling battered and bruised, so I might regret it, but I've been cooped up in carriages for far too many days, not to mention the packet boat before London."

Letty shot her a quizzical look from under her eyebrows but said only, "I shall like a gallop, too. This horse you've given me to ride seems to have excellent paces."

"All Grandpapa's horses have excellent paces," Charley said. "Acquiring good horseflesh is a passion that runs in the family. Papa—" She broke off, turning away to hand her reins to Teddy, then added with a forced smile, "Come along now, darling. Let's attend to business. Then, afterward, maybe we can visit Dewy the Baker."

They entered the little shop to hear a strident voice scolding someone in Gallic accents. The sound of a sharp slap followed, then an outcry. Charley exchanged a look with Letty, whose eyes were wide with astonishment, then rang the bell on the counter. A moment later the owner bustled through a curtained doorway from the back.

A tall, faded-blond woman of indeterminate age, whose prettiness had faded over the years, Angelique Peryllys had a natural sense of style that was expressed today in an elaborate coiffure and a simple gown of saffron-colored armazine, trimmed with dark brown piping and edged with a narrow band of ochre lace at cuffs and hem. She greeted Charley with dignity. "Good day, mademoiselle. We were sad to hear of the dreadful tragedy in your family. You have come to obtain mourning dress, I believe."

"Yes, we have," Charley said briskly. "Angelique, this is my cousin, Lady Letitia Deverill. She, too, will need a few things."

"*Bien sûr, mademoiselle.* Black gloves, of course, and two or three little gowns. Will the child attend the funeral?"

"She will not," Charley said. "Nor will I, for that matter. My grandmother does not hold with females attending such ceremonies, and in truth, I've no wish to go." She did not add that, like Lady Ophelia, she believed funerals were a barbaric custom and preferred to remember her parents as they had lived rather than as they had died.

Letty began to explain her requirements, in French, but Angelique cut her off, saying abruptly, "It is my practice to speak only English to my customers, if you please, mademoiselle. I am persuaded that Miss Tarrant will explain your needs to me."

Catching Letty's eye, Charley saw that there was no need to warn her to keep silent. Thinking of how she would have responded at the same age to an impertinent rebuke from a tradesperson made her very glad that Letty's temperament was less fiery than hers had been.

Angelique said with much more politeness, "I have mourning gowns already made up, Mademoiselle Charlotte, just like any other modiste of quality. They require only fitting and hemming, so if you will allow me to take some measurements— What do *you* want?" She hurled the indignant question at a ragged-looking child a year or two older than Letty, who had stepped through the curtain from the back.

"Beg pardon, mum," the child murmured, "but Bess wants to know—"

"Can you not see that I am engaged? When I am finished, you may believe that I will teach you never to interrupt me when I am assisting a customer."

The child paled and clutched her hands together under her limp apron.

At the same moment that Charley noted the red imprint of a hand on the little girl's white cheek, she recognized her. "Jenifry Breton, is that you? Good mercy, I nearly didn't recognize you, you've grown so. Come here, child, and tell me how your mama and papa are getting on. I've just returned from France, you know, so I have not seen them in months." Glancing at the seamstress, she added, "You must know,

Angelique, that Jenifry is the daughter of one of my grandfather's tenants.''

The child gazed anxiously at Angelique, who nodded curtly. Only then did Jenifry say, ''Good day, Miss Charley—Miss Charlotte, I mean,'' she added with a darting look at her stern mistress. ''Mama and Papa are well, I expect, though I haven't seen them in months myself, not since I got apprenticed to Madam Angelique.''

''Good mercy,'' Charley exclaimed, looking at the seamstress. ''Is that not a trifle harsh? Surely, she might have leave to visit her parents from time to time.''

''Not for the first year,'' Angelique said firmly. ''Once our girls know the rules and have shown they can abide by them, and once I know they take well to stitching, then perhaps. Until then, it is not so good for them always to be shifting from Papa and Mama to Angelique.''

''I see.''

''Go away now, Jenifry. I shall speak with you when Miss Tarrant has gone.''

Jenifry blanched again, and Letty said quietly, ''Perhaps she could select some black ribbons for me, Cousin Charley, while Madame Angelique assists you.''

Charley said, ''That's an excellent notion. Lady Letitia will need several widths, I think, Angelique. Sash lengths, and for her hats—and black gloves, as you suggested. She requires only one mourning dress, however, to wear the day of the funeral. No one expects to see a child rigged out like a baby raven for months on end, thank heaven, and gray is one of her favorite colors. She will have plenty of suitable outfits if the trimmings are altered.''

''As you say, mademoiselle. Now, as to yourself, perhaps I might suggest . . .''

Charley allowed herself to be drawn away then, but after making her selections and before arranging for payment, she said quietly, ''I hope you were not intending to punish Jenifry too harshly merely for coming to ask you a question.''

''She will be soundly whipped,'' Angelique said uncompromisingly. "My girls have strict orders never to enter the shop. She must learn to obey my rules, miss."

"Nevertheless, Angelique, I would take it kindly if you were to let her off with a scolding this time. I could not, in good conscience, continue to patronize a shop where a child from Tuscombe Park is harshly used. Much as I should dislike having to travel all the way to Bodmin or St. Austell . . ." Pointedly, she let her words trail to silence.

Angelique nodded. "It shall be as you wish, mademoiselle, certainly."

Having arranged for delivery the following day of two gowns suitable for deep mourning, and a few accessories, Charley and Letty took their leave.

"How glad I am that I had this black habit made for me in London," Charley said. "Now that Kerra has removed the pink epaulettes and piping, and replaced the mother of pearl buttons with jet, it is perfectly suitable. Oh, but how vexatious! Dewy the Baker's shop is closed now. I wanted to buy you a special Cornish treat."

"Thank you, but I don't feel like enjoying a treat right now, in any event," Letty said. She remained silent after that until they had left the cobblestones and the resulting clatter of hoof-beats behind them. Then she said fiercely, "I am very grateful to have been born a Deverill, believe me!"

"I suppose you are thinking of Jenifry. I have known her since she was born, you know. Their cottage is on the edge of the moor near the river. I used to ride up there and play in a pool nearby. In fact, her father, Cubert, taught me to swim."

"Papa taught me," Letty said. "Cousin Charley, do you know that awful woman beats the girls who work for her? Not just when they are naughty but for setting stitches too far apart or for getting a fingerprint on the material. Jenifry says she makes them pick up their skirts behind and takes a switch to their bare legs. If she complains to her husband about them, their punishments are even worse."

"Good mercy," Charley said.

"Jenifry and Bess are the only ones left to do the work right now, too. There was another girl, but I think she must have run off. I don't think Jenifry was supposed to tell me about her," she added thoughtfully. "She kept darting looks at her mistress while we talked, and that was one of the times Angelique looked back. Jenifry didn't say another word, except about ribbons."

"I'm sure it is a hard life," Charley said, "but if Jenifry learns the business from Angelique, one day she may have a shop of her own. She might even go to a bigger town—even London—and make her fortune. It's too bad she angered her mistress today, but I took care that she won't be whipped this time. I believe that if she works hard and always does her best, one day she will be very thankful for her training."

Letty did not look convinced, but when Charley suggested a gallop, she agreed with alacrity.

Their mourning gowns arrived the following day, and the day after that, the Earl of St. Merryn breathed his last breath. Charley was with him when he died, and she felt abandoned, even a little angry, but she experienced almost none of the profound grief she had expected to feel. St. Merryn had played a large part in her life. Now he was gone, but she felt only the same empty numbness she had felt since the accident. It seemed strange, but she did not allow her thoughts to dwell on it for long. There were too many other details to attend to, no time to contemplate mere emotions.

Stephen Kenhorn arrived from Bodmin that afternoon. He met with Charley in her grandfather's library, a spacious room lined with books that she doubted the hunting-mad earl had ever read. Kenhorn, a thin, wiry man with a habit of wringing his hands together, seemed almost put out with St. Merryn for dying before his arrival.

"I'd have come last night, Miss Charlotte, but for the unfortunate circumstance of my having had business yesterday in Truro. Everything there is in a great bustle, you know, thanks to all the preparations in train to consecrate the new cathedral."

"What must we do next, Mr. Kenhorn?" Charley asked, having no patience for amenities. She had already sustained a trying hour with Lady St. Merryn, who clearly believed her husband had died to make her life more difficult than it was already.

The solicitor primmed up his lips. "Fortunately, you had the good sense to describe his lordship's condition when you wrote of your parents' deaths, so I came prepared for the worst. I'm just sorry I could not get here sooner. Your father, I regret to say, made no will. He had no private fortune, in any case, only the allowance Lord St. Merryn gave him each quarter. Still, I had hoped I might get here soon enough to remind his lordship of that fact." He clicked his tongue in frustration.

"What about my mother's money?"

"Well, Mrs. Tarrant had her marriage portion, of course, but if there is a penny left of that, my dear, I shall own myself astonished. Your parents were not careful with their money, never were."

Recalling many arguments between the two over that painful subject, Charley sighed. "I suppose you mean I am entirely dependent upon what Grandpapa left me."

Mr. Kenhorn looked uncomfortable. "Ah, as to that, my dear, I should be talking out of school if I were to reveal details of his will before the proper reading. That must take place, of course, directly after the funeral. And that will be . . . ?" He raised his brows quizzically.

"They'll all be buried tomorrow," Charley said. "There is no point in waiting longer. The family is too spread about to expect anyone to come, and I refuse to pack all the bodies in ice merely so that more relatives can see them put underground."

"Just so," he said, glancing at her with undisguised concern. "Just so."

"I suppose you think me callous, sir. I am not. I am merely practical. My grandmother is most distressed by all this, as you might imagine. It will not help her to know that her son, her husband, and her daughter-in-law are all stored away down in the ice house, awaiting the gathering of a proper funeral party."

"Perhaps you would prefer to sit down whilst we finish our little talk," the solicitor said with a worried frown.

"If you like, certainly." She gestured toward a chair near

the hearth, where a cheerful fire crackled, and took its twin for herself.

"Have you no one to support you, my dear?" he asked gently. "No older female—or even better, a male relative?"

"I'll manage on my own, Mr. Kenhorn, thank you. And that's just as well, since I know of no male nearer than Paris, or perhaps Edinburgh, whom I'd trust to make decisions, and no female nearer than London. Now, do stop fretting, and tell me what I must do. As you must know, I have never had to deal with such a situation before."

"Few people are ever called upon to deal with a situation like this one," he said. "And—forgive me for speaking frankly—you are quite young, Miss Charlotte, to take on such a burden."

"Nonsense, sir. I am four-and-twenty, an old maid quite contentedly on the shelf, and I've had the benefit of an excellent education. What must I do first?"

"In point of fact, ma'am, there is very little that you *can* do except see to the burials and keep the household running smoothly until the new heir arrives. Petrok Caltor will keep the estates in trim, and I will see what we can arrange about sales of sheep and such like events that must be seen to before probate is complete. No one can sell any of the property unnecessarily before then, as I hope you know."

"What a good thing I hadn't planned to sell the house," Charley said.

He smiled weakly.

"What of the house in Plymouth that my parents used from time to time?"

"As you doubtless know, it has been hired out to a family for the year. We'd be in breach of contract if we tried to evict them."

"I was not suggesting that we should. I just wanted to know. Really, Mr. Kenhorn, I would be much obliged if you would not treat me like an idiot."

"I hope I am doing no such thing, but the fact is, my dear, that there is no dower house at Tuscombe Park. Until we complete probate and the new heir has decided what to do with you, I'm afraid that you and Lady St. Merryn—and Miss Davies, too, of course—will be obliged to remain under this roof.''

Since it had not occurred to Charley that she might have to leave Tuscombe Park, especially if her father had been unable to provide her with an independence, she was somewhat taken aback by his concern, but she rallied quickly. ''I shan't require a great deal, sir. As you must know, I do not intend to marry, and have long looked forward to reaching that stage in my life when I shall be considered old enough to set up housekeeping with a reliable female to lend me countenance. Since Papa and Grandpapa have always known that to be my intention, I daresay there will be enough. It is not as if I were expecting a large dowry to see me properly married, after all.''

Mr. Kenhorn looked very unhappy, and the following day, when the family gathered in the drawing room at the end of the gallery to hear the reading of St. Merryn's will, Charley discovered why.

Letty was not present, since the will did not concern her. When Charley, Lady St. Merryn, and Miss Davies had taken seats, Kenhorn said apologetically, ''There is a great deal in this document that no longer pertains, I'm afraid, since his late lordship quite understandably expected his son to survive him. In the event, I shan't bore you to death by reading the whole thing unless you particularly wish me to do so.''

''On no account whatsoever,'' Lady St. Merryn said, languishing on the sofa. ''My salts, Ethelinda!''

Miss Davies, a stout lady with frizzy, graying blond hair, hovered over the older lady, plumping pillows and straightening shawls until Lady St. Merryn was sufficiently bolstered to sustain the ordeal.

Kenhorn glanced at Charley. ''Miss Charlotte?''

''I shall want to read the whole later, sir, but for now, the salient points will do.''

He blinked, then turned his attention to the document. Raising a pair of horn-rimmed spectacles to his eyes, he said, ''First, there is her ladyship's jointure. That, of course, was settled at the time of their marriage, and his lordship believed it was adequate. It is not a vast sum—''

"It is a pittance," Lady St. Merryn said, sitting up indignantly. "Surely, that is not all he left me, Kenhorn!"

"I regret to say that it is, your ladyship. Please, bear in mind that although his lordship was aware that in the natural way of things, and notwithstanding your ladyship's precarious health, he might well predecease you, he also expected his son to look after you and see that you lacked for naught."

"Don't fret, Grandmama," Charley said calmly. "You will continue to live as comfortably as ever. You still have your share of the Balterley money, after all."

Lady St. Merryn brightened. "Quite right. I had forgotten that."

Kenhorn cleared his throat. "As to that, ma'am, I am happy to say that there is still a good bit of principal left of your marriage portion. Nevertheless, you will recall that you signed a large amount over to your husband several years ago to help settle some difficulties at one of the mines. Moreover, the amount I previously mentioned includes the income from what remains of your marriage portion."

"Good God." Turning pale, Lady St. Merryn collapsed against her cushions.

"His lordship left Miss Davies three thousand pounds," Kenhorn went on.

"Goodness me," Miss Davies said, blinking. "H-how generous."

"Fustian," Charley snapped. "Three thousand a year might be thought generous, Cousin, but a mere three thousand pounds after all the years you have so faithfully served my grandmother is absurd. I wish I might have had five minutes alone with Grandpapa to tell him what I think about that."

"Charlotte!" Lady St. Merryn raised her vinaigrette and breathed deeply.

Miss Davies was flustered. "You are too kind, Charley dear. But really, you must not say such things, not at such a sad time, you know."

"I could say much worse," Charley said, turning back to Kenhorn. "I scarcely dare to ask, sir. Did he leave me anything?"

"He left ten thousand pounds to each of his two daughters, the Lady Susan and the Lady Daintry," Kenhorn said, avoiding her gaze, "but I am afraid he expected your papa to provide for you, Miss Charlotte. He did leave you the pick of any horses currently in his stable. He also left three thousand pounds to augment whatever dowry your father arranged for you, but only in the event that you were married at the time of his death or married within a year after it. That is all. I might add that you are the only one of his grandchildren to whom he left a penny. The residual portion of his private fortune, along with all the entailed property, goes directly to his heir."

"And who is the heir, sir? I confess, I haven't a notion."

Before Kenhorn spoke, Lady St. Merryn said, "It must be one of the Norfolk Tarrants, for St. Merryn had no brothers. We don't know them."

"Quite right," Kenhorn said, "but there is actually some question as to which one it is, I'm afraid. The earl saw no reason to add that information to his will while young Charles lived, but I shall have it sorted out very soon, I expect. In any event, no one can alter anything here at Tuscombe Park until we complete probate, so you can all go on as before until the new heir arrives to set things in order."

Charley said, "I am disappointed in Grandpapa. He knew very well that I have no intention of submitting my body or my mind to any man's direction, because I decided that much when I was a child. I told him many times—and Papa, too— just how I want to live my life. It is as if they never took heed of my wishes at all."

"I am afraid you are right, Miss Charlotte, but in fairness to your grandfather, your wishes must have appeared rather foolish to him. Many a young lady has said she never intends to marry, only to find that marriage is her best course. There is no place for single, independent females in our society. When all is said and done, a woman needs a man to look after her. Surely, you must agree. Moreover," he added before she could set him straight, "I can tell you that your grandpapa assumed that you would have married long before he departed this earth. He did once say, however, that if through some mischance, you had not done so, you should apply to your Great-Aunt Ophelia to support your"—he hid a smile—"your knaggy notions. That's what he called them. He said she should look after you, since she put them into your head in the first place."

Charley pressed her lips together for a long moment. Then she said calmly, "I wrote at once to inform her of Papa and Mama's death, and again when Grandpapa died, but I cannot imagine throwing myself on her mercy or asking her to set me up in a house of my own. Nor do I wish her to die. In the event, I know she will leave most of her fortune to my aunts, for she will also have expected my father to provide for me." She stood and held out her hand to the solicitor. "Thank you for coming, sir. Do you remain another night with us, or do you mean to go straight back to Bodmin?"

"Straight back," he said, clearly relieved that she had not become hysterical. "I will set matters in train at once to notify the new heir, but I daresay it will be six weeks or more before you hear from him."

Mr. Kenhorn was wrong. Less than a fortnight later, Mr. Alfred Tarrant arrived from Norfolk, bringing his wife, two small children, and his unmarried sister with him.

"Came at once," he informed the three astonished ladies who greeted his arrival in the drawing room. "Soon as I read that the whole estate was being looked after by a mere female, I knew there was not a moment to lose!"

Chapter Four

Suppressing the first words that leapt to her tongue as unacceptable, Charley turned to Medrose, who had announced the newcomers in his usual stately fashion. "Please send for Mrs. Medrose," she said. "Ask her to help our guests get settled."

"Not guests, my dear," Mr. Alfred Tarrant said firmly. He was a squarely built, rather fleshy man of medium height with two chins. Charley judged him to be some five years older than herself. His condescending attitude grated as he continued, "I'm afraid that from this moment you are the guests here, not us. Not but what you aren't welcome, of course. I stopped in Bodmin to have a word with Kenhorn, you see, so I know exactly how matters stand. You and your grandmama"—he made a stately bow in Lady St. Merryn's direction—"and, Miss Davies, is it?" He made another bow, to which, clearly flustered, Cousin Ethelinda smiled weakly in response. "Yes, well," he went on, as he turned back to the butler, "you are all quite welcome to stay here with us until we can make other arrangements. Medrose, I want you and the other servants to know that I mean to make no changes here for the present, so—"

"No one can make changes until probate is completed," Charley said tartly.

"Quite right, my dear," Mr. Tarrant said amiably. "Now then, Medrose, if you will just ask Mrs. Medrose to have the mistress's chambers prepared for Mrs. Tarrant, and the late Earl's ditto for myself—"

Outraged, Charley snapped, "Do you intend, the moment you step into this house, to turn my grandmother out of the bedchamber she has occupied since she came to Tuscombe Park as a bride! Good mercy, sir, what manner of monster are you?"

"Why, no monster at all," he said placidly. "Surely, the dowager Lady St. Merryn expected to give up the primary female bedchamber when the new heir arrived. If there were a Dower House here, which I am told there is not, she would surely be making preparations to remove to it."

"Are we expected to address you as Your Lordship?" Charley demanded.

"Oh, not just yet," he said. "Time enough for titles when probate is complete, and Kenhorn has one or two small matters to look into before he can accomplish that."

"What matters?"

"Nothing you need trouble your pretty head about, my dear. Kenhorn has it all in hand, and I doubt you would understand such things if I tried to explain them to you. Now, how are the children to address you, I wonder? I believe Kenhorn said you like to be called Charley by members of the family. I do not hold with masculine nicknames for females, myself, but if that is what you like—"

"How old are the children?" she said, smiling at the two toddlers hiding their faces in the skirts of the younger of the two women who had entered in his wake.

Tarrant said, "Our Neddy is four, I believe, and Jane is two."

"They can call me Cousin Charlotte if you prefer," she said, "or Charley if you will allow it." Turning from him, she held out her hand to the older of the two women with him, and said, "Forgive me if I seemed to forget my manners. We did not anticipate your arrival for some weeks yet, you see, but you are certainly welcome. You, I need not add, may call me Charley if your sensibilities are not disturbed by such nicknames. And your name is . . . ?''

"Edythe Tarrant, with a 'y' and an 'e,' '' the woman said, standing straight and looking down her nose. She was not much older than Charley, but she was at least six inches taller and carried herself like a haughty dame with fifty years' experience behind her. Indicating the slender, light-brown-haired girl to whose skirts the children clung, she added, "This is Mr. Tarrant's sister, Elizabeth, spelled the ordinary way. She makes her home with us, their parents being deceased. I must say, Charlotte, my dear, since I do not believe in mincing words, that I am astonished to see a young woman of quality putting herself forward in such an unbecoming way as you have done today."

"Are you, ma'am? Well, when you have come to know me better, my behavior will not surprise you at all. As you can readily see, my grandmother does not enjoy robust health, so it has fallen to me to look after things here since my parents and my grandfather died. Now then,'' she added in a brisker tone, "I will be glad to show you over the house when you have got settled in. Mr. Tarrant" she added, turning back to Alfred, "I will gladly arrange to help you become familiar with estate matters, too."

"You must call me Cousin Alfred, Charlotte," he said. "As to estate matters, I assure you, I do not require lessons in management from a scrap of a girl. Kenhorn has promised to visit me to attend to all that. In the meantime, I'll want to speak to one Petrok Caltor. Quite an outlandish name, but I am told he is the late lord's steward. Kenhorn tells me he is capable enough, and I don't suppose he named himself."

"Petrok Caltor's is a good and well-respected Cornish name, sir, and he is an *excellent* steward, I might add."

"I expect we will see about that in good time."

Charley ground her teeth together, noting that Lady St. Merryn had collapsed with her salts bottle and seemed to have no intention of speaking to the newcomers. She was grateful when Medrose chose that moment to return.

"Here is Mrs. Medrose, Miss Charlotte," he said from the doorway. Then, turning to Edythe Tarrant, he said, "Do the children have a nursemaid, madam?"

"Ain't arrived yet," Alfred said before Edythe could reply. "We met with a dashed heavy fog rolling in from the sea, which doubtless delayed the second carriage. Nonetheless, our baggage and servants cannot be far behind us and ought to arrive before nightfall. In the meantime, our Elizabeth will look after them, won't you, Lizzie?"

"Oh, yes, Alfred, of course I will," the girl said in a soft voice. "Come, children. We will find a warm fire and perhaps some cinnamon toast. Oh!" The exclamation came when she looked toward the doorway.

Turning to see what had startled Elizabeth, Charley saw Letty come in with Jeremiah perched on her shoulder.

"Upon my word," Alfred exclaimed. "What the devil is that?"

Calmly, Charley replied, "Cousin Alfred, everyone, this is my cousin, the Lady Letitia Deverill. Letty, dear, this is Mr. Alfred Tarrant, who says he is the heir to Tuscombe Park." Having taken the measure of at least two of the newcomers, she added, "Letty's paternal grandfather is the Marquess of Jervaulx, Cousin Alfred."

"Is he, by God? And does he allow monkeys in his drawing room, miss?"

"Why, yes, he does," Letty answered in her usual matter-of-fact way. Making a careful curtsy, so as not to startle the little monkey, she added politely, "How do you do, Cousin Alfred? I am pleased to meet you." She looked expectantly at the others.

When Alfred Tarrant did not introduce his family, Charley said, "This lady is Mrs. Tarrant, Letty, and that one is Cousin Alfred's sister, Elizabeth Tarrant. The children are called Neddy and Jane."

Edythe, ignoring Letty's polite greeting and eyeing Jeremiah with acute disfavor, said almost before Charley had finished speaking, "Surely, that wild animal is not safe to keep in a gentleman's house."

Letty said, "Jeremiah generally lives at the British Embassy in Paris, ma'am. I assure you, his manners are excellent. He does not bite, and he is very clean."

"Nevertheless," Alfred said in a too-hearty tone, "in my house, livestock live in the stable. I don't want to see that little devil in the drawing room again, young lady."

Charley said, "As I understand the matter, this is not yet your house, Cousin Alfred. And since my grandfather saw no harm in Jeremiah, may I suggest that perhaps a compromise is in order for the present?"

"Nonsense, monkeys do not belong in civilized homes."

"Jeremiah does not belong in a stable, where he might catch a chill and die," she said firmly. "I might add, sir, that the marquess is extremely fond of Jeremiah." She paused. When he did not immediately reply, she added gently, "You may safely rely upon Letty to see that he does not disturb you or Cousin Edythe."

"Very well," he grumbled. "But it is a very odd thing, upon my word, it is!"

"Cousin Charley, what a plumper that was!" Letty said in astonishment when Mrs. Medrose had taken the others to see their bedchambers. "You know perfectly well that Grandpapa Jervaulx barely tolerates Jeremiah. I was putting it strongly to say he allows him in the drawing room. He has done so, but only as a very special treat."

"I know. I daresay I behaved badly, but that man is a pompous mushroom. To think that he will take Grandpapa's place here makes my blood boil."

Lady St. Merryn, gathering her many shawls and preparing with Cousin Ethelinda's assistance to go upstairs to her sitting room, muttered bitterly, "I daresay that odious woman will want every room that I consider to be my own."

"Never mind her, Grandmama," Charley said. "You may depend upon it that Medrose will put them both in guest chambers until we can sort out what's best to be done. The children can have the nursery rooms, of course. But is the outside enough for them to demand your chamber or Grandpapa's before Alfred has proven his claim to the title and estate.'' She would have gone on, but the drawing room doors opened again. When Medrose entered, she said wearily, ''What is it now? Surely, those odious people have not contrived to make more difficulties already.''

''No, Miss Charlotte,'' the butler said, avoiding her eye as he turned toward Lady St. Merryn. ''My lady, I beg to announce the arrival of Lord Rockland.''

Lady St. Merryn had recourse to her salts again.

Charley, looking in astonishment at the grinning young gentleman who appeared from behind Medrose, exclaimed, ''Rockland, what on earth are you doing here?''

''Knew you'd be delighted to see me, my treasure. You ought to be grateful I didn't get swallowed up by that dashed thick fog outside. It's consumed this house and everything for miles around. Now, I've already greased Medrose in the fist to tell me why the front hall is rapidly filling with baggage, so I know you've been invaded, but this house looks big enough to hold one more—two, counting my man. Daresay you'll look upon me as your knight in shining armor, come to rescue you in the nick of time. Your servant, ma'am,'' he added, making a profound leg to Lady St. Merryn. ''And yours.'' He made another to Miss Davies.

Lady St. Merryn looked puzzled. ''Rockland? Do I know you?''

''Not yet, my dear ma'am. But I hope and trust that one day you will know me very well, the day my adored one grants me leave to take her as my wife.''

Letty said, ''Do you want to marry Cousin Charley, sir?''

''I do,'' he replied. ''That is the dearest wish of my life.''

''Stop talking nonsense, Rockland,'' Charley said. ''There is not one thing you could do or say to change my mind about marrying. You ought to know that perfectly well by now. Indeed, I don't know what we are going to do with you. However, if you have brought word from Great-Aunt Ophelia, I will be glad of that, at least.''

''Good gracious,'' Lady St. Merryn exclaimed. ''Don't tell

me Aunt Ophelia is here! Oh dear, how very uncomfortable we will be, for I cannot help but think that she will take those dreadful Norfolk Tarrants in aversion. Oh dear, oh dear.''

"Great-Aunt Ophelia is not here, Grandmama," Charley said, raising her voice. With a quizzical look at Rockland, she added, ''You didn't bring her, did you?''

"Alas, I could not bring her up to scratch," he said. "Told me the funerals would be over and that weeping and wailing over dead bodies was a barbaric custom, and not one anyone could expect a woman of her years to take pleasure in. I must say, my treasure, to have made Lady Ophelia's acquaintance has made up for a great deal that was missing in my life," he added with a broad grin.

"Why does Cousin Charley not like you?" Letty asked him.

He shrugged, holding out a finger to Jeremiah, who shook it solemnly. "I don't know, poppet. I can tell you that she insists she likes her horses better. If I were to tell you some of the things she has done to them—to the stallions, chiefly— well, perhaps it is as well that she don't pretend to like me.''

Letty giggled. ''I don't think she would order a gentleman gelded, sir.''

Fortunately, Lady St. Merryn did not overhear the exchange.

Rockland rolled up his eyes in mock horror and turned to Charley, saying, ''I see that you've created another in your image, my goddess.''

Charley grimaced. ''Letty, darling, you simply must not speak of such things in Grandmama's drawing room, or in any drawing room, for that matter. Medrose, show Lord Rockland to a guest chamber, please. I expect he means to stay for a few days.''

''For as long as it takes,'' Rockland said with a speaking look.

She sighed, but in the event, she was grateful for his presence at the dinner table that evening. He behaved in his usual carefree manner and talked as easily to the haughty Edythe as to the shy Elizabeth.

Edythe instantly took exception to Letty's presence at the

table. "That child belongs in the nursery with our Neddy and Jane."

Charley said, "Letty is accustomed to dining with adults, Cousin Edythe. Since we dine *en famille* tonight, there is no cause to exclude her. She would feel quite out of place with your children, both of whom are still in leading strings, after all."

"She could help to amuse them," Edythe pointed out.

"No," Charley said. "Not unless she expresses a wish to do so. Letty is my guest, not a nursery maid."

Rockland said, "I say, Tarrant, someone told me that you and your family hail from Norfolk. I was at Holkham Hall once, for the sheep shearing. Dashed amazing place."

"Our home, Grappen Hall, does not pretend to the glories of Holkham, I'm afraid," Alfred said. "All the same, it's a tidy property. We've another smaller estate in Lincolnshire, as well."

Rockland kept the conversation going in this vein for some time, even managing to draw Lady St. Merryn into it at one point before Alfred said, "I took a tour of the stables before I dressed for dinner. I must say, I can't think what St. Merryn was about to keep so many horses, all of them eating their fool heads off."

Stiffly, Charley said, "Some of those horses are mine, sir, but both Grandpapa and my father were avid hunters. Grandpapa owns a hunting box in Melton Mowbray."

"Well, Cornwall is humbug country, and I don't aspire to ape the Melton men, so I daresay we'll sell most of them," Alfred said. "Do you hunt, Rockland?"

It was as well that Rockland managed to respond quickly, for Charley knew she was near to losing her temper. She left all conversation to him after that, and after dinner, she went straight to her bedchamber. The room, which she had inherited years before from her Aunt Daintry, was cheerful and well lighted, and the mock India wallpaper with its brightly colored flowers and birds rarely failed to cheer her. This evening, however, it did nothing to lighten her mood.

Letty entered a few minutes later. "Our new cousins are not

very obliging, are they?'' she said, sitting on a chair near the window and folding her hands in her lap. ''One might almost think they came here intending to put everyone out of temper.''

Charley sighed. ''I know, darling, but we must make the best of things. I expect I ought to be in the drawing room now, being polite to Cousin Edythe and Elizabeth, while they wait for the gentlemen to finish their port. But I simply could not abide them a moment longer. I don't think Elizabeth has two thoughts in her head other than to say yes and amen to whatever the gentlemen say, and Cousin Edythe wants to find fault with everything. I only wish I might have been a fly on the wall when Medrose told Cook—if he dared—that Mrs. Tarrant means to provide her with a recipe for raspberry fool that she will agree is superior to her own.''

''It was a very good fool, I thought.''

''Cook's raspberry fool is famous throughout Cornwall.'' She hesitated, aware that she should not share her feelings with the child. But when Letty stared expectantly at her, she said with a sigh, ''I feel like a coward. It is the most lowering reflection to know I am relying upon Rockland to entertain Cousin Alfred and his odious family. I've left strangers to occupy our drawing room, and although I hope I would have supported Grandmama and Cousin Ethelinda had they stayed with Edythe and Elizabeth, I thank goodness they retired to Grandmama's rooms instead.''

''Are you as set against Lord Rockland as you seem to be?'' Letty asked.

''Let us just say I have as little desire to speak to him as to the others.''

''Is that because you truly dislike him, or . . .'' Letty paused, then gave her a shrewd look. ''I am only a child, of course, but I have observed that people usually grieve when someone close to them has died. I've even seen some get amazingly angry. But you've said practically nothing about all that has happened to you. At least,'' she amended, ''you have said nothing to me, and I have not observed that you take anyone else into your confidence. Papa and Mama say it is always better to talk about things than to stuff them all down inside, but of course, if you do not want to talk to Rockland, or to anyone else . . .'' Again she paused. Perched on the edge of her chair, she looked like a red-headed bird expecting crumbs.

"I have not had the time or the inclination to weep or wail," Charley said. She turned to pick up a hairbrush from her dressing table, then set it down again. Unless she took the pins from her hair, she could not brush it.

Letty's words brought thoughts sharply to mind that she had struggled to bury in its nethermost regions. With the arrival of Alfred Tarrant and his family, she had felt yet another blow. First her family had abandoned her—for so it seemed—and now her home was to be taken away. To be sure, Cousin Alfred had said she would be welcome to stay, but already Tuscombe Park felt less like a home and more like a battleground.

She soon sent Letty to bed and retired herself, refusing to allow her mind to dwell on her troubles. She hoped that things would soon sort themselves out, that with a period of quiet, life at Tuscombe Park would return to normal.

The following morning, when she descended to the morning room, she found the breakfast servants buzzing with excitement. "What is it?" she asked as she moved to examine the dishes on the sideboard.

The chambermaid replied, "Oh, Miss Charley, they do say there's a ship be a-going to wreck soon, right in the bay! The fog outside still be as thick as muck!"

"What's that you say?" Alfred demanded from the threshold.

Charley greeted him politely and explained, adding, "Shipwrecks are not uncommon in these parts, sir. As you may know, the tides and currents on both coasts of Cornwall are extremely treacherous. If a storm comes, or heavy fog, a ship may easily come to grief on our rocks and reefs. I might add that it is quite a sight to see. On occasion, hundreds, sometimes thousands of men and women swarm the wreckage, like ants. Long before anything can be done to stop them, they carry off not only the cargo but sometimes every vestige of the ship herself."

Rockland entered a moment later with a broad grin. "I say,

one of the servants told me a ship has wrecked in St. Merryn's Bay. Shall we go have a look at it?''

"If you want to go, certainly," Charley said. "They say the fog is still thick, but if you'll give me time to change into my habit, I'll go with you. Medrose," she added when the butler looked in to see if all was going smoothly, "send orders to the stables to saddle horses for us. Cousin Alfred, do you want to come? Perhaps Elizabeth would like to, or Cousin Edythe," she added conscientiously.

"Upon my word, a shipwreck is no place for gently born females," Alfred said.

Charley smiled. "We don't intend to join the scavengers, Cousin, merely to watch the activity. You will have the chance to meet nearly all your neighbors there, I expect. We rarely get to see such a sight so near to us."

"Surely, what they are doing is against the law!"

"I expect it may be, but the magistrates are powerless to act, there being no one to enforce their commands. The military and Customs House officials provide the only effective deterrent. Unfortunately, the former can seldom reach the scene in time to do any good, and the latter interest themselves primarily in wrecks carrying goods subject to duty. I'll be back in a twink," she added, turning back to Rockland. Then, seeing the butler awaiting final instructions, she said, "Horses for Mr. Tarrant, Lord Rockland, Lady Letitia, and myself, Medrose." Then, before anyone could countermand her orders, she practically pushed him from the room, and hurried off to find Letty.

When they rejoined the gentlemen—without Jeremiah, who had been consigned again to Letty's bedchamber—Alfred looked disapproving but said nothing more about the impropriety of their going. Charley's groom, Teddy, accompanied them.

Thinning fog soon let them increase their pace along the path to the cliffs. It also allowed them to see that many others were riding and walking in the same direction. After a time, Teddy drew his horse alongside Charley's. Raising his voice to be heard above the thudding hoofbeats, he said, "A lot of chaps done went to the bay already and come back to get help,

Miss Charley. Some did say there was still men aboard that ship.''

"I hope they got them off safely," she called back.

Alfred, hearing her, shouted, "If the ship is wrecking in heavy seas, how can they save anyone?''

"They might not," she said, slowing her mount again when he did, so they would not have to shout. "Still, Grandpapa spent a good deal of time and effort training the men hereabouts to save lives rather than just to take what they could get.''

"I've heard it said that Cornish wreckers are greatly feared,'' he said.

"Many are, but hereabouts we've begun to win a reputation for saving ships and lives. We keep lifeboats on hand in the bay for just such occurrences as this one.''

When they arrived at the cliff's edge some forty minutes later, however, the scene below appalled her. The tide was ebbing, and they saw the ship's broken hull on the rocks. Only the mainmast remained whole. The others were broken.

Rockland said as they drew rein, "Looks like three or four hundred tons.''

What it looked like to Charley was an anthill. Men swarmed over the wrecked vessel, armed with pick-axes, hatchets, crow-bars, and ropes, breaking up and carrying off whatever they could. Hewing sails and masts, they carried them away. On shore, men shouldered casks. Others broke open barrels, spilling the contents into buckets, jars, earthenware cooking vessels, or anything else they could fill. Men and women alike lined up to get their share. Even children helped. A multitude of people from nearby towns, villages, and parishes crowded the shore and the cliff edge, with many scrambling down to the beach to join the scavengers.

As she watched the ship being dismantled, Charley was shocked to see one of the men aboard fling something black and white into the gray waters of the sea. It struggled frantically to swim in the pounding surf.

"That's a dog," Letty cried. "Oh, it's going to be drowned! Can't we go down and save it, Cousin Charley?''

"Certainly not," Alfred snapped.

Rockland said more gently, "We should never get to it in time, poppet, but surely in all that crowd of folks, there must be—yes, by God! Look, poppet, someone is going after it now."

Charley saw the rescuer, too, and thought there was something familiar about him. He leapt from rock to rock, almost as if he disdained to notice the waves rising high and crashing around him, threatening to sweep him away.

Letty said suddenly, "Isn't that—?"

"I can't see who it is," Charley cut in swiftly, her heart thumping as she watched the struggling dog and the brave but surely foolhardy man trying to rescue it. Nearly certain, even from such a distance, that the man was Jean Matois, she kept her knowledge to herself and shot a warning look at Letty to do likewise.

"Miss Tarrant?"

Reluctantly dragging her gaze from the scene below, Charley saw that she was being addressed by a very large, neatly dressed man on horseback who seemed vaguely familiar. "I am Miss Tarrant," she said. "You must forgive me. I am afraid—"

"James Gabriel, ma'am, mayor of Lostwithiel since last October." He removed his hat, revealing a bushy head of thick brown hair, as he added, "We met briefly at Tuscombe Park House one afternoon some months ago, before you left for London and the Continent. I had called to discuss with your grandfather some details of the cathedral consecration in Truro. He was kind enough to make me known to you."

"Yes, I remember you now, Mr. Gabriel." Judging his weight at over twenty stones, she recalled feeling sorry for any horse he rode, and was glad to see that the bay carrying him now was sufficiently large and sturdily built "You are the man who is refurbishing the ancient chest that will contain the communion vessels, are you not?"

"Fancy your remembering that," he said. "The Seraphim Coffer it's called, and I am indeed the man they asked to fix it up. I did not like to intrude on you today, but I knew your father, too, you see. Since you quite naturally did not attend the funeral, I wanted to take the opportunity to express my condolences on your great loss. His lordship and Mr. and Mrs. Charles Tarrant will be sadly missed in these parts.''

''Thank you,'' Charley said, unable to resist looking back toward the beach. With relief, she saw that Matois had somehow managed to snatch the dog from the surf and was jumping from rock to rock, making his way back to shore. When a huge wave crashed against the rocks, spewing froth so high it seemed to swallow him, she gasped in horror.

''They are safe,'' Letty assured her, her voice trembling. ''He's still there.''

The surf ebbed, and Matois stood upright, the dog safe in his arms.

Beside her, Gabriel said, ''I saw what they did to that poor thing. Blasted fools doubtless thought they were doing no more than making their actions legal.''

Alfred had been eyeing Gabriel with disapproval from the moment the large man had first spoken to Charley. He said bluntly, ''How can that be?''

Recognizing her duty, Charley said, ''Forgive me, Cousin Alfred, and you, too, Rockland. This gentleman is James Gabriel, the mayor of Lostwithiel. Mr. Gabriel, this is Lord Rockland, and Mr. Alfred Tarrant.''

''Soon to be the sixth Earl of St. Merryn,'' Alfred said, holding out his hand.

''Excellent, sir, for you are the very man I want to speak to. You see, the old earl had invited Wellington and his advisors to dine at Tuscombe after the ceremony, but now . . . Well, it's soon to be asking what your own wishes are, of course, but—''

''Upon my word, sir,'' Alfred said, turning pink with pleasure, ''it will be my very great honor to receive him. I shall write at once to assure him that he need not alter his plans. Now then,'' he added in a much friendlier tone than the one in which he had begun the exchange, ''what nonsense is this about making the wreckers' actions legal?''

'' 'Tis an old law, sir,'' Gabriel said. ''I take it, you're a foreigner.''

''Aye, out of Norfolk.''

"Well, hereabouts they believe that a ship is not derelict if on board her is found any live creature—man, woman, child, dog, or cat. I've investigated the matter, and those are the very words used in an obsolete Act of Parliament passed under one of the early Plantagenet kings. Most folks forgot about them centuries ago, but these wretched wreckers still bear them in mind as living fact."

"Upon my word," Alfred exclaimed. "Do you mean to tell me they pitched that poor mongrel into the sea because they believed if it remained aboard they were not legally entitled to salvage?"

"Precisely. One cannot help wondering how many shipwrecked sailors have been murdered merely to render their vessels legally derelict. Hundreds, I daresay, for one cannot imagine an Act of law better calculated to turn the avaricious wrecker into a brutal, cold-hearted killer. I do not hesitate to say that it must be the worst piece of legislation ever enacted in this country."

Listening with half an ear, Charley was still watching the man she believed to be Jean Matois, and she breathed a sigh of relief when he leapt safely back to the shingle and set the dog down. It promptly shook itself and seemed none the worse for its terrifying ordeal. When Matois strode off into the milling crowd of people, who were still removing goods and parts of the ship, she was amused to see the dog trot briskly after him, apparently in the belief that it had found a new master.

Chapter Five

As Alfred and Mr. Gabriel continued talking about the wreckers, Charley heard the latter say, "Many of these folks have been here for hours. Hearing of the ship's plight, they crowded to the cliff tops early this morning, long before the fog began to lift, in expectation of seeing her dashed to pieces against the rocks. It is hardly credible to me that human beings can be so lost to humanity and justice as to wish for the destruction of their fellow man, merely to plunder his property."

"Dreadful, dreadful," Alfred interjected. "But perhaps—"

"There is worse, sir. I have heard of incidents in which they did not even wait for a ship to founder. Wreckers have devised ways to draw unwitting ships onto a reef just so they'll break to bits and render up goods for scavenge. I do not believe that is what happened today," he added fairly. "Apparently, that ship was making for Fowey and its captain misjudged his distance from the reef at the entrance to this bay."

"Most unfortunate," Alfred said. "Were there any survivors?"

"Everyone aboard, thanks to heaven and the old earl's lifeboats. Most were got off before the ship hit the rocks. I've sent for the Lloyd's of London agent, and I'm hopeful that he and his customs men will arrive in time to save something for the underwriters. What we really need, of course,'' he added bitterly, ''is a full squadron of soldiers to prevent a repetition of this disgraceful scene each time a ship founders in these waters.''

The Lloyd's agent from St. Austell appeared on the scene a half hour later. Although he had ten customs officers with him, he took one look at the teeming beach and gave it as his opinion that there was too little left of ship or goods to make risking his men's lives a profitable course of action.

Mr. Gabriel, clearly disgusted with that decision, repeated his assertion that a strong military presence was the only deterrent that might prove effective. ''That, or convincing a few Cornish juries to convict them when they're caught.''

The men continued talking in this vein, but Charley soon became bored with the conversation, and with watching the diminishing activity on the beach. When hunger pangs reminded her that she had eaten practically no breakfast, she informed Rockland that she and Letty were ready to return to the house.

''As you wish, my treasure,'' he said at once, ''but perhaps we ought to discover first if Mr. Alfred Tarrant is ready to go back. I believe he has invited the mammoth Mr. Gabriel to take luncheon with us. One hopes there will be enough food.''

''You do as you please,'' she said. ''Letty and I are leaving.''

The three men caught up a few minutes later, apparently still deep in their conversation about the wreckers. Gabriel asked Alfred if he meant to follow the late earl's policies regarding the wreckers, or those of other coastal landowners.

''What do you mean?'' Alfred asked, frowning.

''Certain local landowners,'' Gabriel said, ''pounce like vultures on every ship stranded on their estates. They claim ancient privilege to justify their actions.''

''Privilege?''

''Aye, sir. They claim local wrecking rights. They believe such rights give them legal title to their plunder. The right to wreck belonged originally to the Crown, but lords with coastal estates usurped it. To this day, they vigorously enforce their claims. I'm happy to say that his late lordship took a more civilized attitude. He not only refused to support wrecking but encouraged local Lloyd's men and consular agents to protect their property. We've seen little wrecking in St. Merryn's Bay these past few years. This business today doubtless results from his lordship's death and a hope that no one else will interfere. They'll be wanting to know, sir, what stand you will take."

"Upon my word," Alfred said. "I can scarcely be expected to take a stand before I've investigated the matter. Still, I'll be glad to learn all you can tell me."

Charley stopped listening to them. Calling Rockland and Letty to join her in a gallop, she gave spur to her mount, soon leaving Alfred and Gabriel far behind. Alfred's pompous attitude galled her. Thus, when they returned to the stables to find his carriage horses occupying stalls that previously had housed St. Merryn's prize hunters, she reacted even more forcibly than she might have done otherwise.

Ignoring Rockland's hint that she not raise the subject until after Alfred had eaten his lunch, she sent Letty upstairs, then lingered in the front hall to await his return. Shaking his head, Rockland stayed with her, although he opined more than once during the next twenty minutes that she was making a grave mistake.

The moment Alfred entered the house with Gabriel, Charley confronted him, despite the presence of the other two men. "Look here, Cousin," she said as he and Gabriel handed coats, hats, and gloves to a footman, "if you or your people want to make changes in the stables, I think you should discuss them with me first. Your man has turned four prize hunters worth upwards of eight hundred pounds each into an open field without so much as a by-your-leave, to make room for ordinary carriage animals."

The footman fled when Alfred exclaimed in outrage, "How dare you speak to me so! I warn you, Cousin, that is not wise. Recall that in future you will depend on me for practically every penny you spend." Flicking a glance at the interested Gabriel, he added grimly, "Miss Tarrant recently discovered that her grandfather failed to leave her an independence." Turning back to Charley, undismayed by her now speechless fury, he added, "I think we can forgo your company at luncheon, miss. Go to your room at once and consider how you will apologize to me." With that, he took Gabriel's arm, saying, "Come along, my dear sir. I want you to meet the rest of my family."

Rockland was a silent but appreciative audience. As Charley watched the other two stroll away, he said, "I foresee victory in my future. A little more of that Turkish treatment and you will accept any proposal of marriage, even mine."

"Don't be daft, Rockland. I am not going to marry anyone. But did you ever before encounter such a coxcomb? How dared he speak so to me! And in front of you and Gabriel, not to mention Jago. Alfred Tarrant is an unmannerly beast."

"In all fairness, my treasure, you took him to task in front of the same audience."

"Well, that's true," she said, reluctantly admitting the point. "But surely, he cannot be so lost to all common sense as to wish harm to those hunters. The financial loss in the end could be his, after all."

"There is no accounting for his behavior. Still, it does just occur to me that he tends to run counter to any advice you offer him. You might be better advised to try conciliation, or even flattery, instead. A few feminine wiles might go farther with our Alfred than your habitual plain-speaking."

"Don't be an idiot," she snapped. "I've never employed a feminine wile in my life, and I don't propose to begin with Alfred."

"Do I take that to mean you don't intend to retire to your bedchamber to contemplate a proper apology?" he asked sweetly.

Charley's response being more in the nature of a growl than a civil reply, Rockland had the good sense to take himself off to join the others in the dining room.

With the help of Kerra, her personal maid, Charley managed to obtain a plate of saffron buns and a pot of tea, which she and Letty consumed in the privacy of her bedchamber. However, her spirits had sunk to a new low. Even Letty failed to raise them, and the child soon left her to her own devices.

Kerra, coming to collect the plates, said, "Begging your pardon, Miss Charley, but Mrs. Medrose said you'd be wanting to know that they be moving her ladyship."

"What?" With effort, she focused attention on the maid's evident distress.

"That new Mrs. Tarrant gave orders that Lady St. Merryn and Miss Davies are to remove to that suite of rooms at the east end of the second floor. Mrs. Medrose did say her ladyship be a mite put off by the notion."

Certain that Kerra was understating the countess's anguish, Charley changed quickly out of her riding habit into a simple muslin afternoon frock, recently dyed dark gray, and went to see what she could do. Finding she had judged her grandmother's lacerated sensibilities correctly, she set about trying to soothe them, and listened with as much sympathy as she could muster, while the countess bemoaned her lot. Since a number of Lady St. Merryn's complaints arose from the thoughtlessness of the two men who had left her to such a fate by dying before their time, Charley soon ran out of platitudes and went in search of a less tiresome way to expend her energy.

Having finally decided that nothing would help if she remained within doors, she donned a cloak and gloves, intending to walk around the small lake at the foot of the sweeping front lawn. She would let the sea breeze clear her mind. Halfway down the main stairway, she was startled to hear a female voice speak from above.

"Cousin Charlotte, good heavens, where can you be going?"

Stopping and turning on the stair, Charley saw Elizabeth peering at her over the gallery rail. "I am going out," she said curtly.

"But surely Alfred told us at luncheon that he had ordered you to your bedchamber!" Then Elizabeth's countenance lightened, and as one realizing that she must have made an error, she exclaimed, "Oh, can it be that you have seen the wisdom of apologizing to him for your bad manners?"

"I have not apologized, nor do I intend to apologize," Charley snapped. "Nor do I mean to waste what's left of the day in my bedchamber. Your idiot brother is keeping eight splendid hunters in an open field merely because he is too pig-headed to listen to wiser counsel. You people came here like a Mongol horde riding out of Norfolk, attempting to take over this house and everyone in it before you had the right to do any such thing, turning everything upside down. You are—all of you— rude, obnoxious, and encroaching!" She was vaguely aware that Rockland had appeared behind Elizabeth, his usually cheerful face looking grave and concerned, but she ignored him.

Her volatile temper had taken over, and suddenly it was as if the explosive fury she felt had taken on a life of its own, as if she were observing the scene rather than participating. While she stood there, shaking in anger, some other person went on speaking, shrilly, unleashing all her pent-up frustration and rage at Elizabeth. Words flowed without thought, and when she saw tears well into the other girl's eyes, instead of stemming the tide, they intensified it.

"What the devil have you got to cry about?"

"Please, Cousin Charlotte, you must not carry on so. Surely you know you have no choice but to submit to Alfred's authority. We females are not at all suited to making important decisions, and dearest Alfred has only your best interests at heart."

"Dearest Alfred is a fool," Charley said scathingly. "So are you if you are stupid enough to think he knows more than I do about running the Tuscombe Park stables just because he chanced to have been born a male. Men, my dear Elizabeth, are not the superior sex they would have us believe them. On the contrary, were it not for women like you, kowtowing to their idiotic notions of supremacy, they would long since have learned how inept they are. They cannot survive without us, but the Amazon tribes proved long ago that women can easily survive with only men enough to make procreation possible. They keep them as pets, like Jeremiah. That is all most men *are* suited for if the truth were told."

"I don't know about Amazons, but—"

"You don't know anything ! You're a fool! Women like you make me want to commit murder, because that is what you are doing, *killing* other women's chances of improving their lots in life!''

Flushing deeply, Elizabeth burst into tears and fled.

"Very pretty behavior," Rockland said grimly. "She did not deserve that."

Recovering with difficulty from the emotional fit that had overcome her, Charley blinked at him, trying to collect her wits. She soon rallied enough to say, "She should not have reproved me. She had no right to do so."

"Still, you said far too much, and if you do not intend to go after her and apologize for that tantrum, I shall do so on your behalf."

"Will you, by God? Good. Then I need not apologize at all." She glared at him, feeling betrayed by his instant siding with Elizabeth against her, and humiliated to think he would dare apologize for her actions. Although she knew she had overstepped the line, Rockland had pretended to care for her, and she believed she had some right to expect his loyalty. When he turned away to follow Elizabeth, she said impulsively, "If you thought I was being so horrid, damn you, why didn't you stop me?"

He looked back in surprise. "How the devil could I stop you? No one can stop you when you take the bit between your teeth."

Frustrated and more furious than ever, she turned on her heel and ran down the remaining steps. Leaving the house, angrily brushing tears from her cheeks, she headed automatically for the stables despite the fact that she wore only her afternoon frock beneath her cloak, and not a proper riding habit.

No one questioned her order to saddle her favorite horse, Shadow Dancer, at once. The stableboys had long since developed a healthy respect for her temper, and needed only a glimpse of her to know they had better obey. Even Teddy, who, having served her most of her life, was accustomed to take a few liberties, made only a token objection when she said curtly that she did not want him to go with her.

"I'll take a pistol, as usual," she told him. "I lost mine in the accident, so I'll have to use one of Grandpapa's now. I don't need you as well.''

Once she had left the stable yard and spurred the black roan to a gallop she felt a sense of freedom, but not until she slowed again to let the horse choose its own pace, did she begin to relax. Her sense of ill usage remained strong. However, before long, guilt stirred when she thought about the scene with Elizabeth. Having managed to stay relatively calm with Alfred, she could not imagine why she had lost her temper with the least obnoxious of the Norfolk Tarrants. That she had done so seemed strange, but the slight remorse she felt did nothing to ease her irritation with Rockland.

"Cousin Charley!"

She had been aware of sounds behind her for several moments but had dismissed them as the cries of shore birds. Looking over her shoulder, she saw Letty galloping after her, alone.

Reining in, she waited until the child had drawn up beside her before she said, "You are supposed to ride with a groom, young lady. Where is Jeb?"

"I sent him to find Teddy," Letty said, twinkling. She had come out without a hat, and her curls were windblown, her freckled cheeks the color of pink roses. "I saw you ride off alone," she said, "so I thought you would not welcome Jeb's company. Fortunately, Teddy had gone to his cottage, so I sent Jeb to ask him where you were going. I had seen from my window that you were headed toward the cliff path, so I just rode off when Jeb left the yard. Are you vexed with me? Must I go back?"

Just then Jeremiah's small head popped out from beneath Letty's cloak. The quizzical look on his face was so much a reflection of his mistress's expression that Charley smiled. "I guess we all need to escape for a while," she said. "We'll deal with the consequences later."

"Good," Letty said. "Where are we going?"

"Just along the cliffs," Charley said. "I did think I might just . . ." She hesitated, thinking now that her notion had probably not been such a good one, after all.

"Did you want to see where the accident occurred?" Letty

asked. "I thought about that when we were looking down at St. Merryn's beach this morning."

Charley glanced at her ruefully. "Would you mind?"

"No, for this morning was not the first time I've wondered about it. Can we get down to the Devil's Sand on horseback?"

"There is a trail of sorts. Melissa and I rode down sometimes when we were children. It is not as good as either of the two paths leading down to St. Merryn's Bay, but we can manage. We'll have to hurry though, or we'll be awfully late getting back."

"Perhaps they won't even know we've gone," Letty said. "I was helping Grandmama and Cousin Ethelinda settle into their new rooms when Cousin Edythe came in and looked down her nose at me as if I had been a toad. She said little girls ought to be in the schoolroom at such an hour. When I asked, very politely, what I ought to do there, since my governess did not accompany me from Paris, she said she wondered that you had not seen what an imposition it is to have a little girl foisted onto the household at such an inauspicious time. I loathe being called a little girl."

"So did I. When I was your age, nothing could more quickly put up my back."

"I do not think that Cousin Edythe remembered that Grandpapa Jervaulx is a marquess, either, until Medrose called me 'your ladyship,' which he practically never does. He said it as if he were addressing a royal duchess, too. Even then, Cousin Edythe just said she hoped I could amuse myself because she wasn't accustomed to entertaining little girls."

"Utterly loathsome," Charley said sympathetically.

"Yes. That's when I made my curtsy and fled to my room, for although Mr. Gabriel had gone and Cousin Alfred had retired to the library after lunch, Rockland and Cousin Elizabeth were talking in the morning room. He was commiserating with her. I don't know why, but he did say, as if he were joking with her, you know, that Mr. Gabriel had been making dreadful sheep's eyes at her all through luncheon. So, even though I couldn't imagine Mr. Gabriel doing such a thing, I did not think they would welcome me, exactly. Besides, I knew Jeremiah would be missing me,'' she added, reaching inside her cloak to stroke the monkey.

"You were probably wise to leave them alone,'' Charley said, glad Letty had not overheard enough to understand why Rockland was comforting Elizabeth. They cantered after that, alternating their paces so as not to tire the horses. When they reached the cliffs above St. Merryn's Bay, she saw with astonishment that no sign of the wrecked ship remained. The beach was empty, and the tide was in.

Not long after that they reached the headland, but when Letty would have turned toward Seacourt House, Charley stopped her. "The trail to the beach is farther along the cliff road, darling. I don't think there is a safe way down the east side of the headland, and with the tide in, we cannot ride around the point. You'll see more clearly how it is when we ride on.''

Ten minutes later, Letty gave a shudder and said, "This side of the headland is just steep black cliffs and scree. I'm ever so glad I didn't see it in full daylight before. If I'd known what it was like when I was trying to move about in the dark, I think perhaps even my sensibilities might have been stirred to quaking.''

"Here's the trail now,'' Charley said. "Let your horse pick its own way.''

"I know.''

They remained silent as they cautiously followed the zigzag trail down to the central portion of the beach. Then they turned their mounts back toward Seacourt Head. The shingle was bare, without a sign of the wrecked carriage or the dead horses.

"I know men brought the . . . that is, that they brought back Uncle Charles and Aunt Davina, and the coachman,'' Letty said in a puzzled tone, "but surely—''

"I, too, thought there would be signs of the wreckage,'' Charley said. "Maybe scavengers came here, as well, and bore off what was left.''

"Mowysy tek,'' said a rough voice behind them. *"Hag mergh da kekefrys.''*

Turning, they saw four men, ruffians with unshaven faces, standing on the shingle behind them. The noise of the waves and cries of gulls had covered the sound of their approach. That Charley had not seen them before did not surprise her, however. She knew from experience that the cliff face was riddled with caves, many large enough for a number of men to lie hidden.

Though she did not recognize any of them, she said calmly, "I understand quite enough Cornish to know that you are being impertinent. Do you know who I am?"

"Can't say we do, lass," the one who had spoken said. "Makes no never mind, though. All I said was you be pretty girls wi' pretty horses, which we could see at once. We'll be knowing you both much better before we tire of ye, I'm thinking."

"I am Charlotte Tarrant, granddaughter of the Earl of St. Merryn, and this is my cousin, Lady Letitia Deverill. You interfere with us at your peril."

"Seems to me we heard the old earl had a palsy stroke, and his son died afore him," the ruffian said. He exchanged a look of amusement with the others that made Charley wonder if they could be the highwaymen responsible for the carriage accident.

She could not think of that now. Quietly, she said, "It is true that both my father and grandfather are dead, but their heir has arrived at Tuscombe Park, and you would be foolish to anger him. Moreover, my cousin is also granddaughter to the Marquess of Jervaulx." Seeing at once from their expressions that she had made a mistake, she carefully slipped a hand under her cloak, which concealed the saddle holster from view. At the same time, to divert the leader's attention, she said evenly, "If you know of me, you must know that my horses have been particularly well trained. You will not be able to ride them unless I command it."

The leader was licking his lips, however. He said thoughtfully, "The marquess, eh? I remember him. Gone to Gloucestershire, howsomever, so he don't trouble me none. Expect he'd pay a tidy sum to get his little lass back though, wouldn't he, lads?"

"Aye," they said in chorus, beginning to move closer to Charley and Letty.

The pistol now firmly in hand, Charley withdrew it and aimed it directly at the leader. "I can shoot the pips out of a playing card at a greater distance than this," she said grimly. "Stand back now, and tell your friends to let us pass."

"You'll only get one of us, lass," the man said, putting his hands on his hips.

"Will you care how many I shoot if you are the first to fall dead?"

He hesitated. The others, clearly doubting that she would shoot, began to sidle away from him, edging around behind her. She held the pistol steady, hoping to convince them she would shoot him, and wishing she had brought more than one pistol.

Chattering excitedly, Jeremiah poked his head out from Letty's cloak.

All four men gaped at him. Letty steadied her nervous horse.

The leader said, "What in the name of the Virgin be that?"

"A monkey," Letty said. "He is very tame. Would you like to shake his hand?"

Fascinated, the four seemed too frightened to approach nearer, especially when Jeremiah climbed to her shoulder. One said, "Think I seen one of them at a fair once."

Hearing barking from farther up the beach, Charley glanced briefly away from the men to see a rider approaching at a canter on a buttermilk-colored horse, preceded by a shaggy black and white dog.

Chapter Six

The dog raced excitedly around the horse, then dashed toward them, only to stop in its tracks when Matois whistled. Apparently recognizing him, the four ruffians stepped back a pace or two and waited until he drew near.

One of the men said with scorn, "Can tell the Frenchman ain't no fisherman, a-whistling like that this close to the sea. Thanks be to God, it ain't nightfall!"

"Clear out, you lot," Jean Matois said evenly as he drew rein. "You've more important business at hand than to be annoying *les demoiselles*."

"Listen to him," another of the men sneered, pushing his own nose in the air with one finger. "Don't he sound a proper gent?"

Matois looked at him, and the man fell silent, finding sudden interest in his feet.

The leader said, "Don't take no pet now, Frenchman. The lad meant no harm. We was just admiring the ladies' horses, and they was a-showing us that strange beast what the little 'un's wearing on her shoulder. Never seen the like afore."

"Well, now you have, *mon ami*, so be on your way. I will

see *les jeunes filles* safely back to the road." His accent had thickened noticeably.

"You do that, Frenchman," the chief ruffian said. He stepped back, gesturing for the others to do likewise.

"After you, *mesdemoiselles.*"

Silently Charley returned her pistol to its holster and urged her horse toward the path to the road. The dog, she noted, trotted gaily at Annabelle's heels.

Letty tucked Jeremiah back under her cloak. Charley had seen her smile at Jean Matois in welcome, but the smile soon faded in the face of his heavy frown. Since Charley likewise felt disinclined to enter into conversation with him, they rode back to the cliff top in near silence. It lasted only until they reached the road, however.

"You were fools to have come here alone," Matois said as he guided Annabelle in beside Charley's horse. "Surely you must know about the wreck this morning. All manner of people have been clambering about on these cliffs."

"We saw them," Letty said. "We saw you rescue the dog, too, but we did not tell anyone that we knew you."

"So you do have some sense." He glanced at the dog, presently chasing a butterfly that flitted just beyond reach of its snapping teeth.

Charley said, "He seems to have adopted you."

"Yes. He's a lunatic, lean-witted fool, and I'm a relenting one. I call him Sebastian, after Viola's shipwrecked twin in *Twelfth Night.*"

She chuckled. Then, seeing him frown again, she said quickly, defensively, "I knew the scavengers would be gone by now. They don't hang about after they've been wrecking, for fear the Lloyd's agent or a customs rider will confiscate their booty."

"Nonetheless, you were fools to ride down onto Devil's Sand without so much as a groom to protect you," he said bluntly. "And don't try to cozen me into believing your father or grandfather allowed you to do such things. I won't believe you."

"A gentleman does not contradict a lady," Letty murmured,

astonishing Charley so much that she did not blurt out the annihilating retort that had leapt to her tongue.

Matois said, "Since I am no gentleman, *ma petite,* such strictures do not silence me. Even if your cousin happens to be accustomed to riding about on her own, she should not have brought you, not without more protection than she can provide."

"We were in no danger," Charley snapped. "I had my pistol, and as you saw, those men feared Jeremiah." When Matois looked at her with much the same flintlike expression he had directed at the ruffians, she shifted uncomfortably. She knew she had been wrong to leave Teddy behind, and even more mistaken to have encouraged Letty to escape Jeb. She looked away, unable to meet that stern gaze any longer.

Gently, Matois said, "Just how many bullets does your pistol hold?"

"Two, but I have more in a pocket stitched to my saddle."

"Excellent. I feel sure they would willingly have waited for you to reload."

Charley bit her lower lip, then grimaced and tossed her head, saying, "How loathsome you are. I daresay you are quite right, however, at least in saying that I should not have let Letty accompany me. The truth is, however, that unrest has long been a fact of life in Cornwall. One either learns to deal with it, or one stays indoors, wrapped in cotton wool. I frequently ride alone, especially when I am in a temper, and have done since I was a child."

Meeting his gaze again, and reading disbelief in his expression, she added ruefully, "You are right when you say Grandpapa and Papa did not approve, but in truth, they scarcely ever noticed my absences. On those rare occasions when Papa decided to act like a parent, I suffered the consequences, but being rare, they did not deter me for long. Papa's attention span, where I was concerned, was short." Pushing thoughts of her father to the nethermost region of her mind, she drew a breath, looked Matois in the eye, and said firmly, "I learned long ago to trust my pistol, my name, and my wits to protect me."

"I see." They were riding three abreast by then, and Jeremiah chose that moment to poke his head out again from Letty's cloak. With scarcely a pause, the monkey jumped to Jean Matois's saddle. As Matois shifted so the monkey could hunker down between his legs, its forepaws resting on the pommel, he said to Letty, "And your papa, *ma petite.* Does he also pay no heed to what you do?"

"No, sir. He would be vexed, I think, if he knew what we had done today."

Charley, remembering times in the past when she had vexed Letty's papa—or had been present when her Aunt Daintry had vexed him—experienced a sudden vision of Gideon Deverill that was not at all comforting. Worse was to come, however.

Letty said in a small voice, "Perhaps I had better not mention this particular incident when next I write to them at home."

Taking a deep breath, Charley said, "Of course, you may tell them, darling. Just be sure you add that your Cousin Charley has at last learned the lesson your papa tried to teach her when she was just about your age. We will always take our grooms after this. You must be sure to say, too, just how Jeremiah frightened those men. That will make your papa laugh. Then, perhaps, he will not be so vexed." Encountering a twinkle from Matois's eyes, she grimaced rudely at him.

He chuckled. "Am I mistaken, *mon ange,* or do you have a healthier respect for *le père de la petite* than you had for your grandfather or your father?"

"Gideon has a way of making people mind him," Charley said, smiling across him at Letty. "Your words, and Letty's, made me remember that little fact just now, but I think even Gideon would admit that I am generally able to look after myself."

"I am sure that you are."

She looked at him, searching his expression for irony or mockery, but he seemed perfectly sincere. He caught her gaze and held it until she felt unaccustomed heat in her cheeks. Then he said thoughtfully, "You said a moment ago that you frequently ride off alone when you are in a temper."

"I did say that." She eyed him warily.

"Was that the case today?"

She looked straight ahead. "If you mean to tell me that people who act hastily and in an emotional dither are unlikely to use good judgment, I don't want to hear it."

"I'm not surprised. What a coxcomb you must think me to believe I would say such things to you, even if they were true."

She looked at him again, but he met the look easily, and this time her sense of humor stirred. Smiling wryly, she said, "I suppose you think you are very clever."

"Not at all. You have just proved that you are as intelligent and sensible as you claim to be. I have no need to tell you what you already know, *mon ange*. But that is not why I stirred these coals. I want to know why you were in a temper. I have heard, by the bye, that your grandfather died suddenly. I'm sorry."

"Thank you. The news of my father's death, and my mother's, proved too great a shock for him," she added. "But if you know of his death, perhaps you also have heard that the new heir arrived yesterday."

He did not respond at once, and for a moment she thought she had surprised him. But he said only, "I had not heard that. I merely wondered what fool would upset you after all you have so recently endured. You say he arrived yesterday?"

"Yes, and it's not just one person but five. Mr. Alfred Tarrant brought his wife, Edythe, his two children, and his sister Elizabeth."

Letty said, "The children are still in leading strings, sir, and not particularly amusing." With a sigh, she added, "Most unfortunately, Cousin Edythe seems to think I ought to spend my time helping the nursery maid mind them."

"Does she? So you do not approve of these interlopers either, *ma petite?*" Jeremiah sprawled across his upper thigh now, dozing.

Letty said, "It is not my business to approve or disapprove, sir. But I must say, I like Lord Rockland much better than any of the Norfolk Tarrants. Although," she added thoughtfully, "Cousin Elizabeth seems pleasant enough, even if she does believe that men are all-knowing and that females must always look to them for guidance.''

''I collect that you do not believe that.''

Letty looked at Charley.

Thinking it an odd conversation to have with a man who wanted them to think him a French wrecker and smuggler, Charley said only, ''The females in my family are more sensible than that. If we look to someone for guidance we do so because she, or he, is worthy to give advice.''

''And Mr. Alfred Tarrant does not fall into that category?''

''He does not.''

''If I am not being too inquisitive . . .''

''He put four extremely valuable hunters out into a field to make room for his commonplace hacks in the stable. His odious wife has ordered my grandmother—whose age alone ought to command more respect—to move out of the rooms she has occupied since she came to Tuscombe Park as a bride. Alfred Tarrant does not think a mere female capable of looking after *his* estates, nor is he willing even to discuss things with her that she knows more about than he does. And he expects me to be *grateful* to him for agreeing to provide a roof over my head!''

''But, *mon Dieu,* surely your father and grandfather provided for you!''

''Not a sou. Oh, no, I am mistaken. My grandfather very kindly left me three thousand pounds. There is just one small condition. Either I must be married at the time of his death, which I am not, or get married within a year thereafter.''

''I see.''

''Well, I do not! I can understand Papa's thinking he would live a long time yet and have plenty of time to put his affairs in order, but I do think he ought to have made *some* provision for me. And Grandpapa had no excuse. Both of them knew perfectly well that I do not intend to marry, although I must say, if the only alternative is to make my home with Cousin Alfred and Edythe—'' She broke off, giving herself a shake. ''I cannot think why I am overflowing onto you like this. It is most improper.''

"I asked you," he said simply. "I begin to see why you fled in a temper today."

"In fairness, that was not due to Cousin Alfred but to Rockland," she said.

"Just who the devil is this Rockland?"

"My most persistent suitor," Charley said, smiling mischievously. "In truth, he is a fool, because I told him years ago that I won't ever marry, but he is useful to have around, particularly in London. I frequently stay there for the Season with my great grandaunt, Lady Ophelia Balterley, but she is a bit past the age mark for gallivanting. Rockland is very good about organizing parties when I want to go to Astley's, or to a play or concert, or some such thing."

"I see. How far, precisely, is Lady Ophelia past the age mark?"

Letty said with a giggle, "Great-Aunt Ophelia is ninety, sir, but she doesn't even require spectacles to read, and if one does not pay attention when she speaks, she bangs her stick on the floor. And she does not think well of men," she added.

"Not even of this Rockland chap?"

Charley said, "Great-Aunt Ophelia finds him useful, too, I expect. At least, when she traveled to Scotland to visit my Aunt Susan—the one whose daughter owns the house on Seacourt Head—Rockland escorted her and attended to all the details."

"If he's so devilish considerate, how did he put you in a temper today?"

Charley hesitated. Up to that moment talking to him had seemed extraordinarily easy, but she had no wish to tell him about the scene with Elizabeth. Nor did she want to discuss that incident with Letty listening.

Their companion glanced at the child, who said instantly, "May I ride ahead? I don't like to gallop when I've got Jeremiah. I'm afraid it will frighten him. But since you are holding him, sir, and since a wonderful straight stretch of road lies ahead that leads well away from the cliffs, may I gallop now, if I don't ride out of your sight?"

Charley said, "Just beware rabbit holes, darling."

Letty gave spur to her mount, and watching her, Matois said, "She's a wonderful little horsewoman."

Charley kept silent, expecting him to pick up the conversation where he had left it. Instead, after a brief pause, he said, "Tell me more about the house on the point. You say it belongs to one of your cousins, but it lies empty."

"Seacourt House belongs to my Aunt Susan's daughter, Melissa. She is a year younger than I am and lives with her husband and his family in Hampshire."

"It seems a pity it's unoccupied. The view is spectacular from up there."

"It is a good view." Her memories of that house not being particularly good ones, she fell silent again, waiting uncomfortably for him to repeat his earlier question, wondering what she would say to him.

He was watching Letty, but at last he said quietly, "Forgive my curiosity, *mon ange.* It has been a long while since I have spoken of private matters with anyone. I did not mean to intrude."

"It was not an intrusion," she said, relaxing. "I brought up the subject myself, after all. The truth is that when I flew into the boughs I was in the wrong. I don't much like having to admit that to anyone."

"You say it was this Rockland who put you in such a temper?"

She sighed. "He merely pointed out that I was acting like a shrew, and I took snuff. The fact is, I lost my temper with Elizabeth Tarrant over a trifle. It's not like me to do such a thing, but the way she agrees with everything Cousin Alfred and Rockland say merely because they are men is utterly maddening. She told me that I must learn to submit to Alfred's authority, and the fact is that if I find myself beholden to him for every groat I spend and every crumb I eat, she is quite right about that. However, I don't think I can do it, and when she ran away in tears, and Rockland took me to task, and even said he would make my apologies for me—"

"Now that was wrong of him."

Grateful for his understanding, she said eagerly, "I should say it was! He is *my* friend, after all, not hers. He should have sided with me."

"He should have insisted that you apologize for yourself, and at once, *mon ange.* Where he sides is his business. Or do you count as your friends only those who agree with you?"

His words shocked her like a blast of ice water. Feeling sudden constriction in her throat, and a burning sensation in her eyes, she could neither look at him nor speak. He was forcing her to see herself more clearly than any mirror, however, and she did not like what she saw. He remained silent. At last, taking control of herself, she said, "Y-you must think me dreadfully arrogant and conceited."

He did not answer at once, but when she braced herself to look at him again, he smiled. His voice was surprisingly gentle when he said, "Not arrogant, and certainly not conceited. I think only that St. Merryn and your father let you grow too hot of hand, *mon ange,* but the right hand on the bridle would gentle you soon enough."

Speechless, Charley choked back a sudden, unexpected bubble of laughter, but she was glad when he showed the good sense not to pursue the topic. Instead, they talked about the weather and the capricious habits of the sea until Letty rejoined them and took back Jeremiah, tucking him under her cloak again. Soon afterward, they came within sight of Tuscombe Park House, and Matois bade them good-day.

"I like him," Letty said, waving as he rode off, trailed by the faithful Sebastian.

Charley liked him, too. She found herself, in fact, oddly attracted to him. He was the first male she could call to mind who had talked to her as if she were his equal. He could be uncivil and much too blunt of manner, but he did not treat her like a child or a half-wit. He listened when she spoke, and he seemed to value her opinions. What a pity, she thought, that she would most likely never see him again.

* * *

Antony glanced back a few minutes later, not knowing if he hoped Miss Tarrant would do the same or not. When she did not, he sighed, recognizing his disappointment.

He had never met a woman like her. She stirred his senses every time she smiled, and when she snapped, he wanted to soothe her and make her smile again. To be sure, at present, she had little enough to smile about. He could not decide whether her eyes were more beautiful when they glinted with anger, or when contemplation turned them into deep mysterious, aquamarine pools.

Sebastian had dashed on ahead. Then, apparently noting that Antony had not increased his pace, the dog dashed back again as if to inquire about the delay.

"I am doubtless as much a fool as you are," Antony said.

The dog's ears perked up at the sound of his voice.

"I am not learning things as quickly as I had hoped," Antony murmured.

The dog yipped, clearly believing Antony had invited an opinion.

"Thank you for your concern," Antony said. "Lord knows, nothing else has helped. I've sent them damn all in my reports, and time is passing. Nor will my action today help the cause. Doubtless my master will think me as great a fool as I think you."

The dog barked again and dashed off after a rabbit.

Speaking now to himself, a habit developed during years of relative solitude for sorting out his thoughts, Antony went on, "Damn these Cornishmen. Michael refuses to trust me, but I cannot blame him for that. Indeed, he remains a mystery, too, for he reveals little about himself, and while the others think I am one of their French compatriots, I can hardly inquire into details of Michael's identity or background. Nor can I go about prating of assassinations. They would instantly become suspicious, and rightly so. Today's business will make matters worse. Giving way to fundamental instinct is always foolish. I must take care that I don't ruin all on a quixotic whim."

* * *

"Cousin Charley!"

The note of warning in Letty's voice caused Charley first to look at her, then to follow the direction of her gaze to the stable yard.

Alfred Tarrant stood by the stable door with Rockland, feet apart and arms crossed over his chest, watching them. His posture was enough to tell her he was angry. When they got near enough to see the expression on his face, she knew it was more than anger. Alfred was furious.

He leapt forward when they reached the yard and grabbed Shadow Dancer's bridle, as if he feared she would ride away again.

Charley accepted Rockland's aid to dismount, and seeing Teddy come from the stable, she gestured to him to take the horses.

Alfred scarcely waited for her feet to touch the ground before he demanded to know where she had been. "What the devil do you mean by going off without so much as a word to anyone, and staying away the better part of the afternoon?"

"If you do not mind, Cousin," Charley said, stripping off her gloves, "I would prefer that you have the goodness to wait until we go inside before you ring a peal over my head. I do not relish hearing my affairs shouted out in the stable yard."

"Now, look here, young woman. I'll say what I want wherever I want to say it, and the sooner you learn to obey my orders, the better it will be for you."

"I am not a child, Cousin. I am four-and-twenty, and I have been giving orders on this estate since I learned to talk. You would do better to recall that you are the newcomer here, and learn to seek advice from those who can help you learn your way. Now, if you will excuse me, I want a word with Teddy before I go inside."

"No."

She had already begun to turn away, but that single flat word jerked her around to stare at him. "*What* did you say?"

"I said *no,* and you had better learn the meaning of the word.

Indeed, unless you mean to beg some other relative to take you in and provide your food and shelter, you had best accept me as master here, and right quickly. Moreover, my dear Charlotte, I will expect you to earn your keep. In my opinion, you have been sadly spoilt, but we can soon rectify that, believe me.''

"You are not master here yet," she reminded him between gritted teeth.

"I think you will find that the servants do not share that belief. I have given orders that you are not to take out any horse without my permission. Nor will young Letty. It don't suit my notions of propriety for girls under my care to go careering over the countryside without so much as a groom to look after them. You'll both go to bed without supper for that, and if you attempt to join the family, no food will be served to you. You may not be a child, Miss Charlotte Tarrant, but you will soon learn that you have no more influence than any other female beneath my roof. And, lest you think to try your will against mine, let me make plain to you what will happen. Any servant foolish enough to obey your orders instead of mine will find himself without a position or a character when I take control, and so I have told them, one and all."

Stunned, suddenly seeing herself in Cousin Ethelinda's role, albeit serving the cold and haughty Edythe rather than Lady St. Merryn, Charley stood gaping at him for several shattered moments before she gathered her wits. Then, turning to Rockland, she said urgently, "See here, sir, do you still want to marry me?"

Though he had clearly been an uncomfortable witness to Alfred's fury, he looked utterly astonished now.

"Well, do you," she demanded, "or has all your talk of undying love for me been nothing but stupid prattle?"

"Good God," he exclaimed, "of course, I want to marry you! It is the dearest wish of my life. If I am stunned, it is because I had given up hope."

"Then hope does indeed spring eternal," she said bitterly, "for I mean to marry you just as quickly as you can get a license."

Alfred said testily, "You've got a full year of mourning ahead of you, my girl, before I will consent to any marriage."

"I don't require your consent," Charley snapped. "I am of age, and you are not my guardian or my trustee. And know this, Alfred Tarrant. I would throw myself off the highest cliff in Cornwall before I would let myself dwindle into a poor relation dependent upon you for bed and board. Rockland, if you love me, get that license at once, but arrange for a very discreet ceremony."

"To be sure, my treasure." He looked pale and still disconcerted, as if he were unsure of what to do next. But if he expected to embrace her or discuss their plans at length, he soon discovered his error, for his betrothed turned on her heel and strode angrily toward the house, with Letty running to keep up with her.

Charley sent the child to her room, then went to visit the housekeeper. Mrs. Medrose shook her head when she saw her, and said, "Oh, my dear, what a pass we've come to! I hope you won't countermand his orders, for I couldn't gainsay you. Mr. Tarrant's made it clear that it's worth our places to disobey him."

"Never mind," Charley said with a sigh. "I won't ask you to take my part, but he's ordered Letty to forgo her supper, too, and she just had the bad luck to be with me. If you can see that she gets some bread and meat, or some fruit at least, I'll be grateful."

"I can do that, and gladly, for I doubt if Mr. Tarrant will inquire about the child. But as to you, my dear . . ."

"Did he discover that Kerra brought food to me earlier today?"

"No, thank the fates, but I dare not let her do it again."

"Well, I won't starve overnight," Charley said, taking leave of her and going up the servants' stair to her bedchamber.

Not until she had shut herself in and flung herself onto her bed did she give thought to what she had done and wonder what had possessed her to do it, deciding at last that simple pride was to blame. Just the thought, at present, of writing to anyone in her family to reveal her wretched circumstances, let alone beg them to take her in, made her feel sick. Anywhere she went, if not at once then certainly in time, she would become that despised member of the household, the poor relation. Better marriage any day, to *anyone,* than that. Rockland would not be so bad, she thought. He was already in the habit of catering to her wishes, so she could be fairly certain he would not become a domineering husband. Why then, she wondered, did the prospect depress her so?

She kept to her room the following day, not wanting to see anyone, and despite its being Sunday, Alfred made no objection, allowing her meals to be served there. Monday morning she went down to breakfast at her usual time, and exerted herself to be polite to him. He was just finishing his meal and seemed to find nothing unusual in her behavior, taking her apparent submission as his due. She did not ride, however. She refused to request his permission, and since he had left her little to do in the house, that day and the week that followed passed with depressing slowness. She had all she could do at first to keep memories of the past from intruding.

Rockland, though frequently repeating his intention to obtain a special license, used first the poor weather and then an incipient cold as excuses to delay his search. Charley suspected that he had no real wish to marry, that his protestations sprouted from habit, but she could not bring herself to release him from their hasty betrothal.

To avoid painful memories, she busied herself with Letty, and read whenever she could, forcing herself to concentrate. She encountered some opposition from Alfred, who did not approve of females reading the *Times,* but she resolved that by asking Medrose to keep the newspaper for her after Alfred had read it. She also sorted through her clothes, insisting that Kerra dye one dress after another until the maid begged her to stop.

"All your gowns will be death black, Miss Charley. 'Tis a shame, it is!"

"They'll be out of fashion when the year is out," Charley said.

"Not all," Kerra protested. "Come six months, you can wear the dark ones."

Finding it too difficult to argue, Charley agreed. She felt as if the morning fog that had become almost a daily visitor to south Cornwall had closed around her, even indoors. Yet sunlight, when it appeared, scarcely affected her. Her thoughts seemed vague and purposeless. She could not work up the energy to press Rockland about the license. Even Letty's comments generally failed to amuse her, and she found sitting with her grandmother and Miss Davies more trying than anything else.

The following Saturday afternoon, after a full week without riding, she forced herself to walk briskly around the entire garden for exercise, avoiding everyone else until they gathered in the drawing room in the late afternoon. Elizabeth and Edythe were polite, if distant, but Rockland, joining them and sitting near Alfred, told Charley that he had learned the whereabouts of a bishop at last. "Not only can he provide a special license," he said, "but I daresay he'll be willing to marry us as well."

"Excellent," Charley said. "You must speak with him at once, sir, tomorrow."

"I can hardly go hunting the fellow on a Sunday," he protested. "Moreover, he's dashed busy at present, making preparations to consecrate the new cathedral. Still and all," he added with a wary look, "I'll do what I can."

With ponderous humor, Alfred said, "I hope you mean to lay down the law to this puss, Rockland. She'll soon have you living under the cat's paw if you don't."

Rockland smiled and seemed about to reply when Medrose flung open the doors and announced in his most stately tone, "Sir Antony Foxearth-Tarrant, madam."

On the words, a very English gentleman dressed in the highest kick of masculine fashion stepped into the room. He made a profound leg. Then, straightening, he raised a gold-rimmed quizzing glass to one light blue eye and surveyed the company.

"Dear me," he drawled, looking mildly astonished, "am I related to *all* of you?"

"Who the devil are you, sir?" Alfred demanded, leaping to his feet.

"Why, my dear Alfred, you cannot have been attending, for

that excellent fellow, the butler, announced my name quite clearly just now. Even if you have decided to forget my existence, you of all people must recognize my name." He paused, then added gently, "I am just awfully sorry to spoil your amusing charade, little man, but I *am* the sixth Earl of St. Merryn, and I've come to claim my estates. You will no doubt, in due course, derive some small amusement from introducing me to your neighbors and what few friends you may have as the long-lost heir."

Chapter Seven

No one stirred for a full minute. When the newcomer raised his quizzing glass again, and turned it toward Charley, she automatically lifted her chin at the impertinence. The glass remained fixed on her.

In the aristocratic accents of a man with Eton and Oxford behind him, the gentleman said, "Upon my word, but you are a beauty, my dear. May I know which of my relations you might be?"

"I am Charlotte Tarrant," she replied stiffly, looking at him more searchingly.

His dark hair had been masterfully cut and arranged in an elegant, swept-back style. His stiffly starched shirt points and exquisitely tied cravat forced his chin to an unnatural height, making him appear to look down his nose at all he surveyed unless he bent slightly at the waist.

His attire was suitable for a royal drawing room. The well-cut black pantaloons and frock coat clearly had been tailored in London by a master. His linen was snowy white, his shoes polished to perfection, and the gold signet ring on the third finger of his right hand looked expensive. Moreover, as Charley noted, his clothing revealed rather than concealed a muscular, well-built body.

Edythe looked outraged, Elizabeth astonished, and Rockland looked faintly amused. Alfred, stunned at first, collected himself to declare furiously, "Whoever you are, you are not Antony Tarrant. He's dead."

The elegant gentleman picked an imaginary bit of lint from his sleeve. "So I have been given to understand. In my experience, however, it is wise to have proof of death before announcing a man's demise to all and sundry, my dear chap."

"What makes you think we have no such proof?" Alfred demanded.

"If you do, my presence on this mortal coil certainly disputes its accuracy. Come, come, my dear Alfred, surely you must recognize your own brother."

Charley gasped, but it was not the gentleman's extraordinary claim that startled her, for she knew that must be false. A prickling of familiarity had stirred when he peered at her through his glass. Only her instinctive withdrawal from such impudence had kept her from seeing then what she saw so clearly now. Sir Antony Foxearth-Tarrant was none other than her old friend, Jean Matois.

At that moment, Letty entered the drawing room behind him, clutching her gray cloak close about her in such a way as to tell Charley, if no one else, that Jeremiah was concealed beneath it. With a direct look, Letty said urgently, "Forgive me for interrupting, Cousin Charley, but could I just have a word with you? Straightaway?"

Charley said calmly, "Letty dear, do allow me to make you known to Sir Antony Foxearth-Tarrant. Sir Antony, this is my cousin, Lady Letitia Deverill."

"Letitia *Ophelia* Deverill," Letty said, making her curtsy and adding as she arose, "I am pleased to meet you, Sir Antony." Her eyes widened when her gaze met his. "Tarrant? Are . . . are you related to us, sir?"

"He is *not*," Alfred said angrily. "He is a damned infernal impostor."

"Now, dash it," Rockland said, "you can't speak so to a

child. Moreover, the man says he's your brother. Seems a dashed odd thing to say if he ain't.''

Alfred stiffened. ''Are you calling me a liar, Rockland? Because if you are, I'll throw you right out of this house. The fact that you've gone and got yourself betrothed to Charlotte won't stop me for a moment. That you can depend upon.''

''But, dash it all, Alfred, is it your house?'' Rockland asked, raising his eyebrows. ''Appears to me this fellow's raising some question about that.''

Aware that the so-called Sir Antony's gaze had been fixed hard upon her from the moment Alfred mentioned her betrothal, Charley kept her eyes on the latter as she said, ''Just tell us this, Cousin. Could a missing brother be that minor detail of probate into which you said Mr. Stephen Kenhorn is looking?''

''What if it is?'' Alfred said. ''I tell you, this fellow's no brother of mine. Don't you think I'd know him if he were?''

Rockland said, ''Man's got a point there, by Jove. Didn't I just say the same not two minutes ago? Moreover, Miss Elizabeth has been sitting there staring at this chap for nigh onto five minutes now, and she don't look as if she's seeing a ghost.''

Elizabeth smiled at him, saying in her gentle way, ''But I would not recognize our Antony under any circumstance, my lord. I was no more than six when the French war ended, you know, and Antony was home only briefly. I cannot even call his features to mind, for I do not believe I have ever seen a portrait of him at home. Do you know what our brother looks like, Alfred dear?''

''I know what he *don't* look like,'' Alfred said scathingly. ''Antony was no damned prick-me-dainty fop.''

Charley said, ''Please remember that Letty is in the room, Cousin, and moderate your language accordingly.''

''Now, see here, young woman—''

''As hot-tempered as ever, I see,'' Sir Antony said, raising his quizzing glass again. ''I do not believe Miss Charlotte's request was unreasonable, dear fellow.''

Alfred glared at him, then said abruptly, ''Look here, stop calling me your dear fellow. Have you got proof, anything at all, to show who you are?''

"Proof? Ah, yes, 'to have a bliss in proof—and proved, a very woe.' Wouldst have 'ocular proof' or 'proofs of holy writ,' sir?" Without waiting for a response, Sir Antony added in a musing tone, "In point of fact, I do not believe I am in any way bound to present such proof to you. Time enough for that when I can meet with that fellow looking to complete probate of St. Merryn's will, don't you know."

Alfred's eyes had narrowed suspiciously. Now, angrily, he demanded, "What the devil do you mean to do in the meantime?"

Sir Antony raised his glass again, this time surveying the room at large. "Why, I believe I shall stay here and become acquainted with my inheritance—and my family, of course." The quizzing glass turned toward Charley again as he added, "I've a mind to study some of its more decorative ornaments."

Giggling, Letty said hastily, "Excuse me, please," and hurried from the room.

Still seething, Alfred looked at Edythe, but she was staring in undisguised chagrin at Sir Antony and paid him no heed. It was Elizabeth who said quietly, "Sir Antony, have you brought servants and baggage with you?"

He smiled at her, and when Charley saw his eyes crinkle at the corners she wondered how he could have fooled her for a moment. He said in a less haughty tone than he had employed so far, "My man Hodson has everything in train, I believe. The butler assured us that there is room in the carriage house for my coach, and a stall in the stable for my hack. I trust my arrival will not put anyone out. This house seems large enough to accommodate one or two more inhabitants, and since I have as much right to be here as Mr. Alfred Tarrant, I will certainly stay."

Alfred said testily, "I don't suppose I can stop you. Kenhorn will have to sort this out, but I hope you don't think you're going to sleep in the earl's bedchamber!"

"Now, my dear fellow, did I not say I've no wish to put anyone out? I believe the best solution is to allow the servants and tenants to carry on as they have done for years, without interference, until—Kenhorn, is it?—sorts us out, as you say."

"An excellent idea," Charley said warmly. "Rockland, since you are nearest the bell, ring for Medrose, and ask him to have Sir Antony's gear taken to the large guest room in the east wing. His man can have one of the smaller bedchambers nearby."

"Right you are," Rockland said, getting up at once to obey her.

Charley turned back to Sir Antony. "Perhaps you should next meet my grandmother, sir. She keeps to her private rooms these days, but I daresay she will want to have a look at you."

He smiled appreciatively, but Alfred said, "See here, Charlotte, whoever is master of Tuscombe Park, it ain't you. You ought more properly to have asked Edythe where she thinks this impostor ought to sleep. It ain't right, you just up and giving orders like that. What's more, I don't like it."

Charley looked at him, fighting her temper. Since she had scarcely laid eyes on him for days, except for mealtimes when she avoided all but necessary conversation, she had nearly forgotten how easily he could irritate her. It was all she could do now not to snap at him. As it was, she said with more bluntness than tact, "I doubt that you or your wife have as yet had time to learn all the rooms in this house, let alone which is most suitable for our guest. I was not putting myself forward. I was merely trying to be helpful, but as usual, Cousin—"

"The green bedchamber, did you say?" Sir Antony appeared to realize belatedly that he had interrupted her. Gracefully begging her pardon, he gestured toward the doorway, where Medrose stood awaiting orders.

Charley looked pointedly at Alfred, who said pompously, "Have Sir Antony's trappings taken to the green room in the east wing, my good man."

"They have already been taken to that chamber, sir," Medrose replied.

"Excellent," Sir Antony said before anyone else could react.

Alfred said, "I daresay you'll be wanting to go up at once. We dine at six."

"Yes, I was afraid you would keep country hours," Sir Antony said with a sigh. "I do not have any particular desire to sit in my rooms till six o'clock, however, and I can see that you won't insist upon enjoying my company. Perhaps I can prevail upon Miss Charlotte to show me the gardens, or the principle rooms, or some such thing.''

"Miss Charlotte is betrothed to Rockland here," Alfred said, indicating that gentleman. "You should perhaps first seek his permission."

"How do you do?" Sir Antony said, shaking the hand that Rockland held out to him. "My felicitations on your extreme good fortune, sir."

"Oh, I'm a lucky fellow, all right and tight," Rockland said. "You won't credit it, but I've been dangling after the chit for nearly four—no, by Jove, it's six—years now. She's only just given me the nod this very week."

"Indeed? I am emboldened to ask what brought her up to scratch at last."

Rockland grinned. "She recognized my sterling virtues. What else?"

"Well said. Do you object if I steal her away long enough to show me the gardens and stables? I promise you, I'll not attempt to cut you out."

Rockland sighed. "Couldn't do it if you tried. Take her where you will, my dear fellow. It's as much as your life is worth to attempt to trifle with her."

As they walked down the front steps toward the sweeping lawn and the lake beyond it, Sir Antony murmured, "Yet another fellow who thinks you can take care of yourself, *mon ange.*" He chuckled. "It occurs to me that it might be both wiser and safer if I call you just plain *angel* now."

"Good mercy, sir, not if you do so where Alfred can hear you. How did you dare to attempt such an imposture? How did you even know he had a brother? I don't know how I kept my countenance when I saw it was you. Letty and I had long since decided that you were not quite what you would have had us believe, but—"

"I was afraid of that," he said, putting a hand under her elbow as they walked along the gravel carriage drive to the garden entrance.

"Letty recognized you, too, you know. Far more quickly than I did."

"I daresay she had seen Annabelle. She was in the stable yard when I arrived. I saw her when I emerged from my carriage."

"But where did you get a carriage? I own, sir, I am consumed with curiosity, so I hope you do not mean to fob me off with Banbury tales. I know you are not Alfred's brother. If he actually has got one, and he's not dead, he is no doubt just as odious as Alfred is. But won't they find you out rather quickly?"

"I think I can keep Kenhorn busy long enough to see to the business that brought me to Cornwall," he said. "Must we continue to walk, or can we sit on that bench?"

"We had better walk," she said. "I would not be surprised if Edythe were watching us from some window or other to observe every move we make. She would like nothing better than to make trouble for me, I think."

"In that case, we will walk. Are they all still driving you to distraction? I must suppose you have made your peace with Miss Elizabeth, at least, so why did you agree to marry Rockland? I thought you were set against the whole idea of marriage."

"I was." She hesitated, suddenly uncomfortable, because after the scene with Alfred, she had not even thought about apologizing to Elizabeth. She saw that he was watching her, and needing to say something, she blurted, "Alfred wants to turn me into a poor relation. You know the sort I mean. Expected to wait upon others, determined to please, always living under threat of being cast out and left destitute, having nothing to look forward to but pity and perhaps a small legacy if one is lucky. I couldn't bear it!"

"You didn't apologize to Elizabeth, did you?"

He sounded disappointed, and she wished very much then that she had apologized. She wanted to tell him everything, that the confrontation with Alfred and her impulsive betrothal to Rockland had put all thought of the scene with Elizabeth out of her head. Somehow though, when she opened her mouth to explain, she could not do it. The unspoken words seemed inadequate, no more than weak excuses.

"I'm afraid not," she said quietly, "not yet."

"Ah, well, I expect there hasn't been an opportunity. No doubt you will speak to her in your own good time."

His tone was even, the words sounding reasonable, but knowing as well as he did that she had enjoyed a full week of opportunity, Charley felt as if he had roundly scolded her. She wanted to defend herself; but he had said nothing to warrant defense, and she knew her behavior was indefensible.

He said, "What a fine knot garden that is. Someone put a great deal of time and trouble into laying that out, I'd say."

She glanced at him and saw that he was not looking at the knot garden but at her. When her gaze met his, the expression in his eyes warmed. Encouraged, she said, "The first Countess of St. Merryn designed it about a hundred years ago. She had a great fondness for gardens."

"I, too, have a fondness for gardens. This one is particularly pleasant." He was still gazing at her.

"Who are you, sir? You said you would explain this imposture of yours. Why are you here?"

He sighed. "Having said it, I am now forced to make good, I suppose. I am not in the habit of explaining my actions. For that matter, I trust very few people."

Charley opened her mouth to tell him that he could certainly trust her, but she shut it again. She could give him no good reason to believe her. A cool breeze ruffled her hair, blowing strands across her face. She pushed them away. The pebbles of the path crunched beneath their feet, and songbirds twittered from trees and bordering tall hedges. Looking down, she saw that his well-shined shoes had acquired a patina of dust. He remained silent.

"If you feel that you cannot trust me," she said at last, still looking at his feet, "I will understand."

"It's not that. I did not realize this would be so difficult. I am here in behalf of Wellington, you see."

She looked at him then in astonishment. "The Duke?"

He nodded. "He is to attend the consecration of the new cathedral in Truro on the fourteenth of June, and he received

an anonymous warning that someone intends to assassinate him
either before or after the event.''

"Good mercy!''

"Just so.''

"But what part do you play?''

"I ... ah ... the fact is that I am expected to discover
the plotters and unhinge their plot before the Duke arrives in
Cornwall.''

"Is that all?''

He grinned. "I own, I had expected to make more progress
than I have. I managed rather quickly to insinuate myself into
the group most likely to be party to useful information. Once
I discovered that the smugglers and wreckers on the south coast
of Cornwall are not only organized but in league with their
French equivalents, I knew I was on the right track. I am still
certain I'm looking in the right place, but so far I've learned
little other than that they thumb their noses at the authorities
and are, to a man, strongly opposed to any civilian police force
in England. I suppose, however, that you don't know much
about the Metropolitan Police Bill that Robert Peel is attempting
to pass through Parliament.''

"Oh, but I do! I am an avid reader of the London *Times,*
sir, although Cousin Alfred does not approve of females reading
anything in the newspapers other than what he chooses to read
aloud to them. At all events, I have found the Parliamentary
debates on the police bill fascinating. I know it has encountered
many delays, and that Mr. Peel means to recommit it early next
week. But that bill affects only London, so I do not see how
it can upset men in Cornwall.''

"They know that what begins in London will soon spread
throughout the land. According to the Duke, that is indeed their
plan for the future.''

"Then I can understand why Cornishmen would oppose it.
At present, when it appears to the Lloyd's agents or to customs
riders that too much smuggling or too many wrecks have
occurred in a given area, they call in the military, especially
when goods liable to duty are involved. That slows things down
for a while, but then the soldiers go away again, and the gangs

return to business. It is still hard to convict them in a Cornish court, you see. Some landowners, like my grandfather, changed things a little when they refused to support the plundering and began training men to rescue ships, cargo, and crews. Juries still won't convict, but magistrates will now, and penalties can be severe. No doubt, the coastal gangs fear that with a sustained civilian police presence, they will find it far more difficult to enjoy the success they now enjoy.''

"That's it, of course." He smiled at her. "I did not expect you to know so much about it. Most females of my acquaintance have no interest in such matters.''

"Most females," Charley retorted, "are trained from birth to take no interest in such things. My Great-Aunt Ophelia believes that men purposely keep women from reading about and understanding important issues. She says men are afraid that women will prove to be as intelligent and capable of discussing them as they are themselves, that given the slightest opportunity, women could provide intelligent solutions to many of our problems, and might even insist upon having a say in our government.''

He chuckled. "I hadn't thought about that, but your great-aunt may well be right. We've had queens who were far more capable of running this country than many of our kings, certainly.''

She regarded him with no little amazement, unaccustomed to hearing such amiable responses to opinions that others were quick to call radical.

He returned her look, his lips twitching almost as if he were going to smile, but there was no humor in his tone when he said, "I need not tell you that I am placing my life in your hands by being so frank with you.''

"I will try to be worthy of your trust," she said.

"I'm not worried about that, but I could scarcely blame you if you refused to trust me. I have, after all, proven myself capable of deception merely by the roles I play. Such deceit does not sit well with most upright British citizens.''

"Good mercy, I quite understand that you cannot walk bang

up to a smuggler and ask him if he is plotting to kill the Duke of Wellington.''

"No, I can't do that," he said, smiling. "In fact, I have blotted my copybook as it is, because my intervention on the beach that day caused some of them to question my loyalty. I introduced myself to them, you see, as a French smuggler with an unsavory reputation. Stepping in and then riding off with you and Letty undermined that position, I'm afraid."

"Are you in danger?"

"Perhaps. At all events, I decided to run this rig. No one will suspect a claimant to the St. Merryn earldom of belonging to the coastal gang, and no gang member will look for Jean Matois at Tuscombe Park. With luck, I can play both roles, manage to stay alive, and gather twice as much information."

Charley said, "Letty suspected you weren't what you seemed that first night, you know. She said Matois means cunning, like a fox. And in the course of her conversation with you, she said you spoke drawing-room French as easily as you spoke the argot of the streets."

He grimaced. "That child wants a keeper, but it certainly explains why she kept calling me *sir.* I hoped it was just that she was an exceedingly polite youngster. What are her parents about to let her learn so much at such a tender age?"

"They believe in teaching her all she can learn," Charley said. "However, from what she said about her father's reaction to some of her less tasteful French vocabulary, I collect that even they are not aware of the depth of her knowledge."

He shook his head. "I'd already met with difficulty maintaining the character of Jean Matois here in England. It was not hard in France, because I associated generally with men of the lower classes. Here I find myself slipping into old language patterns all too easily. I have only to hear proper English spoken to begin speaking it myself. That's a very dangerous thing in my line of work."

"Was the Duke also threatened in France?" Charley asked.

He looked confused.

"You said it was not so hard to play your role there," she reminded him.

He hesitated, then said glibly, "He was the supreme commander, after all. He was threatened many times. Would you like to show me the stables now? We did say we would not be away too long. I don't want Rockland to call me out for spending too much time with his betrothed."

"He won't. Will you let me help you?"

"In what way?"

"At least you did not instantly deny that there is any way I can," she said with a wry smile. "I have lived here all my life, you know, and I am acquainted with nearly everyone. People will tell me things, I'm sure, that they would not tell a stranger. It will be easy to bring up the cathedral consecration, and the Duke's visit, because everyone is undoubtedly talking about those things."

"They certainly are, although no one has mentioned an assassination."

"Of course not. I daresay that when all is said and done, you will find the warning was no more than a prank. Everyone is excited about the consecration, because it means the return to Cornwall of a set of famous sacred vessels removed from a disestablished abbey during the Reformation. That is why the Duke is taking part. He will present the vessels, as a gift from the whole nation, in the historic Seraphim Coffer, an ancient Cornish chest said to date to the twelfth century. Mr. James Gabriel, the mayor of Lostwithiel, is refurbishing the coffer for the occasion."

"The mayor?"

"He was thought to be the best person, you see. The chest was discovered in Lostwithiel, and Mr. Gabriel's late father was the clockmaker there. He did marvelous cabinetwork and trained his son to follow his trade. Although Mr. Gabriel has moved up in the world and is likely, my grandfather said, to be granted a knighthood for his work with the Methodists to aid miners in Cornwall and to oppose the coastal gangs, he is thought to be nearly as skilled at cabinetry as his father was."

"Sounds like a noble fellow," Antony said. "No doubt he'll marry well and give up trade altogether."

She chuckled. "He is a widower, I believe, but you may be

right. He joined the family for luncheon the day of the wreck. I was not present at the time, but Letty said he made sheep's eyes at Elizabeth. I don't think Alfred likes him much, however.''

"He wouldn't. From what I've seen of our Alfred, he will seek a bigger fish than your Mr. Gabriel for his sister.''

"Well, Mr. Gabriel seems to be a fine man, and he will be distressed if anything happens to the Duke in Cornwall. Have you discovered *any* clues to the plotters?''

"Nothing specific, though I do suspect that more than one faction is involved. This coastal gang—some members of which you have been privileged to meet—has numerous connections in France, for one thing.''

"I can understand why the French might hate the Duke. He defeated their emperor, after all. But I don't see why good Cornishmen would plot against him.''

"Annoyance over Boney's defeat lingers in France because Wellington put an end to the most lucrative period the French smugglers had ever known. I daresay the same feeling pervades much of Cornwall. One thing few people realize is that the commodity most frequently smuggled to France was English gold. With English money paid for duty-free goods the French bought guns to shoot English soldiers.''

"Men of Cornwall would never have done that!''

"I'm afraid they did,'' he said. "Each time a Cornish smuggler helped land French lace, brandy, and other smuggled goods, a Frenchman got paid for them. It would be a bit different if they had bartered with Cornish cream or wool, but they did not. Even now, smugglers bring more into the country than they take out. They say they smuggle or wreck because of unfair duties, poverty, or an uncaring government. They blame anyone but themselves. Good English money still goes to the Continent. Wellington, in opposing them, may have set himself up as a target.''

"That's dreadful,'' Charley said, "but wouldn't the Duke be safe with a proper escort? Surely a large military unit would deter plotters and protect him completely.''

"Not against a truly determined effort,'' he said. "In any case, such an escort is something he wants to avoid. If even a whisper of this plot reaches the public ear, the military will *have* to be called in. Wellington is the nation's greatest living hero, cherished by all. His address at Apsley House is Number One London, you know.''

''To match his status in every heart in Britain,'' Charley said. ''I read that, but he is not living at Apsley House just now.''

''He is putting up at Number Ten Downing Street till alterations are completed at Apsley House. To return to the matter of the military, however, he believes they are the last force to be charged with keeping peace. Unfortunate incidents have occurred in the past when a military force tried to restore peace to a community.''

''Peterloo.''

He smiled. ''Just so. That's why he and Peel want civilian police. The problem, of course, is that most people can't imagine how an unarmed constabulary could keep the peace. But the Duke and Robert Peel believe that if they can establish an example in London, they'll soon bring people around to their way of thinking.''

Charley would have liked to continue the discussion, for she found not only the topic to be fascinating, but her companion as well. At that moment, however, they realized they were being hailed from behind. Turning, she saw Elizabeth hurrying along the path, waving at them.

They walked toward her, and when they were within earshot, she said, ''Mr. Gabriel has called, and dearest Alfred was kind enough to invite him to stay and dine with us. He—Alfred, that is—sent me to tell you that he is having dinner set forward an hour to accommodate him—Mr. Gabriel, that is. Alfred thought you would both want to come inside at once to change your attire. Oh, and Cousin Charlotte, Alfred asked if you would kindly inform Cousin Letitia that, since we are dining in company, she must take her dinner in the nursery with the other children.''

''I'll tell her,'' Charley said. The request was reasonable, although she knew Letty would be disappointed not to dine with Sir Antony.

Sir Antony said haughtily, "I must say, Miss Elizabeth, I quite look forward to meeting this Gabriel chap. Sounds like quite a noble fellow to me."

"Noble?" She wrinkled her brow. "He has been the mayor of Lostwithiel for some months now, sir, but I do not believe he is a nobleman."

Sir Antony avoided Charley's eye as he said cheerfully, "Nonetheless, a fascinating chap, I daresay. Said to be devilish interested in everyone's welfare."

"Oh, yes, I am sure you must be right, Sir Antony." Elizabeth smiled at him. "Mr. Gabriel seems very well spoken and interested in many things, which one quite understands, for without his civic interests, one fears he would lead a lonely life, poor man. His wife died many years ago, you see, and his daughter has moved to London. You must forgive me if I did not quite understand you at first. Like so many other women, I can never understand more than half of what you gentlemen talk about."

Charley struggled to suppress a retort and thought she had full command of her countenance. Thus, she was disconcerted to meet a steady look from Sir Antony.

Holding her gaze, he said blandly, "Miss Elizabeth, I believe Miss Charlotte has something of a private nature to say to you. Therefore, if you will excuse me, I'll just go on ahead and find someone to show me to my room."

Chapter Eight

Seething with indignation and trying her best to conceal it, Charley watched Sir Antony stride toward the house. His figure was as admirable from the rear as from any other angle, she noted grimly, but just then she wanted to smack him.

"What is it, Cousin Charlotte?" Elizabeth asked politely.

"What?" Charley turned toward her, her mind still obsessed with what she might do to teach Sir Jean-Antony Foxearth-Tarrant-Matois a well-deserved lesson.

"Sir Antony said you had something of a private nature to say to me," Elizabeth reminded her. "I am sure I have no idea what that can be, for we have scarcely exchanged more than a few words since I arrived. But if Sir Antony says it is so, it must be so. So what is it, if you please? We cannot tarry long, you know, for dearest Alfred will be sorely vexed if we keep them all waiting when he has been so obliging as to order dinner put forward to accommodate Mr. Gabriel."

Charley blinked. Then, realizing that Elizabeth had either paused for breath or had said all she wanted to say, she said bluntly, "Look here, do you believe whatever a man says to you?"

Elizabeth tilted her head a little to one side, clearly giving the question more consideration than Charley knew it deserved. At last she said thoughtfully, "I have been given no cause, I think, not to believe anything a gentleman tells me. They are generally so much wiser and better educated than any mere woman, you know. Surely, it behooves us to seek their guidance. After all, my dear cousin, gentlemen have—most of them—been about the world much more than we have. More than I have at all events," she amended hastily. "Dearest Alfred—and I think little Letty, too—said you had journeyed all the way to France. Dearest Alfred does not hold with foreign travel for females, of course—"

"Of course," Charley interjected evenly. "A man who does not allow females to read the *Times* could hardly think otherwise."

"Goodness, do you *want* to read the *Times?*" When she did not reply, Elizabeth looked uneasy. "I suppose you do. You disagree with him about so many things, but I was going to say I think you were very brave to go to a country that is so . . . so—"

"So French? It's a perfectly civilized country, you know. Some people actually prefer it over England."

"Now I know you are teasing me. No one of sense could think France better than England. Why, only a few years ago they were our greatest enemies. I mean, I'm sure that life there is all quite peaceful now, and I've got nothing against France myself—well, except that it's full of foreigners who don't speak proper Christian English or understand our ways, but—I beg your pardon. Did you say something?"

Forcibly restraining her irritation, Charley said, "I didn't exactly speak. I choked. I expect I must have breathed in a bug or something. Do go on."

"Well, I haven't really got anything more to say on that subject. I did think you began to speak."

Goaded, Charley retorted, "Do you actually believe all that you say, Elizabeth? Because if you do, I've got to say it's utter drivel. There are just as many Christian Frenchmen as Christian Englishmen, though I must admit that most of the former are Catholic. That probably won't improve their credit with you."

"Goodness, no! Mercy me, Cousin Charlotte, did you actually have to speak to any Catholics when you were there? Because if you did, I beg you not to mention it to our dearest Alfred. He would be so displeased. Alfred thinks the Prime Minister was very wrong to support Mr. Peel's Catholic Emancipation Act. I don't know what that was, precisely, but Alfred says that since the Catholics are to blame—"

"Spare me what Alfred says," Charley said tartly. "You might try thinking for yourself, Elizabeth. Read a few good books. I can recommend any number just chockful of information that will astonish you. You might also take a look at a newspaper now and again, as well. You don't seem to be entirely lacking in intelligence—"

"Thank you," Elizabeth said dryly enough to show that she did have claws, albeit well-sheathed ones. "Was that the private matter that you wished to discuss with me?"

Snapped to her senses by the question, Charley felt an unfamiliar stirring of chagrin. Sir Antony—or whoever the man was—had basely manipulated her into the tête à tête, but she could blame no one but herself for the position in which she found herself with Elizabeth now.

Collecting her wits, she said ruefully, "Believe it or not, I wanted to apologize for losing my temper the other day and shouting at you."

"Oh, but you need not give that another thought. I have not, I promise you."

Instead of feeling reassured, Charley felt annoyed. She wanted to snap that Elizabeth *should* give it more thought. The woman was too maddeningly biddable and submissive. One fairly ached to take her in hand and show her the right way to manage her life. Containing the impulse with difficulty, she said carefully instead, "I was wrong to take my anger out on you, Elizabeth. I'm sorry I was rude."

"Indeed, Cousin Charlotte, you need not dwell on the matter. I assure you, once dear Lord Rockland explained matters, I forgave you instantly."

"So he explained matters, did he?"

"Oh, yes. He explained how you get a bit hysterical, you

know, as we females so frequently do, I'm afraid, when we are tired or out of sorts, and assured me that you did not mean a word of what you said. Lord Rockland is very wise, don't you agree? You are a most lucky young woman to be blessed with a man like him to guide you through the trials and tribulations of life. I quite envy you your forthcoming marriage."

Fortunately, since for once in her life Charley was rendered speechless (and thus was unable to inform Elizabeth that both she and Rockland were idiots), Elizabeth went on to say that they really must walk more quickly if they were not to vex dearest Alfred.

"For you will want to change your dress, I know. Indeed, I do not know how you will ready yourself quickly enough as it is. We should not have dawdled so long talking nonsense. Oh, look, here comes dear Lord Rockland now, no doubt anxious to speed us along. It is just like him to concern himself with our well-being."

"Isn't it?" Charley snapped her mouth shut, determined to say nothing more that she could not in good conscience repeat to Sir Antony. That she even had such a thought was enough to make her grit her teeth. Nonetheless, she did not want him to make her see herself in the same harsh light as he had before. Therefore, she greeted Rockland in an even tone, resisting the temptation to ask sweetly if he had come to hustle them in like schoolgirls, to tidy themselves and wash their hands before dinner.

Annoyance stirred again, however, when she saw him look uneasily from her to Elizabeth and back, as if he were concerned about the state of their relationship. Again managing to control her first impulse, she refrained from blurting that she had not yet scratched out Elizabeth's eyes or flayed her with her tongue. Instead, she said simply, "Did you have a particular purpose in seeking us out, Rockland?"

That he had rushed out upon discovering they had been left alone together became even more obvious to her when he flushed and said, "No, no, not at all. That is, Alfred did say he hoped you and Foxearth would not keep us waiting, because that Gabriel fellow's staying to dine. Oh, and Miss Elizabeth,

Mrs. Tarrant was looking for you. She said something about your having promised a treat to the children.''

"Mercy me, I must fly. I quite forgot I had promised our dear little Neddy that I would read a story to him and Jane after their supper. They eat earlier than we do, you know,'' she added, "so pray forgive me, both of you, if I must hurry away.''

"Do that,'' Charley recommended. "I promise, we won't mind a bit.''

Elizabeth picked up her skirts, and although she did nothing so unseemly as to run, she did hurry back to the house.

Unable to suppress her feelings a moment long, Charley said, "Good mercy, Rockland, you're practically panting. Did you think I'd murder her?''

"You nearly did before,'' he retorted. "I don't know what got into you then, so you can hardly expect me to guess what you were doing just now. Not but what you must have seen for yourself by now just how sweet and gentle she is, and how kind.''

"She talks utter bilge,'' Charley snapped. "Idiotic, prattling bilge! What that girl wants is education. Do you know that she thinks women *need* men to guide them through life? That she actually believes men—just by virtue of being born male, mind you—are better suited to think and to make decisions than women are?''

"Didn't I just say how intelligent and sensible she is?''

"You did not! You called her sweet and gentle, and kind. I don't know her well enough yet to know if she possesses those virtues, but I am perfectly willing to take your word for it. None of that makes her any the less a half-wit though. Why, Letty's got ten times more sense in her little finger than Elizabeth Tarrant has in her entire body.''

"I think you are too harsh. Elizabeth understands what it is to be feminine, is all, and she don't need a lot of dashed fool notions crammed into her head to change that.''

"Good mercy, Rockland, you're as much of a noddy as she is. You think she's wonderful because she looks up to you and thinks you all-knowing, just because, through mere happenstance of nature, you possess a penis!''

"Good God, Charlotte! What will you say next?" He looked hastily around, clearly very much shocked.

If the truth were known, Charley was shocked at herself for letting such a word leap from her mind to her tongue. Perversely though, she wondered if Sir Antony would have been shocked. She had a notion that he would not have been, though he might have advised her not to say such things where others might hear. Even as the thought crossed her mind, however, she revised it. She rather thought Sir Antony would trust her not to say such words where anyone they would offend might overhear her. Nor would she. Rockland was not offended, after all, merely shocked.

Glancing at him, she said curiously, "Do I frequently shock you, Rockland? Because if I do, marriage to me could prove rather uncomfortable for you."

He grinned at her, and said as they began walking again, "I find you fascinating, my treasure. Moreover, just think how the lads will all stare when I tell them I've captured the most elusive filly in the marriage stakes."

"Good mercy, is that how you think of me?"

"The biggest prize of all," he assured her. "Dowry or no dowry."

"Well, I hope you don't make a practice of apologizing for me after we're married," she snapped. "I did not like it one bit when you took Elizabeth's side against me the other day, then hared off afterward to console her."

"But, dash it, you were wrong!"

She stopped on the path and caught his arm, making him face her. "Tell me this. If I think you are wrong in a dispute with another man, will you mind if I go to him and say you're just being hysterical, and then offer an apology on your behalf?"

He grimaced. "Dash it, Charley, you make a practice of saying what you think whenever you think it. You've never once hesitated to tell the whole world when you think I'm wrong."

"Not behind your back, I don't. At least," she amended, "not to anyone who would repeat what I tell them. Do you apologize to others for your male friends when you think they are in the wrong?"

"Dash it, I did nothing wrong in talking with Miss Elizabeth. You behaved badly. You must know you did. So don't rip up at me."

He sounded like a sulky boy rather than an adult, and she nearly smiled before she remembered that she was going to marry him. "Don't take a pet," she said with a sigh. "I just wanted you to know how you made me feel. The fact that you apologized also made it difficult for me to do so just now. She's got it into that muddled head of hers that she's already received an apology."

"I should think you'd be grateful then," he said sullenly.

"Well, I'm not. Look here," she added, "when are you going to speak with that bishop about our special license?"

"I told you, he's in Truro, and I'm not going looking for him tomorrow. It's Sunday, dash it. He'll be as busy as the devil in a high wind."

"Good mercy, Rockland, what a thing to say about a bishop! I should think you'd be wanting to get this over—that is, to set a date as soon you can."

"Well, of course I do, but the fellow travels about a good deal, you know. They say he will be in Lostwithiel in a sennight. What's the great hurry?"

"If the bishop will be in Lostwithiel, then he can easily perform our wedding here, but you must make the arrangements beforehand. You can't just go to him in a week's time and say you want a ceremony performed at once. And if I seem to be in a hurry, it's just that I don't want to submit to *dearest* Alfred's self-proclaimed authority one minute longer than necessary, that's all."

"Well, if that's all it is, you're fretting without cause," he said. "Now that Sir Antony's entered the picture, as I see it, he's got as much right as Alfred has to give orders around here. Leastwise, until Alfred can prove he's the real heir."

"Perhaps, but I don't want to submit to Sir Antony either,"

Charley said with feeling. "He is even more puffed up with himself than Alfred is. Only look at him! I own, he does pay some heed to my opinions, but I expect he does it only to be polite."

Visibly relaxing, Rockland chuckled and said, "He's bigger than Alfred, too, come to think of it. I daresay he strips to advantage, too, for all his painted puppy ways. Still, he don't look as if he has much of a temper, or as if he's much in the habit of ordering females about."

"Or of giving a thought to what they really think," Charley said, realizing that she ought to do what she could to help the false Sir Antony establish himself in the role he had chosen to play. The thought of him stripped of his stiff shirt and well-fitting jacket nearly put every other thought out of her head, however. She agreed that he would strip to advantage and thought the sight might be well worth seeing.

Rockland gave her a nudge toward the house. "We are going to be late for dinner if we don't step lively," he said. "I've still got to change my neckcloth and get my valet to polish these shoes again. Just look at the dust on them. One would think that one could stroll through a garden on a tidy gravel path without collecting a lot of muck. But just look at them!"

Caring little for dust, or real muck for that matter, Charley only shook her head. Inside, they parted on the gallery landing, and she hurried to her bedchamber, where she rang for Kerra. With the maid's help, she changed to a dark-gray gown suitable for dining, and was ready before the footman downstairs had rung the second bell for dinner. Nonetheless she found the others waiting for her, with one notable exception.

"Where is that damned fellow?" Alfred demanded fretfully. "The joint will be cold, not to mention the side dishes."

Edythe said, "Indeed, my dear sir, it has seemed to me these ten days past that the servants in this house make no effort to bring our food hot to the table. You must speak sharply to them. They pay little heed to me."

Elizabeth said lightly, "You forget that at Grappen Hall we rarely got food even half so warm as what they serve here,

Edythe, on account of the kitchens being so far from the dining parlor. I think the service here has been excellent.''

Charley smiled, feeling almost in charity with her for once.

Elizabeth went on earnestly, ''But I do not mean to set my opinion against yours, Edythe, certainly. If you are not perfectly satisfied with the servants, I am persuaded that our dearest Alfred will soon get matters sorted out. Won't you, Alfred dear?''

''You may be sure of that,'' he growled.

Standing like a large, silent shadow beside Alfred, James Gabriel seemed to have eyes only for Elizabeth. He had nodded at Charley and murmured a polite reply to her greeting, but then his gaze shifted right back to Elizabeth.

''There you are,'' Alfred exclaimed suddenly, causing every eye to turn toward the grand stairway.

Sir Antony descended gracefully, every hair in place and looking, in Charley's opinion, complete to a shade. Pantaloons and a coat of soft dove-gray superfine made his eyes seem a deeper blue than usual. His neckcloth was arranged in the intricate Obaldeston with a sapphire stickpin nestled in its folds, and he wore a Chinese silk waistcoat embroidered with pink butterflies, green vines, and leaves. Observing that he had become the cynosure of every eye in the hall, he raised his quizzing glass and peered back at them.

''Dear me,'' he drawled, ''have I kept you all waiting? I am so sorry. Behold me abject with apologies. I had to change every stitch, of course. All that dust! Really, someone ought to order the gardeners to wet down those garden paths at least twice a day. At all events, you will agree that I was left with no other alternative.'' He descended the last few steps, then paused before James Gabriel. Raising his quizzing glass, he said, ''I do not believe we are acquainted.''

Alfred said brusquely, ''Mr. Gabriel is the mayor of Lost-withiel.''

''Ah, yes,'' Sir Antony said. ''I believe I have heard you described in glowing terms, Mr. Gabriel. I make you my compliments. No doubt your position is one of vast importance and responsibility, requiring the expenditure of great energy.''

Charley, watching him, could see no sign whatsoever of Jean Matois. Not only was there not the least vestige of a French accent in his drawling speech, but he looked bored and rather sleepy, an English aristocrat exerting himself to be pleasant.

Mr. Gabriel beamed at him, saying, "I am pleased to make your acquaintance, Sir Antony. My position as mayor is indeed a great responsibility, but I am a man who believes in getting things done, sir. As to the energy it takes, why, I've little else to do with my time these days. My dear wife passed on many years ago."

"So sad," Elizabeth said sympathetically.

"Yes," Gabriel agreed. "Perhaps if she had given me a son to raise, I might have put much of my energy into seeing him ascend to heights even greater than those I have attained for myself, but alas, she bore me only a daughter."

With an edge to her voice, Charley said, "No doubt you love your daughter dearly and have found her to be a source of great comfort, Mr. Gabriel."

He blinked at her. Then, with a softening smile, he said, "I care for her very much, Miss Charlotte. As a child she was my dearest delight. But alas, she inherited my ambition, I fear, for she ran off some months ago to seek her fortune elsewhere."

"I hope she was successful," Elizabeth said doubtfully. "Where did she go?"

"It's kind of you to take an interest, ma'am," Gabriel said. "However, I've yet to hear from the minx, I'm afraid. It's not really been so long as it seems, though."

Elizabeth stifled a small cry of distress.

"You are too calm, Gabriel," Sir Antony said. "I fear Miss Elizabeth believes you lack a proper sensibility."

"Well, sir, I certainly don't want to distress so sweet a young lady, but I own, I don't spend much time worrying about things I cannot change. Others engage in a deal of bother and talk, I've found. There are not many like James Gabriel, who believe in action when action is wanted. Still, I must say, Sir Antony, meeting you is an honor. Had someone told me when I was a child that I should one day enjoy the company of such men as yourself, I would have stared in disbelief. But here I stand, though my father were naught but a simple clockmaker, a tradesman who worked with his hands."

"Not a simple man, surely," Sir Antony murmured politely. "I have been told that he was a very fine craftsman."

"To be sure," Charley said. "Mr. Gabriel's papa made the clock in the drawing room, and Grandpapa said the work compares with that of Chippendale or Sheraton."

"Many people have said so," Gabriel agreed.

Edythe said, "Ah, here is our good Medrose. No doubt he has come to inform us that we may repair to the dining room. As you see, Medrose, we are quite ready at last. You can begin to serve at once."

"Yes, madam," the butler said after a brief glance at Charley, who nodded.

The exchange had not escaped Edythe, for she pressed her lips tightly together, but she did not say anything.

Medrose's glance went a long way toward soothing Charley's lacerated feelings, and she smiled at him. Just then she encountered Sir Antony's gaze and saw a distinct glint of amusement in his eyes. Although she did not know if he was laughing at her or at Edythe, she realized at once that she would do better not to betray her small sense of triumph to anyone else. Assuming a more modest expression, she glanced at him again, only to see him graciously offer his arm to Edythe.

Oddly annoyed by the gesture, she was even more irritated to see Rockland look suddenly doubtful. As the male of highest rank, he generally escorted Edythe when Lady St. Merryn did not dine with the family, and he was clearly uncertain now if he ought to escort his betrothed or Miss Elizabeth Tarrant.

Charley said, "Rockland, for goodness' sake, don't stand like a stock. Cousin Alfred is starving for his dinner. Mr. Gabriel, will you be so kind as to give your arm to Miss Elizabeth. Indeed," she added with an airy laugh, "I cannot imagine why we are all standing on such ceremony. Shall we go in?"

Mr. Gabriel assured all and sundry that he was more than willing to escort Elizabeth. But although Rockland promptly offered Charley his arm, he muttered, "Dash it, my pet, I wish you would not fling orders at me like that. It ain't seemly."

"My dear sir, if you stand about like a moonling, you must expect someone to give you a hint."

"You don't hint, Charley. You dashed well shove a fellow."

Alfred, behind them, said testily, "Do you two mean to stand nattering, because if you do, I shall never get my dinner."

In the dining room, Alfred instantly went to the head of the table, and Charley wondered if she was the only one who noticed the challenging way he looked at Sir Antony. When Sir Antony did not appear to notice, merely taking his place beside Edythe at the foot of the table, Alfred's expression changed to smug contempt.

No sooner was everyone seated, however, than Lady St. Merryn appeared, swathed in yards of black crape. She was supported by the footman Jago on one side and by the ubiquitous Miss Davies on the other.

As servants scrambled to lay covers for the two ladies, the dowager glanced around the candlelit room. She said faintly, "Were you not expecting me? I daresay you were not. Dear me, how inconvenient for you, but I was told we had company to dine, and also that a new claimant to the earldom had presented himself. I am persuaded that the latter case cannot be true. Surely someone would have taken the trouble to mention that to me, and to present him. Ah, thank you, Medrose," she added when the butler, betraying a slight frown on his normally wooden countenance, pulled out her chair with his own two hands.

Charley had known Medrose all her life. Watching him now, her instincts honed by the guilt she felt at having failed to present Sir Antony, she experienced a flash of insight that made her look at Edythe Tarrant. The resentful expression she saw on that woman's face when Lady St. Merryn took the place at Alfred's right confirmed a dawning suspicion. Without thinking, Charley said, "Why, I believe you neglected on purpose to tell Grandmama that we were entertaining guests. And I'll wager you told the servants that she chose not to join us!" Not waiting for a reply, she turned back to Lady St. Merryn, saying remorsefully, "Pray forgive me, ma'am, for I fully intended to bring Sir Antony up to you directly when he arrived. Other considerations intervened, however. Then, when dinner was set forward and you did not appear, I'm afraid I simply assumed that you had elected to dine in your room."

Lady St. Merryn said fretfully, "No one even told me that dinner had been set forward. I like to be told these things, you know."

Edythe said haughtily, "You must forgive me, ma'am. I quite thought you would prefer to dine in solitude, since we were merely entertaining strangers."

"You were mistaken," Lady St. Merryn pointed out with gentle emphasis. Shaking her head at a platter of sliced beef that Jago held for her inspection, she said to him, "Just a little soup and perhaps a morsel of chicken, I think."

Edythe, intent on defending herself, said, "To be sure, I suppose Mayor Gabriel may be known to you, but not this other man, pretending to be Antony Tarrant."

"Is that who you are?" Lady St. Merryn peered myopically at Sir Antony. "I don't know any of the Norfolk Tarrants, I'm afraid."

"Nor should you, ma'am," he said instantly. "A sorry and encroaching lot, they are, I'm sure."

She blinked in surprise. "But did not she just say that you are one of them?"

"Indeed, I once thought I was," he said. "The Norfolk lot cut the connection long ago, however, and by and large, I think they were wise. In fact—or so I am told by Alfred here—they put it about that I had died abroad. Therefore, I have quite decided to resurrect myself as a worthy *Cornwall* Tarrant instead."

"Have you, indeed?" Lady St. Merryn said faintly.

Elizabeth stirred impulsively and said in the falsely bright tone of one determined to avoid social disaster, "Do tell us, Mr. Gabriel, had you a particular purpose in visiting us this afternoon, or was it purely a social call?"

Like everyone else at the table, Gabriel had been staring in bemusement at Sir Antony. He rallied quickly, however. Smiling, he said, "To be sure, Miss Elizabeth, I had a purpose. You see, the late earl's sudden death has presented me with a quandary, which I came here to discuss with your brother." He turned to Alfred. "I had meant to ask you to take his lordship's place, sir, since you seemed to be the obvious choice to do so. But now," he added, looking at Sir Antony, then back at Alfred, "I own, I'm at a loss as to what we should do now. It's the Seraphim Coffer, you see."

He looked confidently from face to face, but if he hoped for universal understanding, he did not get it. Everyone at the table gazed blankly back at him.

Chapter Nine

Charley was the first to recover her power of speech. She said, "The Seraphim Coffer is the chest that will contain the sacramental vessels Wellington means to present to the cathedral, is it not?"

"It is, indeed," Gabriel said.

Elizabeth said in astonishment, "Goodness, Mr. Gabriel, are you making the very box that will protect those sacred vessels?"

He smiled fondly at her. "Not *making*, Miss Elizabeth. I fear my skill is not so great as to warrant that honor. This coffer is older than the vessels are, and although it is not so magnificent as others I've seen, it is certainly worthy to contain them. I have been entrusted only with its refurbishing, no more than a little glue, a new peg or two, and new strapwork. One more layer of oil, a good polishing, and the task is done."

"But is the coffer not painted?" Charley asked. "I heard it was quite colorful."

"To be sure, it is. It's a bit gaudy, in fact, but I should not have dared to touch the artwork. That has been protected over the years by layers of varnish and lacquer, you see. It required no more than the removal of one or two layers to make it look nearly new. One can now see the blond curls on each seraph's head, whereas before, one saw only blurred figures in a shadow. I make my task sound too simple, however," he added, helping himself from a dish of grilled crabs. "It is the interior of the coffer that presented the greatest challenge, for it had to be padded and arranged so that each vessel can have its own little nest. I daresay it would surprise you to know that I am nearly as clever with a needle and thread as Miss Elizabeth and Miss Davies are said to be."

Rockland murmured to Charley, "I notice that he didn't say 'as clever as Miss Charlotte is known to be.'"

Annoyed, she said sweetly and without lowering her voice, "If you wanted a wife who would spend her days stitching seat covers for every chair in your house, Rockland, you should have asked someone else to marry you."

Her words created more of a stir than she had intended, for Lady St. Merryn gasped, and even Miss Davies looked mildly shocked. The countess said, "Charlotte, what on earth are you saying? Has Lord Rockland asked for your hand?"

"Many times, Grandmama." But Charley squirmed, realizing that she had said nothing to Lady St. Merryn about her betrothal.

Rockland said dryly, "The difference this time, ma'am, is that she consented."

"I offer my felicitations, my lord," Gabriel said. "May you both be very happy."

"Aye, we'll hope so," Rockland agreed. "Many thanks, Gabriel."

Miss Davies said brightly to Lady St. Merryn, "And our dear Charlotte will be a ladyship at last, just as you'd hoped she would, my dear ma'am. Not Lady Charlotte, of course, but Lady Rockland is a quite unexceptionable title, I believe."

Lady St. Merryn said in her fretful way, "Yes, yes, that's all very well and good, Ethelinda, but why did no one *tell* me?"

Ruefully, Charley said, "We ought to have done so, of course, ma'am, and I am completely to blame. I have not been thinking clearly, I'm afraid. So much has happened, and I was perhaps overly conscious of the need to be discreet. I simply have made a point of not speaking about it to anyone, and I daresay no one else thought it necessary to tell you, believing that I must have done so. Please, forgive me.''

"But you cannot marry anyone just now, Charlotte," the countess said weakly. "Not with your grandfather and parents barely cold in the ground. You must not think of such a thing, my dear, not for at least a year. I simply could not bear it.''

Alfred said instantly, "Just what I told her myself, ma'am. It mustn't be thought of, I said. Full mourning for a whole year before I could see my way clear to consenting to such a thing, that's what I told the minx. But would she listen?''

When Lady St. Merryn bristled at his tone, Charley interposed calmly, "Fortunately I do not need his consent, Grandmama. I am of age, and can make decisions without asking permission from Cousin Alfred or anyone else. At least, at present I can. Lord only knows what a fix I shall find myself in if I have to depend on him for every crumb I put in my mouth. That will likely be the case, too, since neither Grandpapa nor Papa left me much of anything. I refuse to dwindle into a poor relation, however. Even marriage to Rockland must be better than that.''

Miss Davies bleated a small cry of protest.

At the same time, Rockland muttered, "Thank you very much, my pet.''

Hearing them, Charley flushed and apologized for offending them. Then she said, "But you want me, Rockland. You have told me so over and over again. *And* you promised to take me on any terms at all. I, on the other hand, have never pretended to be in love with you. I thought you were as pleased as Punch by this arrangement.''

"Which just goes to show," Sir Antony murmured to no one in particular, "how easily pleased some men can be. I confess, the vision of Miss Charlotte Tarrant enacting the role of a strident Judy is not what I should define as wedded bliss. But doubtless you know what you are doing, Rockland.''

Charley flushed, but before she could think of a suitable retort, Sir Antony smiled across the table at Lady St. Merryn and said blandly, "Do not let her impulsive nature distress you, ma'am. Though I have known your granddaughter but a few hours, I have seen enough to know that she would not willingly cause you pain. If she does marry Rockland, I am certain she will see to it that the ceremony is conducted with complete discretion and solemnity."

Lady St. Merryn blinked uncertainly at him but was unable to resist his smile.

Nodding approval, Miss Davies said, "No doubt you are quite right, Sir Antony. Gentlemen may be depended upon, in my experience, always to get right to the heart of the matter. It don't seem right—really, it don't—that our dear Charlotte should, by the most unfortunate set of circumstances, have been placed in a position that she dislikes and was not raised to anticipate. Of course," she added with a heartfelt sigh, "no one really anticipates such an eventuality, and so few are as fortunate as I was." She smiled at Lady St. Merryn. "I am persuaded that no one could have been kinder to one thrust into the bosom of her family than my dearest cousin was to me. But I talk too much," she added abruptly, shrinking back into her chair. "Pray, forgive me."

Charley wanted on one hand to reassure Miss Davies that she had not meant to offend her, and on the other to shriek at them all that she would never—no matter what other fate befell her—become another just like her. She was sure that if the silence lasted, she would say something she would regret. Thus, she was relieved rather than annoyed when Sir Antony said gently, "How well you put the matter, Miss Davies." He glanced at Rockland. "And how brave you are, my lord."

Rockland's laugh sounded strained, and his tone was doubtful as he said, "I'll hold my own. I am not a man to live under the cat's paw, never fear." Then, as if he expected someone to dispute his declaration, he turned to Gabriel and said hastily, "By Jove, tell us more about this ceremony of yours. Sounds downright fascinating."

Gabriel smiled, making Charley yearn to kick Rockland under the table. He sat beside her, so she could have done it, and it was not the knowledge that he was likely to cry out if she did that stopped her. Sir Antony's presence kept her twitching foot firmly on the floor, and she knew it. Even as the thought flitted through her mind, she realized that Gabriel, in obeying Rockland's request, had mentioned her grandfather again.

"The earl worked with us a great deal on the ceremony," he said. "It's to be the grandest event to take place in Cornwall in living memory, don't you know. Though the cathedral is in Truro, every town in the county is to have its role."

"That's true," Charley said. "Women in many towns and villages have been stitching prayer cushions and wall hangings."

"Aye," Gabriel said, "and other towns have contributed memorial pews, and plaques, and carved screens. Our task, in Lostwithiel is to provide the Seraphim Coffer to store the vessels when they are not in use. I shall have the honor of placing them in their nests myself, and the duty of taking them under guard to Truro for the ceremony."

Rockland said, "I thought someone said you were a Methodist, Gabriel."

The big man shook his head. "Most likely what you heard, my lord, is that I've worked with the Methodies to help the miners and to end criminal enterprises. I don't believe in their religious practices, but I do believe in doing whatever I must to get an important job done." He smiled diffidently.

Sir Antony said, "I believe you mentioned some sort of problem, Gabriel."

"I did," the big man agreed. "It's this, sir. At the critical time, just before the Duke of Wellington presents the vessels as a gift from the nation, the Earl of St. Merryn was to unlock and open the coffer." He looked from Antony to Alfred. "I came here today intending to ask you, Mr. Tarrant, to perform that role for us. However, since it appears that we do not know yet whether you or Sir Antony here is the rightful heir, I confess that I'm at a standstill now as to what we should do."

Edythe said, "My dear sir, we've nearly a month left before that ceremony. Surely, my husband's claim will be proved long before then."

"I wish we could be certain of that, ma'am," Gabriel said.

"The plain and simple fact is that even in cases with little question about who will prevail, these matters take time."

"But this man is an impostor," Edythe snapped. "He should be clapped into irons, not rewarded for his impudence."

"That will do, Edythe," Alfred said, flushing.

"Yes, my dear," she said placidly. "Pray, forgive my outspoken manner, Mr. Gabriel. As you might imagine, this is a difficult time for us."

"Certainly, ma'am," Gabriel said. With an oblique glance at Sir Antony, he added, "I trust, however, that you all can see my dilemma."

Sir Antony said mildly, "I should think the solution must be obvious, Gabriel, if you will forgive my saying so."

"Obvious, sir? But how so?"

"There is one person who can take the late earl's place in the ceremony without drawing the least controversy or condemnation."

Gabriel frowned. "I own, sir, I cannot think who that might be."

"Why, Miss Charlotte Tarrant, of course."

Charley, and everyone else at the table, stared at him in astonishment.

Gabriel said, "But, Sir Antony, Miss Charlotte is female. The consecration is to take place in the cathedral, a holy place, sir! It is a sacred ritual."

"Such ceremonies generally are," Sir Antony said dryly. "But surely, the mere opening of the casket—excuse me, the coffer—containing these historic vessels, is in no way a sacred act. It cannot take place at the altar, for the Duke is also a lay person, and he will be enacting a primary role in that part of the ritual."

"True," Gabriel agreed, frowning. "The bishop will carry the vessels to the altar after the presentation. Still, I've never heard of a female taking part in such a rite."

"Under the circumstances, however," Sir Antony said reasonably, "I should think that Miss Tarrant must be far and away the most appropriate person to represent her late grandfather. I would, of course, have suggested Lady St. Merryn—"

"Oh, no," Lady St. Merryn said, reaching for her vinaigrette, which Miss Davies promptly produced. "I simply cannot be expected to do such a thing. So very public, you know, and so soon after . . ." She inhaled deeply.

"Quite so, ma'am," Sir Antony agreed. "Since your health and state of deep mourning will not permit you to act, some other member of the family must do so."

"Very unusual," Gabriel said, "but if Miss Charlotte is willing . . ."

Everyone turned toward Charley. She glanced at Lady St. Merryn, uncertain of how much such participation by her grand-daughter would distress her. The countess appeared to be entirely preoccupied with her vinaigrette. It was Edythe who objected, strenuously, pointing out that Miss Charlotte was likewise in mourning.

About to declare that St. Merryn also would have been in that state, had he survived the news of his son's death, Charley fell silent in astonishment when a firm hand pressed warningly against her right knee. Exerting herself not to demand what Sir Antony thought he was about to take such an extraordinary liberty, or even to look at him, she sat rigid and silent.

Sir Antony said in his haughtiest tone, "I cannot imagine how Miss Charlotte's opening a painted box in a church is in any way a betrayal of her state of mourning. Surely, my dear madam," he added, gazing at Edythe in much the same way she tended to look at Letty, "you would not have us suppose that such a ceremony will occasion anything but the greatest decorum."

"Certainly not," she said. She tried to match his air of hauteur but, thanks to her deepening color, failed miserably to do so.

Rockland, who had remained unnaturally silent throughout the discussion, said cheerfully now, "Can't see the harm, myself. By and large, every member of this family is in mourning at present. But if anyone fears that such a thing might somehow offend someone, we can just ask Bishop Halsey what he thinks about it."

"A very wise notion, sir," Elizabeth said approvingly.

"Don't you agree, Alfred dearest, that we ought perhaps to ask the bishop if Charlotte should do it?"

"Very well," Alfred said impatiently. "Can't think why we're still talking about it, myself. I'll have another slice off that joint, Jago. Step lively, man. You ought to see that I've finished the bit on my plate."

The rest of the meal passed uneventfully, and when Edythe announced that the ladies would leave the gentlemen to enjoy their port, Charley accompanied her grandmother and Miss Davies upstairs to the countess's sitting room.

As Miss Davies helped Lady St. Merryn arrange herself on a claw-footed sofa that had been carried there unbeknownst to Edythe (along with much of the rest of the countess's favorite furniture), Charley drew up an armchair for herself. She did not perform the same service for Miss Davies, knowing it would only fluster that excellent lady to be waited upon. But as soon as the countess had settled with her vinaigrette close to hand, the fire screen set to protect her from the heat, and the cushions behind her plumped to Miss Davies's exacting standard, Charley said apologetically, "I hope you are not vexed with me, Grandmama. I truly meant to make Sir Antony known to you before dinner, and as for my betrothal, I . . . Well, I don't know what to say."

"You were very thoughtless," Lady St. Merryn said. "I believe I am still entitled to know what's happening in this house, you know, even if I am now expected to be no more than a cipher here. I will speak to Medrose, too."

"Yes, ma'am," Charley said, seeing nothing to be gained by assuring her that it was unnecessary to speak to Medrose. The butler had clearly taken Edythe Tarrant's measure and would not allow his mistress to be snubbed again if he could prevent it. Moreover, she rather enjoyed seeing a spark of animation in her grandmother's eyes.

Half an hour later, leaving Lady St. Merryn to the tender care of Miss Davies, she went to Letty's bedchamber, where she found the child curled up in a wing chair by the fire, reading a book. Jeremiah was asleep in her lap but awoke when Charley shut the door. Stretching much like a human, the monkey looked at her over the chair arm. Letty put down her book.

"Don't get up," Charley said. "You look very cozy, the pair of you. I just came in to bid you good-night."

"It's still early," Letty pointed out, glancing at the little ormolu clock on the nearby dressing table.

"I know. I came up with Grandmama, but if I go downstairs again, I am sure to say something offensive to Cousin Edythe or Cousin Elizabeth. Grandmama is content without me. Cousin Ethelinda is reading to her."

Letty's eyes twinkled. "How did Sir Antony manage at table?"

"As if he were to the manner born," Charley said, twinkling back at her. "I found myself wondering if he might really be Sir Antony Foxearth-Tarrant."

"He isn't, is he?"

"No, I don't think so. He is running a rig, as he calls it. I had better explain how it is, so that you will take extra good care not to unmask him." It occurred to her that the gentleman they were discussing might well take exception to her decision to confide in Letty, but she knew she was safe in doing so. The little girl had lived her life in the diplomatic world. If she knew anything, she knew not to speak indiscreetly.

"Why Foxearth, do you suppose?" Letty asked when Charley finished.

"I haven't a notion, but Alfred did not question it, so Sir Antony—as we must now think of him—must have got it right. I'll ask one of them about it tomorrow."

The depression that had enveloped her for days seemed to have disappeared, and when she awoke the following morning, she felt quite cheerful. The sun was shining, and the moor beckoned. Finishing a cup of chocolate and a bun in her room, she sent word to Letty to join her, went straight to the stables, and ordered the first groom she met to saddle Shadow Dancer. Only then did she realize that she had forgotten one small detail.

The groom, a new one, said respectfully, "Beg pardon, Miss

Charlotte. I've got no orders yet from the master to saddle any horse today.''

"Where is Teddy?'' she demanded. "Or Jeb?''

"I'm sure I can't say, miss, but our orders from the master—''

"Alfred Tarrant is not yet master of Tuscombe Park, much as he likes to pretend he is,'' Charley snapped. "Until he is, you would do well to obey orders given you by anyone in the family. Now, either send for Teddy or saddle Shadow Dancer yourself. He is the black roan gelding with the white blaze.''

"Mr. Tarrant said that horse is to be kept for Miss Elizabeth to ride,'' the groom said doggedly.

"Oh, did he? And has Miss Elizabeth ever done so?''

"No, miss, but Mr. Tarrant said that gelding were most likely the best-trained for a lady. He said we wasn't to let no one else ride it, only her.''

"Shadow Dancer,'' Charley said grimly, "is my horse, not Mr. Tarrant's. He is mine now, and he will always be mine, for my grandfather left me my choice of the horses in his stables. Moreover, if you let Miss Elizabeth try to ride him, you'll soon see how well trained he is. For that matter, *you* try to ride him. My horses accept no rider but me without a command to the contrary, so do as I bid you, and fetch him out. The Lady Letitia's chestnut mare, as well,'' she added. "She will be joining me.''

"It'd be as much as my place is worth, miss. I dassn't!''

"What is the trouble here?''

Charley jumped at hearing Sir Antony's voice so near. Turning, she saw him standing in the stable doorway with Letty beside him, both dressed for riding.

"This dolt,'' she said, "refuses to saddle my horse or Letty's, and I don't know what's become of either of our grooms. Alfred gave a lot of stupid orders the day we rode to Seacourt Head, and I haven't ridden since then. I forgot about them.''

"That's right, sir,'' the groom said. "The master gave orders that—''

"When I want to hear from you,'' Sir Antony cut in, "I will inform you of it.''

"Yes, sir." Flushing, he looked at his feet.

"Does this man know which horse you prefer, Miss Charlotte?"

"He does, although he informs me that Alfred has declared that Shadow Dancer must now be reserved for Elizabeth," Charley added testily.

Letty chuckled. "I wish I may see her ride him."

Her amusement eased Charley's irritation. "It would be a sight."

"And Lady Letitia's mount," Sir Antony interjected. "Does he know it as well?"

"He does. The chestnut mare in the stall next to Shadow Dancer."

"Then I quite fail to see any problem." Sir Antony raised his quizzing glass and peered through it at the groom.

"Please, sir," the lad begged, shifting his feet uneasily, "I've got my orders."

"Miss Charlotte has countermanded them," Sir Antony said, speaking very softly. "You will saddle her horse, you will saddle the buttermilk mare for me, and you will saddle Lady Letitia's mare. You will do all that right speedily and without any more backchat. Furthermore, when you receive orders from any member of the family, or any guest, you will do your best to carry them out. Is that clear?"

"Aye, sir, but what am I to tell the master?"

"I don't much care what you tell him," Sir Antony murmured, taking a snowy handkerchief from his waistcoat pocket and using it to polish his quizzing glass. The groom hesitated. Glancing at him again, Sir Antony said with a sigh, " 'Duller must thou be than a fat weed.' "

"Sir, the master—"

"You know, I should dislike very much being put to the task of teaching you respect for your betters, but if you do not fetch those horses . . ." Letting his words trail ominously to silence, he returned the handkerchief to his pocket, shot the wavering groom a stern look, then added in quite a different tone, "At once, you egregious ass!"

Turning pale, the groom said, "Aye, sir." And with a tug of his forelock, he fled.

"He has probably run to complain to his odious master," Charley said bitterly.

"I doubt that," Sir Antony replied.

"Egregious ass?"

"I rather liked the ring of that, myself."

Antony saw from her expression that she still was not convinced the groom would obey him, but the lad soon returned with two others, and they quickly saddled the three horses. Miss Tarrant remained uncharacteristically silent, as did the child, and Antony felt a strong desire to teach both the obstreperous groom and his master a lesson in courtesy. Such tactics did not suit the role he was playing, however, so as much as the exercise might relieve his temper, he could not afford to indulge himself.

He continued to watch Miss Tarrant, his eyelids half-closed so that she would not too quickly become aware of his scrutiny. Anger had put fire in her cheeks, and her dark eyes showed lingering sparks. Admirable. She was a beauty, and no mistake, but she seemed unconcerned with her looks. Since she was old enough to have enjoyed a number of London seasons, and since she had also spent time with the diplomatic and aristocratic sets in Paris, he knew she must be aware of her charms. He could not imagine her entering a room without every eye instantly turning her way.

He watched her approach the black roan. It pranced and tossed its long mane in evident delight, then nuzzled her shoulder and bosom in a familiar way that made Antony wish he could exchange roles for just a moment or two. Collecting himself, he stepped forward, intending to give her a leg up. To his astonishment, the roan knelt, the chit put a foot in the stirrup, and as the horse rose again, she arranged herself with such speed and dispatch that he knew she had done so many times before.

Letty had been watching him and when he caught her eye,

she grinned at him and said, "Is Dancer not clever, sir? He is descended from a stallion my papa owned for many years, but in fact, all of Cousin Charley's horses are trained to kneel. That way a lady can mount without a block."

"Very sensible," Antony said, lifting the child to her saddle before the groom could do so. "What other tricks has she taught them?"

He glanced at Miss Tarrant, hoping his provocative tone might draw her into their conversation, but she was still silent, her lips pressed together. Clearly, the lady still bore some resentment at having her will crossed.

Letty's voice reminded him that he had asked her a question, but as they rode into the sunlight, he caught only the end of her reply. ". . . all manner of things," she said, "even to stop still when she makes a certain sound."

"She can make a horse stop on command?" This time he caught Miss Tarrant's gaze, but although she looked steadily back at him, she did not speak.

"Oh, yes," Letty said, "and many other things as well."

Goaded now, determined to get a rise, Antony said as they left the stable yard and turned toward the moor, "It is a good thing I brought Annabelle with me. I daresay that if I were riding one of Miss Tarrant's horses, and she became vexed with me, she would crook her little finger and I'd find myself flat on the ground. A dreadful blow to one's dignity, don't you agree?"

Letty laughed. "Do you think you would land on your *dignity,* sir?"

Even Miss Tarrant's eyes were twinkling now, but she still seemed reluctant to release her resentment altogether.

Looking from one to the other, Letty said, "May I gallop, Cousin Charley?"

"If you promise to keep a sharp eye on the road."

"I will." Eagerly, the child urged her mare forward.

Guiding Annabelle in beside the black roan, Antony said, "Have you recovered yet, *mon ange?*"

She shot him an oblique look. "Recovered?"

"From the sulks."

"I do not sulk!"

"Forgive me. I quite thought you were indulging yourself, but if you say you were not, I will not contradict you. As young Letty so wisely pointed out to me some time ago, a gentleman does not contradict a lady, even when she is wrong."

She shot him another look. "Is this your notion of how to tease me into a better humor? Because if it is, you might as well spare your breath. I don't believe in acting as if I feel one way when I feel another. If you don't approve, perhaps you would prefer to ride alone. I don't recall inviting you to come with us, in any event."

He was silent for a moment, considering his reply. Then he said evenly, "First, I don't exert myself to tease spoiled children out of the sulks, whatever their habits of courtesy or the lack may be. Second, I don't think it would be kind to let you return to the stable without an escort. Being subjected to another of Alfred's blustery tirades would not hurt you, but I cannot think Letty deserves to suffer the consequences of your actions yet again, through no fault of her own."

She did not reply at once, and he saw that she nibbled her lower lip thoughtfully. Imminently kissable, those lips, he thought, the way they looked firm and shapely one moment, soft and vulnerable the next.

"I'm sorry I was rude to you," she said, surprising him.

Shifting his gaze swiftly to her eyes, he expected to meet with irony or mockery. Instead, she looked anxious, almost childlike, and sincere. He smiled. "I had begun to feel sorry for Rockland, but now I don't think I'm sorry for him at all."

She relaxed. "I suppose you felt sorry for him because he does not set his will against mine. He knows better than to do so, I expect, but I daresay he rarely has the impulse. He is lazy, sir, and prefers not to make decisions. I think he truly enjoys obliging people, if only he knows what they want him to do."

"He must be a joy to his family," Antony said.

"I don't know much about them," she said. "His father is long deceased, I believe, and his mama lives retired somewhere in Somerset, and never goes to town."

"But if you intend to marry the man, surely—"

"Oh, good mercy, surely you must know that I agreed to marry him because it was that or living under Alfred's thumb forever. Females of any sort have few choices in this world, sir. Impecunious females have none. If we do not marry, we must depend on more fortunate relations to support us. At least by marrying I shall have some small independence."

"And so you mean to marry a fool who will let you rule the roast."

She shot him an angry glare. "Do you think I will make him unhappy? I promise you I won't, and if I had any doubts before, this morning's little ordeal put them to flight. I'm not accustomed to servants questioning my orders, and I do not intend to suffer longer than necessary in a household where they do so."

"I don't think you are accustomed to seeing your will crossed by anyone, *mon ange,*" Antony murmured.

"Don't call me that. It is most improper."

"Ah, but you see," he replied, "I am not in the habit of asking permission for what I do, any more than you are."

Before she could retort, they heard a shout from Letty and saw her riding toward them at a gallop. At the same time, they heard barking behind them.

Reining in, they turned, and seeing the shaggy black and white dog hurtling toward them in full cry, Antony sighed with exasperation and said, "There is one who does not give a click of his toenails for my will and consent. Yes, Sebastian," he added as the dog leapt excitedly around Annabelle's legs, making the mare twitch its ears nervously. "I can see that you are delighted to have found me again, but much as I wish I could share your delight, you are quite out of place in the image I wish to project."

Chapter Ten

Charley chuckled at Sir Antony's dismay, and Letty, reining in alongside of them, laughed and said, "I saw him coming, sir. I have been meaning to ask what you had done with him, but I forgot."

"Sebastian, down," Sir Antony said firmly. The dog ceased leaping and barking, but its tail wagged furiously.

Charley said, "It is clear to the meanest intelligence that he worships you. Where did you leave him when you came to Tuscombe Park?"

Sir Antony sighed. "My man, Hodson, said he had found a family willing to keep him. Clearly he was mistaken, but what am I to do with Sebastian now? Did you not say that Alfred was with you when I rescued him?"

"I did," Charley agreed. "Still, I doubt if he would remember, for he has not seen Sebastian since, and there is—if he will forgive my saying so—nothing particularly memorable about him. Cousin Alfred saw him only when he was dripping wet, too, and he looks as if he's been brushed and well fed in the meantime. I daresay that if Sebastian will consent to live in the stable, no one will pay him any heed. There are lots of dogs at Tuscombe Park. Cousin Alfred cannot know them all."

Letty said doubtfully, "But the others will not exhibit such delight in Sir Antony's company, you know. If Sebastian follows you into the house, sir, Cousin Edythe won't like it. She doesn't hold with animals indoors."

"That explains why I have not seen Jeremiah," he said. "I did not like to ask."

"He stays in my room unless I take him outside," she said.

"That settles it; I shall teach Sebastian to be a lap dog," Sir Antony said, smiling at her. "I detest that woman."

"We do, too," Letty said. "Don't we, Cousin Charley?"

"We do, absolutely," Charley said. "Although I've got the most lowering notion that neither your mama nor your papa would want me to encourage such disrespectful comments from you, young lady."

"No, ma'am."

They looked at each other and grinned.

Sir Antony said sourly, "I cannot think you are providing a good example for this impressionable child, Miss Tarrant."

"Very likely not," Charley agreed with a rueful sigh, "but her parents have both known me for a very long time, so they will understand, I hope."

He smiled at her. "May I ask where we are going?"

She had turned her horse away from the road, onto the open moor. Grinning back at him, she said, "I mean to have a gallop. Then we are going to chat with some of Grandpapa's tenants to see what we can discover about plots." Seeing him glance quickly at Letty, she added, "She knows as much as I do, for I told her. I'm sorry if you are vexed, but she spends most of her time with me, you see, and I could not imagine how to go about talking to people without confiding in her."

"If you'd rather not trust me," Letty said in a small, dignified voice, "I shall quite understand, sir."

To Charley's relief, he looked amused and said, "I believe I can trust you with my life, Lady Letitia. If the whole truth were known, I daresay you've already learned one or two diplomatic secrets that you would never divulge to a soul."

She nodded, her expression serious. "My papa explained when I was very young that it is obligatory never to reveal to others what one learns by overhearing conversations at the embassy. Since I do not always remember whether I was asked to keep silent or not, I just don't speak of matters that affect other people.''

"A wise child." He glanced at Charley. "Do you mean to introduce me to these tenants of yours?''

"I do, if only to put a spoke in odious Alfred's wheel by telling them he might not be the true heir. I just wish you were who you claim to be. The notion of Alfred filling Grandpapa's shoes is almost more than I can bear. He is an encroaching toad.''

"May I remind you," he said, raising his chin, "that you speak of one who is nearly related to me?''

She grinned more widely than ever. "Your brother, in fact.''

"Just so.''

"I just wish he *were* your brother. Something tells me you would have taught him better manners.''

"Ah, but he was still in leading strings when I went off to school, you see. At least,'' he added with a thoughtful air, "I'm sure that's how it must have been.''

Charley gave him a sharp look, but saw only quizzical amusement in his expression. She thought he might admit his true identity if she asked him, but she did not want to put that to a test just yet. Understanding him well enough to know he enjoyed the roles he played, she knew, too, that it would amuse him to know there were moments when she found herself believing he was really Sir Antony Foxearth-Tarrant. She was not ready to give him the satisfaction of knowing that, however.

Giving spur to Dancer, she leaned forward, urging the roan to a gallop, putting everything from her mind except the thudding of hooves on the turf, the cool morning air, the gentle rise of the nearby hills, and the colorful and shadowy undulations of the terrain ahead. Only when she heard echoing hoofbeats did she glance back to see her companions in hot pursuit. She noted with approval that Sir Antony rode as if he were part of Annabelle. She had known he rode well, but she had not seen him at speed before. Well aware that a stone wall lay not far ahead, she did not take her eyes from the moor for long. As she topped a low rise, the wall came into view. Glancing back again, she saw Letty draw her mare to the left, to jump the wide wooden gate instead of the wall. Sir Antony did not follow her. Nor did he pull right to take his own line. He was letting Charley give him a lead.

Pleased and a little surprised, she took the wall easily, and reined in shortly afterward to wait for the others.

Sir Antony said, "Where now, Miss Tarrant?"

Having expected a compliment on her riding, she hesitated. Then, catching his gaze and observing his amusement, she saw that he knew exactly what she had expected, and purposely had not catered to her vanity. She realized then that, except for the exaggerated admiration he had expressed when he first stepped into the drawing room in his guise as the haughty fop, he had never complimented her. She realized, too, that she wanted very much to win his approval.

Astonished at herself for reacting in a way which she despised in other females, she managed to respond evenly, "We'll see Cubert and Wenna Breton first, or Wenna at least. You may have met Cubert yourself, for I think he occasionally helps the free traders. More to the point, you said your assassins may have friends in France, and I know at least one Frenchwoman hereabouts who may still have family there."

"Angelique," Letty said promptly.

When Sir Antony raised his eyebrows, Charley explained that Angelique was the dressmaker in Lostwithiel who had supplied her mourning gowns.

"Not that habit, surely!"

"No, I had this made in London, but Angelique is quite skilled."

"If she is the connection, why do we visit these other people?"

"Their daughter, Jenifry, is apprenticed to Angelique, and I was disturbed to learn that she had not seen her parents since she began to work there. I want to tell them I've seen her, and suggest that perhaps we can arrange for them to do so as well. And, of course, they ought to know more than I do about Angelique, since they apprenticed their daughter to her."

Sir Antony said, "I do not think we are looking for a woman, you know. Assassination is not generally a feminine act, and although I have known you long enough now to realize that you believe women capable of anything—"

Charley cut him off with a chuckle. "I don't suspect Angelique of wanting to murder Wellington, sir. She is married, however, and it does occur to me that her husband might be someone who could tell us something useful. I do not know how they met, of course, but he could well have friends in France. We can talk to him, perhaps, and even to Angelique herself, but I believe Wenna Breton might be an even better source of information. She is a very fine spinster, you see, and spins yarn for other families, as well as for her own. Since she mixes a lot with others, she might give us some very helpful information."

The Bretons' small thatched cottage lay nestled in a hollow at the edge of the moor. A patch of garden rimmed with blackberry brambles sprawled in back with a sheep run behind that. Wenna Breton, a sturdy woman of about fifty, with sunburned cheeks and the deeply lined face of one who spent as much time outdoors as in, opened the door herself.

She exclaimed, "Miss Charley! What a treat. Come you in, lass, come you in."

"Sebastian, stay!"

"Lordy, he can come in, sir. My husband's dogs fair make themselves to home wherever they please."

"Wenna, this is Lady Daintry's daughter, Lady Letitia Deverill."

" 'Tis an honor, your ladyship," Wenna said, making her curtsy. "You would be Lord Gideon's daughter then, as well, would you not?"

"I am, indeed," Letty said, looking around. "What a cozy home this is!"

"Thank you, my lady. My girls and me, we fashioned them throws and coverlets and cushions. They do brighten a place." She looked expectantly at Sir Antony.

Charley introduced him, adding sweetly, "He may be Grandpapa's heir, Wenna."

"Be that so, then? I did hear there be some question about it. But come you in, and I'll fetch out cakes and cider, Miss Charley. You'll like that after your ride."

When they had taken seats in the cottage's main room, which served as kitchen and sitting room, and the cider had been poured, Wenna passed a basket of warm saffron buns.

Charley said, "We won't be at all offended if you want to continue your spinning while we visit. I know you have much work to do, for you always have, and I can see that you were working when we arrived."

"Thank you, Miss Charley, I will." Setting the bun basket conveniently near Sir Antony, she settled herself on a low stool by her spinning wheel. A fluffy plume of white wool dangled from its spindle.

Wenna reached into a large basket of raw wool on the floor beside her and pulled out a handful, stretching and pulling it, her quick fingers picking out bits of detritus missed in the carding. This done, she held the mass near the dangling plume and began rhythmically to press the floor pedal. Using one hand to hold the wool and the other to feed it to the plume, she looked up at her guests again. Yarn appeared as if by magic from the spindle, winding its way to the bobbin below.

Fascinated, Letty got up from her chair and moved closer to watch. "Don't you have to twist it?"

"Bless you, my lady, 'tis the wheel does the twisting." Wenna smiled at Letty. Her hands continued their smooth, practiced motions without pause.

"Is it hard to do?"

"My Jenifry's been spinning since her fifth year, my lady. Near all my girls started young. B'ain't nothing to it but feeding the wool steady and keeping the rhythm. Even four-ply can be the work of a youngster."

"Could I learn?"

The woman stared at her in apparent consternation, though her hands did not stop. "Spinning's a chore for common folk, not for ladies of quality."

"Oh." Letty sounded so disappointed that Charley said, "Wenna spins to put food on her table, Letty, not for her amusement. If she takes time to teach someone who can't help her, she will not finish all the work she needs to do.''

Wenna smiled. ''It ain't that, Miss Charley. I'd teach her in a twink. I just thought her own folks wouldn't like it.''

Letty shot a mischievous glance at her cousin and said, ''They won't mind a bit. Moreover, if my hands were busy, I could let Sir Antony have the third saffron bun. He's eaten two already and seems to be eyeing that last one as if he were starving.''

''He can have as many as he likes,'' Wenna said, getting up to let the child sit on the stool.

''He cannot,'' Charley said. ''We mean to ride into town from here, Wenna, and I'm going to buy some pastry pigs from Dewy the Baker. He can have some of those. I meant to get some the last time we went to town, but we spent all our time at Angelique's, and Dewy's shop was shut up afterward. I've loved pastry pigs since I was a child, and no one makes them like Dewy.''

Wenna had been showing Letty how to hold the raw wool while Charley talked, but mention of Angelique, she looked up. When Charley fell silent, she said, ''Our Jenifry be apprenticed to Miss Angelique, Miss Charley. I don't suppose . . .''

''I saw her, Wenna, a few days before the funeral, when I went into Angelique's. I was surprised to hear that she has not been allowed to visit you.''

''We knew about Miss Angelique's rules, Miss Charley, but we did think we'd be able to see our Jenifry if we went into town. But when Cubert went, he were told that were agin the rules as well. It don't seem right, but Michael Peryllys himself were there, and he did show Cubert where it said as much in them papers he signed. He didn't get so much as a peek at our Jenifry. It don't seem right,'' she said again.

''I don't know people in Lostwithiel as well as I know them in Fowey,'' Charley said, seeing without much surprise that Sir Antony seemed to be paying more attention to the conversation than to saffron buns, now that they were discussing Angelique. ''We're nearer to Fowey for one thing, and it's so much smaller. How well did you know Angelique before you agreed to the apprenticeship?''

''Not at all, miss, her being foreign and all. Cubert knows Michael, of course, for they've . . . they've worked together now and again for years, at the mines and such.'' Glancing away, she went on hastily, ''We knew Miss Angelique makes dresses for many ladies hereabouts, and we hoped she could teach our Jenifry. Jenifry be a dab hand with a needle and thread, and she got her head set on making her own way in the world. Says she don't want to depend on getting herself a husband, but I don't know, Miss Charley. 'Tis a fact and all that I never knew how much I'd miss her, and it fair terrifies me to think of her going into womanhood without a man to look after her.''

Conscious of Sir Antony's steady gaze, Charley forbore to explain her views on feminine independence, although in truth, those views had undergone some slight alteration since the reading of her grandfather's will. She said, ''I can well believe you miss her, Wenna, and I daresay, if I ask to see her, they will not refuse me. As I said, we mean to ride into Lostwithiel from here. Would you like us to look in on her?''

''Oh, if you would, miss! I just want to know she's happy. Though, truth to tell, if she ain't, I don't know what we'll do. Them papers what Michael made Cubert sign did say she must serve Miss Angelique for seven whole years and a day.''

''We'll deal with that if she proves to be unhappy,'' Charley said. ''If she likes sewing, and works hard, one day she could set up her own business, Wenna.''

''Mayhap she could,'' Wenna agreed, but the thought did not seem to cheer her. They remained a few minutes longer, and Charley noted that Letty had picked up the basic principles of spinning. Her motions were nearly as sure as Wenna's had been.

''That was fun,'' she said as they bade Wenna good-bye. ''May I come to visit another day, and try again?''

''Bless you, my lady, come whenever you've a mind. I'll enjoy the company.''

''I think I'll ask Papa to buy me a spinning wheel,'' Letty

said as they rode out of the cottage yard, followed by the faithful Sebastian. "I think it would be fun to spin one's own yarn and then use it to hook a rug or knit a shawl. Just think, the whole thing, from sheep to shoulders!"

Sir Antony laughed. "Do you intend to shear the sheep yourself?"

Letty wrinkled her nose thoughtfully. "Sheep are rather large. I could maybe shear a lamb, but I'm not certain about a sheep. I've never seen one shorn."

"Well, I have," Sir Antony said. "When I was about your age, my father took me to Holkham Hall for the shearing. It was a tremendous occasion with visitors from all over, like a large market fair. Big burly men did the shearing. They grabbed the sheep and held them upright between their knees, racing each other to see who could shear the greatest number in a day. It was a noisy, smelly business. I liked the splendid dinners much more, believe me, and the dancing bears and trained dogs even more."

Conversation turned to dancing bears and other oddities the three had seen at fairs in England and in France, but Charley had not missed the casual reference to Holkham Hall, the famous home of Mr. Coke of Norfolk. So Sir Antony had at least visited that county. It did not mean a great deal, of course, since Mr. Coke was indeed widely known for his hospitality. His guests for the annual shearing were known to come from as far away as Ireland and Northern Scotland. Still, she filed away that piece of information with the rest of what she had learned about him.

He was a pleasant, easygoing companion. She liked him and was rapidly developing an odd sense of contentment in his company, finding his even temperament a refreshing change after her dealings with Alfred. Remembering then the hard look in Sir Antony's eyes when he had intervened with the groom, and the way he seemed able to influence her with no more than a look or a touch, she found herself having second thoughts. Clearly, Sir Antony might not always be so easy of manner as he appeared.

When they reached Lostwithiel and she turned along the

cobblestoned High Street toward Angelique's, he reined in, saying above the ringing clatter of hoofbeats, "I'll meet the pair of you at Dewy the Baker's in twenty minutes. I daresay I can find the place easily enough."

Eyeing him in surprise, Charley said, "You won't have any difficulty at all. Anyone can tell you where his shop is to be found. But don't tell me you are afraid you will feel out of place in a dressmaker's shop, for I won't believe you."

"You would be right," he said with an impudent smile. "In truth, I think you were right, too, about Cubert Breton helping the free traders. Wenna mentioned a name I've heard, and common though the name is, if your Angelique should also chance to have friends amongst that lot, I'd as lief not meet any of them at present."

"Do you think they would recognize you? It never occurred to me that Cubert might, if we'd met him. I think anyone would have to be very discerning to do so."

"Perhaps, but someone might recognize Annabelle or Sebastian more easily."

"I hadn't thought of that. Of course, they might." She thought anyone would remember the well-mannered mare.

She and Letty were disappointed, however, to learn at Angelique's that Jenifry had gone out of town with her mistress to help with a fitting. The girl who assisted them seemed nervous, and recalling that Angelique was a harsh mistress who did not allow her assistants to enter the front part of the shop, Charley decided the girl was afraid of offending a favored customer who might later complain. Hoping to put her at her ease, she said kindly, "Will you tell Jenifry that I brought greetings from her mother, if you please?"

"Yes, miss. I will if I'm allowed."

"But why would Angelique not allow you to give her a simple message?"

"I-I didn't mean nothing by it, miss," the girl said, rubbing her hands on the plain apron she wore. "There just be so many rules, and a body do be forgetting. One way or another, I'll tell Jenifry, I promise."

"See that you do," Charley said firmly. "I do not believe we have met before. What is your name, please?"

"I-I be Bess Griffin, miss. With Jenifry gone, I'm the only one here, since Annie was . . . since she run off to London. It's the first time Miss Angelique done let me talk to customers. Oh, pray, don't be vexed! Miss Angelique and the master, they . . ." Recollecting herself swiftly, she said in more controlled voice, "I won't forget, miss."

"That's all right then, thank you, Bess. Come along, Letty."

"She was frightened," Letty said as they collected their horses and led them up the High Street toward Dewy the Baker's.

Charley agreed. "We'll come back soon," she said. "I begin to think Jenifry might be better off with another mistress. Here is Dewy's," she added. Then, having asked two boys playing on the flagway to hold their horses, she said, "It hasn't been nearly twenty minutes yet, but we'll go inside anyway."

Sir Antony was nowhere in sight, but she guessed that if he was really worried about meeting someone who knew Jean Matois, he might decide to wait until she and Letty were on their way out of town again before he rejoined them.

"We want a dozen pigs, Dewy," she said when the baker greeted her and she had introduced him to Letty.

"Right you are, Miss Charley," the baker said, grinning at Letty as he began to wrap their purchases in brown paper. "And here's the thirteenth for her ladyship, so she won't have to steal one."

"I wouldn't," Letty exclaimed, looking shocked.

Charley smiled, saying to the baker, "She's not from Cornwall, but her papa grew up at Deverill Court, so she ought to know the rhyme." To Letty, she said, "The one about 'Tom, Tom, the piper's son'?"

" 'Stole a pig and away he run!' " Letty looked at the pig-shaped pastry. "Is this the sort of pig he stole then?"

"It is," the baker and Charley said in chorus.

Charley added, "It's got currants inside. Dewy's papa was a pieman, who sold pig pies from a cart."

"Well, good gracious," Letty said, breaking it in half to

examine the filling. "I always had a picture in my mind of a boy, staggering along with a full-sized pig over his shoulder. I wondered how he could have eaten the whole thing before they caught him. Oh, Sir Antony, look!" she added when the door to the tiny shop opened and that gentleman strolled in. Obligingly, he raised his quizzing glass and peered at the pastry pieces she held up for his inspection. Seeing his bewilderment, Letty grinned and said, "It's a pig, sir, like the one that the piper's son stole in the rhyme. *You* know."

"Is it, indeed?" His manner was haughty in the extreme. Drawing back a little, he added in a finicking way, "I trust you have got something to wipe your fingers on, child. Until you do so, I pray you, do not let them venture too near this coat of mine!"

"I won't," she said, twinkling at him. They left the shop, and were soon back on the road. Sir Antony maintained his haughty demeanor until Letty said in a teasing voice, "Are you still afraid of soiling your coat, sir, or do you want to eat a pig?"

Charley smiled, but Sir Antony said with mock severity, "I hope you don't mean to put that question to everyone we meet. It has a rather off-putting ring to it."

Chuckling, Letty said, "Well, if Sir Antony doesn't want one, Cousin Charley, I'd like another, please."

"Greedy girl," Charley said, but she untied the string and extricated three pigs from the paper, handing one to each of her companions and biting into the third herself. "We did not learn very much, I'm afraid," she said when her mouth was no longer full of pastry and currants, and she could speak again.

"Unfortunately, gathering this sort of information takes a great deal of time," Sir Antony said, taking out his handkerchief and wiping his fingertips. "Have you got more of those things, or are you saving them for other members of the household?"

"I bought a dozen," she said, untying the string again. "Letty?"

"Yes, please. Sir Antony," she added as she accepted the pastry, "how can you learn all you need to learn while you are at Tuscombe Park? Cousin Alfred and his family won't be of much help to you, I'm thinking."

"On the contrary, they will be a dam—dashed nuisance," he said. "I had hoped to chat with the gentry as Sir Antony and still be able to go about as Jean Matois to chat up the lower elements, but Alfred is so blasted suspicious of anything I do, that I fear he'll watch every move I make. Furthermore, as I realized today, I can hardly ride Annabelle everywhere as both characters. And my other companion," he added bitterly, gesturing toward the black and white dog trailing behind them, "is even more likely to give me away if I can't think of a way to outwit him."

"Sebastian might indeed present a problem," Charley said, "but as for Annabelle, you are welcome to ride any of my horses or Grandpapa's whenever you like." Catching a quizzical look from Letty, she added with a grin, "I'll teach you a command that will allow you to mount them. Good mercy," she added, "is that not Rockland riding toward us? You don't suppose Alfred sent him in search of us, do you?"

"We have been away rather longer than we led that impudent groom to believe we would," Sir Antony pointed out.

But Rockland had not come looking for them. "On my way to Truro," he announced virtuously when they met. "Alfred received a letter with his morning post, apparently informing him that no more can be done about his claim to the estates until the lawyers receive certain documents from London. That put him out of temper at once, of course, so when he asked me if I really meant to arrange for our wedding—"

"I was beginning to wonder about that myself," Charley said.

"She is so looking forward to wedded bliss, you know," Sir Antony said gently.

Rockland, scenting an ally, grinned and said, "I wish I might think so. One minute she's demanding to know when I'll fetch the license, and the next she's giving me pepper for something else. She don't know the first thing about me, but when I ask if she's sure she wants to marry me, she says she does. Women! I ask you."

" 'Sometimes too hot the eye of heaven shines,' " Sir Antony said, interrupting Charley as she bristled and opened her mouth to tell Rockland he ought not to speak so of her. When she shut it again, Sir Antony went on blandly, " 'And often is his gold complexion dimmed; and every fair from fair sometimes declines, by chance, or Nature's changing course untrimmed.' "

"Is that 'Shall I Compare Thee to a Summer's Day'?" Charley demanded.

"It is."

She expected him to smile at her quick recognition of the sonnet, but he did not.

Rockland, who had been eyeing her warily, said, "Shakespeare, eh? Never could understand that fellow. Had to learn reams of his stuff off by heart at school, and the only part I remember now is 'Out, out damned spot!' I ask you! Talking to a spot of blood. Dashed nonsense. What's this 'eye of heaven' bilge you're spouting?"

"Never mind, Rockland," Charley said. "Surely, you don't mean to ride to Truro and back today? You ought to have started earlier. It's well after noon now."

"I know what time it is," he said irritably. "I'll stay the night and come back tomorrow with the dashed license, and we'll have the ceremony as soon as ever the bishop can spare time for it. Have you any other commands for me, madam?"

About to reply in kind, she caught Sir Antony's eye and said graciously instead, "Travel safely, my lord, and take care you don't encounter footpads along the way. Would you like to take my pistol with you?"

He glanced from her to Sir Antony, then grinned suddenly. "Got one of my own, thanks all the same, my pet. Dashed if I don't think someone's been teaching you a few manners."

"Have a pig, Rockland," Charley said dryly, holding one out to him.

That night, when the family had retired, Antony enlisted Hodson's assistance, and slipped quietly to the stable. Saddling Annabelle himself, he led the mare from the yard without disturbing a soul. He was prepared to deal with questions if he had to, and had purposely retained the clothing he had worn to dinner, just in case, but he was grateful to encounter no one. Once away from the stables and house, he met with Hodson again, long enough to become Jean Matois. Then he rode alone to Fowey.

That village, lying beyond the western point of St. Merryn's Bay, where the river emptied into the Channel, was nearer than Lostwithiel. More to the purpose from Antony's viewpoint, Fowey enjoyed the dubious distinction of housing a number of his compatriots from the past several weeks.

As anticipated, he found several of them at a dimly lit tavern on the waterfront. Ordering a half-pint of ale from the tapster, he joined them, noting that they seemed only slightly less taciturn than when he had first insinuated himself into their midst. By deftly manipulating the conversation, he managed within the next hour to add one small detail to what he had learned from Wenna Breton. He was not certain yet how the knowledge would carry him forward, but he found it most interesting.

More disturbing was a comment made by one of the men just before they bade one another good-night. "Been wondering," he said, looking sharply at Antony, "if you knew a chap in France what called hisself a Fox Cub? Some heathenish thing it sounds in the way them Frenchies talk, but they say that's what it means in good Christian English."

"Le Renardeau?" Antony hoped his reply sounded casual. His heart was suddenly thumping so hard that it seemed odd the others seated around the dirty little table couldn't hear it.

"Aye, that'll be it. Know the chappie?"

"I have heard the name spoken in whispers over the years, *mon ami,* but me, I do not know him. There are many Frenchmen in France, *n'est-ce pas?*"

"Point is, Matois, this Frenchie ain't in France. Word is, he's right here in Cornwall. Happen he's looking to cut hisself in on a few things, if you take my meaning. If you chance to hear aught of him, Michael will want to know, so see that you tell him." The man grimaced menacingly. "If you don't . . ."

Nodding agreement, Antony wondered how *Le Renardeau*'s name had slipped into Cornwall. Since it had served only as the rumored source of certain mysterious events during the war (rumors begun by himself), the Frenchman whose name he had given Michael as a reference could not know that Jean Matois and the Fox Cub were one and the same. It was possible, of course, that someone else had usurped the appellation to serve a purpose of his own, even the one suggested.

Antony hoped that was the answer. His dual identity was known only to Wellington, Harry Livingston, and certain other members of the Duke's staff, none of whom, he devoutly hoped, would want to throw the Fox Cub to the wolves.

Chapter Eleven

True to his word, Rockland returned the following afternoon. Special license in hand, he strolled with Sir Antony into the dining room, where the others, except for Lady St. Merryn and Miss Davies, were enjoying a nuncheon. Grinning, he declared that Bishop Halsey had agreed to perform the wedding the following Saturday.

"The devil of it is, I can't be here then," Rockland added with what looked to Charley like a guilty glint in his eyes. "Didn't tell you before, but I put things off because I'd written straightaway to Lady Ophelia to tell her of our betrothal and beg her to come for the wedding. Sent it posthaste, and got her reply in yesterday's post."

Charley stared at him in shock. "*You* wrote to Aunt Ophelia?"

He looked sheepish. "Knew she would want to know. Wasn't sure you'd tell her straightaway. Well," he added hastily, cutting her off before she could reply, "stands to reason you might not. Didn't tell your grandmama, did you? At all events, Lady Ophelia will reach Plymouth Friday evening." Glibly, he added, "Promised to meet her myself, of course, and bring her the rest of the way."

Exasperated, Charley said, "Good mercy, why Plymouth instead of Fowey?"

"The old lady picked Plymouth. Hates packet boats. Said she'd as lief get off as soon as she could without having to stop overnight with the carriage."

"But why did you choose Saturday if you knew she would not be here yet?"

Elizabeth said in her gentle way, "Really, Charlotte, I am persuaded that Lord Rockland must have had a very good reason for that, too."

"*You* would think so," Charley retorted. "For my part, I think he just forgot. We must certainly wait for Aunt Ophelia. The wedding will simply have to be put off."

"Not if you want to have it before the end of June," Rockland said. "The bishop has no time for us between now and the consecration except this coming Saturday."

"Then get someone else!"

" 'Be not self-willed, for thou art much too fair,' " Sir Antony murmured.

She turned on him angrily, but then, realizing she knew the rest of the couplet, she found herself suppressing a gurgle of laughter instead. Meeting an answering twinkle in his eyes, she said, "Do you think I shall be 'Death's conquest' and 'make worms thine heir,' sir? How dare you?"

"Taken on the whole," he said thoughtfully, "it means you are too lovely to be the spoil of death and the prey of worms. The words sprang to my tongue only because they somehow seemed appropriate to the moment."

"Did they?" But her flash of irritation was gone, and when she turned back to Rockland, she was able to say calmly. "Very well, sir, I will acquit you of lunacy. I presume that you have already arranged either for someone else to fetch Great-Aunt Ophelia, or for someone else to marry us."

"Well, I haven't," he confessed. "Now don't fly into the boughs again, for there's not a dashed thing I can do about it. The old lady's accustomed to me escorting her about, even to Scotland if need be, and she's bound to take a pet if I send someone else. As for another parson, I don't want one. Getting a special license from a bishop is complicated enough for one who ain't a resident of Cornwall. It ain't like going to Doctor's Commons in London and plunking down blunt to get a chit signed by the Archbishop. This fellow Halsey wanted to know all about me before he'd agree. Said he had to decide if I was worthy. If he don't perform the ceremony, I'll have to convince some ordinary psalm-singer all over again. I found a better solution."

"And what might that be?" she asked.

"The wedding will be on Saturday all right and tight. Only thing is, I'll have a stand-in saying the groom's bits for me, like when the King got married."

"You mean a marriage by proxy?"

"That's it. Couldn't think what they called the thing."

"Good gracious," Edythe exclaimed, "is that an acceptable way to marry?"

"Acceptable enough for His Majesty," Rockland pointed out. "That's how he married that dashed peculiar wife he had. Daresay that's how I came to think of it."

"But His Majesty wasn't just away for a day," Charley pointed out. "The Princess Caroline lived in Brunswick."

Rockland shrugged, avoiding her gaze. "Nothing stopping him from going to fetch her, instead of sending Malmesbury. Might have worked out better if he had. He'd have seen for himself what a dashed squirrel he was catching, for one thing."

Sir Antony said, "Fetching her did not suit his notion of propriety, I'm afraid."

Alfred, who had been a silent listener so far, said indignantly, "I should say it didn't! Nor would it have suited England's dignity. It is not for the heir to England's throne to go haring off to bring back a wife from foreign parts. Next you'll be saying he ought to have been married in Brunswick."

"But, dash it," Rockland exclaimed, "ain't that just what I *am* saying? He *was* married in Brunswick. He just didn't happen to be there at the time."

"I don't suppose it matters, as long as the ceremony is properly performed," Charley said. She wondered why, under the circumstances, she felt as if it mattered a great deal. "Whom will you ask to stand in for you?"

"As a matter of fact, I've already asked Antony here to do it, and he agreed."

"Good mercy," Charley exclaimed.

"Well, who else would I ask?" Rockland demanded indignantly. "I expect your cousin Alfred here would oblige me, or Medrose, perhaps, or—"

"Stop," she begged, torn between tears and laughter. "Forgive me," she said to Sir Antony, "but it all seems very strange. There must have been a more sensible way to do the thing, if only Rockland had thought of it before arranging this charade."

"Well, I didn't think of one," Rockland said, "and I'm dashed put out to find you don't appreciate the trouble I went to, after pushing and poking at me to get it done."

Alfred said, "That's what comes of letting a female rule the roast, sir. Your trouble stems from giving in to her in the first place. Had you simply put your foot down, you would be a happier man now, I venture to say."

Charley's head began to ache. Much as she wished she could think of something to say to annihilate Alfred, she couldn't seem to think at all. She was angry with Rockland, although his actions did not warrant the depth of anger she felt. She was angry with Alfred, too, but that went without saying, and she was furious with Sir Antony for no cause whatsoever. Feeling trapped one moment, surrounded by enemies or isolated the next, she began to think she had not a single friend in the world.

She had never felt the need of bosom friends. Much of her childhood she had shared with her Aunt Daintry and her cousin Melissa, but Daintry had been more mentor than friend, and Melissa had always depended on Charley more than Charley had depended on Melissa. Rarely alone on the busy estate, Charley felt closer to her animals, and to certain characters in books she read, than to most of the people around her. She had rarely, if ever, felt lonely. Now, suddenly, she yearned for just one close friend who would understand her feelings and explain them to her, a friend sufficiently wise to help her understand and contain the rage steadily growing within her.

Sir Antony's calm voice startled her, and she realized that the others had fallen silent and were staring. Someone had spoken before Sir Antony, but she had been so lost in thought that she did not know which of them it had been or what had been said. She looked at Sir Antony. "I-I'm sorry. What did you say?"

"I merely offered my humble opinion of Mrs. Alfred Tarrant's suggestion that you be ordered to stop dithering, and to obey Rockland's commands."

She felt herself stiffen. "And what did you reply to her?" Her gaze met his, and the others seemed to vanish, leaving her alone with him.

His smile was reassuring. "I pointed out that although Rockland might somehow contrive to force your obedience, he could not force mine. If anyone tries to make you take part in this ceremony against your will, they will have to do so without my help."

"Thank you." Feeling calmer, with her eyes still fixed on him, she said in a much firmer tone, "I am obliged to you, Sir Antony. I assure you, I am not generally given to distempered freaks, and I do intend to carry on with this wedding as long as Rockland is willing. The ceremony he arranged is not what I would have chosen, but he knows that. He knows me rather well, in fact, and despite that, he has been persistent in his attentions. Therefore, I owe him some extraordinary duty now. If you are willing to stand in for him, I shall not oppose his arrangement." She heard someone's breath catch, but she did not turn away from Sir Antony.

He frowned, then said firmly, "You *are* marrying him for no other purpose than to escape a position that is excessively distasteful to you. Is that not the case?"

Without looking away, she answered steadily, "It is. Is that so dreadful?"

"Not at all. I am persuaded that any number of young women marry for the same reason. The ceremony will go forward then.

Will you join me for a brief stroll in the gardens? That is,'' he added, glancing at Rockland, "if you have no objection.''

"None in the world,'' that gentleman replied promptly. "You've a better chance at turning her up sweet than I have, after all.''

Without comment, Charley accepted Sir Antony's arm. She wished she could read his thoughts, but he was a very self-contained man, whose expression rarely gave away what he was thinking. Neither spoke until they reached the lawn and began to follow the path toward the mirror-like lake, but at last, unable to stand the silence a moment longer, she said, "I suppose I have surprised you.''

"Why do you say that?''

"One day I declare to the world that I'll never wed. The next I practically coerce Rockland into marrying me. Then I quibble and question, and . . .'' She bit her lip.

"As I saw it,'' he said, "those first two events took place in a single day.''

She glanced up, expecting to see mockery in his eyes, but he was gazing out over the lake, his expression, as usual, unreadable. It occurred to her then that he surprised her more often than she seemed to surprise him.

"What are you thinking about?'' she demanded.

He looked at her then and smiled. She was struck yet again by how charming his smile could be, revealing something of the boy he once had been. He did not sound boyish, however, when he said, "I've been pondering a question Letty asked me yesterday, about how I can learn what I must if I stay at Tuscombe Park. I had hoped to gain access to more people, but I find I must exercise more care instead, which hampers my actions considerably. The Duke will arrive in little more than three weeks, and I cannot yet guarantee his safety. The most I have been able to report is that I am fairly certain which men to watch closely, but even that is guesswork, I'm afraid.''

"Have you made contact with the coastal gang since you arrived here?''

"Briefly. I managed to slip out last night, because there was something I particularly wanted to know. For some time, I have tried to identify the man to whom I presented my character references, as one might say, soon after I arrived in Cornwall.''

"The leader of the coastal gang? Did you identify him? Who is he?''

They had reached the lake. He said, "I knew him only as Michael.''

"Michael Peryllys! Good mercy, I would have guessed at once!''

"I doubt that, but I won't argue the point. The lads refer to him only as 'our Michael,' which is hardly an uncommon name. I knew they would not welcome much inquisitive interest from me, and in truth I did not think I would find it hard to learn his full name if I required it. The Lloyd's agent, Oakes, helped me get onto him through a chap from Fowey, but I knew Michael did not live there. I've spent uncountable hours hanging about seaside towns and villages, looking for him.'' He smiled ruefully. "It never occurred to me that he lived inland, or that you might know him. He's a thorough ruffian, you see, not a fellow I'd expect to cross paths with a lady of quality.''

Thoughtfully, Charley said, "I must confess, the few times I have met him, he was civil enough. Still, I think you might have followed your Michael home from one of those meetings you had with him. You'd have known then.''

"Our meetings were at night, and I always had an escort to a meeting place unknown to me beforehand. A very untrusting lot, your Cornish smugglers.''

As they began walking back toward the house, she said, "What did make you think Angelique's Michael might be your Michael? You never saw hers.''

"You mentioned that she was French just before we reached the Bretons' cottage, so I got a prickling when I learned her husband's name, for I had reason to suspect any Michael with a tie to France. That's why I didn't escort you to the shop. I've taken care never to let him see me in a good light, but I did not want to chance walking bang into him as Sir Antony, just in case he did prove to be 'our Michael.' ''

"I can readily believe he would support the gangs, for many in Cornwall do, but I can't imagine him as their leader. He once handed me into my carriage after I had visited Angelique, and his manner was perfectly civil." Looking up at him, she added, "Apparently, you are not the only one who is adept at playing a double role."

"So it would seem." He was silent for a moment, then said, "I ought to have learned about Angelique before now. If I'd investigated her—"

"I told you about her only yesterday, for mercy's sake. If she were the only Frenchwoman in Cornwall, you might have cause to berate yourself, but that is not at all the case. French émigrés are not common hereabouts, but neither are they a rarity, and since you believed your Michael lived near the sea . . ."

"I won't castigate myself," he said, smiling again when she let her words trail to tactful silence. "I'm just glad I did not discount her altogether. In all honesty, when you first mentioned your Angelique . . ." This time, he paused, looking apologetic.

"You assumed she probably wasn't French at all," Charley said, chuckling. "I know just how it is, for I suspected the same myself when she opened her shop some years ago. One encounters so many modistes in London who claim to be Bernadette or Cerisette, but who turn out to be plain Polly Flinders or Moll Smith instead."

"Yes, that's it. Look here," he added abruptly, "we've nearly reached the house again, and I must know. Are you determined to marry Rockland?"

She stopped, turning to face him. "So that did surprise you."

"I am never surprised by the things other people say they will or won't do," he said. "Only actions matter, and in the end, what men and woman say rarely agrees with what they do. Thus, their actions never surprise me much either."

"Then why ask me if I am determined to marry Rockland?"

"Because I want to know your answer, of course."

"But if what I say has nothing to do with what I will do . . . If, in fact, you believe I will do other than what I say I will do—"

"Spare me," he said, holding up a hand in the gesture used by fencers to indicate surrender. He looked amused. "I don't want a war of words with you. I want only to know if you care more deeply for Rockland than you have admitted to me or to the others, and if you are committed to this marriage.''

She opened her mouth to inform him that she was a woman of her word and that whatever she had decided to do she would do without explaining herself to him or to anyone else. But something in the way he looked at her kept her from blurting out the words. Instead she said honestly, ''My feelings for Rockland are what they have always been. He amuses me, and I like him, but I am committed to the marriage for exactly the reason I have given. It is the only acceptable way I know to escape Alfred's tyranny.''

''There must be a more satisfactory way to do that.''

''If there is, I don't know it. In truth, sir, until Mr. Kenhorn explained my position, it never occurred to me that could find myself a poor relation dependent upon near strangers for my bed and board. Marriage must be a better fate than that.''

''But you have other relations, who are not strangers at all. What of young Letty's parents, your cousin and her family, or this great-aunt of yours in London?''

''Great-Aunt Ophelia?'' Charley smiled. ''I am very fond of her, but she admires independent women, not clinging ones. Her father arranged through the Chancery Court for her to retain control of her fortune whether she married or not, and having a poor opinion of the male sex, she chose to remain single. I expected Grandpapa or Papa to settle money on me the same way, but they did not. I daresay Aunt Ophelia may leave me something when she dies, but she is still full of life and energy, and I will not hang on her sleeve. Nor will I throw myself on the mercy of any other close relative. In many ways, that would be even worse than Alfred *or* Rockland.''

''But why Rockland? I cannot believe you have received no other offers.''

She smiled. ''I've had my share, I suppose, though not as many as you might think. I frighten them off, or so Rockland has told me. He is forever telling me he loves me, and more importantly, he does not constantly set his will against mine. Since I cannot imagine myself as the sort of wife who would constantly alter her thoughts and opinions to match her husband's—I beg your pardon. Did you speak?''

''I coughed.''

She grinned saucily at him. ''Why did you invite me to walk with you?'' she demanded. ''Did you do it only to laugh at me?''

No responding twinkle answered her. He said evenly, ''Since I have agreed to play my part in this wedding of yours, I wanted to be certain in my own mind that you were not having second thoughts.''

''Well, I'm not. I daresay Rockland will make as good a husband as any, and quite possibly a better one than most.''

''But you don't love him.''

She shrugged. ''Love is nothing but a state of mind. One responds at some emotional level to another person, briefly, then learns more about him, and the emotion eases. If one is lucky, it eases to friendship. If not . . . Well, in my experience of other marriages, it most often leads to a sort of armed truce. At all events, I am persuaded that love is sadly overrated. People do the oddest things in its name and become quite irrational. I am thankful never to have been so foolish, myself.''

''At the risk of belaboring a point, what if you should fall in love with someone? What if Rockland does?''

''I don't believe I shall,'' she said, frowning. ''After all, I've been on the town for five years—no, six now—and I have not suffered the slightest twinge of emotional attachment to any man. I'm a lost cause, I fear. As for Rockland, from what I have seen, gentlemen fall in and out of love with the seasons. I daresay he will have his occasional *chères amies,* but as long as he is discreet, they won't trouble me.''

''A very sensible attitude,'' he said.

Detecting an edge in his voice, she said indignantly, ''You don't believe me. You men! You have such an inflated opinion of your worth, thinking women cannot get on without you, that we each want to possess you and to scratch out the eyes of any other female who smiles at you. We are not all so foolish, sir, I promise you!''

''Draw rein, *mon ange.* I said none of that. I do think we

had better go in now, however. There is a small chance that your betrothed might not cast quite so reasonable an eye on our extended absence as you think he will.''

''I wish you would not call him that,'' Charley said impatiently. ''Ours is hardly a formal betrothal. We signed no papers, you know. There are no settlements or agreements to be made. My only dowry is Grandpapa's three thousand pounds.''

''That sounds to me like an excellent reason for signing a few papers,'' he said grimly, as he touched her elbow and urged her toward the house. ''Does it not occur to you that Rockland ought to settle money on you, for your own protection?''

With a flush of warmth in her cheeks, she said, ''Good mercy, no. I can scarcely make such a demand when I practically insisted on the marriage.''

''That is precisely why a female needs a male to make such arrangements for her. I am surprised that Alfred did not suggest himself as intermediary.''

Only the expectant twinkle in his eyes kept her from delivering a withering retort. She made a face at him instead and maintained a regal silence until they reached the house. He made no further attempt to pursue the topic.

As they stepped into the empty entrance hall, a feminine screech sounded from above. Exchanging looks, they hurried up to the drawing room to find Edythe Tarrant backed into a corner, her hands held out to fend off Sebastian. The dog stood panting before her, head extended, nose atwitch, and tail wagging.

Medrose, appearing in the doorway from the next room, looked perturbed but made no move toward the dog.

Charley exclaimed, ''What on earth?''

Excited chattering burst forth from the room behind Medrose. Sebastian barked, then barked again, and Letty rushed into the drawing room behind Charley.

''Jeremiah got out, and we can't find him!''

Fortunately Charley understood what the child had said without hearing every word, for Edythe's screeches and Sebastian's barking nearly drowned out both Letty's voice and the high-pitched chatter from the next room.

"What the devil is the meaning of this?" Alfred thundered, entering behind Letty, and pushing past Sir Antony and Charley. "Edythe, what's that animal doing in here and—" He broke off in astonishment, for Edythe stopped shrieking, and Sebastian stopped barking, whereupon Jeremiah's shrill tirade rang forth from the next room.

Jago joined Medrose on the threshold between the two rooms. "Begging your pardon, Miss Charley," he said, "but that dratted monkey's perched atop the clock and if I reach for him, he begins that heathenish screeching again. Will he bite, miss?"

"I'll get him," Letty said, moving toward the opposite door.

"One moment," Alfred said, grabbing her arm and giving her a shake. "I told you, did I not, that I did not want to see that animal again, and here you've let him run all over the house. Worse than that, you've let him frighten my wife. I think what you need is a good, sound whipping to remind you to do as you are bid."

Charley snapped, "Release her at once, sir. You have no authority over her, let alone the authority to raise a hand to her."

"How dare you speak so to me!"

"I'll dare more than that," she retorted, stepping toward him. "Release her."

He did so, saying pettishly, "It goes beyond all the bounds of courtesy for a chit like you to speak to me like that in my own house."

"Your house?" Sir Antony had remained silent, but now he raised his quizzing glass and peered through it at Alfred. "My dear fellow, unless you have heard something new in the past hour, I believe that point is still in grave dispute."

With a dismissive gesture, Alfred said, "That is beside the point. For all Kenhorn says he must see some document or other, you know as well as I do that you are no brother of mine. Hello, Rockland," he added when that gentleman wandered into the room, looking mildly curious. "Come and collect your betrothed, will you? And silence that damned dog," he added when Sebastian, taking exception to yet another newcomer, began to bark again.

Edythe, hugging herself, began to weep, and Rockland stared from one occupant of the room to another in growing astonishment. "By Jove," he said, "I thought we'd been invaded. What's all the commotion?"

"Silence, sir!"

"Me?" Rockland shifted his astonished gaze to Sir Antony. That gentleman said, "You, sir? Why, no, I merely hushed the dog."

Alfred said testily, "I came in upon a scene of utter pandemonium, Rockland, evidently because that damned monkey—"

"Alfred," Edythe said in weak protest.

"Sorry, my dear. That dratted monkey got loose because young Letty here insists on keeping it in a gentleman's house. Where is she?" he added, peering around as if he expected her to reappear out of thin air.

"I'm here," Letty said in a small, dignified voice. She stood beside the footman, holding Jeremiah. "I got him to come down, but I think he's afraid of Sebastian."

"Take Sebastian outside, Jago," Charley said. "Letty, you must take Jeremiah back up to your room."

"Here now," Alfred protested, "I'll give the orders here. Just because you've got away with acting the shrew once don't mean you're taking command, you know."

Sir Antony's quizzing glass went up again. He said, "Do you think her behavior shrewish, my dear Alfred? To my mind, she was most quiet-spoken, given the circumstance. As Petruchio said of Kate, 'She is not hot, but temperate as the morn.'"

Alfred shot Sir Antony a sharp look, then turned away from him to glare at Rockland. "If you take my advice, sir, you will take her home immediately after you are wed and teach her proper duty to a husband."

His words prodded the rage that of late seemed to lie just beneath the surface of Charley's emotions, but before she could utter the hot words that sprang to her tongue, she chanced to encounter a look of amused expectation from Sir Antony. Not wanting to provide further entertainment for him, she swallowed her anger and said to him, "For goodness' sake, help

Edythe to a chair, sir. She looks as if her knees will betray her at any moment, while you so-called gentlemen stand about making idle conversation. Rockland, when do you mean to depart for Plymouth?''

''Plymouth?'' Keeping an eye on Sir Antony, as that gentleman assisted Edythe to a chair, Rockland collected himself and said glibly, ''Oh, yes, Lady Ophelia. I daresay I shall depart Friday morning, don't you know. Alfred here has given me leave to take your grandfather's traveling carriage. I sent ahead to bespeak bedchambers and a private parlor, so I can await the arrival of the evening packet in comfort, and so she can have time to recover after her voyage. She won't want to leave before Saturday morning, in any event, if she can even be got up to scratch then. I'm hoping her dislike of Sunday travel will turn the trick. She won't want to wait until Monday to see you, after all.''

''You make it sound as if she were arriving from India rather than London,'' Charley said, managing a smile, ''but I know she will appreciate your thoughtfulness.''

The rest of that day and the following one passed without incident. Charley spent much of her time making lists of things she would have to do before she and Rockland could leave. She asked him once how soon that would be, and where they would go, but he only smiled mysteriously and said she must wait and see.

His departure Friday morning brought home to her the enormity of the step she was about to take. There could be no going back now, she thought as she watched the carriage roll down the white-pebbled drive toward the main gates. Even if she were the sort of woman who could ignore a promise, she knew she could never jilt a man who was not present to defend himself.

She slept fitfully that night, waking often, once with a memory of words she had spoken to Sir Antony about love. Easy as it had been to dismiss the concept as mawkish twaddle, she wondered what it felt like to be in love. Books made it seem nonsensical. Besotted fools did idiotic, senseless things in the name of love, and counted the world well lost. A woman submitted to a man in the name of love and found herself as much at his mercy as any other of his possessions. That, at least, would not happen to her.

At one point she dozed, then woke in a sweat, having dreamed that Rockland had changed overnight from his easygoing, amiable self to a domestic tyrant. It occurred to her then that his view of the married state might well be different from hers. They had never talked about it. In fact, they had rarely talked about anything important. Though they had been acquainted for a number of years, she knew little about his family and not much more about him. Theirs had been a social relationship, nothing more. The thought gave her pause, but she rallied quickly. She had found it easy enough to keep Rockland dangling on her string. She could certainly manage him as a husband.

She wondered what he thought about children. Having bred horses for years, she understood what a man expected of his wife, but the thought of Rockland mounting her was not one she wished to dwell upon. She slept again, and when she awoke to find the curtains open and sunlight in the room, she felt only relief that the long night was over.

Kerra, turning from the window, cheerfully said that sunlight on a wedding day meant the marriage would be happy. ''Such a pity it is,'' she added as she moved to open the wardrobe, ''that your mama can't be with you today.''

''I'm going for a long ride,'' Charley said more sharply than she had intended. ''I'll put on my habit now, and you can order a bath when I return.''

She rode alone, trying unsuccessfully to gallop away her fidgets. Returning shortly after noon, she avoided the rest of the household and went straight to her room. She bathed in water scented with cinnamon and cloves, after which the maid washed and brushed her hair till it shone like ebony. Because she was in mourning, she chose a gown made for her in Paris of dove gray satin bordered with silk-embossed foliage of the same color. Between the wide-shouldered bodice and flaring skirt, it was nipped in tightly at her waist with a gray satin belt. Her black turban *à la Psyche,* also made in Paris, suffered the removal of several silk monkshood flowers and a bird-of-paradise plume, but fashionable blond lappets depended to her shoulders from each side of it.

"You look a treat, miss," Kerra said, arranging the left lappet so that it rested gracefully on Charley's shoulder.

"Thank you," Charley said, turning when the door opened to greet Letty, who had come to see if she was ready to go downstairs. "I am, indeed. We'll go down together."

Bishop Halsey arrived promptly at three o'clock, and the simple ceremony took place shortly thereafter, in the library, with the family and a few servants in attendance. Standing beside Sir Antony, facing the tall, dignified, white-haired bishop, Charley felt small, even a little frightened. Her thoughts whirled, refusing to focus, and she paid scant heed to the solemn words the bishop intoned until he said, "Antony, wilt thou have this woman to thy wedded wife, to lie together in—"

"Antony," she exclaimed, startled. "But—"

She broke off at a stern look from the bishop, who adjusted his spectacles and peered at the papers he held. "I've distinctly written Antony here," he said. "I'm sure that's what the gentleman said." He looked at Sir Antony and back at Charley. "Did you not know your betrothed husband's given name, my child?"

"I never asked him," she admitted, flushing deeply. Everyone she knew called him Rockland. It did seem odd that he had never mentioned bearing the same given name as Sir Antony, but Rockland rarely talked much about himself, and she had not asked. She glanced at Sir Antony, but he looked straight ahead. Once again she wished she could read his expression. She had a disquieting notion that he was amused by the fact that she had not known Rockland's given name.

The bishop said gently, "Shall I continue, my dear."

"Yes, of course." The ceremony continued, and when Sir Antony put the ring on her finger, Charley's hand shook. When it was over, she stood where she was while he conversed amiably with the bishop. Their conversation was brief, however, for as Halsey explained, he had other commitments. "I cannot linger even to dine, I'm afraid."

After his departure, everyone adjourned across the hall to the dining room, including Letty, who was the only one who expressed any excitement. Alfred hushed her, and conversation during the meal remained quiet, in keeping with his notion of what suited a house of mourning, even on such an occasion. Uncertain of her own feelings, Charley was grateful for the lack of celebration. She only wished she knew how she would occupy herself until Rockland's return.

To everyone's astonishment, that event occurred sooner than expected. Halfway through the meal, sounds of arrival in the hall brought conversation to a halt. Moments later, Rockland entered with Lady Ophelia Balterley on his arm.

Charley leapt to her feet and rushed to greet them. Hugging the solid, squarely-built old lady, she exclaimed, "How glad I am to see you, ma'am! I wish we had known you would arrive so soon. We might have delayed the ceremony."

"What ceremony?" Lady Ophelia demanded. "Pray, who are all these people? I do not know anyone other than your grandmama, Ethelinda, and young Letitia."

Disconcerted by the first question but knowing her duty, Charley introduced the Tarrants and Sir Antony, then said, "Rockland must have explained about our wedding, ma'am. Sir Antony stood proxy for him so he could fetch you as he'd promised to do."

"Nonsense," Lady Ophelia said bluntly. "One cannot marry by proxy in England, Charlotte, only in foreign countries where the law permits such a ceremony, and only when the English party cannot be present. I recall that quite clearly, for it was in all the newspapers when His Majesty was married in Brunswick."

"Good mercy!" Shock swept over Charley. She looked at Sir Antony, but as usual, his face gave nothing away. He was looking at Rockland.

"Knew you hadn't tumbled to it," Rockland said to her, grinning. "You'd have met me with a pistol in hand if you had. Fact is, my pet, you've been ordering me about so, and thinking you can twist me round your thumb whenever you've a mind to, that I decided to teach you a lesson. I said you didn't

know the first thing about me, and since the first thing is my
name, you married Sir Antony Tarrant, not me. Told the bishop
I was acting in his behalf when I filled out the papers, and I
put his names and titles in place of mine. Not to worry though,"
he added swiftly, while Charley struggled to control her fury.
"You need only go to the bishop, explain that I made some
errors, and have the marriage annulled. Then, if you still want
to, we can do the thing properly."

"No," Sir Antony said.

Charley stared at him. "What do you mean, no?"

"I mean that I have no intention of having this marriage
annulled."

Chapter Twelve

Antony half expected Charlotte to strike him, but she only clenched her fists.

"You are utterly mad," she said. "You cannot pretend to want this marriage, and I certainly don't want to be married to you!" Rockland chuckled, and she whirled on him. "And you! I suppose you think you have been quite clever. This is an outrage. What on earth possessed you to play me such a trick? And to involve Sir Antony?"

Still watching her, Antony was aware nevertheless when Rockland shot him a speaking look.

"Don't look to him," Charlotte snapped. "Answer me, Rockland."

Everyone's eyes turned to Rockland then. He shrugged, looking pettish, and said, "I told you, I thought you needed a lesson. Took it as a sign from above when you didn't question the marriage by proxy, because I was as certain as I could be that you would not want to insist that the bishop had got my first name wrong. Still, there was always the chance that someone would tell you a marriage by proxy wasn't legal here."

Charlotte looked from face to interested face. Following her gaze, Antony saw that Alfred looked amused, Edythe annoyed, and Miss Davies bewildered. Lady St. Merryn said weakly, "I certainly could not tell you. I know nothing about such things."

Lady Ophelia snapped, "You'd have known if you ever read the newspapers."

Unsuccessfully trying to stifle his chuckles, Alfred said, "My dear ma'am, do you mean to suggest that her ladyship ought to sully her mind with the sort of stuff one finds in the *Times?* I can guess now where Miss Charlotte comes by her odd notions."

Lady Ophelia looked at him until he squirmed, then turned her attention to Charlotte, saying acidly, "Charlotte apparently never read about proxy marriages."

"I can hardly have read about the King's marriage, ma'am. That took place long before I was born. And, in any event, my lack of knowledge certainly does not excuse what Rockland did."

Elizabeth said, "It all seems most peculiar to me, Charlotte, but I am persuaded that his lordship's reasons must have been good ones."

Antony decided that Charlotte did have some cause to dislike Elizabeth.

Even as the thought entered his mind, Charlotte snapped, "His reasons are quite childish. If he did not want to marry me, he had only to say so, but to mislead the bishop, even to lie to him! Surely, he has transgressed some sacred law or other."

"Didn't lie to him," Rockland said. "Just said I was arranging a wedding, which I was. After all the times you've snapped my head off, I just wanted you to consider for a time how you'd like being married to a man who ain't so easygoing as I am. I saw how he could sweeten that tongue of yours with a look, which is something I never could do. Just thought if I pulled it off, it might give you pause to think, that's all."

"What you have done," Lady Ophelia said in sternly measured accents, "is quite unconscionable, young man. I am extremely disappointed in you. Like most men, you spout a vast amount of nonsense about love when it suits you to do so, and know nothing whatsoever about it."

Rockland flushed, but before he could think of a reply, Letty said, "Are you married to Sir Antony then, Cousin Charley, instead of to Lord Rockland?"

"I am not," Charlotte said sharply, avoiding Antony's gaze.

"But you must be," Elizabeth said. "What a coil this is, to be sure! Indeed, although dearest Alfred has scarcely stopped chuckling since Lord Rockland revealed his prank, it cannot seem amusing to you now. Still, I am persuaded that years from now we shall all laugh whenever we chance to recall this day."

Charlotte glared, but as she opened her mouth, no doubt to go into greater detail about her feelings on the subject, Lady St. Merryn said querulously to Miss Davies, "But I do not understand all this, Ethelinda. I am quite certain that it was Rockland whom Charlotte said she was going to marry, and without even waiting until her parents and my dear St. Merryn had got cold in the ground, I might add, let alone for a proper year. But if the proxy business went amiss, as they say, she should not be married at all. Are they saying now that she has gone and married the wrong man?"

"But, Grandmama," Letty said cheerfully, "even if she is married to Sir Antony, she will still be a ladyship, just as you'd hoped she would be. At least—" She glanced uncertainly at Antony, then said firmly, "Well, isn't she?"

"So it would appear," Lady Ophelia said dryly when Lady St. Merryn only shook her head in distress and reached for the vinaigrette Miss Davies held out to her.

Antony saw Lady Ophelia eye him with a speculative gleam, and decided it was time to take a firm hand in the matter. He said matter-of-factly, "We'll get this sorted out quite easily if I can just have a few moments alone with Charlotte."

"I don't want to be alone with you," she muttered.

"Then the sooner we finish our conversation, the more pleased you will be," he said, taking her hand and drawing it through the crook of his arm. He felt her try to pull away, and when he did not release her, she gave him a startled look. He gazed steadily back at her, however, and apparently realizing that he had no intention of changing his mind, she made no further protest.

As they passed into the hall, he heard a crack of laughter from Alfred and an observation to the room at large that Rockland would be well advised to let the impostor keep the chit. "He was spouting Petruchio's words not long since. Let him play the role if he's got a fancy for it. Maybe he can tame our unruly Kate."

Antony shut the door with a snap.

Charlotte did not look at him. He knew she had heard Alfred's comments, but she did not say anything while he guided her into a stark room at the rear of the hall that looked as if it was generally used to park visitors of the lower classes while servants sought permission to present them. A single, tall, narrow, uncurtained window overlooked the drive leading to the stables, and provided enough light to see easily.

When Antony closed the door, she turned and said, "I cannot imagine what you think you can say that will change my mind about this farce Rockland has created."

Her cheeks were bright, her eyes sparkled with wrath, and she was clearly exerting extraordinary effort to control herself. She was beautiful, and he wondered if she would have exerted such control for Rockland, but he could not indulge his fantasies now. He had a formidable task ahead of him.

"The farce," he said quietly, "began long before I stepped onto the stage. Rockland is not only unworthy of you but he brings out the worst in you. Your decision to marry him was unwise."

"That is water under the bridge now," she said impatiently. "At present I am concerned only with how I can undo this absurd marriage to you. I should think you would move heaven and earth to help me. Instead you make ridiculous declarations about not wanting an annulment. Or did I misunderstand you?"

"You did not misunderstand. I hope, in fact, that you will reconsider your wish to end a union that I consider to be a rather fortunate circumstance. If you will allow me to explain . . ." He paused, watching her narrowly.

She drew a deep breath and let it out again. "Very well, I'll listen. But do not suppose that I shall change my mind, for I expect I will do no such thing.''

"Will you sit down?"

"Stop dithering, and say what you will."

"I need you."

She stared at him. "What on earth do you mean by that?"

"No more or less than what I said. I need you. As I've told you, my movements are severely hampered while I stay here, more than I thought they would be. But by coming here as I did, I have put myself at a distinct disadvantage, because Sir Antony Foxearth-Tarrant would find it hard now simply to disappear.''

"Posing as Grandpapa's heir was foolish. You would have found it more to your advantage to continue going about unnoticed.''

"Perhaps you are right," he said, smiling, "but it seemed a good choice at the time, and it would be more foolish now to waste time condemning what cannot be undone. Then, too, it will be much easier for me to be seen with the Duke, when he comes, if I am already known as Sir Antony.''

Her brow furrowed, and he hoped she would not wonder why he did not simply meet the Duke when he arrived and pose as one of his entourage. To his relief, she said, "I hadn't thought of that. I suppose it is only natural for you to want to be with him, and people certainly won't think it odd to see you with him, because Grandpapa invited him to dine here after the ceremony. Mr. Gabriel mentioned it to Alfred, and I believe Alfred has written to assure Wellington that he is still quite welcome, but I don't think he has received a reply yet. Do you think they'll come?''

"Very likely, but I shall not rest easy until that ceremony is over. Nor would I trust others to keep watch once Wellington arrives in Cornwall. Too much is at stake. As you may have noted in the *Times* yesterday, Robert Peel succeeded in getting his police bill recommitted by excluding the City of London from its influence.''

"That is a good sign, is it not?"

"Yes, because objections from that square mile of ancient

privilege have hitherto presented his main stumbling blocks, so he may well succeed this time. But as a result, Wellington's determination will be greater than ever to prove that Cornwall is safe for him without calling in the army. Since I very much doubt that he'll let me post armed guards within the cathedral to ensure his safety, I mean to be right there beside him.''

"But how does this pertain to me or to this absurd marriage of ours?"

"As my wife, you will lend me credibility," he said. "Not only will my marriage to you allow me to stay in the district as Sir Antony but it will provide me with an excellent reason to position myself near you and the Duke at the front of the cathedral. Recollect that you are to open the Seraphim Coffer for him when he presents the sacred vessels. Also," he added, choosing his words carefully, "our marriage will lend credence to my wish to remove at once from this house."

Astonished, she said, "But why? Where do you want to go?"

He smiled again, hoping his tension did not reveal itself. Much depended upon her cooperation now, and he was not certain enough yet of how her mind worked to know how best to present his case. Instinct told him to be frank. He said, "Thanks to Alfred's insistence upon defending his claim to Tuscombe Park, the necessity to present certain documentary proof, and the time necessary to conclude probate, any decision as to that claim will take a good deal of time."

"Good mercy, do you have documents to produce?" Her eyes were wide. Clearly, she had not considered any possibility of his claim proving true.

He grinned at her. "Anyone, my angel, can produce documents when it is necessary to do so. Indeed, often it is necessary to do no more than suggest that certain documents exist. Whether they do or not, lawyers delight in searching for them. In a case such as this one, the matter was childishly simple."

"Oh, I see."

That she was still puzzled was clear from her expression. He could not tell if she was disappointed, but he could do nothing about it now if she was. He said, "Under most circumstances, people would expect me to remain in the house, guarding my flank, so to speak. However, no one will think it odd in me to want time alone with my bride, so long as I stay near enough to keep at least one eye on Alfred." Putting emphasis on the last phrase, he watched her carefully for her response.

Lingering puzzlement disappeared, replaced by comprehension. "You want to remove to Seacourt Head House," she said. "That's it, isn't it?"

"I knew you had a quick mind," he said with relief. "That is indeed what I'd like, if it is possible. I do not know, however, how close you are to your cousin."

"Close enough," she said. "The Corlans will welcome us with open arms, and we need not fear Melissa's turning us out. She visits only in summer, never during the rest of the year, and no one else will come. Aunt Susan has not set foot in the house since the night she fled from my Uncle Geoffrey, years ago. But I don't know how you can think I'll stay married to you merely to help you remove to Seacourt House."

"Am I so much worse a prospect for marriage than Rockland?"

To his surprise, she hesitated and color flamed in her cheeks. But she rallied quickly. "Whether you are or not is beside the point. Rockland tricked us into this marriage, and you have given me no good cause yet not to end it."

"Let me see if I understand your position," he said, watching her, trying to gauge her feelings. "You decided to marry Rockland primarily to avoid dwindling into a poor relation, dependent on Alfred for bed and board, correct?"

"Quite."

"You do not love Rockland."

"You know I do not."

"Then you can accomplish your purpose as easily by staying married to me."

"But I never wanted to marry you!"

"What's wrong with me?"

She glared at him, clearly unwilling to answer so blunt a question. Twice she opened her mouth and shut it again. Antony could almost hear the mental argument she was waging with herself.

When she did not speak, he said gently, "As I recall it, you said Rockland would make you a good husband because he would never attempt to rule the roast. On the other hand, when he said it would teach you a lesson to be wed to a man less easily led than himself, he as much as suggested that you need to feel a stronger hand on the rein. Are you simply afraid that I might prove less amiable than Rockland?"

Her lips twitched, and to his surprise, her eyes began to twinkle. She said, "I was trying to think of a tactful way to explain how I felt about that, but I daresay there *is* no tactful way. Do you deny, sir, that you would make every effort to call the tune?"

"I am not unreasonable, I hope," he said. "Nor do I think myself a tyrant. In fact, however, a man is legally the head of his household and responsible for the well-being of its members. I would not willingly waive the authority while I must retain the responsibility. To do so would be foolish beyond permission. However—"

"Does it not occur to you that men wrote such laws to benefit themselves at the expense of women?" she demanded.

Tempted though he was to tell her she was being imprudent to pick that quarrel with him just now, he knew he would be wiser not to do so. Instead he said evenly, "I trust you don't accuse me of having a hand in writing those laws."

"Neither have you ever attempted to change any of them, I'll wager."

"I have not. You will have to educate me about these matters. I won't pretend that I am all agog to learn, mind you, or even anxious to change my ways or to question those of men in general. You are far too intelligent to be cozened into believing such things of me. But I will offer you a bargain."

"What bargain?"

"You have clearly realized that no better alternative than marriage exists to free you from Alfred's authority, or someone else's," he said, wondering how long it would be before she realized whose authority that might be if Alfred could not prove his claim. "Even if you renounce this marriage of ours for one with Rockland, marriage still remains your best course."

"I can't marry Rockland now," she muttered. "Not after what he did."

"Hence my offer of a bargain." He was glad she tended to blame Rockland more than himself, but he could not help wondering how long that would last.

She swallowed visibly, squared her shoulders, and said, "Very well, I'll listen."

"Good. As I recall, you come into three thousand pounds upon your marriage. Unlike Rockland, I will engage to settle twice that amount upon you as my wife, now. Further, I will promise to arrange for an annulment of the marriage once Wellington's visit is ended. At that time, I will further engage to provide an independence that will make it possible for you to set up housekeeping on your own, albeit in a modest way."

"How can you do that?"

"By arranging for an allowance unless and until you engage to marry someone else. A husband, even a former husband, has the right to do that, you know."

"But why are you willing to do this? You could easily investigate the plot to kill Wellington without me. Even the odious Alfred would most likely help you if you were to confide in him. Unless, of course," she added with a touch of scorn, "you suspect him of being one of the plotters."

"I don't think that," he said, "but neither do I want to take him into my confidence. Over the years I have learned to trust as few people as possible, and not just with regard to information I acquire." He hesitated. Every instinct, all his experience, warned him not to say what he was about to say. He drew a deep breath. "There is . . . there is more to that than I have told you, I'm afraid. I don't know if you remember exactly what I said to you about my work for Wellington."

"You said you had come to Cornwall to unhinge a plot to assassinate him, and you mentioned that you had played some sort of similar role for him once in France. No, wait," she amended, frowning in her attempt to remember. "You said that because he was the supreme commander, he was threatened many times, so I must suppose you played more than one role on the Continent.''

''I was fairly certain I had not confessed the depths to which I sank in that endeavor,'' he said, watching for signs of reproach and seeing none. ''I believe I did mention that upright British citizens have been quick to denounce these roles I've played, but I failed to mention that one of those upright folks was my own father. He did not see my actions as simple deceit, nor were they. I was a spy,'' he added bluntly, making a clean breast of it at last. ''I am one still.'' He held his breath, waiting.

Contrary to his expectation, she did not shrink away from him. She said only, ''I suppose spying can be a distasteful task, sir, but if your acts helped the Duke defeat Napoleon, I think all patriotic British men, and women, ought to cheer you. No doubt you will say that is merely my foolish woman's way of looking at things . . .''

''I'd never say that to you,'' he said. In his relief, he chuckled at the thought of her likely reaction if he were idiot enough to speak so to her.

Thoughtfully, she said, ''I know you speak excellent French, but how does one succeed as a spy in a country wholly unlike one's own, and in such dangerous times?''

He sobered at once. ''The simple fact is that I played Jean Matois, both in France and in Belgium. I acquired another name, too—*Le Renardeau,* the Fox Cub.''

''Good mercy, how thrilling!''

''Yes, very romantic,'' he said dryly. ''I was a veritable Robin Hood, except that instead of robbing the rich to feed the poor, I spied on the French to help the English. Ordinary French people gave me shelter, even the bread off their plates, and I repaid them by betraying their trust and repeating their words to Wellington's commanders. Not the sort of manners one learns at school, as I'm sure you will agree.''

Her forehead wrinkled again in the way it did when she was giving serious thought to something, so although she did not reply at once, he felt no impulse to fill the silence. It was important to him to know what she would say.

At last, she looked up at him from under her lashes, and

said, "I do see more clearly now why your father and others might have been displeased with your actions, for it does seem shabby to repay kindness of any sort in such a way. Still and all, the fact remains that the French were our enemies and would most likely have killed you had they known you were English." She paused, looking expectant. When he said nothing, she said impatiently, "Well, would they not?"

"All armies shoot spies at once when they are caught," he said. "They take only men in proper military uniform as prisoners of war."

"There, you see. As for being a spy, I'm sure people here were forever talking about French spies in London and elsewhere. They have done for as long as I can remember, so the French, at least, look upon spying as merely an action of war."

"Perhaps. However, among gentlemen—"

"Oh, pooh! How hypocritical! You cannot be speaking of French gentlemen, for how could Napoleon learn what our officers had planned if he never employed gentlemen as spies. As for our own, did they ever reject the information you got?"

"I only meant that ordinary gentlemen—in both countries— do not approve."

"But how absurd. People on both sides gain by their spying, take complete advantage of information that their spies obtain, then condemn them for obtaining it. I have no patience with such hypocrisy, not in France and not in England. But why," she asked shrewdly, "are you telling me all this now?"

"I want you to know the worst of me," he said, forcing the words out. "That's only fair, even if you remain my wife for no more than a short time. Moreover, I heard a rumor the other night that leads me to think someone suspects the presence of *Le Renardeau* in Cornwall. That is, I confess, yet one more reason I hope you will agree to put off the annulment of this marriage. As your husband I will be readily accepted in this neighborhood. We can keep Annabelle and Sebastian at Seacourt Head without undue comment, and I can use that house much more easily than this one as a base for my activities. Come now, what do you say?"

"You leave me little to say that will not sound petulant,"

she said with a sigh. "I own, the promise of an independence of my own is tempting, but it's a bit lowering to discover that I can be so easily bribed. There is one thing, however—perhaps two—that you do not seem to have considered."

"What?"

"Letty, Jeremiah, and possibly Great-Aunt Ophelia."

He could not imagine at first what she meant. Then he knew. When she grinned at him in her usual saucy way, he rubbed his forehead and said ruefully, "I never gave Letty a thought. I ought to have done so, too, for I know you have taken responsibility for her and I cannot imagine that she would be happy to stay with Alfred. That clearly means accepting Jeremiah, but need we take Lady Ophelia? I like her, but she is as sharp as she can stare. Moreover, next you will say we must take your grandmama and Miss Davies, as well."

"On no account," she said, chuckling. "Tuscombe Park has been Grandmama's home since she was seventeen. She will not easily agree to leave it, and certainly not to remove to Seacourt Head, which she thinks sadly exposed to the elements. Indeed, I think Cousin Alfred will have to build her an excessively fine dower house to persuade her to go anywhere. Cousin Ethelinda, being utterly devoted to Grandmama, will not pose any problem. As for Great-Aunt Ophelia, she might decide to remain with Grandmama, too, to lend her support against the encroaching Norfolk Tarrants, but I do think we ought to invite her. That way, she can decide for herself and not feel that we have abandoned her."

"Very well then, but I hope and pray that she will not come. That formidable old lady is shrewd enough to winkle out exactly what I'm up to within ten minutes of her arrival, and I don't want to have to explain *Le Renardeau* to her."

"I doubt she would be as shocked as you fear, sir."

"Even so . . ." He sighed. "Did Rockland know you intended to saddle him with a child, a monkey, and an outspoken old lady in exchange for a wedding ring?"

"I don't know what he expected," she said tartly, "and at present, I don't care."

"Well, you'd better give him some thought, because we need his cooperation."

"What for? I don't ever want to speak to him again."

"I understand that," he said patiently. "However, although almost any tale can be put about publicly to explain our marriage, since your being in mourning made it imperative to be discreet, we cannot have Rockland or any of Alfred's or your people going about telling tales out of school."

"But can we keep them all quiet?"

"I think you'll find that Rockland will agree to keep quiet about the prank once he learns you've changed your mind about marrying him." Antony saw nothing to gain by suggesting that Rockland might well be very relieved to hear that news.

She seemed to consider what he had said. "But what of Alfred and the others? The only servant in the room when Rockland spoke was Medrose, and he won't breathe a word of what happened, but Alfred's people have no cause to keep quiet."

"Alfred will be glad to be rid of us all, I think, including Letty and certainly Jeremiah. I doubt that he will put any rub in our way, or allow his people to do so."

As he expected, that belief soon proved to be accurate, for when he described to Alfred the scandal that would arise if word got around of the outrageous prank, that stern gentleman ordered both his wife and sister to say nothing about it to anyone, including their personal servants. "If any should suggest that Charlotte intended to marry anyone other than Sir Antony, you will simply inform him that he is in error."

To Antony's relief, when it was suggested to Lady Ophelia that she might like to remove to Seacourt House, she said that Lady St. Merryn would be more comfortable if she remained at Tuscombe. "Moreover," she added disconcertingly, "newlyweds ought never to be saddled with a lot of well-meaning relations. You will do much better to have time together without interference, if only to get to know each other better."

Antony exchanged a look with Charlotte, wondering when she would recall that their wedding night lay ahead. The startled look on her face told him the thought had entered her mind at almost the same moment it had entered his. When Lady Ophelia turned away, he said in an undertone, "Now that they know we are leaving almost at once, no one will think it odd if we keep the rooms we have. Plead an incipient cold or some such thing if you think you need offer any explanation to your maid."

Looking relieved, Charlotte said, "I'll simply say I'm tired, and leave Kerra to draw her own conclusions. I am not in the habit of confiding in her."

The next day, being Sunday, passed quietly and without incident, and on Monday they accomplished the move to Seacourt House with little fanfare. Letty, at least, expressed herself delighted to leave Tuscombe Park behind. As they rode along the path to the cliff tops, with Sebastian dashing ahead of them, amusing himself by startling birds from the underbrush, the child said happily, "Cousin Charley, I'm very glad you decided to marry Sir Antony instead of Rockland."

Antony watched Charlotte to see what her reaction would be, but although her cheeks reddened, she said calmly, "Are you, darling? I thought you liked Rockland."

"I do. I just like Sir Antony better. Moreover," Letty added with a mischievous grin as she scratched the little monkey's head, which poked through the opening in her cloak, "now Jeremiah and Sebastian won't have to spend all their time in confinement."

Antony chuckled, but a thought crossed his mind, and he said, "Perhaps you are being too optimistic, Letty. There is every chance, you know, that your cousin Melissa won't want monkeys or dogs running free in her house."

Charlotte laughed heartily, and Antony realized it was the first time he had heard her do so. She raised her face to the cerulean sky and gave free rein to merriment.

Letty watched, clearly bewildered, and finally when Charlotte gasped for breath with tears running down her face, the child said, "But what is so funny? Do tell us."

Charlotte looked from one to the other, still struggling to control her mirth. At last, she said, "I just suddenly saw a picture in my mind of Seacourt House filled with shaggy dogs and noisy monkeys, and us. How Uncle Geoffrey would have hated that! He was Melissa's papa," she said to Antony, "a perfectly horrid man. First, the thought of Jeremiah running free in his house made me laugh. Then I realized Uncle Geoffrey would dislike my living there almost as much as he would have loathed Jeremiah. But Melissa will not mind in the least. She will be delighted when she learns that we are turning her house back into a home, even if it's only for a little while."

Seeing curiosity leap again to Letty's eyes, Antony said hastily, "You must write at once to her, my dear Charlotte, and explain matters to her. Tell her that we wanted a little respite from Alfred and the others, and her house was just too tempting to resist."

"Oh, yes," Letty said. "Once she learns how awful it was living with Cousin Alfred, she will understand entirely why you wanted to leave."

"I wrote the letter yesterday," Charlotte said, "and it went out with the post before we left this morning. I can just see Uncle Geoffrey, bellowing and carrying on. He was much worse than Alfred." When she laughed again, Antony found himself looking forward to the next fortnight with more pleasure than he had expected. Life with the fascinating Charley as his wife was bound to be an interesting challenge.

Chapter Thirteen

What on earth had she got herself into, Charley wondered, as she and Sir Antony, and Letty and Jeremiah, followed Aggie Corlan upstairs to the family wing of Seacourt House. Not only had the child and Aggie accepted her marriage as unquestioned reality but it was rapidly being brought home to her that, although she had avoided the consequences of a wedding night, the marriage was nonetheless real.

She had recited her vows before a bishop of Cornwall, and they were sacred vows. Amongst them lay a promise to honor and obey her husband. That she had not known she was pledging obedience to Sir Antony instead of Rockland seemed a mere quibble now. A new thought occurred to her, and she silently cursed Letty's presence, and that of the housekeeper, as well, because they prevented her from asking Sir Antony the question now reverberating in her mind.

Aggie Corlan approached a tall, ornately carved white door and said as she opened it, ''These be the master's chambers, sir. Corlan and me did clear out the wardrobe and the chests in yon dressing room, and I'm thinking Mr. Hodson has already put your things in their places. We've no proper laundry maid at present, I'm afraid, nor proper chambermaids, for all that.

Just myself and Corlan and the girl what comes to help me with heavy cleaning.''

''Her Ladyship will soon see to hiring more servants,'' Sir Antony said.

Charley had been looking around the spacious, very masculine bedchamber with curiosity, but she turned in surprise when she realized he was referring to her. She remembered that Letty had mentioned soon after the fateful ceremony that she would have a title, but although Sir Antony had stopped calling her *Miss* Charlotte, no one had referred to her since as anything but Charlotte or Cousin Charley, or ma'am.

He went on without hesitation, ''No doubt Lady Foxearth will enjoy seeing this house come alive again.''

Exchanging a look with Aggie Corlan, Charley said, ''I don't know that I can honestly say I've ever seen this house as a lively place. I've been inside it numerous times, to be sure, but I've never seen this room before. I've seen only the public ones, and of course, the old schoolroom, and Melissa's bedchamber. Uncle Geoffrey did not encourage little girls to run free in his house.'' Smiling at Letty, she added, ''I daresay we will put you in Cousin Melissa's old bedchamber. She will require a maidservant, too, Aggie. We've brought no one with us but Sir Antony's man and Kerra, I'm afraid, and Kerra is not accustomed to helping with general housework.''

''Dear me, ma'am, I'd never expect it of her, now she's a lady's maid. No need to fret yourself, however. I've a niece who will be happy to help with the housework and look after her young ladyship, as well, until you find someone more suitable.''

''Excellent. Now, when you have shown me my bedchamber, perhaps you will take Lady Letitia to see hers. Then you can make a list of the servants as we shall require. We shan't need many, for we do not mean to entertain for some time yet.''

''Nor no one won't expect it, my lady,'' Aggie agreed with an uncharacteristic twinkle. ''Not for at least a month, though I'll warrant you'll have bride visits aplenty once word gets round that you've married. Now, Lady Letitia, you come along with me, and after we look at your bedchamber, you shall come down to my kitchen, where I've left some gingerbread a-baking. I'll warrant you and that bright-eyed little critter both have a liking for gingerbread.''

"Oh, yes, please," Letty said. "We've discovered a fondness for saffron buns, too, and we both like fruit. But, please, call me Miss Letty and not Lady Letitia. I'm glad you are not afraid of Jeremiah." As the door closed behind them, she was heard to add cheerfully, "He's quite tame, you know. He will even shake hands if you like."

Sir Antony said, "That relationship promises to prosper."

"It does." The question she had been burning to ask him hovered on the tip of her tongue, but awareness that she was alone with him in his bedchamber held it in check. Determined not to reveal her unease, she said lightly, "Aggie neglected to show me my bedchamber."

"I daresay it is the next room to this," he said, striding to the nearest door and thrusting it open. "No, that's my dressing room. It must be the other one, yonder." Crossing the room, he opened the second door and said with satisfaction, "Here we are, and as fine a view of the sea as can be had from mine. I could grow fond of this house."

"Wait till you experience it in a storm," Charley said. "I spent a night here once in a terrifying thunderstorm. I'll never forget it."

"Are you afraid of storms? The house seems quite solidly built."

"I suppose it is," she agreed, but she was not thinking of the weather. "Look here, sir, I simply cannot sleep in the room adjoining yours. I'll tell Aggie to prepare another one for me."

"You can't do that," he said gently.

"Don't be absurd. There must be a dozen other bedchambers in this house."

"None of which is the mistress's chamber, however."

"What difference can that make? No one else need know." Even as the words crossed her lips, however, she knew word would soon spread, not just through the household but beyond, especially since they would be hiring more servants.

He was watching her, and he said now, "We must maintain

the pretense of a normal marriage, or there is no point to this exercise. All Cornwall would soon be gossiping about us. In order for me to continue to act as Jean Matois when necessary and still be accepted as Sir Antony, there must not be any stirring of local curiosity. I must be accepted as what I appear to be.''

"Look here, sir," she said bluntly, "is our marriage even legal?"

"As legal as legal can be."

"But how can that be? Rockland put what he assumed were your proper names and titles, but since you are cutting a sham—"

"You were married to Sir Antony Foxearth, angel. That is the name by which I have been known for years to folks here in England, and is as legal a name as any other I might possess. As for the title, Wellington himself arranged for my baronetcy."

"Rockland did not put Tarrant, then?"

With a crooked smile, Sir Antony said, "He did not."

"Then our marriage is legal."

"It is. You are Lady Foxearth."

She smiled weakly. "Aggie must have seen how taken aback I was to hear myself called so."

"I daresay she will put it down to nerves and the fact that you have but recently come by the title."

Charley glanced through the open door at the bedchamber that would be hers. She suddenly felt nervous, not just of Sir Antony but of the whole unfamiliar situation in which she found herself.

He seemed to know what she was thinking, for he said quietly, "Tonight will be no different from last night or the night before or the night before that. I will ask no more than that you play your part, *mon ange*. If it will make you feel more secure, there is a key in that lock. You may keep the door locked."

She relaxed, realizing she had no fear that he might try to ravish her. With a half-smile of apology, she said, "I'll keep the key, but I won't lock it without cause, sir. Only think what tales the servants will tell if they find that door locked."

"Thank you," he said. "I promise, you have nothing to fear from me."

She was not so sure. Something about him made her unusually uncertain of herself. Never had she even been tempted to treat him as cavalierly as she treated Rockland. Whenever Rockland displeased or irritated her, she said so at once, never hesitating to speak her mind to him. Indeed, it had been that very factor that had led her to think she might be able to endure marriage to him.

She had thought she felt completely at ease with Rockland, but she knew now that that was not true. She had merely convinced herself that he would not attempt to rule her. He never had tried such a thing, but had he dared, she would have found it easy to oppose him. The thought of setting herself in opposition to Sir Antony stirred a tingling in her midsection. She did not think that would be so easy. Several days later, in the sunny breakfast parlor, when she informed him that she had decided to ride to Lostwithiel that day, she discovered that her assessment of him was correct.

Reaching for the cream pot without so much as glancing at her, he said, "No."

They sat with Letty at a round table in a large, semicircular bay that provided a near panoramic view of the Channel. Except for a few wispy clouds, the sky was clear. The tide was in, and where the sea rolled heavily against the rocks, spray and white foam shot high in the air. The thick walls of Seacourt House muted the rhythmic sound, but they provided a musical background to life at the house, which Charley generally found soothing. Now, however, she was anything but calm. She stared at Sir Antony, now engaged in pouring rich Cornish cream over his oatmeal.

"What do you mean, no?"

"The word is clear enough, I think. Letty," he added, "I would prefer that you not allow Jeremiah to scatter toast crumbs all over the table."

Reminded of Letty's presence, Charley struggled to control her temper, saying with forced calm, "If you have finished

your breakfast, darling, why don't you take Jeremiah outside?
He can throw his crumbs to the ducks in the horse pond.''

"Are we not going riding at all then?" Letty asked, getting
up and settling the monkey on her shoulder. Jeremiah clutched
his toast tightly in his tiny hands.

"We'll see," Charley said, meeting Sir Antony's gaze with
a challenging look.

" " 'Tis a shrewd doubt, though it be but a dream,' " he
murmured.

Charley said no more until Letty had gone away with Jeremiah, and then she said stiffly, "I did not recognize that one,
I'm afraid."

"Othello." He watched her, his oatmeal untouched. It was
the first time since shortly after their arrival that she had found
herself completely alone with him. She and Aggie had been
busy setting the house in order, and she knew Sir Antony
and Sam Corlan had given similar attention to the stables and
surrounding estate. Sir Antony clearly wanted the place to come
alive. He had even sent for Teddy and Jeb, and several of her
horses from Tuscombe Park.

Sir Antony had not forgotten his mission. He had disappeared
without a word several times, and once, she was certain, he
had been away all night. She had tried to winkle information
out of Hodson, but although the man was pleasant and possessed
an air of quiet dignity, he proved to be as close as an oyster
with facts about his master or his master's activities. Being left
to her own devices, she saw now, he had lulled her into a false
sense of independence, but she would allow no one to dictate
her movements.

When he said no more, merely watching her in silence while
he stirred a sugar lump into his coffee, she felt her temper rise.
She had almost forgotten how easily, of late, she could be
stirred to fury, but suddenly she found herself snapping, "You
can't mean to keep me a prisoner in this house!"

"What makes you think I have any such intention?"

"If you think you can keep me from riding, you are very
much mistaken, sir. I ride every morning that the weather
permits. I have done since we came here."

"Not to Lostwithiel," he said flatly. "I have no objection to your riding, provided that you take your groom along if you go beyond sight of the house, and provided that both you and he are armed."

"But I can take care of myself," she cried, aware that she was losing control but unable to stop herself. "I won't beg your permission when I want to ride, any more than I asked for Alfred's. Nor will I submit my destination for your approval!"

"Don't raise your voice to me. I dislike it very much."

"Don't tell me what to do!"

"Now, look—"

"You look!" She leaned across the table, glaring at him. "I won't be told where I can go, and I won't change my habits just to suit your fusty notions of propriety or safety. I've done as I pleased since I was a child, I'll have you know."

"We will leave your childhood out of this discussion," he said. "Things are a little different now."

"Because I've got a husband, I suppose," she said sarcastically.

"That is certainly a point."

"Good mercy, you *do* fancy yourself to be some sort of Petruchio," she snapped. "Well, I'm no Kate for your taming, sir, and I'll thank you to remember that."

"Don't be a fool. Leave us," he added sharply when the new footman looked into the room to see if they required anything more. "I'll ring when I want you."

"Yes, sir," the lad said, effacing himself.

Sir Antony said, "It would perhaps be wise to make certain we are alone before we cross verbal swords, *mon ange.*"

"Don't call me that." Aware that she sounded like a sullen child, she straightened, shooting him a rueful look.

He smiled. "I did not mean to infuriate you, you know. Nor do I have less faith than I had before in your ability to look out for yourself or Letty. However—"

"I knew there would be a *however*. There is always a *however.*"

"Not always. I own, I am perhaps more protective of a wife than I was of a woman I thought was answerable to others, but we must not forget the existence of my unattractive comrades and their uncertainty about the inhabitants of Tuscombe Park."

"What uncertainty?"

"You will recall that your grandfather was not friendly to the free traders. St. Merryn's Bay was more likely to prove a trap for the unwary than a haven of refuge."

"But what has that to do with my riding to Lostwithiel?"

"Only that the coastal gang has yet to take their measure of the new heir."

"Good mercy, they don't even know who he is."

"Just so, but they do know you. Moreover, they know that you are bound to remain of importance, no matter who inherits the estate. I don't want to see you taken hostage to force Alfred's hand, or mine."

"No one would dare try to take me hostage," she retorted. "If they did, they would soon learn their error."

"Nevertheless—"

"There is no *nevertheless,* and there will be no *howevers,* either. I may have agreed to remain married to you, but I did not agree to let you order my life."

"In actual point of fact—"

"Don't quibble!" She stood up, shaking out the train of her habit. "I promised Wenna and Cubert Breton more than a sennight ago that I would make certain their Jenifry is well treated at Angelique's. I mean to go today, because as far as I can tell, no one who cares about Jenifry has seen her since Letty and I did a month ago. I must keep my word. Even you can see that."

"We'll send someone to inquire about Jenifry," Sir Antony said patiently. "But until I can better measure the intentions of Jean Matois's compatriots, you will not ride so far from this house, let alone into the very den of Michael Peryllys."

She stepped nearer, glaring at him. "I will ride where I choose."

"Heaven and earth," he muttered, pushing back his chair and throwing his serviette onto the table, "you'll do as I say for once, and without this infernal debate and cross-talk. How Will Shakespeare could ever have called women frail—"

"A pox on Shakespeare," Charley snapped. Refusing to let the unexpected change in his demeanor make her retreat, she went on angrily, "The only thing he wrote worth quoting is 'What a piece of work is a man!' Unfortunately, he followed that line with a lot of ridiculous claptrap. And don't you dare laugh at me," she cried.

When he only leaned back in his chair and laughed harder, she caught up his bowl of oatmeal in a fit of pure rage and dumped the contents over his head.

A deadly silence fell. Aghast at what she had done, she dropped the empty bowl on the table, turned on her heel, and fled. Glancing back, more than half expecting him to pursue her, she felt strangely disappointed to see that he had not moved.

As she opened the door, he said in carefully measured tones, " 'What a piece of work is a man! How noble in reason! How infinite in faculty! In form, in moving, how express and admirable! In action how like an angel, in apprehension how like a god!' " More furious than ever, she slammed the door shut behind her.

Hurrying to the stables, she wondered at her temerity and wondered even more at his apparently mild reaction. It occurred to her then that he might have remained seated, covered in dripping oatmeal and cream, spouting Shakespearean idiocy at her, because he had already given orders in the stables that she was not to ride without his permission. If he had done such a thing, she knew the stablemen would obey him.

Taking a high hand, she ordered Teddy to bring Shadow Dancer out at once, and when he did so without hesitation, she paused only long enough to be certain her pistol was in its holster before accepting a leg up. Seeing that the groom had saddled a horse for himself, she said, "Are you armed, Teddy? Sir Antony is concerned about certain fractious elements in the district."

"As well he should be, Miss Charley—that is, my lady. Some folks be getting too big fer their breeches." He swung into the saddle.

With a quick glance at the house, Charley spurred Dancer to a gallop. Not until they reached the point where the headland road met the cliff path and the main road to Lostwithiel did she slow to let Teddy catch up.

"That was wonderful," she said when he drew alongside. "What a glorious day!"

"It is, that," he agreed, looking at the clear sky. The air was crisp and a light breeze stirred the trees and the long grass that flanked the roadway.

She followed the main road only until it began to curve east toward Duloe, then left it to ride cross-country, intending to meet it again before Lostwithiel. They passed a wash tin mine, finished and filled up, and several tenants' cottages, before she heard a shout from behind and, turning in her saddle, saw Letty galloping toward them with Jeb in pursuit. Waiting for the child to catch up, Charley felt a twinge of conscience.

She did not doubt that Letty had left without permission, and she could not doubt, either, that the child had simply followed her example. Remembering her suggestion that Letty and Jeremiah feed the ducks in the horse pond, she wondered why she had not seen the child in the stable yard.

"Why didn't you tell me?" Letty shouted when she was within earshot. She was nearly breathless, but when she had closed the gap, she managed to add, "Jeremiah began throwing pebbles at the ducks, instead of toast crumbs, so I took him back inside. When I returned to the yard, they said you had gone. Why didn't you send for me?"

A reasonable question, Charley thought. She smiled ruefully but said only, "Ride a little ahead with me, Letty darling." To the grooms, she said, "Keep a sharp lookout, both of you. Are you armed, Jeb?"

"I am," he said dourly.

She nodded and urged Dancer to a canter. When she and Letty had put enough distance between themselves and the grooms to be certain she would not be overheard, Charley slowed Dancer again. Aware that Letty had been watching her with open curiosity, she said bluntly, "You had better know straightaway that after you left us I quarreled with Sir Antony."

"I was afraid you might."

"You were, were you?"

Letty nodded. "I have observed that you do not like being told what to do. Sir Antony has not given you orders before, so when he did, I expected ructions. I daresay he did, too, so he must have strongly opposed our riding to Lostwithiel."

"If you knew that, why did you follow me?"

Letty shrugged. "I knew you would not mind, and I want to see Jenifry again."

The twinge of conscience this time was stronger than before. A vision of Letty's papa leapt unbidden to Charley's mind, and she found herself giving thanks that the Channel and a good bit of France lay between her and Gideon Deverill. The thought of having to face him as well as Sir Antony sent an icy shiver up her spine. Feeling that she ought to say something stern to the child, she found herself at a loss. Letty knew perfectly well that Sir Antony had forbidden them to go, but to scold the child for doing what she had done herself would be an act of hypocrisy, if not downright lunacy.

In a less than confident tone, she said, "I feel obliged to keep my word to Wenna and Cubert, Letty, but I daresay I should compel you to obey Sir Antony's orders."

"He did not give *me* any orders," Letty said cheerfully.

The words did nothing to ease Charley's conscience, but she did not feel up to arguing. Determined to see Jenifry, she ignored the uncomfortable sensation of prickling guilt, and fixed her thoughts on the task ahead.

In the end, their journey was wasted. Angelique was not in the shop, and when Charley informed Bess Griffin that she wanted to speak with Jenifry, Bess said nervously, "That ain't allowed, miss. Not if it was ever so."

"I am Lady Foxearth now," Charley said, drawing herself up in a fair imitation of Lady Ophelia. She could see that her attitude intimidated the girl, but otherwise it availed her little.

Bess twisted her apron. "I dassn't, my lady!"

"Nonsense, fetch her at once."

Looking frightened, Bess said, "Wait here." She went behind the curtain to the back of the shop, and a moment later, the curtains parted to reveal Michael Peryllys.

Angelique's husband was a burly man who lacked his wife's

more polished manner. He said bluntly, "I'm afraid our girls don't receive visitors, Miss Charlotte."

"I am Lady Foxearth now, Mr. Peryllys, and I am hardly a common visitor."

He shrugged. "I don't set aside good rules, even for the likes of you."

"Have a care," she warned. "I'd advise you not to be insolent to me."

"Would ye now?" He looked her up and down in a way that was more than insolent. "I'd advise you, miss or my lady, to take yourself away out of this shop. You've no call to enter it, without you've come to bespeak a new gown."

"I am amazed if you think you can treat Angelique's customers this way," Charley said, feeling her temper rise. "I must bring her more business than most, too. She won't like it if I take my custom elsewhere."

"Well, you won't be doing that," he said confidently. "My Angelique's the best seamstress there be hereabouts. You'll go elsewhere only if you want second best. Now, if you've no business here today, I've work to do."

"The worst of it," Charley said grimly to Letty as they rode away, "is that the odious man is right. Few seamstresses in Cornwall can match Angelique for skill, and I don't know of a single one even half so close to home."

"What will we do about Jenifry?"

"I don't know, but I'll think of something."

Nothing helpful had occurred to her, however, when they saw a rider coming toward them half an hour later.

"It's Sir Antony," Letty said, shooting her a scared look. "Will he be very angry, do you think?"

"I don't know," Charley said honestly. A man who could quote Shakespeare with oatmeal dripping from his nose and chin was not exactly terrifying. But neither was he predictable, and she was well aware that she had crossed the line of what most men would tolerate. She found herself peering toward the oncoming rider, hoping that for once she would be able to gauge his temperament by his expression.

As usual, she might as well have spared the effort. Although he never looked foppish on horseback, since he rode as if he had been born in the saddle, his attire was as fashionable as could be, and he affected the haughty bearing he generally assumed as Sir Antony Foxearth.

He greeted them, saying, "I trust your journey was successful, my dears."

"We did not see Jenifry, sir," Letty replied, watching him warily.

Noting the look, Charley said at once, "As you see, sir, I brought Letty with me, but both Teddy and Jeb are well armed, so only an army or a fool would have dared to accost us. Happily, no one did."

"No one but Michael Peryllys," Letty said with a grimace.

"What?" There was nothing foppish about the exclamation or the grim way he looked at Charley, and she suddenly felt very nervous. He seemed to look right through her, and his expression made her squirm.

Hastily, she said, "It was nothing, sir. The man did us no harm. He was a trifle insolent, that's all, and he refused to let us see Jenifry. I daresay he was within his rights to do that."

"No doubt." The fearsome look faded as if it had not existed. Nevertheless Charley found herself glancing at him frequently, as if she were affected by a nervous tic. He seemed quite relaxed, and although they talked little as they rode on, he was perfectly civil and amiable. Even so, she had a feeling that he was acting a role.

When they rode into the stable yard and dismounted, the grooms took charge of the horses. Charley walked in silence with Letty and Sir Antony to the house, and inside the front hall, he said to the child, "Run up and change for dinner. I happen to know Mrs. Corlan is serving roast lamb tonight. It won't do to let it cook too long."

Flashing him a relieved smile, Letty said, "I'll hurry."

Hastily, Charley said, "I'd better hurry, too."

"One moment," he said, catching her arm in a firm grip. "I have a few things to say to you."

He seemed suddenly larger than life and frightening. She knew perfectly well that her prickling guilt added significantly to the illusion, but the man facing her now was neither the carefree Jean Matois nor the haughty Sir Antony Foxearth. This man made her wish she had never defied him.

Her moment of weakness was brief, however. She collected herself enough to say, "Do you mean to scold me here, or may we go into a more private room first?"

An appreciative gleam lit his eyes, but he retained his grip on her arm when he said, "The library will do." Urging her toward that room, which lay at the rear of the hall, he waited only until he had shut the door before adding grimly, "If you ever throw anything at me again, madam, I will make you sorry you were born."

She bit her lip but did not flinch. "I own, I amazed myself," she said. "I could not tell at the time if I'd infuriated you, because you just sat there, reciting that absurd nonsense of Shakespeare's, but I'm certainly not surprised that you were angry."

He released her arm, but the look in his eyes was still stern. "Be more respectful of the Bard. You'll learn that I quote him only when I am irritated or angry."

She stared. "Truly? But why only then?"

He shrugged. "I've frequently found it unwise, even dangerous, to reveal my emotions. As a child, I'm afraid I tended to have a rather violent temper. I daresay my father—who disapproved of violence or tantrums from anyone but himself—was as much to blame for my seeking other outlets as anyone. I discovered in school that quoting Shakespeare focused my mind elsewhere than on my anger, at least for a time. My chums soon came to recognize the signs and gave me wide berth when I began to quote the Bard. Over time, I've added much to my arsenal. Though the lines this morning were comic ones, you may rest assured that I was not amused."

She smiled ruefully. "Well, I'm sorry I dumped oatmeal all over you, but it's dangerous to make me angry, too." Turning away, she added lightly, "Besides, if all I've got to fear as reprisal is hearing a lot of silly Shakespeare spouted at me—"

"Don't count on that." He caught her shoulders this time

and, turning her back, waited until she looked into his eyes before he said, "Use your head, angel. Think what more you risk if you infuriate me."

"What would you do?" She no longer felt the least like smiling. To her annoyance, her voice sounded small, but his grip on her arms made her more aware than ever of his superior strength and size. She was glad she had got the words out at all.

"I am your husband," he said, "with a legal right to force your obedience to my will. Think what a pickle you'd be in if I decided to do that."

A vision of her Uncle Geoffrey filled her mind. She knew only too well what husbands could get away with under the law. "But what, exactly, would you do?"

"Whatever I please," he said.

Grimacing, she said, "I doubt that you would beat me. It is not in your nature to hurt someone smaller than yourself."

"You know nothing about my nature," he said, "but there are less violent ways to punish you, I think. Like this, for example." Slipping an arm around her shoulders, he tilted her face up with the other hand and kissed her, hard.

Stunned, she made no effort to resist. Never had a man dared take such liberty with her, but she felt her lips soften against his before she stiffened in outrage.

He raised his head and held her away. Instantly, her hand flew up to strike him.

"Don't," he warned, stopping her with the single word. "You don't know what the consequences will be."

"We have a bargain!"

"Make no mistake, angel," he said, his grim tone sending shivers up her spine again. "I'll do what I must to secure Wellington's safety, and yours. If that means putting you across my knee and giving you what I think your father or grandfather should have given you years ago, I will. If it means giving orders in this household that you find humiliating, I'll do that, too. And before you decide that running back to Alfred or revealing the whole sorry prank to the bishop looks better than staying here and keeping your part of that bargain, let me point out one fact you've overlooked."

"What fact?" She could scarcely get the words out. No one had spoken to her in such a way in all her life, and between fury that he would dare and fear that he meant every word, her tongue seemed suddenly to have tied itself in knots.

"Just this," he said, grasping her chin again and forcing her to meet his stern gaze. "If you run away before you have secured an independent future for yourself, and if my claim to the St. Merryn estates should prevail, it won't be Cousin Alfred upon whom you depend for your bed and board. It will be Cousin Antony."

Chapter Fourteen

Though Charley tried to pretend that Antony's words and behavior had not shaken her, they had, and for the next few days, she scarcely drew a breath without thinking of him. To her dismay, however, it was not his anger that disturbed her. Nor was it his suggestion that she could be dependent on him whether they stayed married or not. It was his kiss.

All she had to do to bring the moment back to life was catch his eye or think of him. Instantly it was as if his lips possessed hers again. Lying in bed at night, she surrendered to her thoughts, wondering what it would be like if he claimed more than just a kiss. These thoughts and others of their ilk entered her mind at the oddest times, disturbing not only her mind but her body as well. Sensations that she had never before experienced threatened now to overwhelm her.

Sir Antony said nothing more about the oatmeal incident, but she almost wished he would. She had not realized how much living with a man day after day would affect her. It occurred to her that being in the same house with Rockland— a situation that had transpired not only at Tuscombe Park but at numerous house parties, and even once at her Aunt Susan's house in Scotland—had never similarly affected her. Firmly, she discounted any similarity of circumstance on the grounds that she had known Rockland for years and was on unusually easy terms with him.

She had certainly never paid much heed to Rockland's moods—or, indeed, to anyone else's, not being moody herself—but she noticed the slightest variation in Sir Antony's demeanor. She told herself it was because he rarely allowed anyone to discern his thoughts, that to do so had become a challenge. But it was more than that. When he was restless or seemed troubled, she exerted herself to soothe him. And although he did not talk to her about what he learned on his frequent sorties, she began to believe she could tell the difference between productive ones and others that were uneventful.

She paid heed to his likes and dislikes, taking care to inform Aggie when a dish particularly pleased him, and when one had not. Despite her attention to him, she did not neglect Letty's needs or her own. She took the little girl riding every day, and with two armed grooms accompanying them, she gave the child lessons in how to train her horses. Soon Letty could make her chestnut mare kneel so that she could mount without aid of a block or a groom, and she had taught it to come when she called.

As Aggie had predicted, ladies in the district began to pay dutiful bride visits once they learned of Charley's marriage and the couple's removal to Seacourt House. Charley realized that some visited out of vulgar curiosity, but most were sincerely delighted for her. In all cases, she kept Sir Antony's mission firmly in mind. Thus, she was able to send her visitors on their way again, confident that they did not suspect that her marriage was unusual or that she had been tactfully prodding them to reveal what they knew about any unusual events, or strangers, in the district.

She and Sir Antony had been settled at Seacourt for ten days before anyone from Tuscombe Park came to call. To Charley's surprise, the first one to do so was Rockland. What was even more surprising was that he brought Elizabeth with him.

When they arrived, Charley was sitting in the drawing room, reading aloud to Letty while the child stitched a sampler for her mama. Jeremiah perched on the back of Letty's chair, supervising every stitch and occasionally offering his version of criticism. Sebastian lay curled on the hearth rug, dozing before the fire.

"Good mercy," Charley exclaimed, rising when the footman announced the visitors. "I thought you must have left Cornwall at least a sennight ago, Rockland."

He bowed over her hand, saying with his familiar crooked grin, "No such luck, my pet. Put out with me though she was, Lady Ophelia begged me to stay, saying she wanted someone sensible to converse with at Alfred's otherwise boring dinner table. It ain't boring to me, I can tell you. You should hear her rake him down when he prattles as he does about the so-called weaker sex."

"I can imagine."

"Yes, but I must tell you, our Alfred's in alt now, because he got a response from Wellington's people at last, and the Duke will take supper with the family the evening after the consecration." He grinned. "Even if Lady Ophelia had not asked me, I daresay I'd have found an excuse to linger, at least until then. That sort of event don't take place every day, you know. It's to be a dashed grand affair."

"Fiddlesticks," Charley said, laughing. "You don't care a particle about the consecration or even Wellington, Rockland. Confess the truth now. You stayed for the same reason you came here today, because you wanted to know if we had murdered each other yet, or worse, if we had concocted a plot to murder you."

Letty chuckled, but Elizabeth exclaimed, "Oh, no!"

Rockland said severely, "Don't be talking foolishness, Charley. You'll frighten the liver and lights out of poor Miss Elizabeth, and all she wants today is to wish you happy in your marriage, since you've decided to stick with Foxearth."

Charley smiled ruefully at Elizabeth and said, "Forgive me if I have distressed you by teasing Rockland. I nearly always come to cuffs with him, you know. Still, it was very kind of you to call. Do sit down. You must be pleased about the Duke."

"Yes, we are," Elizabeth murmured, obeying. "Such a pleasant drive."

"If you came by carriage, it was a long drive," Charley said. Turning to the watchful footman, she said, "Please bring tea and whatever Mrs. Corlan has been baking that might tempt our guests, John. The most delicious smells have been tickling our noses all day," she added, smiling at her guests. "Today is Aggie's baking day, and she creates the most delicious treats for us."

Letty had risen politely when their guests arrived, and noting now that the child was still standing, Charley said, "You may stay with us if you like, darling, or you may go to Aggie and let her give you your tea in the kitchen."

With a flashing smile, Letty said, "I'll go along then. It is a pleasure to see you again, Cousin Elizabeth. You, too, sir. Come along, Jeremiah," she added, picking up the monkey and taking him from the room.

Charley turned her attention back to Rockland, aware that he had been watching her quizzically. "What is it?" she demanded.

He grinned, drawing a chair up between hers and Elizabeth's. "Heard there had been ructions in Paradise," he murmured. "Came to see for myself how bad they are."

"I'm sure I don't know what you are talking about."

"Don't you? Myself, I'd remember dumping a bowl of oatmeal over Foxearth's head. Daresay I'd remember the aftermath even more clearly, come to that. Dashed if I'd have had the nerve to do it in the first place, though. He looks as if he would strip to advantage. Daresay you'll call me a coward, but—"

"Where on earth," Charley demanded, "did you come by that tale? No, don't tell me. The new servants, of course. Several are related to Tuscombe servants. If I put my mind to it, I can probably even tell you who the culprit was."

"So it's true," Rockland said, his amusement clear. "And what, may I ask, was your husband's response to that little display of temper?"

"Goodness, Rockland, didn't your informant tell you that, as well?"

"Told me bilge water. Said Foxearth mopped his brow, then finished his breakfast and his newspaper, whilst you rode off to Lostwithiel as if nothing untoward had occurred. I'll go bail there was more to it than that."

"Will you?" Charley remembered the aftermath again all too clearly, and she hoped her memories did not reveal themselves in her expression. "I'm afraid you will simply have to live with your curiosity, Rockland, for I don't intend to tell you any more. You already know far more than you've a right to."

"You must not tell him anything you do not wish him to know," Elizabeth said gently but with a smile for Rockland. "As I told his lordship during our very pleasant drive here, certain matters should remain private between a husband and wife."

"That's all very well and good," Rockland said, still grinning at Charley, "but I'll wager anything you like that Foxearth didn't take such Turkish treatment with a smile. It was seeing the way he managed her that made me work to convince—"

"Beg pardon, my lady," the footman said as Rockland broke off suddenly. "Mr. James Gabriel wishes to know if you are at home."

"Yes, certainly," Charley said, casting Rockland a searching look. "Show Mr. Gabriel in at once."

Rockland seemed suddenly interested in straightening the black silk ribbon attached to his quizzing glass, and since he rarely employed the glass for its intended purpose, she found his preoccupation highly suspicious and wondered what it was he had so nearly said.

Elizabeth said, "What a pleasant room this is, Charlotte. I do believe, the way this house is positioned, you must enjoy a view of the sea from nearly every window."

"I'm afraid some of them overlook the stable yard, and the hedge garden and headland behind the house," Charley said, amused. "Moreover, as I have frequently said to Sir Antony— who becomes more enamored of the place with each passing day, I might add—one ought not to make up one's mind about Seacourt House until one has experienced bad weather here."

"Mr. Gabriel, my lady," the footman said.

She stood to greet him. "How do you do, Mr. Gabriel? What brings you to us today? You know Miss Tarrant and Lord Rockland, of course."

"I do, indeed," Gabriel said. "I must say, Lady Foxearth, I was most astonished to be greeted by a heathenish, chattering monkey in your entrance hall."

"Oh, dear," Charley said. "I thought Letty was taking him to the kitchen."

"So she said, ma'am. Said she only paused on her way to bid me a good day and that 'twas my great size that set the strange little creature to chattering. Lady Letitia assures me he is quite tame, but he did not take to me at all, nor I to him I must say. Fact is, I ain't accustomed to finding wild beasts in any man's home, let alone that of a gentleman, but I daresay I shall laugh about it all later."

"That is kind of you, Mr. Gabriel. Won't you sit down?"

"Thank you, ma'am," he said, waiting until she had done so before obeying. He glanced at Elizabeth, then back at Charley, saying, "To come right to the point, I want to wish you happy in your marriage, and to tell you I heeded Lord Rockland's advice and spoke with Bishop Halsey about your unlocking the Seraphim Coffer. He approved the notion, I am pleased to say. Gave it as his opinion that since it takes place outside the altar rail, there can be no objection. I do not approve of women involving themselves in sacred matters, but I will bow to higher authority."

"I am sorry you disapprove, of course, but I shall be delighted to have a part in such a ceremony," Charley said. "What, exactly, must I do?"

Obviously pleased to be asked, he said, "The coffer will be in place at the altar rail, for I shall send it to Truro under guard on Wednesday. You will stand to one side of it, ma'am. After the bishop's procession enters the cathedral, he will perform a ritual or two. Then the Duke will address the congregation, whereupon you unlock and open the coffer, then stand back whilst he presents the sacred vessels. The actual consecration will follow, for the vessels must be consecrated, too, before their use."

"Well, I can do that, easily enough. Will you take refreshment, Mr. Gabriel?"

"Why, thank you." He had been casting glances at Elizabeth from the moment he entered the room. Now, drawing his chair nearer to hers, he said, "May I say that it is most pleasant to see you again, Miss Elizabeth."

With wicked amusement, Charley discerned Rockland's startled displeasure. "Mr. Gabriel," she said sweetly, "I must tell you that Miss Tarrant has expressed admiration for the drawing-room clock your father made for Tuscombe Park House."

"Have you, indeed, Miss Tarrant? A splendid timepiece. My father was born of humble stock, but raised himself by means of his skill. I am proud to be his son."

"Do you also make clocks, sir?" Elizabeth asked.

Aware that Rockland's annoyance was increasing, Charley feigned deep interest in Gabriel's reply.

He said, "I can fix most anything that goes wrong with a timepiece, for I learned from a master, Miss Elizabeth, but I lack his creative genius. Thus, I became mayor of Lostwithiel instead. I fancy I've made a rather good job of that, if I do say so myself."

Struck by a thought, Charley said, "Perhaps you might be able to assist me with a small problem I've come across, Mr. Gabriel."

"If I can, my lady. A civic problem?"

"It is more in the nature of an irritation," she said. "The daughter of a St. Merryn tenant is apprenticed at Angelique's shop in Lostwithiel High Street. No one seems to have seen the child for some time, and when I tried to do so, Michael Peryllys refused to allow it. I am doubtless overly concerned, but I will feel better when I can tell her parents I have seen for myself that she is healthy and happy. Perhaps you can advise me as to the best course I should take."

"Nothing easier," he replied. "I've a personal interest in that place, as you might say, and I don't mind telling you I'd like a look at it myself. Moreover, though I may be talking out of school, I've cause to believe Michael Peryllys may be hand in glove with a certain coastal gang that has been causing a deal of trouble on our shore. 'Tis a pernicious business and must be stopped. So when next you visit Lostwithiel, just you come right to me. I'll roust out the constable and some stout men to escort you to Angelique's. You'll have no trouble then seeing the girl, I promise you."

"Thank you, I shall ride to Lostwithiel tomorrow," Charley said.

"Tomorrow, my dear?" Sir Antony stood on the threshold, surveying his guests through his quizzing glass.

Charley started guiltily, but catching Rockland's amused and speculative look, she recovered swiftly and said, "I am glad you have come in, sir. As you see, here are Miss Tarrant, Rockland, and Mr. Gabriel, all wanting to wish us well in our marriage. At least," she added mischievously, "Elizabeth and Mr. Gabriel have come to do so. I think Rockland expected us to have murdered each other by now. He must be prodigiously disappointed to see us both quite alive and well."

"Not disappointed a whit," Rockland said, rising to shake hands with Sir Antony. "I came to see if you had tamed the lioness yet."

"And what lioness is that?" Sir Antony inquired, his demeanor as aloof as ever.

Rockland chuckled. "All right then, have it your way, but I've known her longer than you have, and by Jove, I'm well acquainted with the sharp claws and mighty roar she can produce when she's displeased."

Sir Antony raised his eyebrows. "Dear me, do you refer to Charlotte? But that cannot be, sir, for I have found Charlotte's voice 'ever soft, gentle, and low, an excellent thing in a woman.'" Leaving Rockland gaping (and Charley, too), he turned with aplomb to Elizabeth, whom he greeted with a bow and a polite comment. Then, to Gabriel, he said, "Well met, sir. It is kind of you to wish to pay your respects."

Gabriel said, " 'Twas more than that, sir. I came to inform Lady Foxearth that his eminence, the bishop, has approved her part in the consecration ceremony."

"I believe I also heard you encourage her to visit Lostwithiel tomorrow," Sir Antony murmured, employing his quizzing glass to good effect again. "I am afraid—"

Before he could finish, Charley cut in swiftly, saying, "Mr. Gabriel offered to lend me an escort, sir, including a constable, to compel Angelique and Michael Peryllys to let me see Jenifry. Is that not kind of him?"

Antony looked directly at her, but she met his gaze easily. She did not believe he would forbid an excursion to Lostwithiel when such a ban must sound unreasonable to the others, nor did he. Smiling, he said, "I wish I were free to accompany you, my dear, but I've business in St. Austell tomorrow. Still, I have every confidence in Gabriel," he added sweetly. "He will see that you come to no harm."

Gabriel beamed, but Charley gritted her teeth, not liking the implication that she was unable to look after herself. She hid her feelings, however. Not only did she not want to give Rockland the satisfaction of knowing Sir Antony had irritated her, but she feared Sir Antony might still forbid her to go if she gave him the least cause to do so.

The footman and a maid brought in refreshments, and the conversation became desultory. Charley enjoyed watching James Gabriel flirt with Elizabeth. The man was clearly besotted, but for the life of her, she could not imagine what the attraction was. Elizabeth was her usual quiet self, listening carefully when Gabriel or any of the three men spoke, saying nothing more interesting herself than, "Oh, indeed?" or "How very interesting that is, to be sure."

Charley took little part in the conversation. She had no desire to discuss the weather or the changing colors of the sea, or the habit the gulls had developed of flying near carriages in hopes that someone would toss them a morsel of food. When Gabriel mentioned the coastal gang again, however, she did perk up her ears. She glanced at Sir Antony, but that gentleman said only, "No doubt they have their own reasons. I believe there is much poverty in this area, which may account for a considerable amount of villainy when all is said and done."

"Nonetheless, sir, these pestiferous thieves must be stopped.

I've spoken with Francis Oakes, the Lloyd's of London chap in St. Austell. He agrees with me, but declines to call in the army, even though we both sense that the gang's got plans for something afoot in the near future, so I hope he may alter his decision before long. In any event, I mean to put the matter to Wellington when he arrives. As Prime Minister, he owes it to the people of Cornwall to send at least a division of cavalry to support the local customs agents and revenuers. The Methodists, at this point, are our strongest allies, and they, I need hardly say, are a quite insufficient force against armed villains."

"Oh, Mr. Gabriel," Elizabeth said, wide-eyed, "would you really dare to speak so to our national hero? What will he do, do you think?"

"I must do my duty, Miss Tarrant, and I shall hope and trust he does his."

"That's a false hope if you want the army," Charley said. "Why, if you have been reading the papers, Mr. Gabriel, you must know that the Duke believes the army to be the poorest choice we can have when it comes to peacekeeping. Our military men are trained for violence, not peacekeeping. He strongly supports Mr. Peel's Police Act, which eventually will mean civilian constabulary all over England."

"That," Gabriel said, "might do very well for the city of London, my lady, but it won't do for Cornwall. And as it's planned, I believe it will be only the city of London as will be affected by yon foolish Police Act."

"He's got you there," Rockland said, grinning. "It's called the Metropolitan Police Act, after all."

Before Charley could reply, Elizabeth said, "Charlotte, I am persuaded that Mr. Gabriel must know much more about such matters than you do. You would do well to listen carefully to what he says."

"First of all," Charley said testily, "the *City* of London is in full agreement with Mr. Gabriel. That ancient square mile wants to police itself as it has always done, and its citizens remain fervently opposed to the Police Act, which is why Mr. Peel agreed when he recommitted his bill that they shall not be affected by it. That was very astute of him, too, because the

City represented his primary opposition, and without it, the bill passed in the Commons. Wellington has already introduced it in the upper house.''

''Surely you are mistaken,'' Elizabeth murmured uncomfortably. ''The city of London is much bigger than one square mile, and if Mr. Gabriel says London—''

''My dear Elizabeth, I think it is you who does not understand. Let me explain that the *City* of London comprises only one square mile, the ancient Roman part, of *metropolitan* London, which is much, much larger. Thus, the City of London and the metropolitan aspect of Mr. Peel's bill have little to do with each other. The plan, of course, is eventually to provide a civilian police force for every metropolitan area in England—and Wales and Scotland, too, I daresay, in the end.''

Gabriel said with masculine condescension, ''Even so, my lady, that just goes to prove that Mr. Peel's law has naught to do with us here in Cornwall today.''

''But it does!'' She glanced at Sir Antony but saw that he had no intention of entering the argument. ''Mr. Gabriel, you must see that once the Police Act passes, it will affect all of England, for what serves London will serve us all in the end. We will have civilian police throughout the country, and not just our village constables—who try to keep peace but are unable to do more than raise a hue and cry for a thief or a murderer—but officers with authority to act, to go right out and catch the criminals.''

''We have thief takers to attend to that distasteful task now,'' Rockland said.

''Don't you see how wrong it is to pay someone to recover lost goods? That leads to dreadful fraud and corruption. Only think of the scandals we have had in the past fifteen years. Think back to the last time a so-called thief taker was brought to book for organizing his own gang to steal things and then collecting money from the victim to return the goods. Police should be paid a fair salary to act for everyone.''

''The army could do the same thing,'' Gabriel said, ''and we already pay them.''

Elizabeth said, "How very clever you are to think of that, Mr. Gabriel. I am certain that your arguments must prevail with the Duke of Wellington."

"Well, they won't," Charley said flatly. "You cannot know much about him if you think that, and in view of the fact that he is taking great pains not—"

"That will do, Charlotte," Sir Antony said. He spoke calmly, but there was a note in his voice that stopped her cold. Realizing that she had nearly said Wellington was taking pains not to call in the military, she looked ruefully at him and said, "I beg your pardon, sir. You are quite right. I allowed my zeal to overcome my good sense."

"Your good manners, more like," Rockland exclaimed. "By Jove, you're a Trojan, Foxearth. I never thought I'd live to see this day."

Charley grimaced. "Pray, sir, what day is that?"

"The day, my precious, when you would submit to a stronger will than your own. What a pleasure it is to see it!"

"Is it?" Charley said dangerously.

"Really, my lord," Elizabeth said, "you ought not—"

"Don't deny me this little triumph," Rockland said. "I've waited far too long to see it. Your cousin is one of my favorite people, to be sure, but I don't deny I've found her frequently hot of hand." He turned, still grinning, to Sir Antony and said, "By Jove, sir, you could have knocked me over with a feather when you said you'd take her off my hands. Why, when I first broached— Oh, just so." Breaking off, he looked flustered, glanced at Charley with color flooding his cheeks. Then he looked guiltily back at Sir Antony. That gentleman was watching Charley.

Her gaze swept from one to the other, and as the full import of Rockland's words struck her, she rose to her feet, looked straight at him, and said, "Just what are you saying, Rockland? What did you broach to him, sir? By heaven, if you mean what I think you mean—"

"Be silent, Charlotte." All three men had risen when she did, but Antony's tone was not angry, only warning.

Rockland looked more uncomfortable than ever. Gabriel

glanced curiously from one player to another. Elizabeth remained placidly in her seat.

Charley turned, intending to speak reasonably to Sir Antony, to explain that she had every right to know what Rockland had nearly said. However, one look at his stern expression, instead of steadying her, swept away what little control she had left. Before she knew it was happening, her temper ignited. "How dare you command me to be silent," she cried. "I won't be ordered about by you or by anyone else for the amusement of others. It is my life you have arranged between you, and by heaven, I have every right to know how it was done and by whom. By God, sir, I will—"

"You won't," Sir Antony said. His icy, implacable tone cut right through her diatribe and silenced her. For the few moments before he spoke, she had forgotten Elizabeth's presence, and Gabriel's. She remembered them now, flicking a glance at each before meeting her husband's relentless gaze again. He said in that same chilling tone, "We will excuse you, Charlotte. Our guests can see that you are unwell."

"Oh, yes," Elizabeth murmured with obvious concern. "Perhaps you would like me to go upstairs with you, Cousin Charlotte. I am rarely vaporish myself, but—"

"That won't be necessary," Sir Antony said, "though you are kind to offer."

Charley seethed. She had overstepped the bounds, she knew. But, believing herself to have been strongly provoked, she stood her ground, glaring at Sir Antony.

"Perhaps," he said gently, "you would like me to take you up, my dear."

Her determination collapsed in an instant, and she fled, certain that she heard Rockland chuckle before she slammed the door behind her. She went no farther than the stair landing, where she paced impatiently, wishing the others would hurry up and leave.

* * *

In the drawing room, Rockland's amusement had overcome him. "By Jove, I'd have paid good money to see that. What a shrew!"

"You are speaking of my wife, sir," Antony said evenly.

Rockland sobered at once. "I beg your pardon, I'm sure. It's just that seeing you squash her tantrum so easily when she was practically hurling lightning bolts—"

"I saw no lightning bolts," Antony said. "I heard a lady express her displeasure, as any lady has the right to do. If you heard aught else, my dear Rockland, I suggest that you inform *me* of it before you inform anyone else, for if I were to hear—"

"You won't," Rockland assured him hastily. "No tantrum, no lightning bolts. It shall be just as you say, Foxearth, and no more. Ain't that right, Gabriel?"

"To be sure," Gabriel said, looking from one man to the other in bewilderment. "I do not pretend to understand much of what happened after Lady Foxearth explained the difference between the City of London and London proper. Fascinating, that was. I do hope she will not be too much indisposed."

"I will gladly extend your felicitations to her," Antony said.

Elizabeth stood then and arranged her skirt, saying matter-of-factly, "It is time we returned to Tuscombe Park, my lord. Mama will grow fretful if we are away too long. Will you walk out with us, Mr. Gabriel?"

"With pleasure, my dear Miss Tarrant," he responded instantly. "How well that carriage dress becomes you, ma'am. I protest, I have never seen a gown of just that shade of gray before."

"Gray is gray," Rockland muttered. "Not that she don't look dashed well in that rig." He glanced uncertainly at Antony. "Do you walk out with us?"

"I think not," Antony said, ringing for the footman to show them out.

"I say," Rockland said awkwardly, pushing a hand through his hair, "I hope you don't think I meant any—"

"I think nothing at all," Antony said blandly. "That is my

greatest virtue, Rockland. I never judge by words, you see, only by actions.''

Rockland looked confused, but he said valiantly, ''I don't envy you the next thirty minutes, Foxearth, and that's the truth plain and simple.''

''Therein lies another difference between us, my dear chap. I look forward to the next thirty minutes very much.''

When they had gone, Antony remained right where he was. He did not think he would have to wait long.

Chapter Fifteen

Charley waited only until the front door had closed before she swept back down to the gallery level, flung open the drawing-room doors, and stormed in. "How dare you send me away like that?" she demanded as one door banged back against the wall.

"It is more ladylike to allow the footman to open doors for you," Sir Antony said. "That also prevents doorknobs from crashing into the wainscoting and making holes in it. Please shut the doors properly now."

She kicked them shut. Then, grabbing the first thing that came to hand, which fortunately for him was a pillow from the nearest sofa, she threw it at him, shouting, "By heaven, Antony, don't trifle with me. Did you or did you not know before that sham wedding that Rockland had arranged for me to marry you instead of himself?"

"I did. Now it is my turn to ask a question. Did I or did I not warn you never to throw things at me again?"

"I didn't *throw* the damned oatmeal. I'll show you throwing." She snatched up a book from a nearby table and hurled it at him.

He did not duck, but the book sailed harmlessly past him.

"Don't swear at me," he said. "I don't like it. I am perfectly willing to discuss this if you can do so in a civil manner." He added in quite a different tone when she picked up a six-inch-high marble figure of Poseidon from the same table, "Don't you dare throw that statue."

She threw it as hard as she could.

Catching it easily, Antony stepped toward her.

Charley leapt hastily back, putting the sofa between them. "Don't come near me," she snapped. "I've every right to know the truth, for you tricked me, the pair of you, and most likely you've been laughing up your sleeves at me ever since."

"I am not laughing now."

Out of sheer bravado she caught up the silver-framed miniature of a bewigged Seacourt ancestor and held it poised to fling.

"Put that down."

With every fiber of her body she wished she had the nerve to throw it, but she did not. She was horrified, in fact, at having thrown anything at him. Not since she was four and had flung a mug of milk at her nurse in a fit of temper had she thrown anything at anyone. Nurse had put away the mug, wiped up the spilled milk, and told her she would get no more that day. She did not know why she had thrown things at Antony. She had a notion that if he had never warned her against such tactics, she would not have employed them. His warning had seemed like a challenge instead.

Setting Poseidon on a table, he said, "Put down that picture and come here."

"No." The last thing she wanted was to step within his reach. Remembering his earlier warning and the threat that accompanied it, she felt her sphincter muscle contract. She wondered if Antony ever made idle threats. She suspected that he did not.

"Put it down. Now."

She obeyed this time, watching him warily, paying no heed when the miniature tumbled over onto its face.

"Now you may come here to me."

"I don't want to."

"Nevertheless, you will."

She swallowed hard but remained where she was. "You and Rockland had no right to trick me."

"No, we didn't. It was a scurrilous thing to do. Now, come here."

"You admit it?"

"Of course, I admit it. It's plain fact."

"Then why did you agree to do it?"

"At the time, because it seemed expedient."

"Expedient! You and Rockland cooked this scheme up between you out of expediency?" She was shaking now.

He said calmly, "We did not cook it up together, as you so inelegantly phrase it. He had the notion before he went to Truro, but I didn't know what he'd done till he returned. He told me he believes the notion was reinforced when we met that day, because you took him to task over something and I persuaded you to desist."

"Are you saying he decided to marry me off to you right then because he thought you could . . . could *tame* me?"

"Not at that moment, no. He said the impulse actually to do so came later."

"He acted out of *impulse?*"

"As you did yourself," he reminded her. "Or do you mean to pretend your decision to marry him was not impulsive?"

"Go on," she said through gritted teeth.

"By the time Rockland explained all this to me, mind you, he had convinced himself that his actions were downright noble. He said you were making a big mistake to marry him but that he could not cry off because a gentleman cannot ever do so."

"It is more gentlemanly, I suppose, to trick a lady into marrying someone else."

"I didn't say I agreed with him. I'm merely telling you what he said."

"But, surely, he never said that to the bishop!"

"As a matter of fact, he said the bishop showed him the way."

"What?"

Sir Antony's lips twitched but he said only, "You may recall that Rockland mentioned difficulties that arise when a person from outside the parish attempts to acquire a special license. Apparently, Halsey demanded references from Rockland's home parish before he would issue one. Rockland said it was then that he realized he had not actually said he was speaking for himself.''

"Good mercy, the man is deranged."

"He would tell you it was not lunacy but Providence. He swore the only reason he told Halsey he was acting for me was that he feared arousing your temper again if he delayed the wedding. He said you were interested only in marrying quickly, that you did not care a whit who the bridegroom was. In truth, angel, you said the same to me."

"I did not want to marry you, however, and you are no more a member of the parish than Rockland is."

"Ah, but in my case, that's debatable, you see, because if I should prove my claim to the earldom I'll be very much a member. Moreover, Rockland told Halsey that our marriage was being arranged primarily to protect your future. At that point, he said, Halsey apologized for the 'misunderstanding' and offered no further objection."

"And you simply agreed to go along?" Charley's voice sounded shrill.

"Not at once," he replied calmly. "Rockland next pointed out that you would have two chances to put an end to the scheme. You could scotch it at once if you happened to know that marriage by proxy is illegal in England."

"But I didn't."

"Well, I thought there was a good chance that you *would* know. You are very well read, after all. When you didn't, I pressed him to end the charade, but he said it had been a sign, and that you could still end it the minute you heard Halsey say the wrong name. He insisted that if you didn't know the name was wrong, it would only prove you didn't know him well enough to be marrying him. That's when I decided to go along. I agreed, you see, that in marrying him you were making a grave mistake."

"You should have put an end to the whole thing at the outset."

"Perhaps, but whole tale would have come out if I had. I realized that much when you didn't tumble to the name. I honestly thought he had been wrong about that, but when you did not stop the ceremony, I knew I could not do so either. Not in front of Alfred and Edythe, or the bishop. I thought we could resolve it more quietly afterward. In fact, at one point, I thought you kept silent for that same reason. It was not until Rockland made his announcement that I knew you truly had been fooled."

Bitterly she said, "I assumed that he had fooled you, too."

"I know that now, but by then it had occurred to me that marriage to you would relieve some of my more pressing problems. In my determination to convince you not to demand an instant annulment, I overlooked the fact that you had not accused me of being a party to the plot."

"But I took Rockland to task for tricking you as well as me!"

He shook his head. "You accused him of having dragged me into it. He had done just that, so I assumed then that you knew I was in on the scheme. By the time I realized you didn't know, I had my hands full trying to figure out a way out that would not create the devil of a scandal for all of us."

"It never occurred to me that you could be part of such a thing. As for Rockland—"

"He wanted to pay you out for the way you had been treating him," Antony reminded her. "You had not been very kind to him, you know."

"I know." She had treated Rockland shamefully, but the temptation to do so had been overwhelming at times. He never stood up for himself. It was as if she had wanted to find out just how far she could push him. Well, she thought, she had certainly found out. She wondered if she had been doing the same thing with Antony. That thought sent another shiver up her spine. Antony was not Rockland.

"Now will you come here?" His tone was patient, but she knew his patience was limited.

She shifted from foot to foot. "What will you do if I obey you?"

"I'm making no more bargains, angel. You will do as I bid. Come here."

With a sense of walking to her doom, she moved around the sofa, coming to a halt some four or five feet away from him.

"Not good enough," Antony said.

She gritted her teeth, wishing she were a man. That thought, coming unbidden as it had, nearly made her smile. She did not want to be a man. She liked being a woman, and at the moment, she did not want to be anything else. Beneath her concern about what he might do lay a teeming mass of unfamiliar emotions and sensations. The way he looked at her made her skin tingle. Nerves she had not known she possessed seemed to sizzle just under her skin. Something else deep within her burned like the molten core of a volcano. It was a wonder, she thought, that he did not see the heat rising from her. She was no longer angry with him, but the emotions that threatened to overwhelm her now were easily as hot and as dangerous as her temper.

She nibbled her lower lip, and as she did, she saw the look in his eyes change. He nearly stepped toward her. She was sure of it. But it was not punishment he had on his mind now. Visibly, he tried to collect himself.

"I'm waiting," he said. His voice sounded rougher and came from deep in his throat. Letting her gaze drift lower, she saw his arousal.

Unafraid now, she moved to stand before him. "Here I am," she murmured. "What will you do to me?"

He cleared his throat, and she thought that she had disconcerted him, but then he put both hands on her shoulders and said, "You behaved very badly."

"I know," she said with a sigh. "Of late, my temper just flies away with me, and when I suddenly knew what the pair of you had done . . ." She spread her hands.

"You had cause, but still you must not lose your temper when others are about. You nearly revealed what you know about the assassination plot. In view of Gabriel's desire to bring in the army to deal with the wreckers, you simply must not do that."

"I know. I truly don't know what came over me. First Elizabeth said she was sure Gabriel knew more about the issues than I do, which is nonsense, and then he said what he did about Wellington being sure to take his advice and order in the army. The urge to prove him wrong was utterly overpowering.''

"Poor angel," Antony said, looking into her eyes. "You are learning the pitfalls of secrecy. It is quite human to want to puff off one's knowledge, either to prove one's point, or to win an argument by hurling an absolute clincher at your opponent. Unfortunately, in my line of work, that can be a deadly flaw in one's character."

"How do you avoid it?" she asked, unusually aware of his warm hands on her shoulders, and wondering wickedly how they would feel on other parts of her body.

"I rarely discuss politics, and I try never to commit myself to a fact or point of view. It is too difficult to recall if one learned a detail from a newspaper or from secret sources, or because one was entrusted with a military confidence."

"I rarely think things through before I speak," she said, biting her lip.

"You're blushing," he said softly. "You did no harm today, but you must try harder to act like a conformable wife, or folks will begin to wonder why I don't exercise a husband's authority. You may force me to act in ways you won't like."

The implacable note was back in his voice, but this time it did not chill her. She knew he had good reason to issue his warning. He could not allow her to jeopardize his mission. Wellington's safety must always come first.

She leaned toward him, pressing against the strong hands on her shoulders. "I won't apologize to Rockland, but must I apologize to Elizabeth again, and to Gabriel?"

"I think perhaps you should return Elizabeth's call," he said. "You'll want to see your grandmother and Lady Ophelia in any event. I'll take you there myself, I think. It will do Alfred good to see that I've not abandoned my claim to the estate."

"I'm going to Lostwithiel tomorrow," she said, watching for a reaction.

"So you are," he said equably. He was still looking into her eyes.

She moistened her lips.

"Charlotte, I—" He broke off, and his lips must have been dry, too, for he licked them.

She pressed closer. "Yes, Antony?"

"Damn," he said, and his hands slipped from her shoulders and down her back as he drew her closer and kissed her.

This time, although it began the same way, with the pressure of his lips hard against hers, his movements were more urgent than before. His lips felt hot against hers. She could smell the citrus water he put on his face after Hodson shaved him, and she could smell the soft woolen scent of his coat. His breath was warm against her cheek. Then she became aware of changes taking place in her body as his lips softened and moved more caressingly, tantalizing her to respond.

Feeling her lips yield beneath his, she kissed him back hungrily, enjoying the sensation of his hands on her back, one between her shoulder blades now, the other lower, near her waist. He pulled her tight against him. She felt the warmth of his hands and body through the thin material of her frock, and just as ardently, she felt his arousal and comprehended his urgency.

Having bred horses for years, she understood the male sexual urge very well, and had no reason to think it stirred the human male differently from the way it stirred a stallion. Just as stallions were dangerous when the urge was upon them, so too were men, even gentlemen. For that reason, she had long since learned to keep gentlemen at a proper distance and to dampen their ardor when necessary. Until now, she had not had to contend with a husband, of course. And until now, her passions had not formed any part of the equation, for the simple reason that she had felt none.

With Sir Antony, at that moment, the equation altered drastically. She wanted him to kiss her. More than that, she wanted to feel his hands on her body. She wanted him to catch her up in his arms and carry her off to some fortress, like a knight of old in a Gothic romance. When his hands moved, pulling her even tighter against him, and the lower hand moved lower yet, to the flare of her hip, she pressed her mouth against his, inviting him to continue, to do what he would.

The touch of his tongue on her lips was a shock but not an unpleasant one. Daringly, she touched her tongue to his, smiling as she did. He was watching her, and his eyes gleamed with a mixture of amusement and raw lust. When he raised his head a moment later, she pouted.

He chuckled. "This is a dangerous game we play, angel."

"I know." Hoping he would not stop, she licked her lips invitingly. "You are my husband, sir. People will think it odd if we never touch each other and always keep a polite distance. I should at least become accustomed to your touch, I think."

She could have sworn she heard him groan. He said, "I can see how you drove Rockland to distraction."

"I never said such things to him."

"Perhaps not, but I don't doubt that you enticed him one moment and set him at a distance the next. Nor do I doubt that, like me, he wanted to shake you till your teeth rattled one moment and to make love to you the next."

"Which do you want now?" she asked, looking at him from under her lashes.

In answer, he crushed her against him again and kissed her in such a way that she knew he wanted to possess her. Responding with enthusiasm, she remained certain that she could stop him—and herself—at will.

When he picked her up and carried her to a sofa, sitting with her in his lap, she sighed with pleasure and relaxed against him. Stroking his face with her hand, she delighted in the prickling sensation of his incipient beard against her palm.

He tilted her chin up so he could begin kissing her again, and his fingers tickled her throat as his tongue pressed once more against the opening between her lips.

She parted them willingly, savoring the warmth of him, the tingling shock of invasion. His fingers were warm on her throat, stroking the tender skin there, moving lower to the hollow at its base, then to the topmost ribbon on her bodice. So entranced was she with his tongue's exploration of her mouth that she scarcely heeded what he was doing until he untied the ribbon, then the chemise ribbon beneath it. Deftly, he laid both garments open.

Feeling the kiss of cool air against her breasts, she gasped, but in her mouth his tongue became more demanding, more possessive, until she responded in kind. She felt fire rushing through her wherever he touched her, and through places where no one had touched her in her life. The sensations overwhelmed her, and when he bared her breasts completely, she felt no embarrassment, only increasing passion. The touch of a finger on the tip of her left breast made her arch her back, demanding more.

Abandoning her mouth, Antony bent his lips to her breast, stirring new fires. Charley moaned. One hand drifted to her lap, his fingers gathering the material of her skirt, raising it higher and higher. Slipping beneath the skirt, his hand inched upward, then stopped. He raised his head. Cooler air caressed her wet nipple, making it tingle.

"What the devil have you got on?" he muttered.

"French drawers," she said, realizing what he referred to from his impatient tug on the lacy garment. "I bought them in Paris."

"They're an infernal nuisance, and damnably in the way."

Suddenly, she felt nervous and less confident about what they were doing.

"Antony?"

"What?" he shifted his gaze to see her face.

Passion warred with common sense, and she could think of nothing to say.

He kissed the tip of her nose. "You don't look much like an angel now," he said. "I doubt that they fly about with their breasts so enticingly displayed."

She chuckled. "That's a sacrilegious comment, if not a profane one, sir. If this were Spain you'd have to answer to the Inquisition for such impudence."

"If we were in Spain, you'd have been hanged long ago for witchcraft."

"I'm not a witch!"

"Are you not? You've cast a witch's spell, I think." As he bent his head, his intention clearly to begin again where he had left off, monkey chatter in the hall startled them both. Moving so quickly that her fist caught the point of his chin, Charley snatched the two bits of her gown together, tying the uppermost ribbon faster than she had thought possible, despite being dumped without ceremony onto the sofa seat.

Antony stood, then sat again immediately, taking time only to snatch up the book Charley had heaved at him earlier. He laid it open over his lap.

Charley stifled a giggle as the door opened and Letty came in with Jeremiah perched as usual on her shoulder.

"Hello," she said, looking from one to the other.

"Hello, yourself," Antony said. "Were you looking for one of us?"

She seemed to be examining them, and for an awkward moment, Charley wondered if she could possibly know what they had been doing. She dismissed the thought just before Letty's gaze came to rest upon her breast. The child said, "I am not certain if this is the sort of thing one mentions or not, Cousin Charley, but your chemise ribbon is poking out between two of your bodice laces."

Taking care to avoid Antony's gaze, Charley looked down and said with commendable aplomb, "Good mercy, so it is! How very untidy!" She tucked the white silk ribbon back into its proper place, adding, "Before I wear this frock again, I shall have Kerra replace the ribbons on my shift with ones to match this gray satin. Then I shan't worry about being embarrassed before company. I certainly hope," she added, "that it hasn't been poking out like that all afternoon. I should never be able to look Rockland or Mr. Gabriel in the eye again."

"It wasn't," Letty said, eyeing her shrewdly. "I'd have observed it before if it were. It must have worked its way out while I was in the kitchen."

"I'll wager you did not come in here to assure yourself that my ribbons were in place," Charley said, sensing repressed laughter in her companion and again taking good care not to look at him. "What did you want, darling?"

Letty glanced at Antony, then sighed and said, "I know curiosity is a vulgar habit, because Grandpapa Jervaulx has told me so times without number—nearly every time I ask him a question in fact. But I have observed that if one does not indulge in some curiosity, one frequently does not find out what one wants to know. The truth is that I heard you shouting. Then there was utter silence, so I wondered—"

"Yes?" Antony prompted.

"If there had been murder done."

Both Antony and Charley burst out laughing, but their moment of intimacy was over. Charley tried to convince herself that she was relieved, but she knew she was deceiving herself. Antony had awakened a new curiosity, and as Letty had so kindly pointed out, curiosity, once stirred, rarely slept until knowledge had quenched it.

After dinner that evening, expecting Antony to go out again, she retired to her dressing room and sat down at the dressing table to let Kerra take down her hair and brush it out. The task was half completed when Antony strolled in through the doorway from her bedchamber.

Charley nearly betrayed her shock before she saw him wink.

"Good evening, sir," she said, hoping her voice sounded calmer than she felt. "I thought you were going out."

"Not tonight, my dear, though I do have some matters of business to attend to before I can retire for the night. I did hope for a private word with you before then."

She had relaxed, but these words brought tension flooding back. Keeping her poise with difficulty, she said, "You may go, Kerra. I'll ring when I want you again." When the maid had gone, she exclaimed, "Good mercy, I might have been half-dressed! What were you thinking?"

"I knew there had not been time for that," he said, smiling.

Picking up the brush Kerra had set down, she said more sharply than she had intended, "And just how long does it take a lady to disrobe, Master Expert?"

"Sheathe your claws, my lioness. Rockland hit the mark there, I must say."

"I hope you did not tell him so after I left the room."

"You know I did not," he said, reaching to stroke her hair. When her startled gaze met his in the looking glass, he said gently, "You hit the mark, too, you know, when you said we had better grow accustomed to touching each other if people are to accept our marriage as a normal one. By the same token, the servants must begin to observe that we are developing some intimacy between us. Hodson knows the truth, for there's precious little I've kept from him over the years, and your woman may have guessed, but the rest of the servants must not, and they'll soon know something's amiss if we don't exert ourselves to pull the wool over their eyes."

"If you think I'm going to sleep in your bed to convince them, you'd best think again," Charley said.

"That's what I thought," he replied. When she gasped, he chuckled and said, "Not that you should sleep there, that you had not intended me to think you would."

She bit her lip, realizing no one could blame him if he had assumed from her behavior earlier that she wanted to share his bed. Even now she was not certain of her feelings about that, one way or another.

Leaning a shoulder against the wall, he folded his arms across his chest, watching her for a long moment before he said, "There is something I think you ought to know."

"What?"

"I think that although your experience is limited, your curiosity is boundless. It occurred to me that since we are legally married, and since after the annulment you do not intend to marry again, you might come to believe a certain opportunity exists to explore and satisfy that curiosity."

"Is that what you thought I ought to know?" she demanded, uncomfortably wondering if he could read her mind.

"What I thought you ought to know," he said, "is that it is well nigh impossible to get a marriage annulled if it has been consummated."

"Good mercy, would anyone dare to ask us if it had?"

"They would."

"Are you sure?"

"I am."

"Oh."

He was silent for a moment. Then he straightened, saying, "In view of that, I think we should be grateful that Letty came in when she did."

"We should, indeed," she said, wondering why she did not feel grateful. The truth was that, yet again, her wayward emotions threatened to overcome her. She wanted to cry. When Antony left her a few minutes later, that is precisely what she did, though she could not have given a single reason for her tears.

When she had dried her eyes and washed her face, she got ready to retire without ringing for Kerra. Then, blowing out her candles, and climbing into bed, she lay there, staring up into the darkness. The plain and simple fact was that, other than marriage itself, no acceptable scheme existed whereby women could learn firsthand about the delights or terrors of the conjugal bed. She wondered briefly what her mother had thought about such things, but her eyes only pricked again. Not wanting to dwell on the past, she pushed the uncomfortable thoughts ruthlessly aside.

She had not changed her mind about wanting an annulment, certainly; although, had Sir Antony been the man he presently claimed to be, and in love with her, she might, admittedly, have a few second thoughts. That, she decided, was only being honest. He intrigued her more than any other man she had met, but he did not love her. He did not even make a pretense of doing so, for she was certainly wise enough to know the difference between sexual attraction and love.

With horses, after all, there was no question of love. A stallion had only to catch a whiff of a mare in season to plunge into rut. Men were no different. She had frequently observed, during the various London Seasons in which she had taken part, that men required little more than slight encouragement from any passable female to fling themselves at her. Moreover, it was well known that men took their pleasures wherever they chanced to find them. She had presented an opportunity for Sir Antony, and he had very nearly taken advantage of it. That was all there was to the matter.

Having sorted this all out to her complete satisfaction, she settled back on her pillows and waited for sleep to overtake her. Long into the night she lay, pretending she was not listening with all her might for movement in the bedchamber next door.

When Kerra wakened her the following morning, she had no idea how long she had lain awake before dozing off. She knew only that she had not slept long enough.

"Go away," she muttered, turning over. "I don't want to get up for hours yet."

With an unusually sympathetic note in her voice, Kerra said, "I beg your pardon, my lady, for I know the master kept you awake much later than usual, but you did say as how you was intending to ride into Lostwithiel this morning."

"Aggh," Charley moaned, burying her head under the pillow.

Chapter Sixteen

Not until half an hour later, while Kerra was straightening the short train of Charley's riding habit, did Charley realize exactly in what manner the maid thought she had spent the night. Her sense of humor stirred, for she knew that by not ringing for Kerra to return, she had led her to believe Sir Antony had stayed all night.

Charley wondered if she ought to tell him, and if the news would make him laugh. Had she seen him at once, she might have mentioned it, but he was not in the breakfast room when she entered.

Deliciously enticing odors wafted from dishes set out on the sideboard, and as she examined their contents, a maid entered to see if she required anything more.

"Just tea, please," Charley said, helping herself to some sliced ham, and eggs scrambled with onions and mushrooms. No sooner had she sat down and begun to eat than Letty bounced in, dressed for riding, with Sebastian at her heels.

The child went at once to fill her plate at the sideboard, saying over her shoulder, "Do we leave immediately after breakfast, Cousin Charley?"

"Letty, darling, did you think you were to go with me? I don't think that would be a good idea this time."

"But I want to see Jenifry! I liked her. I want to know that she is safe."

"I'll tell you as quickly as I know for myself that she is," Charley said.

"But you let me go with you before."

"That is not quite true. You followed without permission."

"But you let me go."

An unfamiliar, plaintive note had entered Letty's voice, and Charley heard it with some dismay. Was this what her influence had achieved? Neither Daintry nor Gideon would thank her if the well-mannered child they had sent to England with her returned to them a spoiled and whining brat. She was about to utter a sharp reproof when Sir Antony entered the room. She said calmly instead, "I did let you go with me last time, darling, but in truth, I ought not to have done so. Indeed, were it not for Mr. Gabriel promising to provide me with a properly authoritative escort to deal with Michael Peryllys, I should hesitate to go, myself."

"Or I to allow it," Antony said, entering the room. "You won't go alone, as it is."

"But—"

"I am going with you," he added, smiling. "That is why I stayed up till all hours. I had a letter to write, but Hodson will see it off, so I am at your disposal for the day."

Letty carried her plate to the table, tossing a scrap of ham to Sebastian as she took her seat. Happily, she said, "That is wonderful news, sir. Now I can go, too."

"No," Antony said, as he examined the offerings on the sideboard.

"But I want to see Jenifry again."

Her tone was wheedling but more acceptable than before, Charley noted thankfully. Although tempted to enter the conversation, she held her tongue, certain that Antony would prevail.

He said, "When we know what is going on in Lostwithiel, I will see what we can do about your seeing Jenifry again, but today you will not go with us. And before you say anything more, Letitia, let me add that although I have respect for the general excellence of your manners, your tone when you spoke to your cousin a moment ago was quite unacceptable. I shall not refine upon the point, however, because I am certain that I will never hear it again.''

''No, sir,'' Letty said in a small voice. Although she did not hang her head, meeting his gaze directly, her manner was subdued.

Antony ladled oatmeal into a bowl and brought it to the table just as the maid returned with Charley's tea. He said, ''I'll have some coffee, Daisy, please.'' As she poured it for him, he said more cheerfully to Letty, ''Perhaps you would like to ride to Tuscombe Park today to pay your respects to your grandmama and Lady Ophelia.''

Letty wrinkled her nose thoughtfully. Beside her chair, the dog thumped its tail in hopeful anticipation of more food. Dropping another morsel of ham, she said, ''May I really ride all that distance alone, sir?''

''Not all alone, for you will have your groom. You must promise faithfully to obey him without question, too. Will you do that?''

''Yes, of course. You sound like Papa,'' she added with her customary twinkle.

''Excellent,'' Antony said, flicking a speaking look at Charley as he added, ''You may be just as bored at Tuscombe Park as you would be here, of course.''

Letty chuckled. ''Perhaps I will,'' she said, ''but I'll enjoy the ride over and back very much. I can take Sebastian, but I expect I'd better not take Jeremiah.''

''Not unless you are prepared to leave him in the stable when you get there.''

''He doesn't like that. I'll just leave him here and play with him a bit more than usual when I get back, to make up for abandoning him.''

''That's a good notion, darling,'' Charley interjected. ''Just take care to play with him outside when you do. When he enjoyed himself at Tuscombe Park House, if you recall, he ran up the curtains. Mrs. Medrose said later that he had damaged some of the fringe. It won't do to let him destroy things here in Cousin Melissa's house.''

"Mrs. Medrose fixed the fringe," Letty said.

"So she did," Charley agreed. "Very well then, enjoy your day and we'll tell you all about ours when we get back."

"We'll return by way of Tuscombe Park, and meet you there," Antony said, shooting Charley another speaking look. "It is time we paid our respects, too."

They finished their breakfast quickly, and as Charley accompanied Antony to the stables a short time afterward, she found herself looking forward to the ride even more than she had before. Until Antony had declared his intention to go with her, she had looked ahead to the moment she would force Michael Peryllys to produce Jenifry. Now, like Letty, she looked forward more to the ride itself, and their return, than to the confrontation at Angelique's.

They all left the stable yard together, Charley riding between Letty and Antony, their grooms trailing behind. The scent of the sea was strong, and the sunlight crisply brilliant where it spilled across the landscape from the east, painting white and golden highlights on the eastern sides of trees and shrubs along their way. Black-headed gulls wheeled above them, crying plaintively, and in the distance, over St. Merryn's Bay, a kittiwake banked wildly and cut a white-fringed wave with its wing tip. The air was crisp, with a light but sharp breeze that penetrated Charley's habit coat, but after they had ridden for a while, she felt warmer and found the nip in the air invigorating.

Since Letty and Jeb were to take the cliff-top path, while Charley, Antony, and their grooms would follow the route Charley had taken on her previous trip, the two groups parted when they reached the main road. Content to walk the horses for a time, Charley and Antony rode without speaking, enjoying the soft morning air.

They had two hours of riding ahead of them, but before long Charley leaned forward and lightly spurred Dancer, urging the gelding to a trot, then to a canter. To her delight, Antony rode with her as if he had anticipated the impulse. When she drew rein again ten minutes later to allow their grooms to catch up, she was laughing. "I never intended to gallop," she said. "It just felt so good that I wanted to go faster and faster."

"Our horses can stand it," he said with a smile that sent a surge of warmth through her. He was not riding Annabelle today but one of her bay hunters instead.

"Indeed they can," she said, fondly patting Shadow Dancer's neck. The black roan was not even breathing hard, though she had pushed it to its fastest pace. "Both of them are good for a twenty-mile point. On a road like this, I daresay they could easily run for an hour or two."

He grinned. "It would not do for the haughty Sir Antony Foxearth to arrive in Lostwithiel looking as if he had been blown there by a gale."

"Well, I am in no hurry. The day is too fine not to enjoy it." He was looking fine, too, she thought. He had dressed more for displaying himself in Rotten Row, Hyde Park, than for a gallop across the Cornish moor. His exquisitely cut coat fit his broad shoulders and trim waist like a superfine glove, and his snowy white linen shirt and neckcloth were starched and ironed to perfection. Pale cream stockinet breeches molded to his thighs so well that each powerful muscle asserted itself as he rode, and his top boots shone like polished obsidian, their light turned-down tops a shade darker than his breeches. His left hand rested lightly on his thigh. He held the reins in his right, moving lightly and automatically, his gold signet ring occasionally flashing light from the sun.

When he glanced at her and caught her gaze upon him, she felt heat flood her cheeks, and said quickly, "Do you mean to be seen today at Angelique's, sir? If Michael Peryllys is indeed leader of the coastal gang . . ." She saw no need to finish the sentence.

"There could be someone above Michael, but I'm as certain as I can be that Michael Peryllys is involved," Antony said. "The Michael I've met professes to hail from St. Austell, but I never trusted that information, because Francis Oakes, the Lloyd's man, doesn't know of him, and he knows seamen from St. Ives to Polperro. It's the inland folk, the ones who began as receivers, whom Oakes doesn't know. Lloyd's, after all, is less concerned with smuggling than with wrecking, and now that an organized gang has merged the two activities, the Lloyd's people are as frustrated as the customs agents.''

"Such organization is unusual in Cornwall," Charley said. "I know of only one other instance, when the mayor of St. Ives, Mr. John Knill, formed a gang of villainous smugglers. I remember Grandpapa ranting about it when I was fourteen or so. Knill was collector of customs at St. Ives, you see, as well as being mayor, so he held not one but two positions of trust. Everyone believed him to be a man of great public virtue and rectitude, but all the while he was in league with the very smugglers whom it was his duty to suppress. Many find the story difficult to believe even now, and say he was an innocent victim of the droll-tellers. It is true that they delight in weaving their tales around the name of any well-known local character, but nearly everyone with cause to know the truth believed without reservation that Knill was guilty. Wouldn't it be ironic if the leader of the present coastal gang turned out to be Mr. Gabriel?''

She felt rather pleased with herself when Antony's eyes crinkled at the corners and he laughed, for she had known he would find comical the notion of Gabriel as a smuggler. It pleased her to think she was beginning to anticipate his moods at last.

He said, "That would resolve my problem, wouldn't it? I could simply drop Gabriel over a cliff, the gang would disintegrate without leadership, Wellington would be safe, and—" He broke off abruptly, looking at her, all trace of amusement gone.

His words had stirred a memory flash of a carriage careening off a cliff, but she pushed the mental image away, certain that he had not meant to remind her. She knew the moment his gaze met hers and he stopped speaking that he had read her thoughts and recognized his lack of tact. Rather than try to make him believe he had not upset her, she finished the sentence for him, saying bluntly, "And then we could get our marriage annulled and be done with all this, could we not?''

He did not reply. She knew she was being tactless now and

mentally scolded herself. It was hardly his fault that he looked forward without any reservation whatsoever to the day when Wellington would be safe.

Collecting her wits, she said with a forced smile, "It would shock everyone very much if Mr. Gabriel *were* the ringleader, I think."

"It would not shock Rockland," he said lightly. "He'd be as pleased as Punch."

"Because of Elizabeth? Good mercy, do you think he really cares for her?"

"Would it bother you if he did?"

She thought about it, but only briefly. "I don't suppose it would. Perhaps I would feel a twinge, but only out of pique, I'm afraid. A lowering reflection, too, that I should want to keep him on my string when I don't have more than ordinary affection for him. Despite his faults, Rockland deserves better than that."

Antony chuckled.

"What?"

"I've never known anyone who speaks her thoughts as easily as you do."

"Perhaps I should not, but—"

"Don't stop on my account. I find it singularly refreshing."

"Except when I blurt out things I ought not to say."

"Except then," he agreed.

She sighed. "I don't suppose Gabriel *is* the ringleader."

Smiling again, he shook his head. "I'm afraid not. He's hand in glove with the Methodists, for one thing. Moreover, he wants salvage rights to wrecked vessels to be allotted by turn rather than by right of first boarding. His plan would no doubt save a few lives aboard the wrecked ships, but the wreckers don't think much of it."

"I think they enjoy the competition. Besides, if rights were set by turn, the local folks would be cut out. Now, they flock to the shore whenever a wreck occurs, knowing they will be allowed to take away what they can carry. Under Gabriel's scheme, wouldn't they be stealing from someone?"

His eyes glinted with amusement. "According to Gabriel

and Lloyd's of London, those people are stealing now, because if the insurers cannot recover the goods, they have to pay out a much greater sum to the owners. Gabriel wants to award salvage contracts, but he says that all too often the country people are able to get on board before any person competent to make a contract can arrive and do so. Then all goes to ruin, and what the scavengers cannot carry off they destroy.''

"I don't pretend to understand how insurance works," Charley said, "but I do know the local people depend a good deal on what they can salvage. You still have not said if you mean to let Michael Peryllys see you," she added.

"I'm more concerned with my wish to see him," Antony said.

Falling silent again for a time, they did not push the horses but varied their gaits, cantering for a time, then trotting, and occasionally increasing the pace to a gallop. Once, when they slowed to a walk after a heady run, in the near silence that surrounded them, Charley heard the hoofbeats of their grooms' horses as a poorly coordinated echo of their own.

Glancing at Antony, she said, "Was it necessary for us to bring two grooms?"

"No." His eyes twinkled again. "They are here to inflate my consequence. I'm hoping that if Michael Peryllys does catch a glimpse of me, he'll be so impressed by my sartorial splendor and my entourage that he won't look too closely at my face. I've taken the devil of a lot of care never to allow him to see Jean Matois, even in the poor light of most of our meetings, without at least a day's growth of beard. Matois always has his hair hanging over his eyes, and either a slouch cap or a knitted one. I rub dirt in my hair to alter the color, and the only clothes Michael's seen me wear are baggy fishermen's togs. I doubt he'd see Jean Matois in Sir Antony Foxearth under the best of circumstances, but I've learned over the years never to take any enemy for granted.''

"I doubt if your own mother would recognize you as Jean Matois, or guess that you play two parts."

His lips twisted cynically, and she realized that although he had once or twice mentioned his father, he had never spoken of his mother. All he said was "You recognized me. So did Letty."

"I don't think you ought to count Letty. She had taken quite a liking to Annabelle, you know, and she saw her in the stable before she met you in the house."

"You had not seen Annabelle, however."

"That's true. I noticed more about you than just your face, I expect." She remembered how quickly she had recognized him from the cliff top when the wreckers were claiming salvage.

He was watching her. "What is it? You've thought of something. Is there aught about me that is particularly recognizable to others?"

"Not really. I was just remembering the day of the shipwreck. I recognized you from a distance when you rescued Sebastian, but I'm not sure why I did."

"Probably my clothing."

"Perhaps." She could not recall that he had been wearing anything noteworthy. Still, she had known him instinctively. She wondered if villains could recognize their foes as easily. She hoped they could not.

When he grew quiet again, the comfortable silence between them tempted her to ask him about his mother. She was curious to know what sort of woman she was. But that thought brought an image to her mind of her own mother, and she quickly rejected the impulse, saying instead, "We're nearly there. Lostwithiel is just over the next rise."

He returned a desultory response, and they chatted about the birds and the rising slopes of Bodmin Moor until they reached the crest of the hill and descended into Lostwithiel. They found James Gabriel at home, awaiting them, with four men, one of whom was the town constable. When Gabriel expressed surprise at seeing Antony, that gentleman looked down his nose at him and said haughtily, "Indeed?"

"No offense, Sir Antony, assure you! 'Twas only that I believe you had said you had other matters to attend to today and could not accompany her ladyship."

"However," Antony said gently, "I am here."

"To be sure, to be sure," Gabriel said heartily. "We'll soon sort this out! I've given the matter much thought, I can tell you, and although I might not have felt the same way when I was no different from any common citizen with a daughter looking to improve herself, as mayor, one must act when one sees the need."

"Indeed," Antony said agreeably.

"Aye, sir. Shopkeepers in big cities may have to set strict rules for apprentices, but they needn't do so in my town. As mayor, when I'm told a child is not *allowed* to see her parents, or they to see her, why I just bristle, my lady, and that's a fact. Action is called for, and when action is called for, I'm your man. It don't do to let things muddle on when they are flat wrong. A man must do what he can to change them."

He sounded unusually vehement, but Charley agreed with him, and decided he was hoping to impress her. Perhaps, she thought, hiding a smile, he hoped she would inform Elizabeth that he was a man of action.

Catching Sir Antony's gaze, she saw her amusement reflected in his eyes, although to anyone who did not know him well, she was certain he appeared only haughty and unapproachable.

Gabriel looked at the others. "All ready, are we? Shall we go?" He led his men up the High Street ahead of the horsemen to Angelique's shop, but when they arrived, he halted them and approached Sir Antony. "Perhaps it would be best, sir, do I and the constable enter first and order them to produce the young 'un."

Charley said quickly, "I would prefer to speak with Angelique first." She looked to Sir Antony, adding, "We do not yet know that my request will be denied, sir, and I fear Jenifry will be frightened by a show of force."

Nodding, Antony said, "No reason to exert ourselves without cause, Gabriel."

"Begging your pardon, sir, but I don't think you should allow her ladyship to enter yon shop alone. There might well be trouble."

Charley slipped to the roadway from her saddle and handed her reins to Teddy. "Good mercy, I shall be perfectly safe. If I have not returned in ten minutes, you may come and fetch me.'' With that, leaving Gabriel to look agape at Sir Antony, she walked quickly, and alone, into the shop.

Angelique was with a customer, examining a book of patterns. Upon seeing Charley, she left the woman and stepped forward, smiling and saying, ''A good morning, Miss— Ah, *mais non,* I mistake. It is now milady, *ne c'est pas?''*

''It is. Good morning, Angelique. I want to speak with Jenifry Breton, please.''

''Ah, *c'est dommage, madame,* but I cannot allow that. The rules, you know, they are very strict.''

Charley glanced at the customer, still turning over pattern cards. Quietly, she said to Angelique, ''Perhaps you ought just to glance out into the street before you insist upon keeping to your rules. I think perhaps you will alter your conviction.''

The customer looked up. ''Has it come on to rain since I came in? I declare, I've been here an age, but one simply cannot make up one's mind what is best to do.''

''The weather is still fine,'' Charley said. ''Are you not Mrs. Tibbits, the linen draper's wife?''

''I am, indeed,'' the woman said. ''Fancy your remembering me, Miss Tarrant. Oh, but did I not hear that you have recently married?''

Keeping an eye on Angelique, Charley responded politely. The dressmaker looked into the street, but to Charley's surprise, she did not instantly agree to produce Jenifry. In fact, Angelique looked distraught.

''Pardon me,'' Charley said, interrupting the gentle flow of Mrs. Tibbits's polite remarks. ''I think Angelique has turned rather faint.'' Moving to the latter's side, she said in an undertone, ''Where is she? You can no longer refuse to let me see her, you know. Those men are quite prepared to enter and search your entire establishment.''

''Mais, je ne—''

''English, if you please,'' Charley said, still keeping her voice low. A glance showed that Mrs. Tibbits had returned her attention to the pattern cards, but Charley was certain the woman's ears were straining. In a more natural tone, she said, ''Let me take you into the back, Angelique. I am persuaded that you ought to sit down and perhaps drink a glass of water, or even swallow a dose of hartshorn.''

"*Merci, madame.* I should like to sit down. Will you excuse us for a short while, Madame Tibbits.''

"To be sure,'' the woman said. "Indeed, if you are not feeling quite the thing, I believe I shall return later. I want to think more about that gown before I decide.''

"*Merci, madame,*'' Angelique said faintly. When Mrs. Tibbits had left the shop, she said in a firmer tone, "Jenifry is not here.''

"Thank you, but I prefer to discover that for myself,'' Charley said. "You may come with me, if you like. Is your husband at home?''

"No.''

She said it so matter-of-factly that Charley did not doubt her. She felt a twinge of disappointment that Antony would have to wait to see him, would still not know for certain if Michael Peryllys was the man he knew, but at the moment, she wanted only to find Jenifry. As she turned toward the back of the shop, Bess Griffin peeped in. Quickly, Charley said, "I want to see Jenifry, Bess. Take me to her at once.''

Looking scared, the girl turned abruptly to Angelique.

With a gesture of yielding, the Frenchwoman said, "Take her to Jenifry. They will search the house if we do not produce her.''

"Oh, miss,'' the girl exclaimed, looking wide-eyed at Charley, "I'm ever so glad. It ain't right, what they've done to our Jenifry. If it be legal, like Mr. Michael says it be, it oughtn't to be so, and that's plain fact, that is.''

"Where is she?''

"Down in the cellar, miss.'' Bess wrung her hands. "They said she'd been lazy and needed a good lesson, but they've kept her down there two whole days this time.''

"Good mercy!'' Charley looked at Angelique, but the woman only shrugged.

Minutes later, when Bess opened the cellar door and dim light spilled down the steps, Charley gasped to see small Jenifry at the foot of them, tied fast to the wooden railing. The child scarcely moved when the light fell upon her, and Charley ran down the stairs, saying over her shoulder, "Run out and tell Sir Antony and the others to come in at once. They must see this outrage for themselves!"

"Aye, mistress."

"Jenifry, speak to me," Charley said, giving the girl a gentle shake. "It's Miss Charley. I'm taking you out of here. Why have they done this to you?"

To her profound relief, the child's eyes opened, but their expression seemed glazed. "Water," Jenifry gasped.

Hearing footsteps above, Charley barely glanced up as she said to the shadowy figure at the top of the steps, "Get water for her quickly, and send someone down to help me untie her. She's been here two days, so she'll never be able to stand on her own, and I can't hold her and untie the knots at the same time. Don't dawdle!" she cried when there was no sound or movement. "Go!"

The figure turned and murmured to someone else. Then he moved toward her.

"Oh, hurry!"

"Be calm, *mon ange*. The child will recover."

"How can you be certain? You have not even seen her yet. She looks as if she has not eaten in weeks, Antony. How could anyone do this to a child?"

He was beside her now. "Do you want me to untie the knots or to hold her?"

"Hold her. I-I'm shaking, and you are stronger."

"Can you manage the knots?"

"I think so." The child's weight had tightened them, and Charley could not see what she was doing. At first she thought there was simply not enough light in the cellar, but soon she realized her tears were blinding her. Fumbling but determined, she managed to loosen the knots at last, and release Jenifry.

Antony scooped the child into his arms and carried her up the stairs with Charley hurrying in his wake. When they emerged into the front of the shop, where the light was best, they saw that Jenifry's face was pale beneath smudges of dirt, and her eyelids drooped with exhaustion. Brushing everything off the table where Mrs. Tibbits had been looking at pattern cards, Charley directed Antony to lay Jenifry down. He obeyed, reaching for a length of blue wool draped over a chair to cover her.

One of the men handed him a cup of water. Slipping an arm beneath Jenifry's shoulders, he raised her and held the cup to her lips. "Just a taste, little one," he said. "Take it slowly. We'll have you home with your mam as soon as I can arrange it."

Charley sighed with relief when she saw Jenifry try to smile. Then, looking about, she said, "Where's Angelique?"

The man who had brought the water said, "They've took her away, my lady, to ask her some questions. I doubt she had much say in this business, howsomever."

"Why, what can you mean? Jenifry was apprenticed to Angelique."

"She was, that," the man replied gruffly, "but if Miss Angelique ruled the roast in this house, I'll call myself a Dutchman. 'Tis Michael Peryllys who called the tune here, and from what I can see, our Michael has up and disappeared."

"He killed Annie," Jenifry moaned. "He said I would die, too."

Chapter Seventeen

The three adults in the room stared at Jenifry in shock. Sir Antony found his voice first. "Who was Annie?" he asked.

Jenifry whimpered when Charley rubbed her wrists and hands, which were swollen from the bindings. No one pressed the child to speak, and a moment later, looking at Antony, she said, "She worked here when I came. Madame told everyone Annie ran off because she was lazy and disobedient, but . . ." She did not finish.

Bess came back into the shop room just then and apparently heard Jenifry, for she said, "Annie had a sickly constitution, she did. Like her own mother, she said. Couldn't work as hard as they want us to, so they beat her. She did try to run off, but Michael caught her and beat her senseless. They tied her hands behind her back and fastened the rope to the railing in the cellar, like Jenifry, so she could neither stand nor sit. For a sennight they left her like that." Bess sobbed, and tears streamed down her cheeks. "They wouldn't give her food or water. When she died, Michael was just going to leave her body to rot, but Angelique said customers would complain about the smell."

"What did they do?" Antony asked quietly.

"Dunno," Bess replied. "Took her away, did Michael. We never did see what he did with her. But she never run off to London like they said she did."

Jenifry whimpered, her thin little body shaking beneath the wool coverlet.

"Jenifry, are you all right?" Charley asked.

"Miss Charley, must I stay here? I'm afeared of them, I am."

"You'll not stay another minute."

"But me 'denture papers say I must. Seven years and a day, they say!" She had taken several sips of water, and her voice sounded a little stronger.

" 'Tis true," Bess said. "Miss Angelique did say we must do as we're bid. I've five more years to serve, and Jen's got near the full seven to go."

"I don't care what the law says," Charley said. "Jenifry is leaving at once. I daresay you ought to go, too, Bess, and anyone else who works here."

"There be only the two of us left," Bess said. "But where would I go, miss, and how would I dare? Miss Angelique and Mr. Michael say the law does dreadful things to them what breaks their indentures."

"Don't you trouble your head about that," Charley said fiercely. "I'll fix it if I have to put the matter to the Prime Minister himself."

"Coo, miss, could you really speak to him?"

"I can, and I will."

Antony said mildly, "I daresay Gabriel can arrange for their release, you know. There are strict laws about this sort of thing. Indentured servants are not slaves."

Charley nodded, looking thoughtfully at Bess, who was a neatly dressed, intelligent-looking girl. "Have you got your heart set on being a seamstress, Bess?"

"I have not. I can sew a fine seam, ma'am, but what with all the work there is to do, my fingers be well nigh pricked to the bones. But if I don't sew, what could I do?"

"You could go into service," Charley suggested.

"Lordy, miss, I'd have to begin in the scullery."

"I don't think so," Charley said. "As it happens, we are in need of another chambermaid and I could use a seamstress, too. As for Jenifry—" She looked at the child, now sitting up and leaning against Antony. "I have an idea about that, as well."

"I must work, Miss Charley," Jenifry said. "Me folks can't keep me."

"I know, my dear, but how would you like to maid a little girl a couple of years younger than you are? I promise you, she won't be difficult."

Light gleamed in Jenifry's eyes. "The young lady what came with you the last time, Miss Charley?"

"The very same. As it happens, she has not got a maid just yet. I think she would be well pleased to have you, but not until you are healthy and strong again. To that end, I think we will take you straight home to your mama and papa."

Tears welled in Jenifry's eyes. "Oh, thank you, Miss Charley!"

"Beg pardon, my lady," Gabriel's man said, "but that French wench be bound to set up the devil of a screech if you go and take away them what sews for her."

"Let her screech," Charley said coldly.

Antony said, "Perhaps I should just have a word with her. I can . . . uh . . . explain the matter to her in her own tongue, you see."

"Lord, sir, do ye speak them Frenchies' lingo?"

"The curse of a gentleman's education is that one is forced to learn all manner of odd things," Antony said apologetically. "Where have they taken her, if you please?"

"To the mayor's house, I think, sir."

"Excellent." He turned to Charley. "My dear, do what you can for the child. She can ride with me, but we ought to get some food into her before we depart. Not much, mind you, and only something light and easy to digest. Don't try to feed her one of Dewy the Baker's pastry pigs or anything of that sort," he added with a smile.

Bess said diffidently, "I could fix her a bit of chicken broth, my lady."

"An excellent notion," Charley said, but she had seen both girls' eyes light up at Antony's mention of pastry pigs, and she knew he had acquired a fondness for them as well, so at the first opportunity, she sent Teddy to Dewy the Baker's. While she knew Jenifry could not manage a rich pastry at once, the pigs would keep until she could.

Leaving Jenifry and Bess in Charlotte's capable hands, with Gabriel's men and his own grooms to keep watch for Michael Peryllys, Antony went to discover what Gabriel had learned from Angelique. He found the mayor back at his home, standing belligerently over the dressmaker, who sat hunched in a chair, weeping pitifully.

With exasperation, Gabriel said, "She just cries. I haven't got a word of sense out of her."

"Where is your husband, madam?" Antony asked her.

Angelique looked up, tears glistening on her lashes. She looked calculating, Antony thought, like a woman accustomed to getting her way with men.

He shot a look at Gabriel, whose expression remained stern and unyielding. "Who," the mayor asked grimly, "tied that child in the cellar?"

Angelique glanced at Antony but seemed to recognize that he was not an ally. *"Michel,"* she whispered, looking down again at the hands twisting together in her lap.

Antony said, "Did you protest such treatment, madam?" When she did not reply, he repeated the question in French.

Starting, she sharpened her gaze, re-evaluating him. He had met with that look before, many times, and not just from women. She was sizing him up, trying to decide if he was really her enemy, or perhaps a friend instead.

The look tempted him to keep her guessing, for he knew he might learn more from her if he could keep her off balance, but he did not believe the person behind the assassination plot was female. Nor did he think that a man strong enough to merge the coastal smugglers and wreckers into one organization would entrust his secrets to a woman like Angelique, and despite

the possibility that there might be someone higher up, he still
believed Michael was their leader.

Knowing indifference would annoy her, he turned his attention to Gabriel as if she were of no account, and said,
"We are taking the two girls with us. I am not altogether certain
of what must be done in order to release them from their
bonds—"

"You can*not*," Angelique exclaimed. *"Mon Dieu,* would
you ruin me? How shall I manage without them? You are
unfair, you men. Nothing was done to that Bess, and if Michel
punished that Jenifry girl, it was because she deserved it."

"Now you interest me very much, madam," Antony said
sharply in her language. "What can the poor little one have
done to deserve being beaten, starved, and tied up in a dark
cellar to die?"

In careful English, and looking now at Gabriel, she said,
"He exaggerates, sir. Me, I tell you, Michel only punished her
because she did not do her work. She complained that she
wanted her mama and her papa, and so he whipped her a little
and said she should have no supper. That is all."

Antony said grimly, "The child has not eaten in days. It is
a wonder she did not die of thirst or cold in that cellar."
Looking narrowly at Angelique to judge her reaction, he added,
"If she had died, she would not be the first they've killed,
either."

"You lie!" Angelique sat bolt upright, but he saw that her
face was stark white, and her hands trembled in her lap. She
looked fearfully at Gabriel.

"If you know what happened before," Antony said sternly,
"and if you were party to it, you are as guilty of that other
child's murder as anyone else is."

"Murder," Gabriel exclaimed, turning pale.

"Yes, murder," Antony said. "Jenifry believed before they
put her in the cellar that one of the older girls, who was there
when she arrived, had simply run away. But when Michael
punished her, he told her the truth about the other to terrorize
her. I daresay they threatened Bess with the same end if she
ever dared speak out."

"N'en parlez plus, monsieur!" Angelique was weeping again. "Me, I pleaded with him to stop, but he was angry. He said she was just lazy and he would teach her to be more industrious. He said he would kill me, too, if I spoke of it to anyone."

Gabriel said, "We won't hang you yet, madam, but you had best not do anything now to warn Michael Peryllys that we are onto him. If I should learn that he's been home and you've not informed us, I'll order the constable to arrest you and hold you for the summer assize court at Launceston. We'll be wanting to know more about that other girl's death, in any case, but you can go for now." He called through a doorway into the next room, "You can see her home now, Constable."

Angelique got up with more haste than grace, and fairly ran from the room.

When Antony moved to follow, Gabriel touched his sleeve. "One moment, sir, if you don't mind. I'd like to seek your advice on another matter."

"Yes, what is it?"

"I've heard certain rumors, Sir Antony. Like as not they don't amount to anything, but I'd never forgive myself if they proved to be true, and I'd not spoken."

"What rumors?"

"You know that the Duke of Wellington means to lend his presence to the consecration of the new cathedral in Truro."

"Yes, of course. Lady Foxearth is to open that coffer of yours, so he can present the sacred vessels."

"Did you also know the Duke means to take ship from London?"

"Yes, to Fowey. Get to the point, Gabriel. I've other matters to attend."

"They say there's a plot afoot to capture him as he makes for Fowey harbor."

Antony went still, but his thoughts raced. He had heard nothing of such a plot. "Capture? How? He will be well guarded, I can assure you."

"They mean to take the ship, I'm told. I don't know how they aim to do it."

"Who are they?"

"That's the rub, I'm afraid. They say the French are involved, that I do know, and like as not they'll get plenty of help from the lot here. I'm thinking Michael Peryllys, being married to the Frenchwoman and all, is like to be up to his neck in the business. Don't like the man, myself, and wasn't sure before but what my suspicions arose from that dislike. But now we've excellent reason to hunt him down."

"Do you know aught of their plan?"

"If I did, you may be sure I'd have taken it straight to the customs folk or to Oakes in St. Austell. In truth, I'm not even certain there *is* a plan. I've heard only the rumors, as I said, but I'm more suspicious now, what with Peryllys having disappeared, as it seems he might have done. What I'd like to do now is to send for the army."

Cautiously, Antony said, "I'd advise against that course, I think, at this point."

"Well, I don't want to look a fool if naught comes of the rumor," Gabriel said, nodding, "but this ain't the first I've heard of something in the wind, and now I've heard talk of a new leader amongst the Frenchies—fellow called Lee Renardo. Since you know the lingo, you'll know that means little fox or some such thing. Seems he's made quite a name for himself over the years. Tricky, they say. Don't expect you've heard tell of him, though."

"My dear fellow!" Antony raised his quizzing glass and peered through it.

Gabriel smiled weakly. "No offense intended, Sir Antony, assure you."

"None taken," Antony replied. "Look here, I daresay you know precisely what to do about this—"

"Well, but that's just it. I don't. If the old earl were still alive and kicking, I'd appeal to him. He put an end to a lot of the tricks that lot used to cause wrecks. There was no nonsense about lighting signal fires on the beach, or sending out fake light ships from Fowey to draw the unwary onto the rocks. But I'm thinking young Alfred Tarrant's a bit of a lightweight next to the earl. Fact is, till the St. Merryn folk know whether it's him or you that's in charge there, they'll be as likely to look to Miss Charlotte—to Lady Foxearth, that is—as to anyone else to guide them, begging your pardon, sir.''

He looked expectantly at Antony, clearly hoping he would offer some tidbit of information about the St. Merryn puzzle, but Antony felt no impulse to oblige him. Instead, he said, "This rumor of yours—care to tell me where you heard it?"

Gabriel flushed. "Gave my word, you see, and it came so roundabout, I can't see how it would serve you or anyone else to know. The important thing's the date of the Duke's arrival. Can't change that very easily at this point, you know."

"No, we can't," Antony said, thinking of the report he had stayed up to write, which Hodson had taken to St. Austell. It would go off with Oakes's weekly report to London. He went on, "As I understand it, the Duke's ship arrives in Fowey harbor the night before the ceremony, which is Saturday next. I'll have a word with a few people, and see if there is not something we can do to foil this plot."

"Excellent, Sir Antony," Gabriel said with undisguised relief. "I was hoping I might leave it all to you, sir."

"You may," Antony said.

"Still and all, sir, you might just be mentioning to Francis Oakes that a military unit or two would be right welcome, especially with Michael Peryllys having showed himself willing to commit murder. Shocking, that is, and to think we never knew of it."

"Bess said the child was sickly but that Michael called her lazy. He beat her and put her down in the cellar, just as he did with Jenifry. Unfortunately, poor Annie—"

"Annie?" The big man stared at him.

"Yes, did I not mention her name before?"

"You did not." Gabriel looked grim. "You said it were a child, sir."

"I thought she was, but I don't know that anyone said so. Did you know her?"

"Aye, I might have done, but not if it were a young 'un. I'll look into that."

"I expect you will," Antony said, taking his leave. As he

walked back to Angelique's shop, he found his thoughts drifting not to murder, or plots against the Duke, but to the question of just who had introduced *Le Renardeau* to Cornwall.

The romantic identity had been fun to exploit during some of his activities in France, but it would not help him in Cornwall. Jean Matois was also known in France, albeit to a much more select portion of the populace, and Antony had decided that identity would provide the most sensible way to insinuate himself into a gang whose members knew one another and whose Cornish dialect and customs would betray an outsider instantly. A man from London was as foreign this side of the river Tamar as a man from France, and in his favor, Jean Matois had friends among French smugglers who would vouch for him to their Cornish counterparts.

It crossed his mind that some of his old comrades might be involved in the plot, and he wondered why he had not heard a word about it. Even if the local men did not trust him enough yet to include him in the planning, he, like Gabriel, ought to have felt something in the wind. Perhaps, he thought, he had been too preoccupied with other matters. He wondered suddenly if the rumored plan was truly to capture the Duke and hold him to ransom, or if this *was* the assassination plot. In either case, it behooved him to get to the bottom of things, and quickly. There were only a few days left.

Back at Angelique's shop, he walked in on a tense scene. The dressmaker had returned before him and had apparently decided to try one last time to prevent her assistants from leaving.

"You mistake, madame," she was saying when he entered the shop. "There are ways in England to force *les apprenties* to serve out their time."

Jenifry and Bess both stood behind Charlotte, whose face was nearly as white as Jenifry's. But as Antony quickly realized, anger not fear had drained the blood from Charlotte's face.

"How *dare* you to speak so insolently to me," she said in a voice that, though calm, throbbed with fury.

Antony saw at once that she was on the verge of losing her temper again, in much the same way that she had lost it with

Elizabeth and later with Rockland and himself. He decided to cast a damper.

Before she could say more, he said, "I see you are ready to depart, my dear. If we are to return Jenifry to her parents before nightfall, we had best be on our way."

Stopping mid-sentence, she stared at him for a moment as if he had materialized out of thin air like a specter, but she collected her wits swiftly, saying, "It is scarcely noon, sir. It will not take us that long to restore her to her family."

"Will it not?" He watched her narrowly. That she was furious was readily apparent to anyone who knew her. She was very nearly shaking with fury.

Angelique made a last attempt. "It was not my doing, madame, please believe me! It was the work. So much to be done, and English girls, they are so lazy."

"You will have less work in future, I promise you," Charlotte said, her voice still trembling. "I mean to tell everyone I know just how you treated Jenifry, and what happened to Annie. Even if you were not the one who killed her—"

"Ah, madame, you must not believe what that wicked one told you. Annie, she went to London. *La pauvre méchante,* she believed she would become rich there."

"I don't believe you," Charlotte snapped. "Come, girls, we're leaving."

Since Jenifry was too weak to walk, it was as well for the effect of Charlotte's exit that Antony picked the child up and followed, with Bess like a shadow beside him.

They left Lostwithiel at once. Antony held Jenifry, and Bess rode pillion with his groom. They rode directly to the Breton cottage on the edge of the moor, and they rode in near silence, Antony having decided to leave Charlotte to her thoughts, for a time at least, after one look at her set face and trembling lips.

Wenna Breton was home alone when they reached the cottage. She greeted them with mixed emotions, gratitude over Jenifry's safe return warring with worry over the child's condition and the likely consequences of having deserted her position.

Antony hastened to reassure Wenna. "There will be no consequences that need concern you," he said gently. "Angelique and her husband have broken the law, and he will be punished for what he did to Jenifry.''

"But how will she find another position?'' Wenna asked, holding her daughter as if she could not bear to let her go, even to put her to bed. "We've so little money, sir, and other mouths to feed.''

"Get her rested and healthy again,'' Antony said, "and she shall come to Seacourt Head to serve the Lady Letitia.''

"Oh, how good you are, sir. Thank you.''

Charley saw Antony slip Wenna some money, but the sight did little to calm her fury. From the moment she had seen Jenifry tied to the railing, she had wanted to murder someone. Having managed to control herself, first for the child's sake and later for propriety's, she had expected the feeling to ease once she was alone with the two girls, but it had not. Poor, frightened Bess had so frequently expressed her fear that Michael Peryllys would return that Charley had nearly snapped the girl's nose off.

As they rode away from the cottage, leaving Jenifry to her mother's care, she still felt angry and, at the same time, as if she wanted to cry. Trying to ignore the hot prickling of tears in her eyes, she dashed them away with the back of her hand, glared at Antony, and said harshly, "Why did you pretend to Wenna that we've solved all their problems? What happens when Letty returns to France and you and I—''

"Letitia will not return for several months yet,'' he interjected firmly. With a sign to the grooms to fall back, he added, "Curb your temper, *mon ange*. You nearly let the cat out of the bag just then, about our marriage.''

"I don't care.''

"Yes, you do.''

She glared at him again, but the look he gave in return made her decide to say no more. Instead, she gave spur to Shadow Dancer and galloped ahead, hoping to blow the unrelenting fury from her mind. She expected Antony to pursue her. When he did not, she felt both angrier and relieved. She did not want to have to hold her own in a conversation with him, but she thought he should care enough at least to try to talk to her.

When they arrived at Tuscombe Park to collect Letty, Charley forcibly gathered herself, not wanting to reveal her emotions to the child or to anyone else. Sending Bess to the kitchen, where Mrs. Medrose could be counted upon to give her a hearty meal, she took Antony's arm, and went up to join the rest of the family in the drawing room.

To her surprise, they all were present, and she greeted her grandmother, Cousin Ethelinda, and Lady Ophelia with unfeigned pleasure. Her greetings to Alfred, Edythe, and Elizabeth were more restrained, and when she saw Rockland, she grimaced and said, "Are you still here?"

"By Jove, confess that you're glad to see me," he said, grinning at her. "I told you, I mean to stay for the consecration and to dine with the Duke. Alfred won't let me go, in any case. Says he'd never survive in this houseful of women without me."

"Might be the making of him," Lady Ophelia said crisply. Then with a narrow-eyed look at Charley, she added, "What have you been up to? You look perturbed."

Charley forced a smile. "Letty must have told you, ma'am, that Sir Antony and I had business to attend in Lostwithiel."

Alfred cleared his throat noisily, saying, "The child babbled some nonsense about interfering with an apprentice. I hope you did no such thing." He shot an oblique look at Antony, adding, "Not a proper matter to barge into, in my opinion."

"Indeed?" Antony raised his quizzing glass.

Charley said, "We certainly did interfere, Cousin, and I hope if you had seen what they did to that poor child, you would have done the same." Realizing that her voice had begun to shake, she pressed her lips together, wishing someone else would speak. They all seemed to be staring at her.

Cousin Ethelinda blurted, "Have you had any luncheon, dear? Perhaps—"

"I'm not hungry," Charley said, certain she would choke on food.

Tense silence fell again until Letty said suddenly, "When

you came in, I was just telling everyone of an amusing account I read in this newspaper. It's about a man walking on the common near Wadebridge, who suddenly felt his legs grasped by what he feared was an imp from the dominions of his satanic majesty. 'The appearance of the demon was black,' it says here, 'and it had a tail, which it twisted around his leg with great force.' '' She looked up with a twinkle. ''His satanic assailant was a monkey, which footpads had trained to help them rob people. Only wait until I tell Jeremiah!''

''Merciful heavens, child,'' Edythe exclaimed, ''what paper *is* that?''

''The West Briton,'' Letty replied, shooting a glance at Charley.

''That dreadful, common newspaper,'' Edythe said, making a face. ''Wherever did you come by such a thing, child?''

''I don't think I should tell you,'' Letty said calmly. ''I certainly don't want to get anyone into trouble merely for being kind to me.''

''Such impertinence,'' Alfred said sternly, ''only goes to show why females, especially young ones, ought never to be allowed to read newspapers.''

''Pray tell me, sir,'' Lady Ophelia said in a tone of dangerous calm, ''just how does the child's reading about a monkey show any such thing?''

''No good ever came of encouraging females to read,'' Alfred snapped. ''Women are hard enough to handle already, and females who read newspapers stuff their heads with things beyond their understanding. From what little I've seen of *The West Briton,* it's filled with liberal nonsense that no one of sense ought to read, let alone a child.''

Letty said thoughtfully, ''I have observed that men—''

''Hush, Letty,'' Charley said swiftly.

Lady Ophelia said, ''No doubt you fancy yourself a loyal Tory, sir, but I have never understood the idiocy of men who refuse to read what the opposition writes. It is quite the simplest way to know what they are up to. Moreover, *The West Briton* is amusing.''

"You have *read* it, madam?" Edythe exclaimed, clearly shocked.

"Certainly. My woman acquires a copy for me each week when I am in Cornwall. I also read the *Royal Cornwall Gazette* and the *Times,* and I can tell you that when one wants to comprehend a local election, *The West Briton* beats the others all hollow when it comes to printing the facts."

Feeling the onset of a headache, Charley looked at Antony, who said at once, "I fear I must curtail this conversation. If the gray cloud I noticed over the Channel is fog, we don't want it to catch us on the cliff path. Letty, are you ready to go?"

In the flurry of good-byes, Charley managed to steal a moment with Lady Ophelia, begging her to call at Seacourt Head so they could enjoy a more comfortable conversation.

"I'll come," the old lady said with another of her sharp looks. "Is he treating you well? I must say, you look as if you've been run off your pins, but I daresay a good bit of it is lingering grief over your parents' deaths."

"Good mercy, don't fret about me," Charley said, striving to sound perfectly normal. "Why, I've been so busy, ma'am, that I've scarcely had a moment even to think about that, so I promise you, I am not wallowing in grief." Turning to assure herself that Letty was doing all that was polite, she saw a moment later that Lady Ophelia had stepped away and was speaking forcefully to Antony. The scene made her smile grimly. She hoped the old lady was giving him pepper. She had a feeling that not too many people in his life had dared to do so, and she thought it would do him good.

She was a little surprised to see that Antony had spoken the truth about weather gathering over the Channel. It did not look threatening, and the sun still shone brightly, but she knew it could well be fog. Scarcely a day passed this time of year without any.

Letty seemed determined to chatter about her visit, speaking so disdainfully of Alfred that Antony called her sharply to order. Unabashed, she smiled at him and said, "Well, I would not say that to just anyone, you know, but the man has fluff for brains."

Antony said, "It is improper of you to say so, however, even to us."

"I didn't say it. Aunt Ophelia did. However, if you would rather that I not repeat such things, I won't. May I ride ahead? There isn't any fog yet, and I want to gallop."

"Very well," Antony said, signing to Jeb to go ahead with her. His own man and Teddy remained behind, with Bess again riding pillion behind the former. A few moments later, Antony said, "You did want to leave, did you not? I saw the way you looked at me."

Charley shrugged, avoiding his gaze. "Their bickering was giving me a headache, and I felt guilty that Letty had displeased Alfred again."

"Don't. Alfred is a prig."

She grimaced. "I won't attempt to refine upon that assessment, but Letty is getting out of hand, and I fear that I'm to blame. I've encouraged her to speak frankly, and somehow she has begun to go beyond the line of being pleasing."

"She's an enchanting child who is testing her boundaries, that's all."

"I hope her parents will agree with you when she returns to Paris."

"They will. Look here, I've learned something I want to discuss with you. Gabriel has heard rumors of a plot to capture Wellington when he arrives at Fowey."

"Good mercy!" The news diverted her thoughts instantly. "How?"

"He doesn't know, but he believes French smugglers are at the heart of it." He paused, looking at her with an odd expression in his eyes, then added dryly, "Gabriel says they may be led by a chap called Lee Renardo."

Charley stared at him. *"Le Renardeau?* You're joking."

"I wish I were. It is not the first rumor that has surfaced recently about him either, or the first that suggests he is in Cornwall. I just wish I knew the source. In any case, if you have any creative notions about this latest wrinkle . . ."

"But if there is a plot, surely you must have heard of it."

"Not a whisper. They are always plotting amongst themselves, of course, but I have heard nothing to suggest so massive an undertaking. Still, I must treat it as fact and plan accordingly, so if you can think of anything that might help . . .''

"I'll do my best," she promised.

They did not catch up with Letty before she reached the house, but as Charley went upstairs to change after presenting Bess to Aggie, she met Letty coming down. Jeremiah, perched on the child's shoulder and apparently searching for treats in her hair, paused in his search long enough to chatter a greeting at Charley.

Letty said with a grin, "He liked the story of the footpad's monkey, Cousin Charley. I wonder if we could train him to do something like that?"

"Letty, for shame!"

"I just wondered," the little girl said.

"Just keep him out of mischief," Charley said sternly.

"I will."

As she changed her clothes, Charley thought about the smugglers and forgot about Letty and Jeremiah, but when she went downstairs again, she was quickly reminded. Approaching the drawing room, she heard raucous squeals and shrieks, then a crash accompanied by the unmistakable sound of shattering china.

Chapter Eighteen

The first thing Charley saw when she entered the drawing room was what seemed like a thousand pieces of Sèvres porcelain scattered across the floor, some of them still moving. Letty stood amidst them, looking in dismay at the wreckage. Striding angrily toward the child, vaguely aware of Jeremiah leaping from the mantel to the top of the nearest curtains, Charley grabbed Letty and gave her a shake.

"Didn't I tell you to be careful?" she scolded, both hands now on the child's shoulders as she punctuated her words with more shakes. "How could you be so careless? That was Sèvres china, young lady, Cousin Melissa's favorite vase!" Her voice increased in volume, and Letty's eyes widened with alarm. Charley shouted, "You deserve to be severely punished for such carelessness, Letitia, and by heaven—"

"*Charlotte!*" Antony stood in the doorway. He said more calmly, "I want you, please. Letty will excuse you."

Charley scarcely looked at him. "Not now. Letty and Jeremiah just smashed Melissa's vase into a thousand—" Unaware that he had moved, she broke off with a shriek when he scooped her up and pulled her hand from Letty's arm. "Put me down!"

she cried, pounding him with her fists. "Damn you, Antony, put me down at once!"

Holding her with one arm around her waist, he clapped the other hand over her mouth. In the same tone he had used before, he said, "Ring for a maid to clean up the mess, Letty, then catch Jeremiah and calm him down. I'll look after your cousin."

"She's dreadfully angry," Letty said, still wide-eyed. "I have never seen her so angry." She looked down. "She did tell me to be careful. I'm sorry about the vase."

"The vase doesn't matter a whit," Antony said. "We will get Cousin Melissa another one, and you may choose it for her yourself. Now, go and do as I told you."

He removed his hand from Charley's mouth but made no reply when she began to rant again, merely hefting her up under his arm and carrying her from the room. Struggling to free herself, she called him every evil name she could think of, paying no heed to where he was taking her, even when he carried her outside, until suddenly she was airborne. Before she had drawn breath to scream, she heard the panicked quacking of ducks and the chilly waters of the horse pond closed over her head.

She came up sputtering, madder than ever, wanting nothing less than to see Antony dead at her feet. Splashing through waist-deep water to the edge of the pond, she scrambled out and, shoes squishing water with every step, advanced on him with fire in her eyes. "How dare you do such a thing to me! Letty deserved to be scolded, and you had absolutely no right to—*Antony, no!*"

He threw her in again.

This time she swallowed a large mouthful of water, and came up coughing, but she did not pause. Sputtering and gasping for air, she stormed back toward him.

Antony stood at the edge of the pond, hands on his hips, watching her. "Do not speak until you can compose yourself unless you want to go right back into that pond," he warned her, "because that is precisely what will happen, as many times as it must, until you can speak with a civil tongue. I will tolerate nothing less, and the sooner you learn that the better it will be for you.''

''How dare you!'' Angrily, she plowed her way toward the edge of the pond.

He straightened, waiting for her to step out of the water.

Recognizing his intent, she stopped a few feet away in hip-deep water and swallowed hard. ''Very well, I'll apologize, but you made me angry, and lately, when I get angry, I seem to lose every vestige of control over my temper. I c-can't help it,'' she added curtly when a sudden, unexpected ache in her throat made it hard to speak.

He stood looking silently down at her until she felt almost compelled to beg his pardon, to promise him she would behave better in the future. Biting back the impulse, she watched him warily, knowing she looked a mess but knowing, as well, that the way she looked was not what made her squirm before that uncompromising gaze.

He offered her a hand but said in the same quiet way as before, ''I don't think much of your apology, but since you have not had much practice in making them, I suppose it will have to do.''

Unexpected tears welled into her eyes. ''That's an awful thing to say—as if I were a child, or an idiot.''

''If you were a child,'' he said in carefully measured tones, ''and I were your father, I'd have put you across my knee right there in front of Letty and spanked you until you could not sit comfortably for a week. But you are not a child, Charlotte, and I am not your father.''

''No, you are not,'' she snapped. *''My father and mother are dead!''* Bursting into deep, racking sobs that shuddered through her body, she felt her knees give way beneath her. But she did not fall, for Antony was there.

Murmuring, ''At last,'' he picked her up again, gently this time, like a child, and carried her into the hedged garden at the back of the house, where he found a bench in the sun. There he sat down with her on his lap, and let her cry until she could cry no more. He said nothing. He just held her very tight.

For long moments after the last wrenching sob, she remained still, her face pressed against his chest, shivering in her wet clothes one moment, soaking up the warmth of the sun and of Antony's body the next.

When she shivered again, he said, "We had better both go inside and get out of these wet clothes before we catch our deaths."

"Not yet," she said. "Please?"

"Very well. I'm not as wet as you are."

She was silent for a moment, collecting herself. She felt utterly wrung out, but she wanted to make her peace with him while they were still alone.

"Antony?"

"Yes?"

"I-I'm truly sorry. I behaved dreadfully. I just don't know what came over me. It was exactly like the day I ripped up at Elizabeth, and the day Rockland told me you had known about his prank. I can't seem to stop. It's almost as if some other Charley takes over and starts shouting. Y-you don't think I'm losing my mind, do you?"

He chuckled, and she felt more warmed by that sound than by the sunlight. He said, "You are not losing your mind, angel. I didn't realize what was wrong, or I'd have made you let off some of the steam you've collected under your lid long before now."

"What steam?"

"We had a cook when I was still in the army," he said, his voice soothing, calm, and musical to her ears. "He made a stew one night in a heavy pot over a quick fire. The gravy bubbled up around the lid and baked tight, sealing the pot shut. All of a sudden, without the least warning, the lid blew right off that pot and nearly took a young soldier's head with it. The steam inside could not escape, you see, and it built up so much pressure that the lid finally blew."

"Is that what has been happening to me?"

"I don't think it will happen again," he said, "but yes, in a way, I think that is what has been happening. What with trying to look after Letty and manage everything after your parents and grandfather died, you allowed yourself no time to grieve.''

''But I never felt like grieving until just now,'' she protested. ''Then it just washed over me like a huge, unexpected flood.''

''You didn't allow it to happen before. I've watched you, angel. You like to be in control of your world, and you've rarely had to submit to anyone else's authority. It was the thought of having to submit to Alfred, remember, that made you look first to Rockland as a possible husband, and then to accept my bargain as your last hope of escape. Correct?''

''You know it is.''

''Then how could you allow yourself to submit to mere emotions? If you cannot control them, how can you control anything or anyone else?''

''I don't try to control people!''

''Don't you?''

Much as she wanted to deny it, she hesitated.

''What about Rockland?'' Antony prompted.

''That's not control,'' she said scornfully. ''The man cannot make the simplest decision on his own. If I didn't tell him what to do, he'd never do anything.''

''He did at least one thing on his own,'' Antony reminded her with a smile.

''That was an aberration,'' she said, squirming to get off his lap. ''I'm beginning to get cold now. There's clouds drifting across the sun. We'd better go inside.''

''Very well,'' he said, helping her stand up, then getting up himself. He retained a light grasp on her arm, however, and when she would have turned away toward the house, he restrained her, adding gently, ''Don't get the idea that I'm through with you yet, because I'm not. Not by a long chalk.''

''But why? I've apologized, haven't I?''

''I am not the one who deserves your apology.''

Her gaze met his, and although she expected to see sternness, what she saw was understanding. Looking away, she sighed. ''You mean I've got to apologize to Letty.''

''Do you think you need not?''

''It's humbling to think that I must, that's all.''

"Once you have cleaned up and are feeling more the thing, you will manage it well enough," he said.

Glancing at him again, she wondered why she did not resent his insistence upon such an apology. Instead, she felt steadied, and more sure of herself than she had felt for some time. She managed a watery smile. "I won't wait. You are quite right. She deserves an apology, and I mustn't put it off. Will you come with me?"

"Oh, yes," he said. "Didn't I say I'm not through with you yet?"

"But you can't mean to scold me any more! Not when I've already admitted my fault and apologized for it."

"No," he said, putting an arm around her and urging her toward the house, "I won't scold, but we are going to talk about your parents and your grandfather. And don't bristle like a hedgehog," he added when she frowned, "because it won't do you any good. I found early on in my interesting career that the worst thing a man can do if a friend falls in battle is not talk about him. The Irish hold wakes where they drink and carouse and generally celebrate the deceased person's life and memory, and that, my angel, is what we are going to do as soon as we've got you all cleaned up."

Charley did not reply. It was not the thought of talking about her parents and grandfather that silenced her, however. It was the casual way Antony assumed—if she had not misunderstood him—that he was going to help clean her up.

Inside the house, he said to the footman, "Have a bath prepared for Lady Foxearth in her bedchamber, John, and be sure someone builds a blazing fire to go with it. She took a tumble into the pond, and we don't want her to take a chill."

"Yes, sir."

"Where is Lady Letitia?" Charley asked, trying to maintain at least a semblance of her dignity, despite the fact that the footman was taking great care not to look at her.

"She is still in the drawing room, my lady."

"Thank you." Conscious of her squishing shoes, and of Antony's presence behind her, Charley went to the drawing room, where she found Letty curled up on the window seat with Jeremiah, staring out at dark clouds gathering over the Channel.

The little girl turned at once when they entered and got quickly to her feet, leaving the monkey on the seat. Speaking rapidly, she said, "We've got it all cleaned up, Cousin Charley, and I'm very sorry that I broke it, and I've written a note to Cousin Melissa to tell her that it was all my fault and that I'm very sorry, and—"

"Letty darling, hush, it's all right," Charley said. "Come here and tell me you can forgive me for being such a horrid shrew." She held out her arms, and Letty rushed into them, only to jump back again with a gasp.

"You're soaked to the skin!"

"Sir Antony thought I needed to cool my temper."

"He did?" Uncertainly, Letty looked from one to the other.

Glancing at Antony, Charley saw that he was smiling at her. Though Letty clearly was bursting with curiosity, Charley knew Antony would reveal no more than she did herself. Without further hesitation, she said, "Letty, I-I must apologize for shouting at you like I did, and even more for shaking you. You did not deserve that."

"But I wasn't careful, and I did break the vase," Letty said. "It wasn't Jeremiah at all. I was reaching to catch him, and I knocked it over."

"That was still an accident. Even if you had done it on purpose, which you never would, it would have been no excuse for my behavior. Will you forgive me?"

"Of course. I daresay you are very tired after everything that has happened these past weeks, and I have observed that when grown-ups are tired, they do not always behave as sensibly as they might otherwise."

"You observe quite a lot, I think."

"I expect so. Should you not change your clothes? You are shivering."

"I mean to do that straightaway, darling." Giving Letty another quick hug, she turned to go. Antony paused to speak to the little girl before he followed her, then took the stairs two at a time until he caught up with her.

"What did you say to her?" Charley asked.

"I just suggested that a double serving of Aggie's apple tart with clouted cream might tempt her to have her supper in the housekeeper's room."

"But why should she?"

"Because, angel, I don't want our little talk to be interrupted. We'll have our supper up here." He reached ahead of her to open the door of her bedchamber. "Ah, Kerra, excellent. Here is your mistress, dripping wet. Pop her into that tub as quickly as you can, and don't let her out until she's thoroughly warm again."

"You're very decisive this afternoon," Charley said with an edge to her voice.

"I am, am I not? Would you care to contradict my order?"

"Go away, Antony."

"I will for now, but I'll be back in a trice, just as soon as I've told John we want our supper served up here, and to check the windows. I think there's a storm brewing."

"Antony?"

"Yes?" He paused on the threshold, looking back.

She hesitated, aware of the maid and uncertain of him in this mood. He had not lost his temper or argued with her, but he had ordained her every move since she had lashed out at Letty. On one hand, it was oddly pleasant to let someone else make decisions for her. On the other, she did not like being told what to do, and at the moment he was giving her no choice. She said, "Don't come back till I send for you."

"Get into that tub, angel, before your bones start rattling." Then he was gone.

As Charley turned to let Kerra begin stripping her wet clothes off, she caught sight of her own reflection in the glass, and gasped. Her eyes were red and swollen from crying, her cheeks blotched and white from her emotional storm and the cold. Anyone who had seen her in the past few minutes must know she had been weeping.

Looking over her shoulder at Kerra, who was undoing the hooks at the back of her gown, she saw that the maid's eyes were fixed resolutely on her task.

"I expect you must wonder how I became so wet," Charley said quietly.

"It is not my business to wonder, my lady, but as it happens, one of the lads who helped fill yon tub said you had tumbled into the horse pond."

"Oh, he did, did he!" Another score to settle with Antony. "Doubtless everyone at Seacourt Head will know the whole tale by dinnertime!"

"If you will just let me slip this gown off, ma'am, we can get you into the tub."

With a sigh, Charley submitted. She could smell the spicy scent of her favorite bath salts, and she saw that Kerra had set aside the soap she used to wash her hair. Putting her feet in the tub was hard, because the water felt too hot at first, but once she sat down, she leaned back and closed her eyes, relaxing, inhaling the delicious scent.

Remembering her ravaged countenance, she murmured, "Dip a cloth in cold water for me to lay across my eyes for a while before you wash my hair, Kerra."

"I've witch hazel, ma'am. I'll dip some cotton in it to put on your eyelids. The smell will overcome the spicy one, but it will do more for your eyes than plain water."

Moments later, eyes closed, half dozing, Charley felt as if her muscles had turned to warm wax. The first touch of the soap bar on her shoulder startled her, but the lathering was swift and sure, over her shoulders and up her throat to her chin, then down her right arm and over to her left. She let the maid do all the work, and concentrated on relaxing, letting the warmth penetrate to her bones.

When the soap moved toward her breasts, it moved more slowly, caressingly. The motions were unusual, for Kerra had helped her bathe many times, and usually she lathered her shoulders and back briskly, then left her to wash those portions she could reach by herself. Although the maid had not asked her to bend forward so she could soap her back, as she usually did, she thought Kerra had merely respected her evident desire to lean back and relax. The soap dipped between her breasts.

Lethargically, she raised one hand and removed the witch-hazel soaked pad from her right eye to look into her husband's grinning face. "Antony!" In her shock, she sat bolt upright, then slid quickly back down in the water, losing the other witch-hazel pad in the process. "What," she demanded, "have you done with Kerra?"

"Sent her away."

"Well, get her back, and go away yourself. You have no right to come in here while I'm bathing."

"I am your husband, angel. We can begin our little talk at once." His hand rested lightly on the curve of her right breast, and Charley found it hard to breathe.

Swallowing, she said in a gruff voice, "Do you think you are going to wash me all over? Because if you do, you can think again."

He sighed. "A very tempting thought, I'll admit, but I daresay you can wash most of the best bits by yourself. Bend forward, and I'll scrub your back."

Certain she would do better not to defy him, she obeyed.

"How do we wash your hair?"

"*We* ring for Kerra to do it."

"I don't think we need Kerra," he said, unpinning her hair and letting it fall over her shoulders and breasts. "However, if I am not to do something wrong, you'd best tell me what to do. In between, you can tell me about your father. What manner of man was he? Were you fond of him?"

"I didn't really know him very well," she said. From that point, the words flowed more easily than she had thought they would. Between instructions about soap and rinse water, she found herself telling him things she had never told anyone. She described how her parents had spent much of her childhood wrapped up in the social whirl, going to London for the Season, to Brighton for the summer, then to endless house parties during the hunting season, rarely spending time at Tuscombe Park.

"Didn't you mention a house in Plymouth?" he asked her.

"I did. We lived there for brief periods after my cousin Melissa moved away to Scotland, but until I grew old enough to go to London for the Season myself, I spent most of my time with my grandparents and Great-Aunt Ophelia. For that matter, until Aunt Daintry married Letty's father, I spent more time with her than with my parents. After she married, Papa and Mama made an effort to spend more time with me, but . . . do you know, Antony? Before this afternoon, I cannot recall a single time in all my life that I curled up in someone's lap and cried my heart out like that. Isn't that odd?''

"Bend over again," he said. ''I've got to pour rinse water over your hair again.'' When he did, it ran into her ears and she got soap in her eyes. He handed her a cold, damp cloth to take the sting away, and said, ''Tell me more about your mother.''

Telling him was easier than she had thought it could be. She felt as if, just by explaining Davina to him, she began to understand her better, and herself as well. She described her grandfather, a staunch believer in the superiority of the male sex, and told Antony about the vituperative arguments St. Merryn had frequently engaged in with Lady Ophelia, who had made no secret of the fact that she thought the earl an idiot.

"That must have been fascinating for a child," Antony said, holding out a huge towel for her and averting his eyes while she stood and quickly wrapped herself in it.

"Oh, it was," she said. ''They even fought about the Bible. Aunt Ophelia believes ancient men made the whole thing up to suit themselves. She once told Grandpapa she was only thankful to know that had a good English barrister presented the case of Eve's apple before upright English magistrates, the blame must have fallen where it belonged, and Adam would have found himself in prison.''

"Adam? But Eve was the one who tempted him.''

"A bagatelle, sir. Will you hand me that wool robe on the bed, please? You see, by English law, anything a woman does in the presence of her husband is assumed to be done under his command and control. Silly, of course, since many women act in direct opposition to their husbands' commands, but there it is.''

Antony chuckled. "I like your Great-Aunt Ophelia.''

"Do you, sir?'' Charley slipped behind a screen, dropped

the towel, and wrapped her robe securely around her. "I adore her, but I warn you, she terrifies most men."

"I don't terrify easily," he said.

She stepped from behind the screen, her damp hair tumbled about her shoulders and down her back. Smiling, she said, "You don't, do you?"

"Come, sit by the fire. While we dry your hair, you can tell me more about your childhood."

"We've talked enough about me for a time, and you were right, in that I feel much better for it. The pain isn't gone, but it's no longer a huge knot inside me. Tell me about your family, Antony. I know Alfred is not your brother, but I don't know if you've even got a brother."

"I have no family to speak of," he said curtly.

"What became of them?" She was determined this time to find out something about his past.

"They disowned me when it became known that I had spied for Wellington."

"I know you said that your father disapproved of that. I still think he ought to have been proud of you for helping the Duke defeat Napoleon."

"Gentlemen don't stoop to spying," he said bitterly. "England does not take unfair advantage of any opponent."

"Is he the one who said that to you?"

"He agreed with it, but I heard those words first from my mother."

"Oh." She knew in that moment that he had helped her enormously, for the anger that struck her, though sharp, did not threaten to overwhelm her. Carefully controlling her countenance, she turned so the heat from the fire could reach her hair. "As you brush," she said, "pull up so the hair separates as it falls. It will dry quicker."

"Yes, my lady."

Glad she had not distressed him with her questions, she said airily, "That demure attitude won't help you, you know, for I'll get even one day. I don't take lightly to being ducked in a horse pond."

"Then don't give me cause to do it again."

Swiftly, she stood and faced him, saying, "Antony, don't think that because I've agreed that I was wrong this time I shall submit meekly now to your every whim and caprice, because I won't. I deserved what happened today, and . . . and I am grateful to you for stopping me before I'd done or said anything truly horrid to Letty, but—"

"Come here," he said.

"What?"

"You heard me." He held her gaze, but he did not seem displeased. Indeed, a twinkle lurked in his eyes, and she found it oddly disturbing.

"What are you going to do?" The mood in the room had shifted abruptly, and her body, which until a moment before had felt relaxed and warm, now stirred to alert awareness. The sense of warmth deepened and spread through her. She licked her lips, watching him. "Antony? Answer my question."

"Come here."

Only the dressing stool separated them, a distance of no more than two or three feet. Watching him, her gaze locked to his, Charley stepped around the stool without another word, suddenly knowing that, more than anything else in the world, she wanted to feel Antony's arms around her again.

Setting down the brush, he put his hands on her shoulders, drawing her closer. She realized that she had been anticipating this from the moment he had suggested he would help her clean up. His arms went around her, and his lips touched hers, softly, then harder, as if the passion stirring in her were aflame in him. He moaned against her lips before his tongue tickled her lower one. A hand moved to the opening of her robe.

A rap at the door and the sound of the latch heralded the arrival of their supper, and with a start of dismay, Charley whisked back to her seat on the dressing stool and handed Antony the hairbrush. By the time the footman and Daisy entered to lay the covers, Antony was rhythmically brushing her hair again.

Over dinner, they talked of politics and news from the *Times* until the servants left them with their fruit and wine. Emboldened by the latter, Charley looked straight at him and said, "I think your father is a fool, you know, and your mother—"

"Both my parents are dead."

"Then I used the wrong verb, that's all."

"Unfortunately, most Englishmen think like my father. Going through a man's private papers is bad form. Spying on his troops or trying to learn his battle plans is equally distasteful. My father was not the only one to give me the cut direct at Brooks's."

"Good mercy, he never did such a horrid thing!"

"He did. And now, if you please, I should much rather talk some more about Lady Ophelia. I don't think my family boasts anyone like her."

"She is unique," Charley said, shocked that his father had humiliated him in such a public way, and quite willing to tell him more about the elderly feminist. She hoped to soothe away the pain she had detected when he spoke of his parents, but she succeeded beyond expectation, for twenty minutes later, he roared with laughter.

When he could speak again, he said, "I know you told me she thought men had written the Bible to suit themselves, but she cannot have said they molded their notion of God to that same purpose!"

"She did. She said it's clear that they wrote the Bible as proof that God intended men to be superior, because how else could they ever have expected anyone to swallow such a clanker as woman being born of man? Why would an all-powerful God go to all the trouble of creating man first, just to have to cut out a rib afterward to make woman, when all he had to do was create her first and let her give birth to man in the natural way. Mary did not require Joseph, if you recall, to conceive the Christ child, nor, apparently, did God think to create Christ without Mary. One therefore has to believe, according to Aunt Ophelia, either that God was all about in His head to create man in the convoluted way the Bible says He did, or that a few idiot men made the whole thing up."

Antony's eyes danced. "Angel, do you believe these things, too?"

She smiled. "Truly? I don't know what I believe. My parents and grandparents were traditional. Even Aunt Ophelia goes to church on Sundays—to keep up with the latest nonsense being preached and know what the enemy is thinking, she says, but—" Breaking off, she said with astonishment, "Antony, the Duke is much like Aunt Ophelia, is he not? He does not think like your father or those other men you mentioned before. He wants to know what the enemy is thinking. Is that so dreadful?"

"I don't think it is, of course, but then, I'm like you in that I don't know quite what I believe about some things. I used to follow all the proper Anglican teachings. I believed in God and goodness, and that if one followed one's conscience, everything would come right in the end. I was wrong. Tell me more about Lady Ophelia."

She complied, making no further attempt to draw him into talking about his past. She enjoyed both his conversation and his company, and when he stood at last and bent to kiss her hand and then her cheek, she made no effort to conceal her disappointment.

"If I even begin to kiss you like I did before supper, angel, we will very soon have no grounds for that annulment you want," he said, bidding her a firm good-night.

Watching him go, vaguely aware that rain was streaking the dark windows, Charley wondered for the first time if she would enjoy independence as much as she had thought she would. She rather thought she was going to miss Antony.

Chapter Nineteen

Antony lay in bed, staring at the ceiling, feeling noble one moment, frustrated the next. In his mind's eye he tried to imagine Charlotte lying awake too, but he thought it far more likely that she was fast asleep by now. He did not know what time it was, and although the oil lamp on the bed-step table needed only to be turned up to see the little clock beside it, he made no effort to move. He did not care in the least what hour it was.

He had held her in his arms. He had seen her naked body, and he had kissed her. His hunger for her now could not be ignored. He wanted her. He wanted to taste her again, to touch her, caress her, and to possess her. She was his wife by the laws of Britain and the Church of England. By rights, all he need do was crook his finger and she would submit to him. The thought was delicious, tantalizing, stimulating. He would order her to lie back against her pillows, naked, her soft breasts vulnerable to his touch, to his kisses and caresses, her slender legs spread in welcome.

A chuckle rose unbidden in his throat. Charlotte Tarrant would never—not if someone told her the earth would begin to spin backward if she refused—welcome a man in such a way. The image of her rising from the horse pond, splashing awkwardly toward him, not once but twice—with murder in her eyes—was the real Charlotte, and in truth, he knew he preferred the real one.

A distant rumble of thunder reminded him of what she had said about storms at the house on Seacourt Head. He wondered if she was afraid of thunder. Unlikely, given the general level of her courage, but he had seen war heroes cringe and cower when the heavens roared.

The next rumble sounded closer. The storm was approaching fast. He got up and moved to the window, pulling back the curtains. At first there was only blackness more dense than that in his bedchamber, where an occasional crackle from the dying embers on the hearth sent sparks dancing into the darkness. Then a jagged, branched lightning bolt lit up the night. He saw sparkling black water. Crashing waves edged with lacy white foam created a border for the dark cliffs around St. Merryn's Bay. Thunder rumbled, and before the noise died away another flash lit the scene outside like daylight. The crack of thunder that accompanied it rattled the windows. The next flash and boom came only seconds later, and then the storm engulfed the house. Rain lashed the windows and the wind howled, shaking the walls, threatening to blow the house right off its high perch into the sea.

He stood watching, mesmerized by the storm's fury. In a sudden lull, he heard a metallic click and then a soft, "Oh!"

Turning just as another flash lit the heavens, he saw Charley framed in the dark doorway that separated their rooms. In those few brief seconds of light he saw that she wore only her white lawn nightdress. Her feet were bare, her hair tousled, and her eyes were wide with shock or fear.

"What is it?" he asked, taking an anxious step toward her only to see in the next flash of light that she had turned sharply away. "Don't go. Wait!" Only then did he realize he was stark naked.

* * *

With her eyes squeezed tightly shut, Charley hesitated in the doorway. She had been foolish to come to his room, but she did not want to go back. This might well be the only chance she would ever have, yet one glimpse of his naked body had nearly sent her bolting from the room like a skittish mare.

The fury of the storm was already abating. She heard him clearly when he said, "I'm putting on my robe. You can look now. Were you frightened?"

"No," she said without thinking, her eyes still shut tight. Realizing instantly that she ought to have said yes, she opened them again. She had been lying in her bed, staring at the ceiling, wondering if he was awake or asleep. She could remember the feeling of his arms around her, the comfort of his embrace, the wondrous feeling of being cared for, looked after, held. Her memories had skipped uncontrolled from the scene in the garden to that in her bedchamber when she had suddenly realized that he had sent her maid away, to bathe her himself. She had savored those moments of intimacy with him, embroidering them in her mind until her imagination boggled. She simply did not know enough to embroider the scene to its climax.

Having bred horses for years, she understood the mechanics, but she could not imagine them being pleasant. Still, if the way her senses had reeled when he touched her was any indication of the possibilities, she was determined to learn more.

She realized he had not spoken again and, curious, opened her eyes at last. He stood right in front of her, so close that she nearly cried out. He was outlined in golden light, and she saw that he had turned up the lamp on the step table by his bed.

"Are you certain you are not afraid?" he asked gently. "There is no shame in such fear, you know. Even the bravest of soldiers has been known to cringe when thunder crashes overhead and lightning splits the sky."

"I grew up here," she reminded him. "Not in this house, of course, but the storms are as fierce at Tuscombe Park."

"One does not have a sense there, however, that one could at any moment be swept into the sea. Do you think Letty might be frightened?"

"I doubt it. She told me she has no sensibilities, and I believe her. She is probably watching from her window, just as you were. Besides, it's nearly over."

"If you were not afraid, why did you come?"

"I knew you would be awake." She hesitated, cursing herself for a fool. If she had said she was afraid, he would have held her again, comforted her again. Honesty was all very well in its place, but she certainly could not just spit out the statement that hovered at the tip of her tongue. "I want you to cover me."

"What?"

"I can't believe I said that." Laughter bubbled around the words. "Good mercy, what you must think of me! I swear to you, I never meant to say that." She looked at him, but she could not see his face clearly. Realizing that with the light behind him, he could see hers, she looked away, lest he recognize her doubts. She wanted to leave, but her feet seemed glued to the floor. "Say something," she pleaded. "I know I'm making a fool of myself. I had no notion that arranging a coupling could be so hard."

"Good Lord! Well, I knew you didn't want another quilt." His voice sounded odd, as if he were speaking through clenched teeth, or trying not to cough.

"I expect there's another way to put it. I want you to—"

"I know what you want."

Now she thought she could discern amusement. "So help me, Antony, if you are laughing at me . . ."

"I'm not. God knows, I'm not. But if you could manage to think in human rather than equine terms, perhaps we—"

"Equine? You think I'm thinking about *horses?*"

"Don't you always?"

"In actual fact," she said, straining to recover her dignity, "what I know about such matters does come from what I know about horses. When my cousin Melissa married, I tried to get her to tell me about her experiences in the marriage bed, but she always seemed to avoid my questions."

"I'd like to meet your cousin Melissa. She sounds like quite a strong-minded woman if she can ignore questions from you."

"Don't be such a rudesby. Will you do it?" Again, she wished she could see his expression, especially when he did not answer immediately.

A branch of lightning forked across the sky, followed by a long, fading rumble of thunder, but his expression told her nothing. Not until the sound disappeared in the distant night did he say, "I want to be sure I understand you. You merely want to know what happens in the marriage bed. Is that it?"

"Not just *know*. I don't want you to tell me stories or draw pictures for me. I want you to do it, to show me how it's done."

"But we've discussed this. Consummation could make an annulment impossible."

"Could, not must. The point is that since I never intend to marry for real, I shall never know what happens. Until today I didn't much care one way or the other— Except for an occasional surge of curiosity, that is."

"Until today?"

She shifted from one cold bare foot to the other. "In the drawing room, and then again when you were kissing me before the servants brought our supper, I experienced some odd sensations, very pleasant ones."

"That is perfectly normal," he said, "but it is not a matter for simple experimentation, angel. There are bound to be consequences."

"You mean the annulment. Well, I cannot believe anyone would really ask me such impertinent questions, but if they do, I need only poker up as if I were in utter shock at being asked. That's what Elizabeth would do, I know. I don't think," she added musingly, "that I could flat out lie to Bishop Halsey."

"Do you think I could?"

"Quite easily." She moved past him, so that he had to turn, and she was relieved to see that he was amused by her response. She grinned at him. "You've had ever so much practice at telling falsehoods, after all."

"Not to bishops," he retorted.

"Well, mayors are much the same thing, I expect, and you've lied to members of the gentry and the nobility, so even a bishop cannot be beyond your skill."

"My dear, sweet idiot, do you honestly mean for me to believe that *you* would lie to a bishop in a sacred matter?"

"But I've just explained that I won't have to. If necessary, I'll affect a fit of the vapors, and everyone will stop plaguing me with disagreeable questions. Now, Antony, there cannot really be anything wrong about this. We are lawfully married, after all, and I am quite certain that other marriages have been annulled after a consummation."

"There is always Henry VIII," he murmured.

"Exactly." She reached out to touch him, and although her fingertips were light against his chest, she felt him quiver. "I did not think it would be so difficult to convince you," she said, looking into his eyes. "A stallion needs only to know that a mare is willing. In actual fact, even that much is not—"

"Good Lord," he snapped, catching her by the arms and giving her a shake, "do you think I am made of stone? What if you become pregnant?"

"From one time? Don't be absurd?"

"How many times does it take for a mare?"

"But that's because one knows precisely when a mare is in season," Charley said. "With human females, I don't think one can tell as easily. I don't know that for certain, and you no doubt know much more than I do about such things, so do please tell me if—"

With a groan he pulled her to him and silenced her with a kiss. At first his hands gripped her arms with bruising strength and his lips pressed hard against hers, as if he would crush her, but when she put her hands at his waist, he groaned again. His hands slid from her arms to her back, pulling her tight against his body.

She could feel his heat against her, and the pressure of his erection. That he desired her was evident. That he knew what he was doing was also evident. Daringly, she slipped one hand beneath his robe, and when he gasped against her lips, she felt a surge of unfamiliar power. His flesh felt warm and hard and smooth. When he did not try to stop her, she slid her hand around to his back, feeling the slope of his hip and buttock.

She moved her hand upward, letting one finger trace the ridge of his spine.

His tongue touched her lips, pressing for entrance. Welcoming him, she darted her tongue to meet his, delighting at the sound of a moan deep in his throat.

Slipping her other hand beneath his robe, she laid it flat against his stomach, sliding it provocatively lower.

Before she realized he was moving, he caught her roaming hand with one of his.

Her lips felt swollen. She looked up in surprise. "Why did you stop me?"

"We must. I cannot be responsible for what may happen, and while you might well believe yourself willing at present, when the sun rises—"

"I'll feel the same. Damn you, Antony! Why do you insist on making this so difficult. Don't you want me?"

"One of us must be sensible."

"That is *not* an answer."

"Very well then. Yes, I want you. Are you satisfied?"

"What a stupid question! Of course I'm not satisfied. You worry about things that you think I should worry about. You take my burdens on your shoulders when I don't even consider them burdens, because they haven't happened yet. Tell me this. How have you kept other women you've coupled with from getting pregnant? And don't say you've never— How *dare* you laugh at me!"

He made no effort to stop but laughed till he had to hold his sides. Only when she picked up a book from a nearby table and held it threateningly did he control himself enough to say, "If you throw that, I'll put you over my knee. That's Will's *Taming of the Shrew* and I won't have it damaged."

"Your bedside reading, in fact?"

"I own, I did just dip into it earlier."

"Looking for advice about how to deal with me, sir?" Her tone was scathing.

He grinned. "If you like to put it that way. My remedy if you throw that book is the same as Petruchio's for a waspish female." When she frowned, trying to remember the scene, he said, "When Kate strikes him, he threatens to cuff her if she does so again. In some productions, she does. Like Petruchio, 'I will be master of what is mine own.' "

She remembered the rest of that citation, but although it was comforting to imagine Antony shouting, "Touch her whoever dare," she remembered his warning about the only times he quoted from works of the Bard. Although she did not think he was angry with her, she did not want to test his threat. Putting down the book, she said, "Why did you laugh at me just now?"

"Not at you, angel, only at your candor. I cannot imagine that many men would appreciate it as much as I do, or tolerate it, for that matter."

"If it is so intolerable, sir—"

"Not to me. I told you before that I find it refreshing, but it's a very good thing you did not marry Rockland, I think."

"Why?"

"Imagine his reaction if you had asked him about his barques of frailty?"

"Good mercy, does he have any?"

"Most healthy unmarried men past a certain age do, but I beg you, don't ask him."

She was silent, her emotions warring with her thoughts. An unexpected ache at the back of her throat made it difficult to say, "Must I go back to my room?"

"No." His voice was gentle, and when she looked at him, she saw tenderness in his eyes. "I'm going to stir up the fire, so if you'd like to get into my bed, I'll join you as soon as I've finished."

Feeling oddly shy for one who had spent the past quarter hour seducing a man, she looked at the high, broad bed for a long moment before moving slowly toward it with one eye still on her husband. He was not a man accustomed to letting others call the tune for his dancing, and she wondered how much longer he would allow her to do so, if in fact he had allowed it thus far. She had an odd notion that she was the puppet and that Antony still held the strings.

His bed smelled invitingly of the citrus water he used after shaving, and as she slid beneath the covers, she felt both wanton and wary. She knew, in that moment, that the thought of sleeping in his bed had tickled her imagination from the moment of discovering she had married him instead of Rockland.

She watched him stir the fire to life, then glanced at the little clock on the bed-step table. It was past one. She looked back at Antony as he straightened and turned. His robe fell open and when he saw her looking, he shrugged it off, casting it onto the bed. He had a splendid body, but she paid scant heed to the play of muscles in his broad chest and shoulders or his firm, well-shaped thighs and calves. She could not take her eyes from his sex, tumescent and throbbing.

He climbed into bed, bunched pillows behind himself, and slipping one arm behind her, drew her toward him. She trembled but did not resist. Still willing, still curious, she felt nonetheless awed by her temerity. Had it been anyone but Antony—

"Penny for your thoughts."

She started. "I-I was just thinking I'd never have done this with anyone else."

"Just as well. Your husband would object."

"Would you?"

"I most definitely would."

"Oh." She snuggled more comfortably against him. "Well, you are not exactly my husband, after all. It is just a role we are playing for a time."

"A role you seem determined to alter."

"You said you want me."

"No use denying plain fact, angel, but there will be consequences. You seem to have assumed that I'll lie about this to the bishop if I'm asked. I won't. Moreover, it has occurred to me that there might be a more fundamental reason for your behavior tonight than mere feminine curiosity."

"What?"

His arm tightened around her. "You lost control today in a big way. We talked about your determination to control your life, your emotions, pretty well everything around you, and in many ways, you've been losing that control since the day you met me. First, your parents were killed. You couldn't prevent that tragedy, or change it. Then along came Alfred and his family, and when Rockland outmaneuvered you, you ended up, through no choice of your own, married to me. Is it possible that tonight's behavior may be an attempt to regain control over your life? If you can manipulate me, even seduce me, then the power to rule your own life leaps back into your hands."

"I wouldn't! I-I couldn't!" She looked at him, confused and bewildered. "Do you really think that is what I'm doing?"

"I don't know. It is also possible that after such an emotional upheaval as you experienced today, you are just seeking shelter, and the comfort of friendship."

A flash of unholy amusement caught her unaware, and her lips twitched. "I don't think I would ask a mere friend to show me the secrets of the marriage bed, Antony."

"Perhaps not," he agreed, his smile warming her to her toes, "but just in case all this stems from more than vulgar curiosity, I propose that we take matters slowly."

"Can you do that? I thought that when gentlemen were aroused, they had to ease themselves or suffer pain. I saw how aroused you became, you know, and certainly, stallions can become utterly crazed with—"

"Angel, if you don't stop comparing me to a horse, I swear, I'll either kick you or bite you."

She chuckled. "But *can* you go slowly?"

"There are rules," he said. "For whatever reason, you seem peculiarly vulnerable to seduction right now. Friends don't take base advantage of such moments, and we are friends. For lovers, the rules are a little different, but we're not lovers."

"N-no." She felt sad, wishing suddenly that she could say she did love him, or pretend he loved her, wishing she knew what love was, and wondering if she would recognize it if she tripped over it. Lady Ophelia had said more than once that one did not fall in love, one stepped into it rather like one stepped into things in a stable yard. Even so, one ought to recognize where one had stepped.

"It's just as well that we're not lovers," he went on calmly, "since my life scarcely lends itself to any permanent arrangement. Still and all, if you find that you are determined to follow through with this experiment, knowing the consequences and accepting them, I expect it's better to do it now with a man you're properly wedded to than to do it later with someone altogether unsuitable."

"I wouldn't!"

"Curiosity is but lust of the mind, you know, so only time can tell that. Now, however," he added, forestalling argument, "the first thing you'll want to learn is how male and female bodies react to being touched. That will help you recognize and fend off particularly knowledgeable but unwelcome suitors. For example, a lady's arm can be quite sensitive. Here, I'll show you what I mean." He shifted himself a little onto one side, facing her, and raised her right hand to his lips, kissing the back of it. "A simple gesture," he said. "No doubt, some chap or other has kissed your hand in greeting."

"Many times," she agreed, "but they usually wear gloves, and a gentleman does not actually press his lips down like that. He kisses air, mostly."

"True," he murmured. "Still, you feel no particular sensation when my lips touch you there."

He was wrong. She felt his lips and breath in a most extraordinary way, and she wondered if perhaps she ought to tell him her whole body was tingling just from being so near him, but he turned her hand over and pressed his lips into her palm just then. The tingling turned to fire, making her gasp.

"You see," he said, his breath hot against her palm, "a woman's body lends itself to seduction. The inside of the wrist is also rather sensitive," he added, kissing it lightly, "and the forearm. I will just untie this pretty pink satin ribbon and open your sleeve a bit, if you will permit the liberty."

She could not seem to breathe, let alone to object as he suited action to words, his lips tracing a path up her forearm toward the inside of her elbow, his hand gently pushing the delicate lawn sleeve higher and higher. When his tongue touched the sensitive skin at the bend of her arm, Charley moaned and leaned back against his supporting arm, arching her back and then gasping again when the movement caused the material of her nightdress to caress the sensitive tips of her breasts.

Antony smiled. "Your body is alive, angel. It leaps to the slightest caress. I wish now to kiss your neck, just here beneath your pretty little ear. A gentle kiss, like the touch of a butterfly's wing. So. Here, and here."

The kisses tickled, but the tickle was unlike any she had ever felt before, stirring warmth and other, unfamiliar but delightful, sensations throughout her body.

"Do you like that?"

"Good mercy, don't stop!"

"I have only just begun." His fingers trailed lightly around her neck, his lips following until they found the hollow of her throat. Here, she felt his tongue again, warm, like moist velvet, and a strange aching sensation touched her at the fork of her legs. Arching again, she drew a long, shuddering breath.

"Sh-should I be doing something to you?"

"Be still," he murmured. "This is only the first lesson. Do not be in a hurry to learn everything at once" His fingers touched the ribbon near the hollow of her throat.

She tensed. "What are you doing?"

"Relax, angel. 'Tis no more than when I bared your arm. The cloth is in my way." He parted her bodice, trailing kisses over the plump curves of her breasts.

"Are you going to leave that lamp burning?"

"Certainly, I am. It gives me great pleasure to watch you."

She was breathing faster, shallow breaths. His hand was at the second ribbon tie. There were no more. With that tie undone the gown would open to her thighs. She caught his hand but did not try to move it away.

His hand turned beneath hers, and suddenly his was the captor, hers the captive. When she did not resist, he raised hers gently, pressing it back toward her shoulder, where he caught and held it with his other hand. Her right one was still free, and when he reached for the tie a second time, she grabbed his hand again.

He said, "Tell me to stop, and I will, angel. If you don't want that, put your hand down. Touch me if you like, but let go of my hand. I am going to open your gown. I want to look at you. I want you to feel my eyes upon your naked flesh."

Shuddering at the strength of the feelings tearing through her body, she did as he commanded, marveling as waves of pleasure swept over her. Antony parted the gown gently, baring her to her waist. As the cool air caressed her, he bent over her, touching his lips to the space between her breasts, then rising up again to gaze at her, still holding her left hand in his, taking his time.

With his free hand he cupped her right breast, pressing lightly with his fingertips then watching the soft flesh spring back when he eased the pressure. His forefinger moved tantalizingly toward the tip of her breast, but now he was looking into her eyes. When the finger reached the tip, she jumped, and when he caught the nipple between his thumb and forefinger, rolling it a little, pinching lightly, she moaned, shutting her eyes to savor the sensations. When his lips replaced his fingers, she cried out and arched her back again, her breathing quickening to sharper, more rapid gasps. The ache between her legs increased, becoming unbearable, demanding comfort.

His hand was on her belly now. His lips moved from right breast to left as the hand stroked her. He still held her left hand at her shoulder, but her right lay between them, unheeded, as she gave herself up to the sensations he ignited throughout her body. His hand slid lower, closer to the ache. Involuntarily she stirred again, her mind and body silently urging his hand lower and lower. As she strained to savor every new sensation, her breathing remained shallow and quick. Her feet and hands felt numb.

His hand touched the hair between her legs, and when his fingers moved, exploring her nether lips, she cried out again, softly. Raising her right hand at last to touch his chest, she discovered something else. "Antony, I can barely feel my hands or feet, and my face tingles. What's happening?"

* * *

Antony paused in his explorations, raising his head to look at her face. Despite golden light from the lamp, it was nearly as white as her gown. When he released the hand he had been holding, she clutched it with the other one, rubbing them together.

"They tingle," she said, "but my fingers and toes have gone to sleep. What caused it? Does it always happen?"

"No," he said. He saw that she was breathing rapidly and, though he had rarely met with such a reaction, he thought he knew what had happened. Laying her against the pillows and drawing the two parts of her bodice together, he tied the ribbons, saying, "Take slow, deep breaths, angel, and try to relax. I have seen this before."

"Have you, indeed?" She tried to sound virtuously outraged, but he could tell she was still a little frightened.

Lightly he said, "Soldiers waiting for battle to begin sometimes breathe quickly, and their limbs grow numb, too. I don't know exactly why, but I do know the sensation will pass if you relax and breathe normally. I think our first lesson is over, however."

"But that is not all there is, surely."

"There is much more, and if you still want to learn, I will teach you. I don't think this will happen again, now that you know what to expect."

"They are waking up already," she said, grimacing as she rubbed her hands together and moved her legs and feet. "They prickle. Tell me what it feels like to you to do such things to me. Why do you like to watch what you are doing?"

No woman had ever asked him that before, but then he could not remember talking to any of his occasional partners about the act, or having the least desire to do so. Moreover, he was not at all sure Charley really wanted to know what he felt.

He smiled, drawing her closer. He had enjoyed watching her reactions, feeling them, provoking them. He said, "I suppose I feel curiosity at first. When I first met you, I was interested." The word was inadequate to express what he had really felt.

He tried to think of better ones. "I've never met anyone like you. I don't suppose I ever expected to, so there's an enticing wonder, but you are very much a woman, angel. Tonight, I felt an overpowering curiosity to discover just how much woman I had."

"You wanted to see me without my clothes, in fact."

"Since the wedding," he admitted, not quite willing to admit that he had wanted to see her naked from the first moment he had seen her smile.

"Am I desirable, Antony?"

He swallowed. "I think there is no man in his senses who would not find you desirable." She was breathing normally again, and her color had returned. He said, "Can you feel your toes and fingers now?"

"Still a little tingly, but I can feel everything. Will you kiss me again?"

"I will," he said, lightly kissing her cheek, "but then we will sleep, for tomorrow we must decide how we are going to protect the Duke."

She moved against him, turning her face up in clear invitation. He could not resist, and this time when his lips touched hers, her mouth opened and her tongue darted out to meet his, teasing him until it was all he could do not to take her at once. Thinking to teach her a lesson, he plunged his tongue into her mouth, holding her tightly, then pressing her back against the pillows, but she only demanded more.

Clutching at him, she moved her hands over his body as if she were urging him to possess her. Knowing he had awakened innocently sleeping passions, he wondered if she would ever forgive him—if, knowing what she now knew about herself, she could ever be happy as a single woman. She had insisted she wanted the experience, and he had not wanted to deny her, or himself, the pleasure. He knew he would not deny her if she came to him again another night, either, but now he forced himself to pull away, saying firmly, "That's enough. You may sleep here if you like, but before we explore further, I want to know you are not making a foolish choice in the heat of passion.

Believe me when I tell you that things will look different in the morning.''

She glared at him, furious, but she did not argue.

''Good night, angel.''

She sighed. ''Damn you, Antony.''

Chapter Twenty

When Charley awoke the next morning, she was still in Antony's bed, but he was gone. She had fallen asleep quickly and had no memory of dreams or stirring in the night, but now memories flooded into her mind. Clearly, there were things about married life, and about men, that she had never known or considered before now.

The curtains were shut, and since she knew he had not bothered to shut them after she entered his bedchamber, she assumed he had drawn them that morning so the sunlight—if there was sunlight—would not wake her. His bedchamber, like hers, faced west in any case, but the gesture had been a thoughtful one. She was finding, in many ways, that she rather liked being looked after.

She liked other things, too. When she recalled what he had done the previous night, her body tingled all over again. Such a pity, she thought, that it had betrayed her just as matters got particularly interesting. Wishing yet again that she had someone with whom she could talk about such things—another woman, with more experience than she had—she sighed and stretched. She missed Melissa.

Three weeks had passed since she had written, so she knew

a reply must come soon. She had no doubt what it would say, for once Melissa got over the shock of learning she had married, she would insist that Seacourt Head House was entirely at their disposal. But when Charley tried to imagine confiding details to her of the past weeks—and the previous night—she found herself grinning. Even as a married lady, Melissa would not, she felt sure, be entirely receptive to such personal confidences.

She stirred restlessly, trying to recapture the sensations that Antony had awakened in her, but she could not. Remembering his prophecy that she would regret the impulse that had driven her to him, and to his bed, she wondered if he regretted giving in to her even to the extent that he had. Would he be disappointed, or surprised, to learn that far from regretting her impulse, she looked forward to repeating the experience, even to expanding upon it? She did not think he would refuse her a second time.

Wondering where he had gone, she remembered that he intended to find a way to protect Wellington from the men who wanted to capture or kill him. The thought brought her upright, for she wanted to know what he would do. More than that, she wanted him to include her in whatever he planned.

Slipping from the high bed, she hurried to her room where Kerra had opened the curtains to reveal a sky presently clear of both storm clouds and fog. She rang the bell, and when the maid arrived, bringing hot water, Charley said, "Fetch my riding habit while I wash, please, Kerra. Is Sir Antony still downstairs?"

"He was in the breakfast room when I come up, ma'am. He don't dawdle about, but the papers came, so happen he'll be looking at one or another of 'em yet."

He was reading the *Times* when Charley entered the breakfast room, but he lowered it and gave her a long, thoughtful look.

"Good morning," she said cheerfully.

His smile was crooked and did not reach his eyes. "No regrets?"

"Not one." She looked more closely at him. "You look as if you've got a few, however. Vexed, sir?"

"With myself, not with you. We played with fire last night, angel. Fire burns."

"We are not children, Antony. I am four-and-twenty, and you're—"

"Older than that, but the stakes are high, and since this marriage is a sham, it behooves us to take care."

"Does that mean you won't give me any more lessons? You said you would, you know."

"It means that we must beware of the consequences. You don't want a husband, and I don't need the responsibility of a wife and perhaps a child. We both have put more faith than we should in your determination never to marry again."

Before she could reassure him that she never would, the footman looked in to see if she required anything that he had not already set out. "I'll have tea, John," she said, peeking under the nearest lid. "Oatmeal porridge! Don't you ever eat anything else for breakfast, Antony?"

"Toast and coffee," he said. "One thing I missed during my years on the Continent was good oatmeal porridge, and to have it swimming in rich Cornish cream is an added pleasure. Don't you like oatmeal?"

"I'd rather have ham and toast with a boiled egg, or just toast and honey." Taking the honey pot with her to the table, she sat down opposite him. "Do go on reading your paper if you like. Has anything of interest occurred in London?"

"The Metropolitan Police Bill will get a third reading today in the House of Lords," he said, "and Wellington will lead the discussion on Friday. Now his enemies oppose the bill because it does *not* include the City of London."

She chuckled, spreading honey on her toast. When he folded the paper and put it down she said, "Where is Letty?"

"Riding with Jeb, Sebastian, and Jeremiah. Did you sleep well?"

"I did. Have you devised a plan yet?"

His eyes twinkled. "I have not, and I'll thank you not to discuss that particular subject where anyone else might overhear you."

"But I want to know what you mean to do. Moreover, I want to help."

"Very well." The footman returned with her tea, and Antony shot her a mocking look as he said, "That will be all, John. You may shut the door." When the man had gone, Antony said, "We must first think of a way to divert any vessel that might try to waylay the Duke's ship. Have you any notion how we can do that?"

"Wellington means to land at Fowey, does he not?"

"Yes. If I could have got word to him to land elsewhere, like Falmouth, that might have done the trick, but I knew of no way to tell him in time, or of knowing afterward whether he had taken my advice."

"Falmouth would have been more sensible," she said thoughtfully. "It's only thirteen miles from Truro. Why is he landing at Fowey?"

"Because that was his original plan. Not only did your grandfather invite him to dine at Tuscombe Park the evening after the consecration, but Wellington wants the people of Cornwall to see him. He means to travel in style from Fowey to Truro, then take a roundabout way back to Fowey by way of Lostwithiel and Tuscombe Park. Since Alfred renewed St. Merryn's invitation, he had no need to alter those plans. I'd intended for us to meet him in Fowey and travel with his party to Truro, but now . . ." He paused.

Charley was still thinking, listening with half an ear, but when he fell silent she looked up and said, "If he leaves Portsmouth Saturday morning and arrives at Fowey in the middle of the night, as most likely he will unless the wind blows directly from the east—" She broke off, adding, "He will sail from Portsmouth, will he not?"

"Yes, it's the quickest route from London, but although we know it takes about eleven hours by road from London to Portsmouth, the winds, the weather, and the tides will dictate how soon he will arrive in Fowey."

She frowned. "Won't they keep watch for him off St. Merryn's Bay? If you could somehow manage to intercept his ship between here and Plymouth . . ."

"We could never be certain of doing so. He won't be flying the Royal Standard, after all, and there is a lot of water between here and France."

"But won't he sail along the coast?"

"Not likely. Sailing too near the coast can be dangerous, and with capricious winds, it's not unusual for ships to sail nearly to France to reach Cornwall. Locating one ship in particular, at night, would be nearly impossible."

"Then how will the assassins find him?"

"I don't know. The strangest thing about this is that, in all this time, I have not heard a word about any plot against Wellington. No matter how careful they've been, or how secret their plan, I should have heard at least a whisper. I know they expect to land goods of some sort within the next sennight, but if any lad I've talked with knows Wellington is a target, or that the main action is to take place at sea, I've seen no sign."

"You said they don't really trust you," she pointed out.

"True, but most of the lads anticipating work are spotsmen, lookouts, and tubmen, not sailors. They expect their prize to come to them. In any event, as I said, there is no way for them to be certain of waylaying the Duke's ship in the Channel. That is precisely why, if I'd had my way, he would have sailed from London to Falmouth, done the road between Falmouth and Truro in a well-guarded coach, and then we'd have gone straight back to London after the ceremony."

It was the first time Charley had considered the possibility that Antony might leave Cornwall with the Duke. "Must you go back with him?" she asked with an unexpected lump in her throat.

"No," he said evenly. "I have matters to attend to here first."

She caught his gaze and held it. "What matters?"

"Did you think I would simply abandon you, then attend to the annulment and set up your independence after I returned to London?"

His tone challenged her, but she said calmly, "Since it only just now occurred to me that you might return with the Duke,

I hadn't thought about the rest of it at all. Won't some of that business *have* to be looked after in London?''

"Certainly, but there will be papers to sign here, too," he said, getting up.

"Don't go yet," she said, adding quickly, "You haven't said what you mean to do—a-about Wellington, I mean."

He paused, gazing solemnly at her. The silence lengthened before he said, "I want to think more about that."

"You don't intend to tell me!"

"Yes, I will, if only because I don't trust you not to go haring off on your own."

"I wouldn't."

He smiled then. "Will you give me your word of honor that you won't?"

She hesitated, but when his smile twisted sardonically, she said, "I'd give it in an instant if I thought I could trust you to confide your plans to me."

"Touché," he said. "I deserved that, I expect. I've told you before, I don't trust easily, angel, even though I know you would not harm me intentionally. By the same token, however, I need to know where you will be, so your actions don't inadvertently compromise mine. We must also consider Letty. I don't know what I'll be doing during the next two days, and I don't want either of you to miss that ceremony."

"No, I must be there to take my part, and Letty is quite looking forward to it."

"I know, but I can hardly take the pair of you into Fowey and leave you at an inn alone until the Duke arrives. Folks would wonder where Sir Antony had got to, and if he appeared with you, they'd watch us too closely for me to accomplish anything."

"Letty and I could meet you in Fowey early Sunday morning," she suggested.

"You could, but in truth, I'd feel less concerned about your safety, and hers, if you would agree to spend Saturday night at Tuscombe Park and travel to Truro with Alfred's party. If you will do that, then I need only look after Wellington." When she hesitated, he said, "You could suggest to them that I had important business with the Duke, although that might make Alfred squirm if he thinks I am pleading my case for the St. Merryn estates. Perhaps you'd better tell them I'm meeting an old friend, Harry Livingston, whom I've not seen in years, and I feared you would be bored. Harry is on the Duke's staff, and will dine at Tuscombe Park with us after the ceremony.''

"Very well," she said with a grimace. "That was not what I had in mind when I said I wanted to help, but I daresay Alfred won't need much explanation as to why you don't want to be saddled with me or Letty. *He* would think us very much in the way.''

"Then you'll do it?''

"Yes, but now you must tell me what you mean to do about Wellington.''

"I did say that, didn't I?'' When she nodded, he sat down again and leaned back, stretching out his legs and folding his arms across his chest. His eyes twinkled. "The best part of keeping one's counsel is that one need never reveal slowness of mind, and can always look brilliant after the fact without ever admitting to stupid ideas or plans gone awry. Dare I confess now that I haven't got a notion of what I intend to do?''

His humor was contagious, and Charley felt herself responding, wanting to reach out and touch him, to tell him they would find a way together. But touching him might lead to other things, and at the moment, Wellington's safety must come first. "Have you no ideas at all?'' she asked. "How do you usually devise one?''

"The simplest plan is always the best,'' he said. "The problem lies in defining the simple plan, and all we know for certain is that Wellington will be on a ship moving from Portsmouth to Fowey sometime Saturday night.''

"We must hope last night's storm was not the first of a series,'' she said, "but even if it is not, we may have fog, you know. Not only is it particularly common this time of year, but we frequently have thick fog within two or three days after any big storm. At the least, judging by the weather this past fortnight, the sky will be overcast or cloudy. On this coast, even smugglers like a little moonlight.''

"I know they do," he said, grinning, "but wreckers don't."

"No, wreckers prefer strong winds and high incoming tides to sweep their victims ashore. Last night would have been excellent by their standard."

"I've experienced only the one wreck, and that was caused by weather. What do wreckers do if there's not enough wind or a strong enough tide to provide a victim?"

He was watching her through narrowed eyes now, and as she gazed back, a glimmer of an idea stirred. "They misdirect their prey," she said. "There are stories, horrid ones, about wreckers in the Scilly Isles who lit fires to look like lighthouses, causing ships to wreck on the rocks. Cornishmen are even worse, they say. They don't allow them to tend the Scilly lighthouses, out of fear of what they might do."

"They tend lighthouses here in Cornwall, however," he said thoughtfully. "As I recall, the nearest principal ones are on St. Anthony's Head near Falmouth, Gribbon Head west of Fowey Harbor, and the Eddystone Light off Plymouth. Is that right?"

She nodded. "There is a small one at the Deadman, too, and more beyond Falmouth. I believe that ships coming into the Channel from France or the Bay of Biscay use the two at the Lizard, and the Eddystone when they can see it, to orient themselves, but surely you aren't suggesting we darken some lights and create our own? There are other ships sailing Channel waters, after all, wholly innocent ones."

He grinned. "Do you think I could do that, darken the big lights?"

"Couldn't you?"

"I suppose I could arrange it, at that, but we've less than three days now. Still, if darkness would wreak havoc for the scoundrels, what about too much light? Perhaps we could turn their own tricks against them, by adding lights hither and yon."

"That would also wreak havoc for innocent ships in the Channel."

"How did they prevent accidents before they had light-houses? Or after the Eddystone Light was swept into the sea? You know it's not the original one, I expect."

She rolled her eyes. "It's not the second either. The first

went down in a storm, taking its designer and a lot of others with it, and the second burned down. The present stone one ought to stand until Armageddon, however, unless the rock beneath it crumbles. As to how they guarded the coast before, they used lightships similar to our pilot boats, sailed by men who knew the coast, and watched for approaching ships to warn them off.''

His brow furrowed again. Content to watch him, Charley let her thoughts drift until, with a sigh, he looked at her and said, ''We have a number of problems.'' He ticked them off on his fingers. ''First, we don't want to send all shipping off course for a night. Second, we don't want to cause anyone to run aground. Third, we want Wellington to arrive safely at Fowey. Fourth, we don't yet know who is after him, or what they plan to do. Gabriel said the villains are in league with the French, so the first thing I need to discover is what French ships are harbored nearby, and if others are expected. Oakes can help me there, I know. I'll have a talk with him, and tell him what we've learned. For one thing, he can arrange to make sure we have no villains manning our lighthouses.''

''What do you want me to do? If you need signal fires or lightboats, they will take time to prepare. I could begin if we can decide where they ought to be.''

''I want one fire right here on the headland, visible from either side,'' he said. ''It won't fool anyone accustomed to this coastline unless it's a truly dark night, but along with a few others, it might confuse a vessel enough to make it unsure of its location, and unlikely to attack another ship. Wellington's captain will use the Eddystone as his mark, and will expect the next light to be Gribbon Head. Our lights won't fool him, I hope, but the more I think about it, the more likely it seems that the scoundrels must intend to draw them off course somehow. That does make me wish he were landing at Falmouth. With all the traffic in and out of that harbor, they couldn't hope to tell which ship was his.''

''Fowey used to be the major port,'' Charley said. ''When Edward II captured Calais, Fowey sent more ships with him than the rest of the kingdom combined.''

"I'm very glad to know that," Antony said with a teasing twinkle in his eyes.

She stuck out her tongue at him.

He stood up again. "After I talk with Oakes, I'm going to see what more I can find out. I don't doubt Gabriel had information about villainy afoot, but unless they think they can board Wellington's ship in the harbor and take him captive there, I can't imagine how they mean to get him. As for fires, I daresay you'll find that Corlan knows what's wanted, because if this headland has not served the same purpose in the past, I'll eat my boots. On a dark night, extra lights would disorient anyone who doesn't know this coast like the back of his hand."

"I'm still uncomfortable about confusing innocent ships," Charley said.

"No ship will be in real danger," he said. "They need only hold off till morning to get their bearings, or signal for the aid of a pilot boat from one of the ports, but I'll see if I can't arrange for a few extra pilots to be on hand if that will ease your fears."

When he had gone, Charley went to find Sam Corlan, and to her amusement, learned that he knew as much about setting signal fires on the headland as Antony had predicted he would. Leaving him to attend to the business, with little more than a glib explanation that the master wanted some bonfires lit Saturday night as a celebration signal to incoming ships, she ordered Dancer saddled and went to find Letty, to tell her that their plans for the next couple of days had become somewhat unsettled.

When they met on the headland path, Sebastian barked a greeting, and Letty took Jeremiah from inside her cloak and put him on her shoulder. The monkey promptly began grooming her hair. Separating strands with his nimble fingers, he peered at them as if he were examining each shaft for lice or mites. Untroubled as usual by her pet's activities, Letty said, "Is something amiss, Cousin Charley?"

"No, merely undecided," Charley said, watching the monkey with affectionate amusement. "We don't know exactly when His Grace will arrive at Fowey, you see. Sir Antony had planned for the three of us to ride from here to meet the Duke's party Sunday morning. Now he finds that he may want to meet his ship when it arrives instead, which may be late Saturday night. He is a trifle concerned about the Duke's safety, you see, and thinks it might be better to warn him to take special care.''

"When will we know exactly what Sir Antony means to do?''

"That's the problem. He does not know that, himself. I suggested that we could ride to Fowey to meet him early Sunday morning, but he would prefer that we spend Saturday night at Tuscombe Park and go to Truro with Alfred and the others.''

Letty frowned. "How long is the journey to Truro?''

"About two and a half hours at this time of year, barring accidents.''

"What about Sunday night? I know we are expected to dine at the Park after the ceremony, but will we come back here after that?''

"I don't think so, darling. It would be rather late by then to ride back, and taking a carriage means a much longer trip, you know. If I'm not mistaken, Sir Antony will expect us to impose on Alfred's hospitality until Monday morning, at least.''

"Jeremiah will get very lonely without me," Letty said.

"You must help him become accustomed to being with Aggie. He likes her already, because she frequently gives him treats.''

"Yes, but she doesn't like him mucking about in her kitchen," Letty said, unconsciously echoing what Charley knew must have been Aggie's own words.

"Then ask Bess to look after him," Charley said, her mind already moving to other, more important matters. "She is always happy to oblige.''

"I like Bess," Letty said, "but when is Jenifry going to come? If she arrives before we go to Tuscombe, can she go with us? I'd like to have my own companion there. No one pays me any heed unless I go into the nursery, and really, Cousin Charley, Neddy and Jane are entirely too young to be amusing.''

"We'll see," Charley promised. "I expect Jenifry will want to come here as soon as her parents say she is fit to do so."

As it happened, Jenifry arrived early Saturday afternoon with her father. Greeting her fondly, Charley sent her upstairs with Aggie to find Letty, who was supervising the packing of what she would require at Tuscombe. Then, drawing Cubert Breton into a small downstairs parlor, Charley said anxiously, "Is she truly fit, Cubert?"

"Aye, she is, miss, or as near as can be, considering." The man's voice was gruff, and he seemed to have a hard time looking at Charley, but at last, he straightened, squared his shoulders, and said bluntly, "We be much beholden to you, Miss Charley, to you and Sir Antony both. You saved our Jen, you did. There be no way to repay the debt, but if ever you've a need, I beg you will let me do what I can. My Wenna says the same. She sent this coverlet, made for you with her own two hands." Tugging his graying forelock, he gave her the brown-paper-wrapped package he carried.

"Thank you, Cubert. How very kind of Wenna, but I require nothing more than to know Jenifry is safe and well. As it is, now I shall worry about you getting back to the moor safely before the fog catches you. It will be upon us soon, doubtless as thick as yesterday, but as it happens, Lady Letitia and I are riding to Tuscombe Park to spend the night, so you can ride with us. You'd do well to stay at Tuscombe overnight, too."

"Thanking you all the same, ma'am, but I've work to do come morning." His eyes shifted again, not meeting hers, but then he looked right at her, and said, "Happen I'd a bit o' business hereabouts the night, so it were no hardship to be bringing our Jen. She's been fretting at the house. Does too much thinking, she does, and sees that devil Michael Peryllys behind every sheep and shadow. Happen she'll feel safer here at Seacourt House, though, to my mind, there be little to choose betwixt 'em." He hesitated, then said diffidently, "Would Sir Antony be at hand just now, miss?"

His look was intent, and remembering that, like many others in the area, he frequently lent a hand to smugglers for no more than a barrel of wine, Charley wondered if he knew what the coastal gang planned to do. Knowing she must tread lightly, she shook her head in response to his question and said, "I'm afraid he's been gone for two days, Cubert. I don't expect to see him until tomorrow."

He nodded, shot her another sharp look from beneath his thick salt-and-pepper eyebrows, shifted his feet, then said as if he were changing the subject, "Saw Sam Corlan toting wood toward the point, Miss Charley. Would you be knowing his purpose, ma'am? I ain't asking just to be prying like. Give you my word on that."

Charley hesitated. She trusted Cubert Breton despite his reputation, and she did not for a moment believe that after what Michael Peryllys had done to Jenifry, Cubert would aid him in any enterprise. She believed that he felt beholden to her, too, and she did not think he would lie to her. She said, "You know that the Duke of Wellington will be in Cornwall tomorrow, that his ship is due to sail into Fowey Harbor tonight."

Cubert nodded, his intent gaze never leaving her face.

"Sir Antony has heard rumors," Charley said quietly, "that there will be an attempt to capture the Duke and hold him to ransom."

Cubert blinked, and a frown creased his brow. He said, "But who would do such a thing to the great man, and him being our own Prime Minister?"

"They say someone here in Cornwall is in league with French smugglers who have an old quarrel with him. Someone mentioned the name *Le Renardeau,* but . . ."

He shrugged. "I've heard the name, but only fantastic things, ma'am, like droll-tellers' tales. Ain't no one ever claimed to see this Renardo, neither. I warrant as how they made him up out o' whole cloth so as to have someone else to blame when—"

"When what, Cubert? What are they going to do? Sir Antony wants to know."

Cubert grimaced, glanced out the window, then back at the half-open door. Stepping to the door, he looked into the hall, then shut it firmly before he turned back and said, "Miss Charley, I always thought you had a good head on your shoul-

ders and was less likely than any female I ever knowed to fly
into a fuss without cause."

"Cubert, I'm trying very hard to be patient. What do you
know?"

A wry smile twisted his lips, but the wary look that accompanied it told her he had no wish to make her angry. He said,
"Happen there be a ship in jeopardy tonight, Miss Charley.
B'ain't the Duke's ship, howsomever, and if Sir Antony goes
blundering about, not knowing what's o'clock, as you might
say, he's bound to come to grief."

"Good mercy, Sir Antony is out there somewhere, very
likely risking his life to discover what threat exists against the
Duke of Wellington, and here you stand telling me there *is* no
such risk. Who are they after if not Wellington?"

"Merchantman, miss, from Biscay. Michael Peryllys and his
lot mean to wreck her in St. Merryn's Bay or on Devil's Sand.
But it ain't just that, Miss Charley. They say Michael set someone to watching of Sir Antony since the business over our
Jen—said we never had no trouble till he came into Cornwall—
and if Sam Corlan's a-building up a fire for the night, 'tis my
belief he's in on it with the lot of them."

"Sam is following Sir Antony's orders," Charley said, hoping that was so, and that she and Antony had not played into
Michael's hands. The thought that he had set a man to watch
Antony sent chills up her spine. "How will they do it?" she
demanded. "There's little wind, and if the fog comes in, they'll
be as hampered as anyone else."

He shrugged. "Dunno, miss. Happen the Frenchies have got
a fellow on board to steer the ship off course or cause some
sort of accident that'll bring them in closer, fog or no fog.
Wind may pick up some, too, and I heard talk of a pilot boat
out o' Fowey. One way or another, they mean to have the cargo
off that ship."

"How do you know all this?"

He shrugged, but when his gaze slid away from hers, any
thought she had had of enlisting his aid disappeared. Cubert
was grateful that she had saved Jenifry, but he was not so
heedless of his own safety, or that of his family, as to reveal

everything the coastal gang had planned, if indeed, he knew everything. Most likely, he had heard some of the rumors James Gabriel had heard but, with inside knowledge, had more accurately understood them. Or, perhaps, he was simply unwilling to admit personal knowledge of a plot to capture Wellington and either kill him or hold him to ransom.

"Cubert," she said, "I've changed my mind. I will send Lady Letitia and Jenifry to Tuscombe Park with armed grooms to ensure their safety. I'd be grateful if you would be so kind as to accompany them . . ."

"Aye, Miss Charley, I'll do that right enough, but what of you?"

"I have some thinking to do," Charley said. "Wait here, if you please."

Expecting to encounter difficulty persuading Letty to agree to the change in her plan, she hurried to the child's bedchamber, only to discover that Letty had little thought beyond her excitement over Jenifry's arrival.

"I'm sorry you won't be there," Letty said when she had explained, "but since Jenifry can go with me, I won't even mind when they make me dine alone."

"Won't you, darling? I'm glad, for I cannot imagine Alfred or Edythe taking kindly to a suggestion that you do so when the Duke is there. I'm sending Teddy with you, by the bye, as well as Jeb and Mr. Breton. I want you to feel quite safe."

"But won't you need Teddy?"

"No," Charley said. She did not want to have to explain her half-formed intentions to a groom who had known her all her life. The only person to whom she would look for help was one she was certain would not try to hinder her.

When she had seen the girls off with their escort, she went in search of Hodson, finding him in his master's dressing room, putting clothing in a portmanteau. He turned politely, giving her his full attention.

"Hodson, I've changed my mind about tomorrow," she said. "Lady Letitia has gone on to Tuscombe Park, but I mean to join Sir Antony in Fowey in the morning."

The man said mildly, "Do you indeed, madam?"

"Yes," she said firmly. "I expect that you are taking those things to him, so that he can change from Jean Matois back to himself for the ceremony."

Showing no surprise at her knowledge, he said, "That is correct, madam."

"Will you see him tonight?" She could hear the urgency in her tone. So far, she had managed to bury her fears in the need to decide what her actions would be, but her composure was fragile at best.

"I do not expect to see Sir Antony until morning, madam," the valet said, "but he did ask that I bespeak a chamber for him to use then. I sent a lad yesterday to attend to that, and I am going myself now to take Sir Antony's shaving gear and clothing, and to assure myself that all is in readiness for him. Shall I take your things as well? I shall not stay there, because he feared that if I were seen to be in residence overnight at the inn, someone might question his absence. I will gladly escort you tomorrow if you like."

Nodding, she said, "If you should chance to see him, Hodson, tell him I've heard that the coastal gang is after a merchantman, and that a pilot boat might somehow be involved. But don't look for him, lest you put him in danger by doing so. You must come back here if this is where he will expect to find you if he needs you."

"And you, madam, if I might be so bold? May I tell him what you plan to do?"

"I don't know what that is yet. I wish I did. My first impulse was to ride for help, but in truth, I know not whom to trust. I can just imagine trying to convince the constable at Fowey that he must raise a hue and cry over a possible attempt to capture Wellington, or the possible wrecking of a merchantman in St. Merryn's Bay or on the Devil's Sand. He would think me mad."

Tactfully, Hodson said, "I do not believe the master would appreciate a hue and cry over anything just now, madam."

"Very likely not," she agreed, "but I am also afraid that the villains might have realized that Jean Matois and Sir Antony are one and the same, Hodson. What if they have found him out and taken him prisoner, or worse?''

''That, if I might take leave to say, madam, is a frequent worry where the master is concerned. I myself have felt it often over the years. However, I have learned that he nearly always lands on his feet. You will say that, as his valet, I cannot suffer the same level of anxiety as one who harbors more tender feelings toward him, but I assure you that until you hear he has been put six feet under, there is no cause for alarm.''

Remembering that Antony had said Hodson knew the facts of their marriage, Charley nearly reminded him that she was not in love with her husband. She held her tongue, however, because whether she was in love with Antony or not—a phrase that sounded much more like a partnership now—she knew that she cared more about him than she had ever cared about anyone before in her life. If that was love, so be it. In any case, she did not contradict Hodson.

By the time Hodson returned it was dark, and she saw at once that he had not met with Antony. When she asked if he had spoken to the constable, he said, ''No, madam. As I mentioned before, it is best to rest one's faith in the master. I have found that when I did not do so, I took a grave chance of upsetting his carefully laid plans.''

He said no more, but Charley did not miss the warning. She tried to contain her soul in patience, but not being a patient person by nature, she soon found her fears increasing to a point where she could no longer sit still. The more she thought about Michael setting a man to watch Antony, the more frightened she became. She had to know. Only then did it occur to her that Michael Peryllys was a wanted man, that if she could tell the constable where he might be found, the constable would have to act.

Upstairs, as she changed to her riding habit without Kerra's help, her mind raced from one thought to the next. Deciding she could do nothing else until she had learned whether Michael would be at St. Merryn's Bay or on the Devil's Sand, she found her gloves, pistol, and riding whip, then put out the lights and opened her curtains. The sky was cloudy, and she had to wait for the slender moon to peep out before she could see the sweeping beach of St. Merryn's Bay. She saw no activity, but it was early yet, not more than half past nine. She needed to know more before she rode for help.

Hurrying to the stable, she met no one, and no one disturbed her as she bridled Dancer, flung her saddle onto the gelding's back, and drew the cinch tight. Grateful that she was not a female who needed others to perform such tasks for her, she holstered her pistol, mounted quickly, and guided the horse out of the stable. Minutes later, she was cantering along the dark track toward the cliff road high above the Devil's Sand.

On the road, she slowed Dancer to a walk until they were past the headland, then dismounted to walk near the edge, looking down. Her eyes had adjusted fully to the darkness, and although the sliver of moon gave her little light as it played hide and seek with the clouds, she was able to see enough of the silvery sand below to know that the tide was starting to turn. She saw no sign of human movement on the beach.

Commanding Dancer to kneel so that she could mount again, and stilling a sudden fear at being so near the edge, she rode back the way she had come, going past the turning to Seacourt House, and along the path above St. Merryn's Bay. She had not ridden far when she saw a single flicker of light on the shingle below. It was gone in an instant, but it had been enough. Someone was there.

Curiosity stirred, and she told herself that Fowey's constable might not believe her solely on the basis of rumor and one flickering light. Thus it was that although she passed the first and second of several precipitous trails leading down to the beach, when she came to the third, she rode away from it, off the main path, and into a protected hollow. Tying her reins to some scrub shrubbery, she hoped Dancer would remain there undisturbed until she returned, and that any sound the gelding made would be attributed to the gang's own ponies, which must, she knew, be somewhere nearby.

Taking her pistol from the holster on her saddle, she picked up her skirt and hurried back along the main path to the narrow, twisting trail that led down to the beach. She did not mean to go all the way, just far enough so that she could find a spot that would give her a good view of what was happening below. She had taken no more than ten careful steps down the steep path, however, before a dark figure loomed up and grabbed her, and a heavy hand clapped over her mouth.

Chapter Twenty-one

Antony crouched some distance from the opening of the largest of several caves that the sea had carved into the chalk cliff. He knew that Michael's men stood in the entrance, and he did not want to draw attention to himself. Though it had taken time to learn where they would be, he had found them easily enough, but although he had watched most of them enter the cave, he had not seen Michael.

Gabriel had got his signals crossed, he thought, for if these men were after the Duke, they did not know it. They had spoken of him, and a few had done so with some chagrin, but he suspected those simply feared they might miss seeing him. All their attention now was focused on the sea, but in the direction of the Bay of Biscay, and they murmured of a merchantman and riches to be had before the night was over.

He had feared at first that someone might recognize Jean Matois and Sir Anthony Foxearth as one and the same. Earlier, when he had eased his way into their midst, more than one had given him a sharp look, especially when he asked about Michael, but each man with whom he had spoken expected to see Michael on the beach tonight.

Antony soon decided he had not been wrong in thinking the

men had grown more reticent, and he soon understood the reason. For some time he had known that they both liked and mistrusted the fact that he spoke French. It meant they were no longer wholly dependent upon Michael to tell them what the Frenchmen said; however, they did not trust Frenchmen. Now, unless he was much mistaken, they had also heard the rumors of *Le Renardeau*'s presence in Cornwall.

At another time, in another circumstance, he might have found humor in being outmaneuvered by his alter ego. Tonight it was not funny. He could only be thankful that no one had accused him outright of being the elusive Frenchman. He hoped they would continue to assume that someone with such a vast reputation for cunning as the Fox Cub enjoyed would have a more imposing personality than the simple Jean Matois.

Men moved on the beach now, quietly and without lights, except for one idiot who had lighted his spout lantern moments before, only to have another man douse it with a muttered curse. The moon disappeared behind a solid bank of clouds, and the chilly mist made itself felt. As darkness and damp closed around him, Antony wished he had thought to provide himself with oilskins.

The brief glow of lantern light had ruined his night vision, but it was returning. He could see the lacy crests of waves breaking against the shingle now. The tide was rising. He didn't suppose it would make much difference to the wreckers' plan if it began to ebb before the merchantman arrived—if it did arrive. He was still skeptical. That they had set their trap in St. Merryn's Bay instead of further to the east argued that they expected their prey to approach from the west, but without yet knowing exactly what they intended, he did not dare assume that Wellington was safe.

He hoped Oakes and his men were well hidden, and would not move too soon. Moonlight glimmered through a break in the clouds, highlighting waves as they broke on the shingle. The beach appeared deserted, but he knew men hid behind many a boulder, watching the sea.

His thoughts drifted to Charley, and he wondered what she was thinking at that moment. No doubt she was annoyed that he had not returned to Seacourt Head to tell her all he had learned. There would be a reckoning for that, in time, but at least she was out of the business for now, safely abed at Tuscombe Park House.

The man who grabbed Charley had caught her hand and pistol in such a way that she could not have fired the gun if she had wanted to. A gruff voice muttered near her ear, "Not a whisper, my lady, if you would not bring all to ruin."

Scarcely the words of a knave or a brute, she thought, holding still and making no effort to free herself. Her heart was pounding, and she yearned to express her strong displeasure at nearly having the liver and lights frightened out of her. The man knew her. That much was clear. She hoped that, knowing who she was, he would have sense enough not to harm her. Wanting to draw a deep breath, and realizing her left hand was free, she tugged at the rough hand clamped over her mouth.

He said, "I'll want your assurance of silence, ma'am, and I'll keep the pistol for now, if you please."

Definitely not a knave. She nodded, released her hold on the gun, and when he took his hand away from her mouth, she said quietly, "Who are you?"

"Francis Oakes, ma'am. I have the honor to be—"

"The agent for Lloyd's of London in St. Austell," she said. "Sir Antony has mentioned you to me."

"Has he? Then may I take it that you are in Sir Antony's confidence, my lady?"

She wondered about that, and wondered, too, just how much Mr. Oakes knew about Antony. Deciding to take the simplest course and hope he would explain himself further, she said, "I am."

"Excellent. Now we'd best get you away from this track at once, ma'am. I doubt that they can see us from below, but it would be as well to take no chance of it. I want these villains in custody before the night is done."

"It's a merchantman they are after," Charley said, "not the Duke."

"Bless you, so we've been told this very day, ma'am, but I'm wondering how you came to discover it. I know for a fact that Sir Antony has not been at home today."

She did not answer, hoping he would assume she required all her concentration to make her way back up the steep, narrow track without slipping. When they reached the main path along the cliff top, she said, "I left a horse nearby, Mr. Oakes."

"I presumed as much, ma'am. One of my lads will have moved it, I'm sure. We are trying to keep the area hereabouts as quiet as possible, though we've a pretty accurate notion as to who is about and who is not."

"You've been watching then," she said. "I looked down here from my window earlier, but I saw no activity, and since I was unsure if my information was correct, I rode first to see if there was activity on the Devil's Sand."

"If I might be so presumptuous as to ask, my lady, does Sir Antony know you have acquired this habit of riding about at night all by yourself?"

"Where is he?"

"Below, watching for one who might well manage to slip past us. He's done so in the past, I'm afraid."

"Michael Peryllys?"

"The same. And again, I'm wondering—" He broke off with a low chuckle. "Ah, but I am forgetting that you are the one who set young Jenifry Breton free. You'll be knowing the worst about Michael."

"I know he has done murder."

"Aye, young Annie, and mayhap others before her, if we but knew it. Hush now about that, for here's Gabriel coming now, with a couple of my lads."

She saw figures approaching, and when they met, before anyone spoke, Oakes drew them farther away from the cliff path. Despite the darkness, Charley saw enough of James Gabriel's expression to know that her presence had astonished him.

He obeyed Oakes's gesture for silence until they were some distance from the path, but then he exclaimed in an undertone, "What mischance brings you here, my lady?"

"No mischance, Mr. Gabriel. I chanced to discover that your

information was slightly in error, and came to see for myself what mischief was afoot."

"As to error," he said, "we cannot be wholly certain yet that the Duke is safe. Those lads on the beach will take their booty where they find it, and if Wellington's ship should appear first . . ." There was no need to finish. His meaning was clear.

She said, "How many men have you got with you, Mr. Oakes?"

"Twenty, my lady, scattered here and about."

"Will they be enough?"

Gabriel said with annoyance, "We should have ordered up a full military troop."

Ignoring him, Oakes said, "I hope we have enough, ma'am. I didn't dare trust anyone else, not with His Grace coming and all. I just hope and pray that lot below haven't told the whole countryside to expect a wreck in the bay, but I think they'll want to take the best for themselves first, since they've lured it here by knavery."

"You think they intend somehow to run it aground?"

"I do. It was bound for Falmouth, and they have already taken steps to force it off course. But I ought not to be talking with you about such things. With so little wind, we ought not to be talking at all. Perhaps you would like me to provide a couple of my men to see you safely home again," he added diplomatically.

Charley said firmly, "I am not going home, Mr. Oakes. To take away any of your men when they are sorely needed here would be quite unconscionable of me."

"Now, my lady, I am persuaded Sir Antony would say you should go home."

"He is quite right," Gabriel said testily. "Sir Antony would insist!"

"I don't agree. Sir Antony is one of the most reasonable men I have ever met. I think if he were to weigh the cost of reducing your force by the number of men you would think necessary to send with me, against the advantage of having one more person here to help, he would say that since I am here, I ought to stay."

Gabriel gasped, and a strangled sound from Mr. Oakes indicated that that good man had stifled his first, impulsive reply. She gave him full marks for good sense, but he said with obviously forced calm, "I don't know that Sir Antony would say that, ma'am. Nor do I know what help you could be to us in a fracas."

"In a physical fracas, probably none," Charley said frankly. "I'm not nearly large enough to hold my own against desperate men determined to win free. However, if you will be so kind as to return my pistol, I can keep watch from here and engage to keep anyone who ought not to leave from doing so, at least by that trail yonder."

"Nonsense," Gabriel snapped. "Keeping lookout is no job for a mere woman."

"If we are not to fall out," Charley said flatly, "do not let me hear you speak again of *mere* women, sir. A trigger does not know male from female, and I promise you that no man climbing that trail will argue with me. I am too well known in these parts for any one of them to doubt my willingness to shoot him." Choked laughter from one of the shadowy figures was hastily stifled.

Clearing his throat, Oakes said, "I don't doubt your ability, my lady, and nor do I deny that we'll need every man once we begin making arrests. But I'll require your assurance—your word of honor, if you don't mind—that you will stay put and not try to follow us to the beach. I could never reconcile it with my conscience were you to get involved in what is like to be a most violent situation. Nor would Sir Antony forgive me, whatever you say to the contrary."

"I won't dispute that," Charley said, not even wanting to think of what Antony would say if she should appear in the midst of a battle against the wreckers. "May I say, however, that you are one of the first men I've met who believes a woman *has* a sense of honor?" she added. "Generally, if a woman says she does, men laugh at her."

"One has only to meet you, my lady, to know you are woman of your word."

After that, even if she had considered defying him, she knew she would not. Not only would she have Antony's displeasure to face, but to fly in the face of trust so freely given went against everything she believed in.

Suddenly, Gabriel said, "On the horizon, Oakes! There, to the southwest, against the horizon, bearing straight toward us."

Charley saw the pinpricks of light at once, and she saw, too, that lights began to spring up all along the coast. In the mist, she knew the merchantman must be closer than it appeared, for them to see it at all. She knew, too, that the mist would distort the lights along the cliff tops, making it difficult to tell one set from another. The twin lights at the Lizard, normally visible from Seacourt Head, and which many ships used as landmarks when entering the Channel from the Bay of Biscay, were not discernible to her now. If they could be seen from the ship, they must, she knew, appear much the same as other lights along the coast. All the captain would know was that he had entered the Channel. No one aboard would know their exact location.

"How did the wreckers intend to bring it in?" she asked.

"We are not certain," Oakes said. "It is quite likely that they have at least one cohort aboard the ship, but it is also likely that they have suborned one of the pilot boats from a local port. We'll know soon enough which it is. No one aboard that ship would know for certain in this mist, and with all them lights, where Fowey Harbor is, let alone where this here bay is to be found."

"It will be a pilot boat, I think," Charley said, explaining swiftly what Cubert Breton had said, without naming him.

"Aye, you're right," Oakes said a moment later. "There they come now."

Charley had glanced away momentarily to see if the light on Seacourt Head blazed as brightly as the others. An annoying glimmer of an idea stirred in her mind, but she couldn't catch the full thought, and before she could concentrate on it, the glimmer had died. The men around her shifted impatiently.

"Light below," one said. "Quick on and then out. A signal, Mr. Oakes?"

"Yes, so I should think," Oakes agreed. "We'll need to be moving soon, before they see our boats."

Charley said, "What if they have weapons aboard the pilot boat, Mr. Oakes? Could they not board the merchantman and force her to run aground?"

"Perhaps, but most merchantmen have ways of repelling boarders, especially from a much smaller craft like a pilot boat. I'm thinking it's more likely the captain of the pilot will turn tail and run for it if he catches sight of the cutters. We've two in the water, sitting dark and watching for bigger ships. It's as well the merchantman has shown itself. With this mist, if they'd had to wait much longer, they'd have had to light up so as not to be overrun by some unsuspecting, innocent ship. Wouldn't do to have one of His Majesty's revenue cutters creating a hazard in Channel waters. They'll be moving in behind that pilot boat now, and if he shifts a degree off course once he's got the merchantman in his wake, they'll board him. Mark me, lads," he added in a louder tone, "I want this lot below gathered up before they realize their race is run."

"Ought to wait a bit and catch them red-handed," Gabriel muttered angrily. "They all want hanging."

"If you are suggesting, Mr. Gabriel, that I should allow that merchant ship to be wrecked with all its cargo, just to hang this little batch of thugs, I tell you I won't do it. We've enough to charge them all with attempt, because they'll have got their tools with them. No jury in these parts will mistake wreckers for honest fishermen."

"No jury in these parts will condemn wreckers for *attempted* wrecking," Gabriel snapped. "Hard enough to find any who would convict them of the real thing."

"Now, that's where you're wrong, sir, if you'll pardon my saying so," Oakes said. "Opinions have been changing hereabouts, thanks to men like the old earl. It's slow but it's sure. Attitudes change, even in Cornwall."

"We'll see that," Gabriel growled. "We'll get at least one, at all events. I want Michael Peryllys to pay for *all* his crimes. I want that devil hanged at the next Assizes."

"I know that," Oakes said grimly, "and we'll get him."

They watched for a few more minutes before he gathered his men again and gave them their orders, sending a number of them to descend a second trail, which led to the beach near the Fowey end of the bay. A few minutes later, Charley saw a blue flicker in the distance.

"They're set to move now," Oakes said. "Come with me, Mr. Gabriel, and mind now, Lady Foxearth, you're to stay here no matter what occurs below. I've no wish to be threatening a lady, but I think it only fair to warn you that if you do show your face on that beach, I won't hesitate to tell Sir Antony that I gave you strict orders to stay here. And say what you will about him being reasonable, ma'am, I've never known a man yet who takes it kindly when his wife flings herself into danger against orders."

A shiver raced up Charley's spine at the thought of Antony's anger, but she managed to keep her voice calm. "I have given you my word, Mr. Oakes."

"Aye, you have, my lady, and I have agreed to accept it. Forgive me if my fear of Sir Antony's displeasure stirred me to overstep the mark of civility."

"No apology is necessary, Mr. Oakes. I'll walk with you to the top of the trail, and perhaps you could just show me where you hid before, for it was a most effective hiding place. I was completely unaware of your presence until you grabbed me."

"You were watching your step, ma'am, so it's not so odd you missed seeing me. I've been thinking about that, and it seems to me that if you should see or hear someone moving downhill toward the beach, you should let him pass. If you fear he might take us unawares, just let off that popgun of yours once he's well away from you. You will have the advantage over anyone coming uphill, you see, but downhill it's a bit different. You'll be safer then to keep mum, if you'll take my advice on the subject."

"I will," she said. "I can fire two shots, so a warning shot won't leave me unarmed. I've extra bullets, too, but I confess, I am not very adept at reloading under the best circumstances, let alone in the dark."

"That don't astonish me, ma'am, since few men are skilled

at reloading a weapon in the dark. Ah, here is the boulder where I concealed myself. We'll leave you now, and may I say I think you are a very brave woman.''

Watching him make his way down the path with his men and Gabriel, Charley was impressed by the silence with which they moved. She was certain she had made much more noise than they did, though she had been alone. She could not see any activity on the beach because the slope of the cliff face obstructed her view, and she found the silent darkness unnerving. Reminding herself that Oakes believed she was brave, she pretended that she was utterly intrepid, and pretended, too, that she had convinced herself as well as Oakes that Antony would not mind her staying to help.

In the distance, she could see the merchantman. It loomed larger and larger in the mist, and even she could tell now that it was off its course. Sailing into Falmouth Harbor, it would present a side view, for it would be sailing nearly due north from its present position. Instead, she faced its bow head on. The lights of a much smaller boat, the pilot, glinted far below the merchantman's bowsprit light. Though she expected momentarily to see lights of at least two other ships, she saw nothing but dark water and sky. Overhead a few stars twinkled. A breeze stirred nearby shrubbery, but otherwise, except for the muted sound of the surf below, the night was still.

On the beach, Antony saw movement as men began to gather near the eastern end of the bay. It was nearing midnight. Even so, he wondered why the merchantman was so trusting of the pilot. Surely, they would expect to see more lights at Falmouth than they could see now. Catching the arm of a passing man, he said with his best French accent, *"Mon ami,* how is it they think they are sailing into a big port, eh?''

"Keep your voice down, Frenchie. We ain't seen no sign o' revenuers or customs' lads, but it don't do to be calling attention to what we're about.''

"Ah, *oui,* but me, I did wonder, *sais-tu.''*

"If you must know, your own people set this up, and they've

a lad aboard yon merchant ship what's told them all English townsfolk go to bed at sundown. Reckon they can't see Land's End at all in this mist, but word is they'll be told the reason there be lights along the cliffs tonight is that we're expecting the Duke o' Wellington. Your French friends would like to meet him, I'm thinking.''

"Me, I heard it said that Michael could make that possible," Antony said, grinning. "I tell you, *mon ami,* I am sad to think we capture only a merchantman.''

"You won't be when you get your share. Taking Wellington was no more than a ridiculous pipe dream, if it was that. Oh, aye, I heard the tale myself but didn't credit it, and nor did any man o' sense. Dunno who began it. I ask you, who would be so crazed as that? Michael? I wish I may see it. Got too much fondness for his own skin, Michael has. Ain't even here yet, is he?''

"Is he not?''

"Not as I know. Here now," he added in an entirely different tone, "what be all them lights yonder near to our ship? And what the devil's all that row?''

At the sound of shouts and a pistol shot, Antony melted back into the darkness till he found himself against the cliff wall. The last thing he wanted was to be captured or identified as Sir Antony where any of the others might overhear. Hurrying footsteps crunched across the shingle from all directions. Lanterns flickered to life here and there, and already, out on the dark water, the merchantman and her escort were turning.

Carefully, quietly, he made his way toward the nearest trail up the cliff. Then a familiar voice spoke out of the shadows. "I thought you'd come this way, Sir Antony.''

Charley heard the commotion below. She could see more lights at sea, and many more at the end of the beach. Gunshots sounded, first one, then sporadic echoes, enough to make her fear again for Antony's life. Silence followed. She peered through the darkness, but the distant lanterns cast little if any light onto the trail, and the stirring breeze made it hard to tell if anyone was moving nearby. Her skin prickled, and her heart thumped. Desperate to know who was in command on the beach, she held her pistol at the ready, feeling both afraid to move and afraid to stay where she was.

Even in her habit skirt, she knew she would be unable to descend safely without a light if she kept her pistol in hand, but she was determined not to put it down. Thinking that if she could command a broader view of the beach, she could perhaps discern what was happening, she stood up at last. Then, taking care to make no sound, and moving with extreme care, she took a few steps toward the trail.

Noise of sliding stones stopped her in her tracks. Squinting, trying to pierce the darkness ahead, she waited, breathless, hoping against hope that it would be Oakes or Gabriel who came. She made no sound, certain that either of them would speak first to reassure her of her safety. The approaching figure said not a word. Moreover, he moved furtively, as if he were afraid of ambush.

"Halt," she commanded fiercely, "or I'll shoot."

"Angel, if you put a bullet in me, I'll be even angrier than I am right now, so I'd strongly advise you not to do it."

Lowering the pistol, she flung herself at him, crying, "You're safe! I was so afraid they might have—"

"Not yet they haven't," Michael Peryllys snapped from above them at the same moment Antony caught her in his arms. "But he's a dead man now, madam, and so, I'm afraid, are you. Step away from him. Now. Good evening, Sir Antony, or are you Jean Matois tonight, or perhaps even the infamous *Le Renardeau?*"

Startled, Charley whirled in Antony's arms and saw Michael's menacing figure shadowed against the few stars overhead. Without a second thought, she raised her pistol and fired. An echoing shot answered hers harmlessly as the figure fell forward and rolled. Before either of them could move to stop it, it pitched over the edge.

Gasping with shock, she stared at Antony and said, "I didn't realize he was so close to the edge. How did he know you are *Le Renardeau?*"

"I don't know that he did," Antony said grimly. "He was more likely flinging darts in hopes of hitting a mark." He drew a long breath, then added, "By God, madam, if I were a man of violence, or even a sensible one, I'd put you across—"

"I just saved your life!"

"At a considerable risk to your own." Grabbing her shoulders hard, he shook her and snapped, "How dared you leave the house tonight of all nights!"

To her astonishment, Charley found that she did not mind being shaken, particularly since he pulled her tight against him afterward and held her. He was breathing hard, as if he had been running. A moment later, he muttered against her curls, "Give me that damned pistol before you shoot one of us in the foot."

Obeying, she said, "What should we do about Michael? I suppose I ought to feel quite dreadful at having killed him— at least . . . He must be dead, mustn't he?"

Antony said harshly, "You can be sure that he is. No one could survive—" He broke off on an odd, hesitant note, as if he had remembered something.

"What? Do you know of someone who *did* survive a fall like that?"

With no more than a brief hesitation he replied firmly, "No. Michael is dead, angel, never fear. I'll have to go back down and tell Oakes what happened here, but I cannot take you with me. Will you be all right here for another few moments? With Michael dead, you've nothing more to fear, but you'd best keep out of sight."

"I don't know that there's nothing more to fear," she said, wishing she could read the expression on his face. "Are you still angry with me?"

"We'll talk about that when we get home."

"What about Wellington?"

This time his hesitation was clear, and when he spoke there was amusement in his voice. "Damned if I didn't forget him! Still, I've time enough to take you home and get back to Fowey to meet his ship. If there ever was a threat against him, the danger is past now, but he will expect a full report from me before we depart for Truro.''

''We'll both meet his ship,'' Charley said matter-of-factly.

''Will we?''

''We will. Not knowing exactly what would happen tonight, I arranged for Jeb and Teddy to take Letty on to Tuscombe Park without me. She has Jenifry with her, so she is content, and Alfred and Edythe won't miss me. They will be taking a number of carriages, you know, and Aunt Ophelia will be glad to keep an eye on Letty.''

''Stay here,'' Antony commanded. ''We'll talk about this after I tell Oakes how Michael Peryllys happened to collect a bullet and throw himself to the beach.''

''That bullet's in his black heart,'' Charley said, ''if he had a heart.''

But Antony had already gone, and she heard his retreating footsteps, slipping and sliding down the steep path.

Chapter Twenty-two

By the time Antony returned, Charley had begun to wonder if he had run into trouble, but when she saw that James Gabriel accompanied him with a lantern, she relaxed. Gabriel said anxiously, "I hope you were not frightened here by yourself, ma'am. I could scarcely credit my ears when Sir Antony said he had left you alone."

Charley smiled. "I told you, he is a reasonable man, sir." Hoping that her words would act upon Antony in the same way that Oakes's trust had affected her earlier, she added with amusement, "I am not afraid of the dark, you know."

"Well, as to that, ma'am, I must say that if you had been my wife or daughter"—his voice seemed to catch, but he recovered quickly—"I would not be so sanguine at finding you here at such a time, as Sir Antony appears to be. Indeed, I was astonished to learn that *he* was below on the beach. That skirmish was no place for a gentleman, though I confess that if Oakes had not identified him for me, I would have taken him for one of the wreckers, myself. One must admire his zeal, but you will admit that his action was foolhardy. Do you know those villains originally planned to capture the Duke of Wellington? I talked to one of them, and he confessed straight out that they intended to hold His Grace to ransom, and failing that, to assassinate him! I don't doubt they would have killed you as well, Sir Antony, had they caught you.''

"Do you think so, indeed?" Antony said. Despite his grubby appearance, he had reverted to the haughty drawl that had served him so well. He went on, "I hardly knew myself what I was about, Gabriel, so it was a damned good thing Oakes had everything in hand. When the excitement began I nearly tripped over my own two feet in my haste to escape. Fortunately, knowing I would be there, Oakes took it upon himself to watch for me at the foot of the path. I own, though, when he stepped out of the darkness and spoke my name, I nearly screeched like a Scotch banshee out of sheer terror.''

Charley said soulfully, "I think you were very brave, sir." Feeling his hand at her elbow, she expected for a moment that he might take advantage of the darkness to pinch her for her impudence, but he did not. He grasped her arm, and although his fingers tightened warningly, they would leave no bruises.

He said dryly, "Thank you, my love. It is ever my aim to impress you, and now that all danger has passed . . .''

"As to that," Gabriel said when he paused, "I am not sure that all danger *has* passed. Certainly, with that murdering scoundrel Michael Peryllys dead and gone, Cornwall is a safer place, but there are many others like him. I need hardly remind you that that French scoundrel, *Le Renardeau,* is still on the loose.''

"Just who is this chap?" Antony demanded. "I find it hard to believe that such a rascal could flit around Cornwall with impunity. Surely, if he is French—''

"So the men tell me," Gabriel said. "He is said to be extremely dangerous, too, so I would be remiss if I failed to warn you. I mean to get word to the Duke, as well, for with the least threat remaining against his life, one cannot be too careful. If anything should happen to His Grace in Cornwall, we should never live it down.''

"As it happens," Antony said, "Lady Foxearth and I have been invited to travel to Truro in His Grace's party. I can deliver your warning to him, if you like.''

"Well, now, that does solve one problem for me," Gabriel said. "As mayor of Lostwithiel, I had hoped to be on hand to welcome him to Cornwall, but for my own peace of mind, and his safety, I think I must go along to see this lot properly locked up till the Assizes. Fowey is nearest, of course, but it does not boast a jail large enough to hold so many, and with Wellington there, we must not chance one or another of them escaping. The castle prison at Launceston will hold them all easily. His Grace will be disappointed not to have the opportunity to speak with me, particularly to receive my views with regard to the necessity for a continuous military presence in Cornwall to deter crime; however, perhaps I can see him before he leaves the county."

Astonished, Charley said, "But what about the ceremony, sir? You cannot possibly want to miss that!"

"It is because of the ceremony that I must do this, ma'am. Francis Oakes is a very good man in his way, but he is not a Cornishman, and I fear he will not be as alert as I shall be to the possibility of an outside attempt to free these men along the way. Particularly in view of the death of Michael Peryllys," he added grimly.

Guiltily, she said, "I hope you do not think I had any choice about that, Mr. Gabriel. He had his pistol aimed right at Sir Antony."

"My dear ma'am, the man was a murderer," Gabriel replied fiercely, adding in a voice that trembled with suppressed passion, "I wanted to shoot him myself when I learned of our Annie's death. His death tonight took place at God's will, and no one else's. Indeed, if you had not shot him, he would have murdered you as well as Sir Antony."

"But the Seraphim Coffer! All your hard work!"

"I shall be sorry to miss the presentation," he said with more control, "but it is only a ceremony, after all. Oh, and that reminds me, you must have the key to the coffer." He fumbled at his waistcoat pocket, then pressed a medium-sized round-shafted key into her outstretched hand, saying, "I've carried it with me everywhere since yesterday when we placed the sacred vessels inside."

"Good mercy, sir, I thought the coffer must be at the cathedral by now, under guard. I'm sure you said you intended to send it there on Wednesday."

By the lantern's light she saw his wistful smile. "I found I could not bear to part with it so soon, my lady. If you were a craftsman, you would understand how one seeks perfection with yet a bit more sanding, a bit more polish, a tuck in the satin here, an adjustment there. But I set two men to guard it. They will keep it safe at the dean's house and carry it to the cathedral just before the ceremony. Do you recall your part?"

"I think so," Charley said. "It is not complicated."

Evidently still seeking perfection, he said, "Bishop Halsey will accept the cathedral keys from the deacons on the doorstep, and they will enter the cathedral. The Duke will speak, and you will unlock the coffer. Then, once you have done so, you must stand well back and allow him to open it with his own hands, to make his presentation."

Tucking the key safely into her left glove, Charley said, "I'll remember easily enough, although I did think you said before that I should open the coffer as well."

"The bishop believes it will provide a more dramatic moment if the Duke does so," Gabriel said. "He will doubtless explain that to you himself. I shall be sorry to miss it, as I said, but I do think it is important to get these villains safely locked away where they can do no more harm. You will find one of Oakes's lads with the horses yonder," he added, gesturing westward. Then, bidding them farewell, he went quickly back down the trail, holding his lantern out before him to light his way.

Antony still held Charley's arm, and she said dryly, "Do you mean to hold onto me all the way to Fowey?"

"We have not yet determined that you are going to Fowey."

"Well, I am. The only alternative is for you to take me back to Seacourt Head yourself and stay there all night. Since we are presently almost as close to Fowey, and need not get up so early if we are already in the village, it is more sensible to go now. Moreover, our clothing for the ceremony is there, because I told Hodson today that I would be riding to meet you, and had him take mine to the inn as well as yours. What purpose would we serve by going home?''

"I could have privacy to beat my wife," he said musingly.

She chuckled. "If you want to do that, I expect the landlord will turn a deaf ear if he believes you are who you say you are despite those clothes. I daresay he will, too, for although you look a bit rough and seedy, the minute you begin talking in that drawling, condescending way, no one would take you for anything but a gentleman of consequence. But truly, Antony, do you think I should have stayed home?''

"I do," he retorted.

"How unfair, and foolish, too! Michael Peryllys would have killed you if I had not been here." The very thought tied a knot in her stomach and made her shiver.

"You don't know that," he said.

Employing one of his own favorite tactics, she said nothing.

The silence lengthened. Then, with a sigh, he said, "Very well, I suppose he would, at that. I'd give something to know how much he really knew about me."

"Cubert Breton said Michael set a man to watch you—to watch Sir Antony, that is—after he learned of Jenifry's rescue," she said. "It's been only a few days, but if his man saw you leave Seacourt as Matois, Michael might suspect that you play two roles."

"And because Matois is French, Michael connected him to *Le Renardeau?*"

"Well, how many Frenchmen are running around Cornwall whose antecedents are unknown to him? His wife is French, after all. Even without setting a spy to watch Sir Antony, he must have wondered if Jean Matois could be *Le Renardeau.*"

He nodded. "You are right, of course."

She waited.

He released her arm, slipping his around her shoulders as he said, "If you expect me to apologize for expressing my displeasure, angel, you'll have a long wait. That you may have saved my life does not lessen what I felt when I learned that you were here."

Remembering with a glow of warmth wholly at odds with

her opinion of violent men how fiercely he had shaken her, she said, "How did you find out?"

"Oakes, of course. What I said before was true. He was waiting for me, certain I would not want the men who know me as Matois to see me at the same time as his men, who know me as Sir Antony Foxearth. When he and Gabriel told me you were guarding the trail to keep anyone from leaving that way, they scared me witless. I didn't consider Michael then, but I should have. All the lads expected him to be there tonight."

"Cubert would not have warned him to stay away," Charley said as he guided her off the path onto rougher ground. "Could Michael simply have been lying in wait for you, do you think?"

"I doubt it. The more I think about it, the less I believe that anyone connected Matois and Sir Antony before tonight. Seacourt Head is open land, and we'd have heard if any strangers were hanging about. I think it's more likely that Michael was cautious because he knew they were looking for him. He must have overheard us speaking, and recognized me as Matois then. Annabelle is yonder in the shrubbery," he added. "I expect Oakes's men will have moved Dancer to the same place."

They met no one except the agent Oakes had left to mind the horses, and when they had mounted, Antony led the way. He avoided the main path along the cliff until they had passed beyond the far end of the bay, explaining that he did not want to meet anyone coming up from the beach on any of the trails at that end.

Noting that most of the fires along the coast were dying out, Charley said, "What if the French are still lingering nearby in the Channel, waiting for the Duke's ship?"

"These waters are crawling with revenue cutters by now," he told her. "Not only did Oakes send two boats to watch for the merchantman and anyone who accosted her, but he sent several more to warn ships coming from the east to keep clear of the area. They'll hang about this side of the Eddystone to bring the Duke's ship into Fowey when it appears, and now that the mist is clearing, I doubt if they will miss it. At all events, with Michael out of the picture now, the Duke will be safe enough.''

"Except for *Le Renardeau*," Charley reminded him with a chuckle.

"Perhaps I ought to have reassured Gabriel on that head," Antony said. "It's a pity for him to miss the ceremony after he's put in so much time and effort preparing for it, but it's still habit with me not to trust easily, especially where *Le Renardeau* is concerned. And since he can't bring himself to trust Oakes to do his job . . ."

"That does not surprise me," Charley said. "Mr. Oakes is no doubt perfectly capable, but by Cornish standards he *is* still a foreigner."

"I can see that it's a matter of pride with Gabriel to make sure the Duke does not meet trouble in Cornwall, but he is carrying things a bit far now, don't you agree?"

Warmed by his evident interest in her opinion, she smiled and said, "We have worried for so long that it's hard to believe the danger is over, particularly since Mr. Gabriel is still uncertain about that. He does take his position seriously, and I think the lack of a military presence to protect the Duke makes him very nervous. He seems to grow more so each time I meet him."

They rode in silence for a time, until she said quietly, "If you are still vexed with me, Antony, I wish you would say so now, before we reach the inn."

"Why?"

Surprised that he had to ask, she answered with some asperity, "Because I cannot be certain that you will not make me angry, of course. I'd as lief not have to worry about what the inn servants might hear us say to each other."

He chuckled.

"That's not funny!"

"Very well," he said, stifling his amusement with disconcerting ease, "I'll say exactly what I think. You acted impulsively, and unwisely. No, don't argue with me yet. You asked me to tell you, and I will, but I'm tired and so are you, and the last thing I want to do is to quarrel." He paused, clearly to see if she would reply, and when she did not, he said, "You should have brought someone with you, angel, if only Teddy. I don't say that because you are female, either, or for any reason other than that you would have been safer that way. I'd say the same thing to a man."

She doubted the last, but she said, "I expect you are right about its being the safer course, but I wanted Teddy to go with Letty and Jenifry to help Jeb protect them, and I did not know whom else I could trust."

"You sent Teddy with Letty because you knew he would try to talk you out of leaving the house," Antony said. When she glanced guiltily at him, he added, "Now, explain to me why you felt you could not trust Hodson."

She sighed. "I did think he ought to be where you expected him to be, in case you had need of him. You would not send to me for help, I knew, and in truth, I had no plan, sir. I was worried about your safety, and I thought I could get help in Fowey, but I knew I would have to have a convincing tale to tell. I rode out to see what I could see, that's all."

After a moment, he said gently, "Well, I'm not angry anymore, angel, but I was."

"I know." Again she remembered the fierce way he had shaken her. "I have never killed anyone before."

"That was not your fault. Gabriel was right. Michael would have shot us both."

"I know. I just think I ought to feel something, and I don't. Not so much as a tremor of remorse. You don't suppose that I am going to suffer a huge reaction later, do you, like I did after Papa and Mama died?"

She half expected him to laugh, and was relieved when he replied flatly, "No, I don't. What happened then was perfectly normal, because you had not allowed yourself time to grieve for them. You kept telling yourself that you had more important things to worry about. Moreover, you loved your parents, angel, and in a way, I think you were protecting yourself against your deep feelings for them. You don't care the same way about Peryllys, only as you would about any chap who died, and less about him than most. You can say a prayer for his soul, and I daresay that will exorcise any sense of guilt that might linger.''

If she did not do as he suggested, she did send a silent prayer of thanks that she had been able to pull the trigger when she did. Just the thought that Michael Peryllys might have killed Antony sent ripples of horror through her even now.

Their conversation was desultory after that until they reached the inn. Inside, however, they met with an unexpected obstacle when they woke the landlord to request two rooms for the night. Though mine host did no more than blink at Antony's drab jacket and breeches, he proved unable to fulfill their request.

''I regret having to disoblige you, sir,'' he said, rubbing his forehead in apparent distress, ''but I've kept only the one bedchamber free, as your man asked me to do. It's got a small adjoining sitting room, which he said would serve you and her ladyship well enough, since you wasn't expecting to stay the night but would use the rooms only to change your clothing. We didn't expect to see the pair of you tonight.''

''Our plans changed,'' Antony said. ''Now, be a good fellow and see what you can arrange for us. You need not to be choosy, you know. I can sleep anywhere.''

''But I've got nowhere else,'' the landlord said helplessly. ''I give you my word, sir. What with the Duke of Wellington in town tomorrow, folks have come from miles around to see him. I've got bodies lying cheek by jowl in every attic and stable loft. 'Tis the same at the Lugger, across the way, and Fowey's only got the two inns. Surely, since you're married, sharing the bed won't matter. 'Tis a fine, large one.''

Before Antony could reply, Charley said quietly, ''That will do perfectly well, thank you. Indeed, sir,'' she added, smiling at her husband, ''I shall not complain, I promise you. The Ship is said to be one of the best inns in Cornwall, after all.''

Though the landlord smiled gratefully, she thought her husband nearly grimaced, but he said with Sir Antony's customary hauteur, ''Very well, my dear, it shall be as you wish.'' However, when a sleepy chambermaid showed them to their bedchamber, he waited only until she had stirred up the fire and departed again before he said, "I will not sleep on that spindly sofa in the next room, or on the carpet by the hearth. I scarcely closed my eyes last night. My lodgings were extremely rough."

"We *are* married," she said, flicking an amused look at him from beneath her lashes. "Surely, married persons occasionally occupy the same bed without . . . uh, without—" She broke off when she saw that he was grinning at her. "You know perfectly well what I mean!"

"I do," he said, untying her bonnet and casting it onto the top of the bare dressing table. As he reached to untie the black stock she wore around her neck, he added, "Shall I help you unfasten your dress?"

Without a maidservant at hand, unless she chose to sleep in her cumbersome riding habit, she had no choice but to allow him to undo the tiny buttons at the back of the bodice. She removed her coat and the stock, and turned her back, while he stripped off his gloves and tossed them onto the table with her bonnet.

Antony undid the first buttons quickly. Then his progress slowed, and each time his fingers moved to a new one, they caressed her through the thin cambric chemisette she wore under her habit. At last he stopped, his hands resting lightly against her back. His presence behind her was disturbing, his light touch teasing. She wanted to see his expression, but there was something in the moment, a sense of intimacy, that she did not want to disturb. She could scarcely breathe. She wanted to lean back against him, to touch him, to feel his strong arms close around her, but she was afraid any movement would break the spell. When one of his fingers touched bare skin at the nape of her neck, above the narrow lace frill, she shivered, but she was not cold.

The little fire crackled on the hearth, its light joining that of several candles to fill the room with a reddish, golden glow. She could hear him breathe. She could smell the salty scent of ocean waves and coastal wind that clung to his damp wool jacket and breeches. She wanted to look at him, to judge what he must be thinking by the expression on his face, but she did not dare let him see hers. He would think her wanton if he could read her thoughts.

One of his hands, then the other, slipped gently around to the tiny chemisette buttons at her throat, buttons that her stock had hidden. As a finger tickled her chin, stroking gently, the other hand nimbly unfastened the top button. Two more followed, and still she said not a word.

She felt his breath against her right ear before he murmured, "You are not wearing stays, are you?"

"I never do," she said simply.

"Excellent." Two more buttons dealt with. These were larger than the ones that held the frill in place, and soon he reached the curved edge of the habit bodice. So intent was she on his progress in front that she did not realize his left hand had moved until she felt it touch the small of her back.

"Why do ladies wear so much clothing nowadays?" he asked.

"'Tis the fashion, of course." The voice sounded unlike her own.

"A damned inconvenient fashion, if you ask me."

In front, one finger dipped under the edge of her habit bodice, into the opening of the chemisette, touching bare skin between her breasts. She held her breath. If he did not think she was capable of undoing the front buttons herself, she was not going to tell him otherwise. But he knew she was, of course. She began breathing again, a little rapidly, wondering how far he meant to go and if he expected her to stop him.

In back, he dealt with the fastening at her waist, releasing it deftly. She felt the weight of her skirt tugging the bodice. Only her arms in their wide sleeves kept the habit from slipping to the floor. His hand returned to her waist, then moved lower and stopped. In a voice of amusement, he said, "More pantaloons?"

"When was the last time you undressed a lady who wore a riding habit?"

He choked on a laugh and turned her at last to face him. Dancing firelight enhanced the twinkle in his eyes. "What makes you think I make a habit of undressing ladies?"

"You do not seem unpracticed at this, but I only wondered because ladies have worn pantaloons or heavy stockings under their riding habits for a long time. All my life, certainly."

"I prefer those things you wear that have lace edging round the bottom. Very enticing, I thought them, like a well-constructed invitation." His gaze met hers and held it. He looked as if he were trying to read her thoughts.

She wondered what he saw and hoped it was nothing that would deter him. Wanton behavior or not, this might be her last chance to learn what married people did in bed, for now that Wellington was safe, they would soon have to arrange their annulment. Indeed, for all she knew, Antony had already arranged for the bishop to deal with it in Truro after the consecration. The thought made her sad, so she did not dwell on it, fixing her gaze on him instead, willing him to continue what he had begun. When he did not do so immediately, she reached out and put her hand inside the rough jacket he wore, stroking the fine lawn shirt beneath it. When her hand moved lower, toward the top of his breeches, she heard his breath catch. "Aren't you getting hot in that jacket?" she asked, still looking into his eyes.

"If I am, what do you propose to do about it?" His voice was low in his throat.

"I want to learn what married people do, Antony. Teach me."

Shrugging off his jacket, trying to control the surge of desire he felt for her, Antony told himself that he would take care. He reminded himself that she was his wife and he had every right to do as he pleased with her, that even if he should let his instincts rule his better judgment, he would do her no great harm so long as she did not become pregnant. And if she did . . . Even as the thought crossed his mind, she slipped her hand through the opening in his shirt to his bare skin. He stifled a groan. The wanton little baggage intended to seduce him.

Salving his conscience with the knowledge that he had warned her of the consequences, he gathered her into his arms and kissed her gently, beginning slowly to explore her body with his hands, pushing clothing aside as he encountered it. She responded at once, reaching for him, and he wondered if she was in some way reacting to the fear she must have felt before she had pulled the trigger and shot Michael, or if she was merely curious, as she had said. In either case, he had no wish to stop her.

He had wanted to hold her again, and to do much more than that, ever since the night of the storm, when she had come to his bedchamber. Reassuring himself yet again that he would do her no harm, he plunged his tongue into her mouth.

She moaned and pressed toward him, her hungry passion nearly overwhelming him. His fingers seemed to take on a life of their own as he stripped her clothing from her, and without another thought for consequences, he carried her to the bed. His shirt was open, and he knew she must have unbuttoned it, but he had no memory of it. His mind filled with the scent of her, the silken softness of her skin, and the feelings her slightest touch produced within his body. At first he wanted only to stroke her, to kiss her, to enjoy her passion.

She was silent except for the little moans and cries of pleasure she made in response to his touch, but her reactions produced stirrings within him that he had never experienced before. He was not unskilled, but his experiences had been casual, without emotional ties. Had he tried, he would have found it hard to remember a single partner's name. Charley was different. She made him feel different, more alive than he had ever felt before. He kept his eyes open at first, watching her, enjoying the play of the firelight on her beautiful body.

As his hands moved gently over her breasts, making her gasp, her eyes opened wide, and firelight ignited flames of passion in their dark depths. She smiled and murmured, "May I kiss your body, too, the way you are kissing mine?"

"You may," he murmured, his throat nearly closing on the words, "but take care. I'm having all I can do not to ravish you here and now."

"But I want you to ravish me," she replied. "I've never

felt like this before, Antony, and I shall probably never feel like this again. I don't want it to stop.''

"You do understand that this is how people get pregnant."

"Yes, of course, I do. You know I do. But it won't happen, and even if it does," she added, looking mischievously at him, "the worst that will occur is that we shall have to stay married. I daresay even that will not be as bad as I thought, so long as you will engage not to interfere with me. You can do as you please, and I shall remain here and raise my child, and everything will go on as it did before we met." Her gaze slid from his as she said the last words, and he knew she did not mean them, that she simply (and quite foolishly) assumed she would not become pregnant through a single incident. Still, anger that she could think even for a moment that he would abandon her to raise *his* child alone made him want to shake her again.

The anger ebbed swiftly when she began to explore his body with her lips and tongue. Her hand slipped lower, and he soon forgot his objections. When he could take no more, he moved to possess her, hesitating only at the last minute. Afraid to hurt her, he took great care when he entered her, but aside from a moan deeper than those that had preceded it, she did not protest. Taking her, he found it surprisingly easy to read her responses and to stimulate her until she writhed with passion beneath him. His senses reeled, soaring to a peak beyond any he had ever experienced before.

When it was over, he helped her clean herself, surprised but delighted that she did not seem at all shy of him.

"I thought it would hurt more," she said.

"I'm no expert, despite what you think, but I'm told that women often differ in that respect," he said.

Apparently content with the answer, she let him take her in his arms again and carry her back to bed. Not until sometime later, as they lay side by side, utterly sated, did he wonder when it would occur to her that, if she did get pregnant, he would not be the biddable husband of her fantasies. And if she did not become pregnant and still wanted an annulment, he wondered if she thought he would lie to the bishop when the small question of consummation arose. He would not, but he found himself looking forward to the moment, and imagining how she would react. It occurred to him then that, in his mind at least, they were married forever now, whether they liked it or not. The thought warmed him considerably.

Chapter Twenty-three

Charley and Antony were still asleep the following morning when Hodson arrived in a carriage with a driver and Kerra, but when they learned that Wellington's ship was safe in the harbor, they made haste to dress and to break their fast. Upon learning that Hodson and Kerra both wanted to attend the consecration, Antony said with a smile, "Why don't you ride our horses then, if you like, since we don't have our grooms with us? Will that suit you, angel?"

"Yes, certainly," Charley agreed as she stirred sugar into her tea. "Kerra, I will tell you what you must do to make Dancer let you ride him." When they all were ready, they went to the harbor. There was not a cloud in the sky.

To Charley's surprise, they found Rockland and Elizabeth awaiting them near the long dock. Rockland greeted them with his usual mischievous smile, but she sensed at once that something was different between the two. The way Elizabeth looked at Rockland would have given them away even if he had not been looking (in Charley's opinion, at least) like the cock of the walk.

"You're betrothed," she exclaimed.

Elizabeth looked disappointed, and Rockland said with disgust, "If that ain't just like you! By Jove, you're as bad as

Lady Ophelia. She took one look at us, too, and said exactly the same thing. I ask you, what's the use of having a grand announcement to make if no one allows us to make it?''

"Well, I'm sorry, but you oughtn't to go about looking like a pair of cats that shared a cream cake if you don't want people to guess things. Where are the others?''

"On their way to Truro, of course,'' Rockland said. "They were going by way of the Bodmin turnpike, in several carriages. Alfred made one of his usual dogmatic declarations, saying we would take the front seat in that great traveling carriage of his, with him and Edythe, but I thought not. The alternative was to ride with Lady Ophelia and Lady St. Merryn and the paralyzingly dull Miss Davies, or to take Letty with us. Alfred kept saying he did not see any reason for us to ride in a separate carriage. In all truthfulness, I think he believes it's indecent of us, but I told him it was quite all right since we're now betrothed, and that you had asked me to meet you here. I also said,'' he added with an oblique look at Antony, "that *you* had promised to introduce Elizabeth to His Grace. Hope that don't put you out. I thought it likely he wouldn't mind, for by what I hear of him . . .'' He paused with uncharacteristic delicacy.

Charley chuckled. "You mean that meeting one more pretty female won't make a particle of difference to Wellington. Why didn't you just say so?''

"By heaven, I thought marriage would tame that tongue of yours,'' Rockland said, glaring at her, "but I can see that it's done no such thing. I daresay that in another month you'll have put a ring through poor Antony's nose.''

Heat flooding her cheeks, Charley opened her mouth to deliver a hot retort, but Antony laughed and said, "Wellington has never yet refused to meet a lady, and if I present Miss Elizabeth on the occasion of her betrothal, he will be delighted.''

Looking warily at Charley, Elizabeth said to her in a low, rather tense voice, "Does it displease you, Cousin, our betrothal? I know you expected to marry our dear delightful Rockland, and after the shameful prank he played, tricking you into marrying Sir Antony, he must seem dreadfully fickle now.

Indeed I should not be surprised if you are quite livid with the pair of us. I know that you have always disliked me.''

Caught up short by Elizabeth's distress, Charley experienced a prickling of remorse. She had felt relieved, if anything, to find that Rockland had looked elsewhere, and now that she saw them together, she could see that they were right for each other. Summoning up a warm smile, she said, ''Elizabeth, I have behaved wretchedly. I don't dislike you at all, but after the way I've treated you in the past, I can't blame you for believing I do. Please forgive me, and know that I wish you both only happiness. Look,'' she added, seeing a stir of movement on the docks, ''here comes the Duke with his party now. Just to prove that I am not distressed by your news, I want to make you a special betrothal gift. You must take my place in the ceremony.'' When Elizabeth looked shocked, she added firmly,''Please, *do* say that you will.''

Flushing to the roots of her hair, Elizabeth exclaimed, ''I couldn't possibly do that, Cousin Charley. Mr. Gabriel wants you to have that great honor, and I daresay he will be unhappy enough when he learns that I have become betrothed, without my upsetting his arrangements for the ceremony. Perhaps you do not know this, but he has become most particular in his attentions to me.'' Blushing, she smiled at Rockland. ''Indeed, I think that is what caused my darling William to speak up when he did.''

When Rockland grinned, Charley said in amazement, ''William? Is that your given name?'' He nodded, making her grimace, but then she shook her head and smiled at them both, saying, ''Mr. Gabriel will not see you open the coffer, Elizabeth. He felt obliged to escort a host of villains to the castle prison in Launceston today instead.''

Elizabeth looked more gratified than regretful. ''He won't be at the ceremony?''

''No, he won't,'' Charley said. Producing Gabriel's key from the sensible reticule she carried and pressing it into Elizabeth's hand, she added, ''Here is the key. The dean or one of the deacons will tell you exactly where you must stand, what to do, and when to do it. Of course, if you truly don't wish to . . .''

"I shall be deeply honored," Elizabeth said, smiling in obvious delight. As they moved toward the approaching group, Charley heard her say in an awed undertone to Antony, "Is it true, sir, that you are personally acquainted with His Grace?"

"To my sorrow," Antony answered with a wry smile.

Striding forward ahead of the others, Harry Livingston grasped Antony's hand tightly and said, "Well met, Tony. Have you got everything in hand?"

"I believe so," Antony told him. "There was a spot of bother last night—"

"We heard all about it," Harry said, turning his attention pointedly to Charley. When Antony presented him to her, Harry laughed and said, "Your servant, ma'am. Tony wrote that he'd got married, but not that his wife is a raving beauty. Here, sir," he added, turning to the Duke, "Tony neglected to tell us the best part of his news, and to punish him, allow me to present Lady Foxearth to you in his stead."

Antony saw with relief that Harry's antics did not disturb Charley in the least. Nor did she stand in awe of Wellington, whom she doubtless had met in London. She smiled and made her curtsy and was soon talking easily with the Duke.

Wellington had dressed simply but elegantly, as had been his habit since his days in the Peninsula. He had always worn civilian dress in the field, his blue frock coat and light pantaloons making him easily identifiable. Only for formal military ceremonies did he don a uniform. Today he wore a drab cloak and a simple cocked hat, cream-colored knee breeches and stockings, and a dark coat. He flirted with Charley—and with Elizabeth when Antony presented her—as easily as if he were thirty years younger.

They made a tour of the village, allowing its citizens to pay their respects. Then the Duke and his entourage piled into the several carriages awaiting them. Antony and Charley followed in theirs, with Rockland and Elizabeth just behind, and Hodson and Kerra riding in their wake. Charley settled back against the squabs with a sigh.

Chuckling, Antony said, "I hope you aren't exhausted. It will take us another couple of hours to reach Truro, and the ceremony begins at two. Then we've the journey to Tuscombe Park, and dinner with Alfred and the others to get through."

Her eyes twinkled. "If you must know, I was just glad to get away from Elizabeth and Rockland."

"I thought you were pleased by their betrothal," he said, aware of a small knot forming in his stomach.

It disappeared when she laughed and said, "I am delighted, but I got just a little tired of hearing Elizabeth continually referring to *our dearest Rockland* and *our darling William*. I have just as much regard for Rockland as anyone . . . well, nearly as much, but—" She broke off suddenly with an arrested look in her eyes.

"What?"

She shook her head, frowning. "I don't know exactly. Something I said just then stirred a notion in the back of my mind, but it won't come forward." She thought a moment longer, then grimaced with exasperation. "That's the trouble with trying to catch hold of a thought that doesn't want catching. It disappears as if it had never presented itself at all. Talk about something else, Antony. Maybe it will come to me."

They talked of nothing and many things, passing the journey in easy comfort with each other, but whatever the niggling thought had been, it did not reoccur to her before they reached the cathedral. As they drew up in the cobblestoned square, they saw that the party from Tuscombe Park had arrived just ahead of them.

Alfred and Edythe had already emerged from their carriage, and as footmen assisted Lady Ophelia and Lady St. Merryn from the second one, Antony saw Letty, swathed in her voluminous gray cloak and looking like a small, gray nun, jump down from a third vehicle that appeared otherwise filled with servants. Not for a moment did he suppose that Alfred and the other adults had banished her to that vehicle, but he did not blame her for choosing to ride with a few lively servants rather than three old ladies or Alfred and Edythe Tarrant.

Forty minutes later, inside the cathedral, the organ sounded a single chord, and the congregation turned as one to face the great entry doors. In the hush that fell upon them came three loud knocks. From outside, the bishop's words sounded clearly:

"Lift up your heads, O ye gates, and be ye lift up ye everlasting doors; and the King of Glory shall come in."

From their position near the doors, four churchwardens replied, "Who is the King of Glory?" When Bishop Halsey had made the proper response, they opened the doors and presented to him the petition for the consecration, and the keys to the cathedral, saying, "Reverend Father, we pray you to dedicate, consecrate, and bless this church."

Charley, standing between her husband and Letty in the first row of pews on the left side of the central aisle, watched the bishop's procession pass through the doors and along the aisle toward the sanctuary. Bishop Halsey carried the tall, decorated staff with which he had knocked upon the doors.

Having taken part in the ritual circuit of the cathedral's exterior that preceded their approach to the entrance, Wellington followed the bishop, and for once, his attire did full justice to the grandeur of the occasion, because he wore his Garter robes. The sky-blue velvet mantle and crimson velvet surcoat provided splashes of color amidst the black and white raiment of others in the procession. His soft-crowned black hat trimmed with ostrich plumes sat at a jaunty angle, and his gold collar of twenty-six enameled garters coiled around enameled roses, seemed to rest lightly on the ducal shoulders. The Garter itself showed each time he moved his left leg forward. One of the few men in the kingdom ever to hold at the same time both the Orders of the Garter and of Bath, he displayed the latter only in the smaller silver star below the Garter star on his left side.

The procession reached the altar rail, where Bishop Halsey said a prayer of dedication before moving into the sanctuary. The organ sounded again, and the choir and congregation sang a psalm. Then the archdeacon stepped forward. Signing to the congregation to kneel, he sang a portion of the Litany while the bishop, carrying the staff, measured the cathedral from east to west, and from north to south, before tracing a St. Andrew's Cross on the floor at the entrance to the chancel.

From that point a series of prayers and responses followed, and Charley found it hard to keep her mind on her prayer book. The temptation to gaze about her at the magnificent cathedral was nearly overwhelming, but since she had already hushed Letty twice, she felt obliged to keep her eyes where they belonged.

The child seemed unnaturally fidgety, so she thought it imperative to set a good example. At one point, thinking Letty must be hot in her heavy cloak, Charley asked if she wanted to remove it. She refused, and although her reddening cheeks made it clear that she was overwarm, Charley did not press her to do so.

More prayers and the lesson followed, then another hymn, before the bishop, standing near the altar rail, said, "Oh, worship the Lord in the beauty of holiness."

The congregation replied, "And let the whole earth stand in awe of Him."

"Be seated." Halsey turned expectantly to Wellington, who stood at the end of Charley's row, on the center aisle.

Letty seemed to make a squeaking sound of distress, but she turned away from Charley as the Duke stepped forward and moved to face the congregation. "My friends," he said, his voice carrying easily, "I will make no long speeches. This moment, of all moments, belongs to this glorious house of God."

Charley saw that Elizabeth had been expecting him to speak for some time, for his declaration that he would not brought her head up with a jerk. Seated also in the first row of pews but across the aisle, between Rockland and Alfred, she had sat when everyone else had. Quickly rising again, she stepped forward to stand at the altar rail, separated from the Duke only by the Seraphim Coffer, resting just to the right of the central opening in the railing.

Hearing a muffled cry some rows behind her, Charley turned, ignoring a look of disapproval from Lady Ophelia, who sat at Letty's other side. A large, heavily veiled woman four rows back, in apparent distress, was trying to make her way to the center aisle. Charley's first thought was that the poor thing was ill, but as that notion crossed her mind, she became aware of another disturbance nearer at hand. To her shock, Jeremiah's head popped through the opening in the front of Letty's heavy cloak. As the disturbance behind them grew louder, the monkey scrambled free of the child's grasp, leaping to the back of the pew and agilely eluding her frantic attempts to recapture him.

Wellington, cool and collected as always, ignored both interruptions and said calmly, "I shall now present this coffer of sacred vessels . . ."

The veiled figure had reached the aisle, and was striding forward.

". . . as a gift from the British nation . . ."

Jeremiah ran to the end of the pew.

". . . to be dedicated to this glorious cathedral."

The monkey leapt at the veiled woman, snatching at her hat and veil, as Wellington said, "Miss Tarrant, if you will kindly open—"

"No!"

The striding figure broke into an awkward run just as Jeremiah streaked off down the aisle with a hat, a veil, and a wig.

Pandemonium erupted amongst those in the congregation who saw what the monkey had done, and Charley saw that the *woman* was none other than James Gabriel. As he hoisted his skirts and charged toward the altar rail, she turned in terror to Antony.

He had already seen, and with a hand on the pew rail, he swung first one leg then the other over, his gaze catching hers. "Watch Letty," he ordered. Then, turning, he dashed toward the Duke, more than a dozen feet away.

Charley looked at Elizabeth and saw that she had knelt in front of the Seraphim Coffer, her attention so firmly riveted to her own important task that she was deaf to all the commotion.

In the blink of an eye, pieces of the puzzle clicked into place in Charley's mind. Unable to climb over the pew rail as Antony had done, she shrieked Elizabeth's name as Antony grabbed Wellington and shoved him to the ground in a whirl of crimson and blue velvet, covering the Duke's body with his own.

Although Elizabeth must have heard Charley shriek, she had already unlocked the coffer, released both latches, and was opening the lid, oblivious of Gabriel racing toward her. Grabbing Letty, Charley forced her to the floor, protecting the child's squirming body with her own. Lady Ophelia dropped down beside them just before the explosion.

Antony saw Gabriel seize Elizabeth by the shoulders, fling her aside, and throw himself atop the coffer as it exploded. The blast, though muffled by his large body, was still sufficient to shake the altar and send two acolytes tumbling. Pieces of the wood chest shot out from the blast, but when the cacophony of screams and shouting died away, the few injuries proved to be minor. The sole person killed in the explosion was the proud man who had risen from clockmaker's son to be mayor of his town.

The stunned bishop was far enough away not to have been knocked over, but he had grabbed a column to steady himself. Straightening, he gazed uncertainly out over the congregation, but it was Wellington, scrambling to his feet the moment Antony rolled off him, who took command. No stranger to pandemonium accompanied by gore, the Duke began at once to issue orders, and no one questioned them.

"Archdeacon, cast your vestment over that poor devil's remains," he bellowed. "Churchwardens, see to the injured at once. My friends," he added when people realized he was speaking and began to quiet down, "I pray you, remain peaceful and do not further disgrace this house of God. You may be sure," he went on in the same powerful voice that had once carried his commands across fields of battle, "that it was the Lord Himself who protected us from harm this day. You will go forth from here in the knowledge that His house is truly blessed."

When the bishop murmured anxiously that the consecration was not complete, the Duke said firmly, "Then I would suggest that you make a decision as to what you want to do, Bishop. Your choices are clear. You can continue now."

"Surely not, my lord duke," Halsey squeaked. "Not with the body and blood of Mayor Gabriel spattering our altar."

"Your minions can remove Gabriel's corpse to the vestry," the Duke said practically, "and a damp rag will soon remove the bits most likely to offend. However, if you choose not to continue at present, you have only to announce to the congregation just when you do mean to do so. Next Sunday, I should imagine, though I daresay you won't get as large a crowd then as you have today. It will have become something of an anticlimax by then, don't you think? My advice is to get on with it now but to do the thing with dispatch. Surely, there are bits of the ceremony that you can leave out."

As realization spread through the congregation that the danger was past, fear turned to curiosity. Heads strained and twisted to see what was happening at the altar rail. Bishop Halsey, with a glance at the assembly and another at Wellington, moved to confer with the dean and the archdeacon.

Wellington turned to Antony, who was feeling extremely grim, and said, "I collect that you never anticipated this gambit, my friend."

"I never suspected him," Antony admitted, forcing himself to meet that stern gaze. "He kept the Seraphim Coffer at his house to refurbish it. I recall now that he said he would deliver it here on Wednesday but then kept it till Friday, when he must have installed his explosive device. As a clockmaker's son, though he often deprecated his skill, he must have learned enough of his father's art to prepare his mechanism. He tricked me well, Your Grace. When it counted most, I failed you."

Wellington shook his head. "When it counted most, Tony, you offered your life for mine. I won't forget that, or allow you to do so."

Antony grimaced. "In truth, sir, had he not created such a row, I'd have never known what was about to happen, and in fact, I still don't know why, at the last minute, he changed his mind and threw himself over the chest."

"I do," Charley said, putting her hand on Antony's arm and giving it a squeeze. "He cared deeply for Elizabeth. Seeing her so near the coffer shocked him into acting."

Antony had not seen her come forward. The stunning discovery that Gabriel had not been the man he seemed to be, combined with the urgent need to protect Wellington and the shock of the explosion, had put all thought of Charley and Letty out of his mind. He looked at her now in guilty dismay of this second failure, but she smiled.

"I have told you and told you," she murmured for his ears alone. "You can trust me to take care of myself, and to take care of Letty."

"Where is she?"

"Jeremiah fled to the organ loft with his treasures," she replied in a normal tone. "She is trying to coax him down again."

The Duke, who had been reassuring Harry Livingston that he was quite unharmed, turned then and said, "I could not help overhearing you say that Mayor Gabriel was in love with Miss Elizabeth Tarrant, my lady. I quite thought Tony said earlier that she is betrothed to Lord Rockland."

"I did," Antony said.

Charley said, "Mr. Gabriel did not know about the betrothal, however. Nor could he have known that she would be taking my part in the ceremony today, for we arranged that only this morning in Fowey. I daresay seeing her gave him quite a shock, but it is unnerving to think he would not have leapt forward to save me."

Antony said, "He did impress upon you that once you had unlocked the coffer, you were to stand well back and let His

Grace open it to present the vessels. You even questioned him, saying he had previously told you to unlock it and also to open it."

"Yes, and then I told Elizabeth to ask the archdeacon what she should do, and most likely he said to open it. Though Gabriel said it was the bishop's suggestion that I let His Grace open the box, he knew it was no such thing, and just seeing her step forward was enough to terrify him. For that we must all be grateful, but why did he come here at all? He was to have gone to Launceston with the prisoners."

Antony shrugged. "I expect he couldn't bear not to see his handiwork. That is not unusual in such a case, but after all his work, people would have expected him to stand right up front with the other dignitaries, and he would not have wanted to be so near. Therefore, if he was to be here, he had to have a disguise. I daresay he simply took advantage of the arrests last night to provide himself with an acceptable excuse."

Remembering that it had been Gabriel who had revealed the previous night's plot, and who had continued to say the villains meant to capture the Duke, Charley said, "It is even possible, I suppose, that he somehow manipulated last night's events to provide himself with that excuse. But why on earth would Gabriel want to kill His Grace?"

Wellington smiled ruefully, saying, "It is not the first time I have been a target, ma'am, nor, I daresay, will it be the last. My would-be assassins do not always have reasons that we ordinary mortals can comprehend."

Letty's voice echoed through the silence that followed. "Jeremiah, come down at once. We are in enough trouble without you causing more."

Charley exchanged a look with Antony, who turned purposefully toward the organ loft before Wellington stopped him with a touch. "My watch, I believe, Tony." He went to Letty's side, held out his hand, and said imperatively, "Come down at once, sir."

To everyone's astonishment, Jeremiah descended with wig

and veil still clutched in his paws. The hat had vanished. He jumped to the Duke's arm, then to his shoulder.

Letty looked solemnly up at the Duke. "I expect I ought not to have brought him to church, sir," she said.

"No," Wellington replied with equal solemnity, "but I am glad that you did."

"You are?"

"I am. I believe he has saved my life, and perhaps the lives of many others."

"Would the explosion have killed you if Mr. Gabriel had not fallen on it?"

"I believe so."

He reached out a hand, and she put her much smaller one in it. Then she looked at Antony, and from him to Charley. Turning back to Wellington, she said, "I think I will take Jeremiah now, sir, and sit quietly in some corner or other until everyone else is ready to depart."

"An excellent idea, Letitia," Alfred Tarrant said sternly from behind them. "I was never more shocked in my life. I shall have a good deal to say to you later, believe me." In quite a different, much more genial tone, he said, "I am Alfred Tarrant, my lord duke. It is my very great honor to be your host this evening at Tuscombe Park."

As Wellington handed the monkey to a crimson-cheeked Letty and turned to reply to Alfred, Charley gently took the wig and veil from Jeremiah and nodded when Letty asked if she could return to her seat. Seeing Rockland approach, his arm around a still-sobbing Elizabeth, Charley stepped forward to meet them, saying anxiously, "Elizabeth, are you hurt? What an ordeal for you! I'm so dreadfully sorry, but if I had had the least notion that there was to be any danger—"

"I know you would never put me in harm's way, Cousin Charlotte," Elizabeth said, dabbing a handkerchief to each eye. "That is precisely what I told my darling William when he said that if he thought for even one minute that you had—"

"Here, now," Rockland interrupted indignantly, "I never said I *did* think it!"

"No, no, my dear sir, and I never meant to give that impression. It was clearly just as His Grace said, that God Himself intended me to be there. Mr. Gabriel would certainly not have flung himself on that exploding chest to save Charlotte, and only think how many others might have been hurt had he not given his life for mine. He will be rewarded, too, I'm certain. After such a magnificent sacrifice, even the most vengeful God could not refuse to reunite him with his beloved wife and his daughter, Annie.''

''Annie! Good mercy,'' Charley exclaimed, looking at Antony. ''Was Annie Gabriel's daughter? Did you know that?''

''I did not,'' Antony replied grimly.

''The way he said 'our Annie' last night, like one speaks of a family member—that's why, this morning, I . . . I had that odd niggling thought,'' she added, hoping he would remember, that she would not have to remind him that it was Elizabeth's constant references to 'our dearest Rockland' that had begun the niggle. She was not surprised, however, when his next words proved that she need not have worried.

''I remember very well,'' he said. ''It is a pity that you could not quite catch the memory then, although I doubt that we would have realized the extent of his distress even if you had. He must have nearly lost his senses when he learned that Annie had not run away to London as everyone thought, but that, in fact, Michael had killed her. Since he blamed the violence in Cornwall on the lack of a military presence here, and he blamed Wellington and Robert Peel for that lack, it cannot have been much of a stretch for him to blame Wellington for Annie's death.''

''But someone must have known of his plan before then,'' Charley protested. ''His Grace received warning of it, after all.''

''Begging your pardon, my lord duke,'' Bishop Halsey said, appearing from behind Wellington with his dignity apparently restored. ''The remains of that poor man having been removed, and the altar cleaned, we have decided to continue with an abbreviated consecration ceremony, as you suggested earlier.''

''Excellent,'' Wellington said approvingly. ''It does not do to submit to adversity." In a louder voice, he added, "Take your seats, everyone."

Facing the milling congregation, the bishop raised his arms, palms outward, and said in a voice of command equal to the Duke's, "Let us pray."

Chapter Twenty-four

Outside the cathedral after the ceremony, several members of the Duke's party suggested that, in view of the unfortunate incident, he should return to the ship at once by the route they had come. However, Wellington scoffed at these unsubtle hints that he might still be in danger, insisting that although his companions could do as they pleased, he would travel back to Fowey through Lostwithiel, and would dine at Tuscombe Park as he had planned.

"Can't disappoint folks waiting along the road to see us," he said. "Not the way rumors will have been flying after that explosion. If we disappear now, word of my death will reach London before I do. Still welcome to dine with you, ain't we, Tarrant?" he demanded, looking sharply at Alfred.

Before that gentleman could speak, Edythe and Elizabeth said as one, "Oh, yes, indeed, Your Grace." Edythe added, "It is a great honor for us, Duke, as you can well imagine, and you will be very glad to see such a grand estate as Tuscombe, I know."

The twinkle in Wellington's eyes as he returned a polite response reassured Charley that he was no stranger to the unfortunate manners Edythe displayed, but catching Lady

Ophelia's disgusted gaze, she bit her lip to keep from grimacing in reply.

She had been looking for Antony, having somehow become separated from him when the bishop called the congregation to order, and she saw that Alfred was glancing around, too, as if he were also looking for someone. She realized then that he had not spoken after Edythe did to reassure Wellington of his welcome at Tuscombe.

Knowing he must have observed the familiarity with which Antony spoke to the Duke, and Wellington's friendly response, she wondered if Alfred feared Wellington might exert his influence for Antony. Suppressing a chuckle, she decided it would do Alfred good to stew a bit longer before he learned that Antony had simply taken advantage of the situation at Tuscombe to suit his own purposes.

Edythe was still chatting in her haughty way with the Duke, although townspeople frequently interrupted to pay their respects to him. Watching them, wondering where Antony had got to, Charley felt a small hand slip into hers and looked down to see Letty standing beside her, looking contrite. Jeremiah peeped out between the folds of her cloak, alert and curious.

Letty said, "Are you angry with me, Cousin Charley?"

Glancing back at the Duke, Charley saw that he was watching them with a pronounced twinkle in his eyes. Nevertheless, she said firmly, "I think you had better be very well behaved for the next few days, young lady. When I so much as think of the way that scamp leapt out and snatched off that veil and hat—"

"Don't scold her," Antony said quietly from behind them. "If she hadn't brought the little beast along, I shudder to think what the consequences would have been. I remember wondering why she came with the servants, instead of with Alfred or Lady Ophelia," he added vaguely, glancing around at the still excited crowd. "I never thought of Jeremiah."

Relieved to see him, Charley said, "I wasn't scolding her. I know Jeremiah saved the day. I just don't want her thinking she can go her own road whenever she chooses." When his only response was to turn back to her with the same odd searching look, she said, "What is it? Has something else gone amiss? Where have you been?"

"Supervising the removal of Gabriel's body from the cathedral. Can you deal with Edythe and Alfred if I am late joining their dinner party?"

"Of course, I can. Good mercy, sir, they are not vicious, merely bad-mannered. Moreover, I shall have Great-Aunt Ophelia and the Duke to look after me. But why should you be late? Are you not traveling with us?"

"Harry Livingston and I mean to stop in Lostwithiel and have a look through Gabriel's house. I want to talk with Harry, in any case, to discuss all that has happened, and since I daresay you will keep Letty with you, we can't talk in the carriage. Hodson and Kerra can ride with the Tuscombe servants, and we'll take the horses. If we ride ahead now, we won't be far behind you at the end. Wellington is in no great hurry at the moment, but they won't wait dinner for us. He will be anxious to get back to Fowey and away with the night tide."

"Do what you must, sir. We can deal with odious Alfred and his wife."

Antony's attention shifted, and when Charley turned, she saw Wellington approaching. Harry Livingston, just behind him, was doing his best to protect the Duke from his well-wishers. Harry smiled and responded to them, but deftly diverted each one who tried to reach Wellington. The task proved nearly impossible, however, until several other members of the Duke's retinue added their efforts to his.

Wellington, oblivious to the tumult, said without preamble to Antony, "Harry tells me the pair of you want to look into things in Lostwithiel."

"Yes, sir. There are still unanswered questions, and I believe we may find the answers to some of them in Gabriel's house. At all events, it's worth taking a look."

"Very well, very well. Get on with it then. Happy to look after your wife and Lady Letitia. Just don't be too long, will you?"

Antony grinned. "Your ability to withstand boredom is legendary, sir."

Wellington looked at him sharply. "I'd give quite a lot to know just what sort of rig you've been running, you young scoundrel."

The grin faded. " 'What fates impose, that men must needs abide; it boots not to resist both wind and tide.' "

"I know a bit of the Bard, myself, young Antony. Don't forget that 'an honest tale speeds best being plainly told.' "

"We'll see about that, sir. 'Having nothing, nothing can I lose.' " Bidding them farewell, he turned and walked back to join Harry Livingston.

Charley's carriage drew up in the square, and as the Duke handed her inside, he smiled and said, "Very thorough, Tony is. Daresay he's annoyed to think Gabriel pulled the wool over his eyes, but he'll soon come about."

"You aren't angry with him about that, are you, sir?"

"No, no, not in the least," the Duke said. "Very fond of Tony. Like to see him re-established, if only to cure his impudence."

"If he would just show his face in London," Charley said, "I don't think he would find it nearly as hard as he thinks."

"Not now, at all events."

"I expect you mean because he is respectably married," Charley said, wondering how much longer that would be the case.

Patting her shoulder in a manner so friendly as to remind her of his reputation for outrageous flirting with any passable female, Wellington said, "Don't trouble your head about the lad. I shall be most interested to learn what he discovers about our Mr. Gabriel. Now, up you go, Lady Letitia! You, too, Jeremiah. I say," he added thoughtfully, "you don't suppose Mrs. Tarrant would allow Jeremiah to join us for dinner, do you? Liven things up a bit, that would."

Choking back laughter, Charley said, "Don't even think about it, Letty. And you, sir," she added sternly, "can just stop chuckling. That was an unconscionable thing to suggest, and you are *not* to encourage her to think it a clever notion!"

Wellington burst into laughter. "Lady Foxearth," he said when he could speak again, "I don't remember the last time anyone took me to task like that. It's a great pleasure to know you, ma'am. I look forward to improving our acquaintance."

Certain the Duke—known to be a high stickler—would not have been so amused had anyone but Letty overheard, and wondering if Antony would approve of her speaking in such a way, Charley smiled weakly.

Stifling chuckles, Letty said with sudden remorse, "Ought we to be laughing so much after so great a tragedy, my lord duke?"

Wellington leaned into the carriage, patted her knee in a much more avuncular fashion than he had patted Charley's shoulder, and said, "Dear child, when the day arrives that we can no longer find cause for laughter, that will be the real tragedy."

"Well, I have frequently observed that people feel better when they can laugh, but how can a person know when it is seemly to do so and when it is not?"

Smiling, Wellington said, "I begin to think our evening will be far more amusing than I'd thought, my dear. You ponder that question on the way home, for although I must seek my carriage now, I look forward to continuing this conversation later."

Leaning back into her corner as the carriage lurched forward, Letty sighed. "He is very kind, and I'd like to talk more with him, but I am very sure they will not want me at the table tonight any more than they will want Jeremiah."

Charley agreed that Edythe would not suffer a child at her dinner table, on this day especially, but they soon found they had both reckoned without the Duke.

Alfred and Edythe had commanded their driver to go ahead of Wellington's cavalcade, so they could be at hand to welcome their guest when he arrived. Driving more slowly, the ducal party made better time than Charley had expected, but they did not arrive at Tuscombe until nearly seven. As the carriages drew up, footmen scurried to assist emerging passengers. Medrose, standing in the open doorway at the top of the sweeping steps, welcomed them with his customary stately bow, and announced that their host and hostess awaited them in the principal drawing room.

"If you will kindly follow me, Your Grace."

They went up the right wing of the staircase and along the gallery to the end, where a footman threw open the tall double doors. Preceding them, Medrose said, "His Grace, the Duke of Wellington, madam—Lady Foxearth, and His Grace's company."

Alfred and Edythe sat in twin wing chairs near the blazing fire. It was clear from Edythe's flushed face and Alfred's frown that they had been having an argument of some sort, but both of them got to their feet and approached Wellington in a manner nearly as grand as the butler's. Charley instantly recalled her grandfather's bluff heartiness, and knew that St. Merryn would have met so important a guest in the hall, if not outside on the front steps. She never missed him so much as those moments when she found herself forced to watch Alfred Tarrant attempting to take his place.

Alfred said in subdued tones, "Welcome to Tuscombe Park, Your Grace. I regret that our company is somewhat thin for the occasion, but we are as yet still largely unacquainted with the gentry in this neighborhood."

Edythe said grandly, "Indeed, Duke, we were certain, after so tiresome a day, that you would prefer a smaller company and some peaceful tranquillity."

"I'm easy to please, madam," Wellington said. He nodded to Alfred and bowed over Edythe's outstretched hand, but Charley observed that he did not kiss it. Easy to please or not, the Duke's interest did not include females of Edythe's stamp.

"I fear you find me still in some distress, Duke," Edythe said, dabbing her lips with a lacy handkerchief. "So upsetting to see our pretty ceremony spoiled."

"Look at it this way, madam," Wellington said. "Many prettier ceremonies may lie ahead, but none, I venture to say, will be as memorable as this one today."

"Very true," Edythe said. "Won't you take one of those wing chairs near the fire, Duke? They are quite the most comfortable in the room. Charlotte, do sit down. His Grace cannot sit until we do, after all. And Letty, dear, run away upstairs to the nursery now with the other children. Good gracious me, if you haven't brought that heathenish animal inside with you! What were you thinking? Alfred, tell her to take it directly outside again!''

Since Letty looked mutinous, Charley said, "If you will ring for Jago, Cousin Edythe, I believe he will be quite willing to look after Jeremiah. As for sending Letty to the nursery—''

"Must forgive me, Mrs. Tarrant," Wellington said, cutting in smoothly. "Afraid I took the extraordinary liberty of inviting Lady Letitia to sit at my right hand tonight at your table. Knew you'd be on my left, of course, but I'm acquainted with Lady Letitia's father, you see. He served as one of my brigade majors at Waterloo. Captain Lord Gideon Deverill he was then. Saw him now and again on the Continent—his charming wife, too— but this is the first time I've had the honor to meet his little daughter. Hope she'll tell me what Gideon's been up to since I last clapped eyes on him."

Charley could see that Edythe was struggling to overcome indignation, and taking pity on her, she said, "I'll find Jago, Cousin Edythe, and take Letty upstairs to tidy up. Where shall I find Grandmama and Great-Aunt Ophelia?"

"In Lady St. Merryn's sitting room, I believe," Edythe replied faintly. "We dine in fifteen minutes, Charlotte, so please don't dawdle."

Letty said happily to the Duke, "We won't be long, sir."

Chucking her under the chin, Wellington said, "See that you aren't, my dear. I'll be counting the minutes."

Charley was afraid that last exchange might prove too much for Edythe's tattered dignity. But as she swept Letty out of the room, she heard the woman say in much her customary way, "Won't you tell us all about your Catholic Emancipation, Duke? I own, I find it difficult to understand how that astonishing law came to pass."

Outside the drawing room with the doors safely shut, Letty gurgled with laughter. "What a thing for His Grace to say to me! Cousin Charley, am I really going to dine with the grownups?"

"You are, darling, so we must find Jago to look after Jeremiah, and then you must tidy yourself as quickly as ever you can. His Grace ought not to have said such an improper thing to you, of course, but I daresay that with only Alfred and Edythe and his own few people to talk to, he really will be counting the minutes."

Antony and Harry Livingston had not arrived when Charley and Letty returned to the drawing room just before Medrose announced that dinner was served, but Rockland and Elizabeth had joined the group, along with Lady St. Merryn, Miss Davies, and Lady Ophelia. When the Duke offered his arm to a beaming Edythe, Lady Ophelia took advantage of the opportunity to say in an undertone to Charley, "Do you really think it wise to allow the child to join us?"

"We've not much choice, ma'am, for Wellington himself arranged it," Charley said, "but have no fear. Letty has often dined in distinguished company, you know."

"More distinguished than this, for that matter," Lady Ophelia said with a sniff.

"Aunt Ophelia, what a thing to say!"

"I did not mean Wellington, for goodness' sake. Not that I hold with his stand on Reform. A woman would deal much better with that, but he has done well enough supporting Peel on his Police Bill, and he *is* the Prime Minister, after all."

"Quite, ma'am," Charley said swiftly, with a warning glance in the direction of Miss Davies, who was near enough to overhear. It was doubtful that she had done so, however, since her attention, as always, centered on Lady St. Merryn's comfort.

Their numbers were uneven, for no one had known how many members of the Duke's retinue would join him, and the number of ladies was limited. In the end, fifteen covers sufficed. The place at Alfred's left and the one on Charley's right remained unoccupied, awaiting Antony and Mr. Livingston. Lady St. Merryn sat at Alfred's right.

Conversation continued sporadically while two footmen served the meal, and Jago took advantage of a surge in the general chatter to inform Charley that Jeremiah was contentedly exploring a bowl of his favorite fruits and nuts in the housekeeper's room. When Medrose caught Jago's eye, the footman straightened abruptly, saying, "Will you have a bit of the dressed crab, madam?"

"Thank you," Charley said, smiling at him.

She could see that although Wellington did not neglect his hostess, he turned more frequently to Letty, and when one of those unexpected silences occurred that strikes every group from time to time, Letty's voice sounded clearly. "But you never explained, sir, how a person can know *when* it is seemly to laugh, and when not."

With everyone clearly listening, Wellington winked at the child and said, "I wouldn't advise you to laugh in church, my dear."

"No, certainly not," Letty said, giving him a look of disapproval. "I thought you would understand me better than that."

"Letitia, that will do," Alfred said blightingly.

"Nonsense," Wellington said. "I began this. Let her go on."

"I just wondered," Letty said patiently, "how one can know when laughter is seemly again after such an event as we witnessed today. Or after any death. I have observed some people—females in particular—who refuse to laugh for fully a year after someone dies. Is that not excessive?"

"Yes, yes, certainly," Wellington said, watching her now with a fascinated eye.

"Then is six months of gloom not also excessive?"

"Lady Letitia," Wellington said, smiling, "I cannot say how much is enough or not enough. What I can say, sincerely, is that it is most unfortunate that by the time you are old enough to accept suitors, I shall be far too old to be one of them."

"That is not a proper answer, sir," Letty said with another of her direct looks. "Moreover, you are already married, are you not?"

"Good gracious," Edythe exclaimed, "what will the child say next? Certainly His Grace is married, miss. He had the honor to marry Miss Kitty Pakenham, Lord Longford's daughter, some twenty-three years ago. She is said to have been deep in love with His Grace, too. So romantic I always thought it, although people do say—''

"For mercy's sake, be silent, Edythe," Lady Ophelia said tartly. "You don't know the first thing about His Grace's marriage, and to be offering it up like another course to be digested with dinner is the height of bad manners. You make me blush, and I can tell you, with all that I have seen in my ninety years, that takes some doing."

"Well, I declare, ma'am, I cannot think what you mean! To have allowed that child to chatter on at the poor Duke until she must have bored him senseless, and then to reprove *me!* What *can* you be thinking?"

To Charley's relief, Medrose took that moment to announce wooden-faced from the doorway, "Lord Antony Foxearth and the Honorable Mr. Livingston, my lady."

Glancing toward them, undisturbed by the exchange that had just occurred, Wellington said, "Well, lads, did you discover the whole yet?"

"We may never know the whole truth," Antony said, taking the empty chair next to Charley and waving Harry to the one by Alfred. "We did find a journal that appears to be Gabriel's, indicating that he was even more adamantly opposed than we thought to the proposed civilian police force. We brought the journal along for you to see. If we are interpreting correctly the bits we have read, it was Gabriel himself who sent to warn you of an assassination plot."

In the midst of the general consternation stirred by Antony's words, Rockland exclaimed, "Did he, by Jove? But why the devil would he do such a thing if the plot was of his own devising?"

Antony exchanged a look with the Duke, and Charley recalled as he did that the others knew nothing about his mission in Cornwall. When they had fallen silent again, he said quietly, "It appears that he did so merely to convince His Grace that he should have a military escort to protect him during his visit here." To Wellington, he added, "At that time, sir, he was sincerely worried about your safety, a concern that later apparently included fear that certain rumors he heard of a plot to wreck a merchant ship might cover a more deadly plot against you.''

Harry Livingston said, ''We think he told Tony about those rumors, hoping Tony might carry enough influence with county authorities to demand that they bring in the military at last. It evidently had escaped his understanding before then that you, sir, would dislike such an action very much, but at some point he learned that you would.''

''Good mercy,'' Charley said, ''I told him that.'' Looking at Wellington, she added contritely, ''I tried to explain to him your views about the military being more suited to violence than peacekeeping. But how,'' she demanded, turning to Antony, ''could he have thought the wrecking scheme was really a plot against His Grace?''

''He points out in the journal that, had Michael's gang wrecked Wellington's ship, they might have killed all aboard to justify scavenging the cargo, using that old legal precedent he once told us about. He said they could have claimed later that they had mistaken the ship for a merchantman and never known who was aboard.'' Turning to the Duke again, he said, ''We were right to think it was learning of his daughter's death that turned him into a fanatic, sir. He mentions several times that he had warned you of the danger, almost as if, having done so, it was quite fair for him to attack you. Even then,'' he added with a wry look, ''he seemed quite remorseful over the need to assassinate you. Evidently, he had come to believe that an important figure had to die to prove that the military is the only force strong enough to control real crime.''

Over the indignant comments that followed, Wellington's voice carried calmly when he said, ''But you, Tony, have proved Gabriel wrong. You showed clearly that an unarmed civilian officer can protect the populace more efficiently than the army can. The number killed today—and last night, too— might well have been enormous had the military dealt with them. Instead a gang of louts are on their way to the Assizes, and the only one killed was the assassin himself.''

Elizabeth said quietly, ''It seems very sad to me. Though I

could not care for him as he clearly hoped I might, I did think he was a good man.''

"He *was* fundamentally good," Antony told her. "Despite the events of the past week, he did many good things for Cornwall, and he was a good mayor for his town. The journal contained no entry for yesterday or the day before, but the last pages are filled with guilt over his daughter's death. Evidently, he had accepted without question Michael's account of Annie running away to London, just as he had accepted their rules of apprenticeship. He had even been a little ashamed of Annie, feeling that she had not lived up to the standard set by his late father and himself. But his ramblings evolved into a fury against what he perceived as a lack of protection against criminals, a lack that, in his mind, had actually resulted in his daughter's murder.''

Harry Livingston said, "Gabriel disliked Michael Peryllys even before he learned of Annie's murder, and seems to have suspected him of leading the coastal gang. Tony and I thought that somehow Gabriel might even have initiated the plot last night, in hopes of catching Peryllys and his men in the act.''

Charley said thoughtfully, "Still, they did catch Michael Peryllys, and if Mr. Gabriel had not revealed what he knew, Michael might still be at large.''

Smiling at her, Antony said, "That's true. The only part that did not come from Gabriel was the information about the merchantman being the real target. I doubt that we will ever know the whole truth about his activities, but if I had paid more heed to the man, I might at least have recognized the real danger sooner.''

"Don't beat yourself for that, lad," Wellington said. "Eat your dinner now, for you are well behind the rest of us.'' Turning to his hostess, he made a quiet remark, and following his lead, the others lowered their voices to a more formal level.

Antony leaned close to Charley and murmured, "I collect from their silence on the subject that you've refrained from saying you once suggested Gabriel as a villain.''

Astonished, she said, "I certainly never thought him capable of such a fearsome act as he attempted today. I only ever mentioned him in the context of wrongdoing because of those old tales about that mayor of St. Ives who connived with smugglers. Did Gabriel really think that by murdering heaven-only-knows-how-many people, he could bring peace to Cornwall? He must have gone mad.''

"We think he did," Antony said quietly.

Polite conversation rumbled around them again until suddenly Rockland said across the table, "I say, Foxearth, I've been thinking about all you've said, and it seems to me you know the devil of a lot about this business. Did you have all that from this journal you say you found in Lostwithiel? And how is it His Grace calls you Tony?''

In the silence that followed, Charley heard a sharp intake of breath from Antony.

Wellington said, "I say, Tarrant, I believe in taking the shortest route in a charge, and I think you must be the chap who wrote the War Office some weeks ago, inquiring into the whereabouts of one Antony Tarrant, late of His Majesty's army. Ain't that so?''

Taken aback, Alfred looked for a moment as if he would deny all knowledge of such a letter, but the Duke and every other person in the room looked directly at him.

Flushing deeply, he cleared his throat harshly and said, "There was such a letter, certainly. Upon the death of the late Earl of St. Merryn, I required to know my brother's whereabouts, but I regret to say that I have never received an answer.''

Wellington said evenly, "That letter was forwarded to me for reasons that need not concern you, sir, but as you must have deduced by now, I was unable then to provide you with accurate details of your brother's whereabouts. You must have been delighted to learn for yourself, however, that he is very much alive.''

Alfred's start of astonishment and the amazed look he shot at Antony were, in Charley's opinion, much too contrived to have been genuine, and his voice sounded strained when he said, "Good God, sir, are you telling me this fellow really is who he says he is? I must tell you that, receiving no reply from the War Office, I assumed my brother was unknown to them and had left no record. As to this man's claim that he was heir to Tuscombe Park, when I realized just moments ago that he has been acting as your agent, I'm afraid I assumed that claim was a mere pretense to create an identity that would allow him to remain in Cornwall without drawing suspicion.''

The Duke did not hide his disbelief. "Good God, sir, would you pretend you never recognized your own brother?''

"I-I've not seen him since I was a child," Alfred stammered.

"Surely you knew of his service to England," Harry Livingston snapped.

"How could I?"

"Because," the Duke said, glancing now at Mr. Livingston, "I made it a point to write to your father when Tony was granted his baronetcy, to tell him of the services your brother had performed. I was circumspect—had to be, of course. At least, I thought I had been," he added with a more piercing look at Harry, who avoided that sharp gaze this time. "Nonetheless, I did make certain he knew that Tony had served England magnificently, hoping he might see his way clear to forgiving him."

"D-did you, sir?"

"I did, and I tell you to your face, young man, I don't believe for a moment that your father would have thrown my letter away. I believe you read it."

When Alfred did not reply, Harry Livingston said acidly, "I can prove that he did. I shall say no more at present, because it is not necessary to make a gift of the details to the world. However, in light of the use to which he put his information, he certainly deserves to hear *much* more. If Tony hasn't figured out your part in this for himself, Mr. Tarrant, you may be sure that I shall explain it to him before I depart."

Alfred looked sick, and Charley saw that Mr. Livingston still avoided Wellington's shrewd gaze. No one said a word. As she glanced toward Antony, Medrose said with his usual stately calm, "Shall I serve the pudding now, madam?"

Edythe opened her mouth to reply, but before she could speak, Antony said, "Bring our port now instead, Medrose. The ladies can take their pudding in the drawing room if they like, but His Grace must leave within the hour if he is to catch the tide.''

"Very good, my lord. Jago, her ladyship's chair, if you please.''

Lady St. Merryn gave a little cry of joy and clapped her hands together, for once having no recourse to her vinaigrette. "Oh, how delightful! Ethelinda, did you hear?''

Not until Jago stepped up to hold Charley's chair did the full meaning of what had just happened strike her. But when the footman moved to assist her, she realized that not only was Antony the rightful Earl of St. Merryn but she was his rightful countess.

Chapter Twenty-five

An overall feeling of constraint kept even Lady Ophelia silent when the women retired to the drawing room. In the face of Edythe's bleak expression, and Elizabeth's evident distress, the next half hour passed with agonizing slowness in monosyllabic attempts at conversation. The gentlemen made a brief appearance then, but only to take their leave and announce that Rockland and Antony would ride to Fowey to see the Duke off. Briefly fearing that Antony had changed his mind and would return to London with Wellington, Charley nearly leapt to her feet to stop him before he caught her gaze and smiled reassuringly. Edythe had looked up swiftly when the gentlemen entered, but Alfred was not with them.

When the men had gone, Miss Davies began to gather Lady St. Merryn's belongings, and Lady Ophelia said, "I believe I will go upstairs with you. This room is too drafty for my old bones tonight."

At once, Charley moved to help her grandmother rise from her sofa, saying, "Letty, dear, we should go upstairs, too, I think."

Neither Elizabeth nor Edythe objected to the mass departure.

"Poor things," Miss Davies said sympathetically when the doors were safely shut behind them.

"Don't be a ninnyhammer, Ethelinda," Lady Ophelia snapped. "Edythe Tarrant and that detestable husband of hers tried to steal young Antony's inheritance."

"I did think that's what it all meant," Letty said thoughtfully, reminding the others of her presence. "Sir Antony is just who he said he was all along, is he not? When no one said exactly that in the drawing room, I didn't quite like to inquire."

"Sensible of you," Lady Ophelia said bluntly.

Lady St. Merryn said in a stronger voice than anyone had heard her use in a long time, "I should call the child's behavior tactful, myself, but one really cannot blame Edythe, you know. She never knew Antony Tarrant at all. And poor Elizabeth was only a baby when he went away to school. You should be pleased, ma'am," she added, smiling at the old lady. "The villains of this extraordinary play are all men."

"Not quite all of them, Grandmama," Charley said quietly as Lady Ophelia snorted. "Angelique Peryllys is no angel. If she did not contribute to Annie Gabriel's death, she certainly knew the manner of it and did nothing to prevent or report it, and she never did a thing to protect the other girls who worked in her shop."

"I never thought her gowns became you as well as your London ones, dear," Lady St. Merryn said complacently, adding in a matter-of-fact way, "I collect that you are not going back to Seacourt Head tonight."

"No, ma'am. I must wait to see what Antony means to do next, but in any case, we had planned to stay tonight, so Mrs. Medrose prepared my old room for me. I am going to put Letty to bed now, but then I will come to your sitting room, if you like."

"Yes, do," Lady St. Merryn said cordially. "Such an extraordinary business, and we still have much to talk about. You do mean to come, too, don't you, Aunt Ophelia?"

"Certainly," the old lady said, using her cane to steady herself on the stairs. "Nothing like a bout of tearing other people's characters to shreds to provide one with an amusing evening."

Charley left them at the landing, but by the time she got

Letty settled and joined them in Lady St. Merryn's sitting room, she found that her grandmother had changed her mind. A smiling Jago was setting up a card table, apparently for whist. Amazed, Charley glanced at Lady Ophelia.

The old lady shrugged. "I don't mind. I daresay you won't."

"Of course, she won't mind," Lady St. Merryn said tartly. "Don't put my salts bottle there on the table, Ethelinda. I shan't need it, and it will only get in my way."

They played one rubber, but then Lady Ophelia declared herself too old to stay up so late playing for mere chicken stakes, and announced her intention to retire.

Charley said, "I'd better go, too, I expect. Antony will be home soon."

"Not if I know men," Lady Ophelia said. "Even if they got there in an hour and the boat sailed at once, which I doubt, your Antony and that Rockland will have stopped at an inn for something to wet their whistles before returning."

"Antony said they would come straight back," Charley said, smiling.

"Well," Lady Ophelia said, picking up her stick, "I've always said the only man a woman can trust is a dead one, but I'll have to admit your Antony shows more promise than most. You may walk with me, my dear."

Bidding the others good-night, they strolled slowly along the corridor toward Lady Ophelia's bedchamber. Abruptly, the old woman said, "Rockland did you a greater service than he knew, did he not?"

"How much, exactly, do you know about what happened, ma'am?" Charley asked, not certain how else to reply to such a statement.

"Rockland told me, when he collected me, that he had played you a trick but that everything would come right in the end, and I know he meant to marry you properly once he'd taught you a lesson. Had to tell me that much, of course, but then you stayed married to Sir Antony."

"It seemed the best thing to do at the time," Charley said.

"Good gracious, child, I've known you all your life and

been closer to you than most. I must suppose you knew what you were doing.''

''I agreed to stay married to him only because of his duty to Wellington and his need for a plausible reason to remain in Cornwall. And I only agreed under certain ... certain conditions.'' She avoided the old lady's eye, reaching past her to open the door to the bedchamber for her.

Lady Ophelia paused on the threshold. ''I won't ask what those conditions were or if he met them,'' she said mildly. ''I don't think those things matter now. He had his excuse to remain in Cornwall all along, did he not?''

''He means to get the marriage annulled now,'' Charley said, barely able to get the words out. ''I insisted upon it, you see. Now, even if I say I have changed my mind, he's given me no cause to think he has changed his. In any case, he will think—'' She broke off, unable to finish.

''He will think you want to stay married now because it is the only way you can remain Countess of St. Merryn. Is that it?''

Her throat aching, Charley nodded. Tears welled into her eyes.

''You're a fool, child, and if he don't see that, he's a fool as well.'' Lady Ophelia stepped into her room. ''Go to bed,'' she said. ''I won't tell you what to do. I shall leave that to your husband.''

Walking slowly to her bedchamber, Charley knew that she had told at least one untruth to the old lady. She did have some cause to believe Antony cared for her. She had known that much since the night before when he had shaken her. A man who rarely allowed others to touch his emotions did not react violently simply because he believed a woman had put herself in danger. Antony did care, but whether he knew that himself, or cared enough, was more than she could guess.

Kerra was waiting for her.

''Has Sir Antony returned?'' Charley asked.

''No, my lady, but he told Hodson to make up a bed for him in that little chamber at the end of the corridor by the servants' stair, so he won't disturb you when he does.''

Tempted though she was to await his return, Charley knew that he and Rockland might well be several hours yet, so she went to bed. And although she expected to lie awake, plagued by thoughts and memories, she soon fell asleep.

When Antony and Rockland returned an hour later to find that but for a few servants the rest of the house had retired, Rockland suggested a drink in the library.

"Thanks all the same," Antony said, "but I think I'll go to bed."

"Had a surfeit of my company, have you?"

"I'm glad you went with me," Antony replied honestly. "I could not let Wellington go without discussing with him what I mean to do next, and it has been a long day. Without your company, I'm likely to have fallen asleep in the saddle. Yet again I owe you my gratitude, Rockland."

"Again, eh? I take it that you have seen the light then, and wish you luck. You will need it."

"I'm not certain we're speaking of the same thing," Antony said, "but I don't deny that I can use some of that luck. Good night."

Upstairs, he looked into Charley's room and when the light from his candle fell across her face, he saw that she was asleep. He longed to climb into bed with her, but he dared not do so, for he had done much thinking, despite Rockland's cheerful chatter, and had come to a difficult decision. He loved her too much to insist that she stay married to him. If it meant lying to the bishop, he would do it to set her free. He was glad she was asleep, but decided to settle the business first thing in the morning.

Since he neglected to tell Hodson to wake him at his usual time, he overslept, and by the time he scrambled into his clothes and got to Charley's room, she was nearly dressed. His first view was her reflection in the looking glass, and he thought her eyes lighted up when she saw him, but when she turned around, she raised her eyebrows at the sight of his shirtsleeves and wool breeches.

"Forgive my appearance," he said from the threshold. "I didn't wait for Hodson but grabbed the first thing that came to hand, in order to catch you before you went downstairs. You may leave us, Kerra."

"Just a moment, Kerra," Charley said. "She has not finished doing my hair, sir."

"Wear it down, or she can come back later. I want to talk to you."

A flush tinged her cheeks, but she did not look angry. Turning back to her dressing table, and watching him in the mirror again, she said provocatively, "I don't want to wear it down. Do it up the usual way, Kerra. Kerra!"

But the maid, (wisely, in Antony's opinion) bobbed a curtsy and fled.

Glaring, Charley said, "I don't like it when you give orders to *my* maid."

"Do you think you can put your displeasure aside for just one moment and attend to me?"

"What is it?" She looked at him with sudden concern. "Did something else happen? Letty! Has she—"

"Letty is fine. Jeremiah is fine. As far as I know, everyone is fine." A glance showed him that the door had not latched behind Kerra. He shut it, watching Charley. She had turned to face him, but the flush in her cheeks was gone. She seemed pale. He said gently, "In fact, angel, the time has come to conclude our bargain."

"So you really mean to have it annulled?"

Dared he think she was dismayed by the thought of parting? He hoped she was. He did not think he could bear it if she were not. He said bleakly, "I cannot ask you to remain married to a man whom all society shuns."

"That's just as well," she said, glaring at him again, "because I would be most uncomfortable being married to such a man."

"Any woman would," he agreed, but the bleakness vanished.

"She would be a pitiable creature, but she would not be your wife, Antony."

"I don't think you understand how much my past—"

"Oh, piffle, Antony, as if I had not heard all that before. You needn't look daggers at me, either. I know you hate being interrupted. Like that stupid Petruchio, you'd prefer a wife who would pledge such duty to you as a subject pledges to his prince, but I could never be such a wife, and I will *not* listen quietly to such fustian."

"Fustian, is it?"

"It is." She stood up, moving to face him, and he felt amazement again at how much presence she had. Although she had compared him to Petruchio, he had no wish to change a hair on her beautiful head. She was still glaring at him.

She said, "Antony, the world—even the polite world—has changed. In those days, when your father behaved so cruelly, Englishmen favored liberty over order, ignoring reality. One cannot enjoy freedom without order. It was simple masculine idiocy to think England's greatest enemy would abide by our ancient notion of courtesy. When your opponent refuses to abide by rules of fair play, for you to stick to them buckle and thong simply gives him an absurd advantage."

"Well, yes, but—"

"Don't argue with me," she snapped. "You will find that you are mistaken about the reception you will receive in London. In fact, Antony, I begin to believe the Fox Cub has turned coward."

"Now, just a damned minute!" He stepped toward her, pausing only when he saw that her eyes were twinkling in anticipation. "So I'm a coward, am I?"

"Perhaps that's a bit harsh, but you cannot have thought it out logically. Not all of your friends deserted you. There is Harry Livingston, for example."

"He is a fool. It was he, apparently, who added a note to the letter he wrote for the Duke to my father, telling him the French had turned *Le Renardeau* into some sort of folk hero. We learned over the port that Alfred had read that note, found more tales of *Le Renardeau* on his own, and used his knowledge to start the rumors that have plagued me. He swears he meant no harm, but Harry believes he hoped the Fox Cub would be captured and put down by the authorities."

''He cannot have wanted you killed,'' Charley said, growing pale again.

''I choose to hope not, but although he put on a good show of remorse when Harry took him to task, in the course of it, he admitted that he was pretty certain of my identity when he heard me quoting the Bard. Said he had often heard of my habit of spouting the stuff, and it gave him a turn. As I recall, the rumors began only after I arrived here at Tuscombe. Still, it would not suit me to see my brother clapped into prison.''

''He certainly has much to answer for,'' Charley said, ''but you won't divert me so easily. What of Wellington? Is he also a fool?''

Antony was silent but not for the reason she doubtless believed. After years of loneliness, to know now that the woman he loved was fiercely determined to fight his battles, even if she had to fight him, was a pleasure he did not want to interrupt.

She shook her head at him. ''My dear sir, when your idiot father—yes, idiot, and I will not apologize for calling him one. When he gave you the cut direct at Brooks's, Wellington was not in England. Now your father is dead, and the Duke is Prime Minister. You have money and vast estates—at least, I hope you intend to claim the estates. You cannot leave Alfred here.''

''No, I won't,'' Antony said with a smile. ''I'll settle one of the lesser Tarrant estates on him. Grandfather Foxearth's, I think. That will do for him and Edythe.''

''Foxearth is your mother's name?''

''Yes, I adopted it because it was not my father's.''

''I see, but that brings us back to what I was saying.''

''I think I have heard enough,'' Antony said, stepping nearer. ''There is only one more thing I want you to tell me.''

''What do you want to know?'' Her voice was soft, and he heard a catch in it.

''I want to know if you still hold men in such aversion that you could never bear to remain married to one.'' He heard a catch in his own voice then, and it was all he could do to hold her gaze until she answered him.

She smiled and reached out a hand to him, saying, ''I expect it was never the men I disliked so much as the way they made me feel about myself. They give off such an air of superiority, even the least of them, and try to control the women they meet. But I tried to control things, too. You were right about that, and so was Rockland, in everything he said when he tricked me into marrying you. I used feminine wiles to manipulate him, and other men like him. But he was like clay in my hands, so he brought out the worst in me. Since he seemed not to mind the way I treated him in return, I never knew he cared how I behaved toward him, or others, and he never did care enough to stop me when he disapproved."

Antony grinned. "Do you think he could have stopped you, my little shrew?"

She laughed. "He said the same thing, and in truth, I doubt that he could have. He certainly would never have been as rough and ready as you were."

"Perhaps not, but one can scarcely blame him for avoiding that temper of yours."

"I know. I like myself much better since I married you."

"And me? How do you feel about me, angel?"

Looking suddenly and uncharacteristically shy and unsure of herself, she bit her lip, then said, "You've changed, too, you know."

"I know," he said tenderly, "and I also like myself better. I have, ever since I was trapped into marriage with a naughty angel."

"You were not trapped. You knew perfectly well what Rockland was up to. *I* was the one who was trapped."

"Kate the curst," he murmured, adding gently, "You can be free at once if that's what you want, angel. As I said, I am a man of my word."

"You said you would never lie to the bishop," she reminded him, color flooding her cheeks again. "W-we have consummated our marriage."

"I decided last night that if you want to be free, I will do what I must."

"You will?"

"I will, unless— You aren't pregnant, are you?"

His blunt question clearly caught her off guard, and he knew she had not considered that she might already be bearing his child. The thought warmed him. It warmed him more when she smiled mischievously and said, "I think maybe I am."

Summoning up a heavy frown, he said warningly, "Kate the liar."

She shrugged, looked away, then said innocently, "How can I be certain?"

"Easily. I won't touch you again until you know."

Charley moved toward him. "You lie now, my lord." She placed one hand against his chest and looked up into his eyes. "Can you *swear* that you won't touch me? Not the littlest, tiniest touch of your smallest finger? What if I refuse to make a similar promise? What if I touch you here, or here, or—"

"Madam, enough!" He caught her hands and pulled her closer. Looking right into her eyes, he said, "I love you. Now, do you want the damned annulment or not?"

"Not," she said, and with that one word filled him with a joy greater than any he had ever known. Then she bit her lip again, and said earnestly, "You don't think I'm saying that just because I want to be Countess of St. Merryn, do you?"

"I do not."

"Good." She leaned against him, adding, "Because now that I've got a properly trained husband, I do think it would be foolish to turn him loose again." Freeing one hand, she slipped it between them, clearly intending to torment him further.

Stifling laughter, he said, "Angel, I'm warning you. Stop that."

"What will you do if I don't?"

"Put you over my knee."

"I don't think so. Your bed would be so cold and prickly tonight."

"Cold I understand, but prickly?"

"Thistles."

"I see." Without more ado, he scooped her into his arms.

"Antony, put me down! Where are you taking me?"

"To a bed, angel of my consolation, that I know is neither

cold nor prickly, to teach you how to submit properly to your husband.''

"Are you going to throw Cousin Charley in the pond again?'' Letty asked from the doorway. Jeremiah sat on her shoulder, watching them inquisitively.

Antony chuckled. "What an excellent notion!''

"You dare," Charley murmured.

"No annulment?''

"No annulment," she agreed, "but the independence you promised me is quite another matter, sir.''

"Great-Aunt Ophelia says independence is important for a female," Letty said, "because it teaches her to make decisions in matters that affect her life.''

"I was referring," Charley said sweetly, "to a more tangible form of independence, to money, in fact. In my name, sir, at Drummond's Bank.''

"Some men," Antony said thoughtfully, "would call that extortion. Others would call me a fool for letting my wife control any money, since I should then be unable to control her.''

"That, sir, is precisely what Great-Aunt Ophelia means by independence.''

"Tell me you love me first.''

"Now *that's* extortion.''

He laughed and bent his head toward hers, murmuring, "Kiss me, Kate.''

Her eyes danced. "Well, I will, but only because I have been wanting to do so these past twenty minutes. Oh, and I *do* love you, Antony, so much!'' When she could speak again, she said with a wicked twinkle, "But may I have the money?''

"You may.'' He began to kiss her again, thoroughly, forgetting Letty's presence.

The child said, "You called her Kate, sir, but I have read *The Taming of the Shrew,* and I don't think Petruchio would approve of her asking for money, do you?''

"Petruchio," Antony said, chuckling, "never knew your Cousin Charley.''

Dear Reader,

I hope you enjoyed *Dangerous Angels*. Regarding the historical background, although there were several attempts to assassinate the Duke of Wellington while he was Prime Minister and before, none of them took place at a cathedral consecration in Truro. The Seraphim Coffer and the sacred vessels from the abbey on the River Tamar are likewise products of the author's imagination.

The details about the Metropolitan Police Bill are as accurate as I could make them, as are Wellington's political positions and actions (except for his participation in the cathedral consecration). The House of Lords passed the Police Bill the week after this story ends, and it became law in September 1829. Only recently have British police officers begun arming themselves with more than a nightstick.

John Knill was indeed a mayor of St. Ives who was suspected of running a gang of smugglers; and the activities of the Cornish smugglers are taken from actual events, as is the treatment of Annie, Jenifry, and the other apprentices.

If you have not encountered Charley before, and would like to know more about her, she appears as a child with her cousin Melissa Seacourt in *Dangerous Illusions* (Pinnacle, June 1994), and as a young woman—likewise with Melissa—in *Dangerous Games* (Pinnacle, June 1996). I hope you will also watch for *Highland Secrets,* coming from Zebra in October 1997.

Sincerely yours,

Amanda Scott

If you enjoyed *Dangerous Angels,* be sure to look for
Dangerous Illusions, and *Dangerous Games,* available
now at bookstores everywhere. And for a taste of Amanda
Scott's next fabulous book, coming next fall from Zebra
Books, turn the page for . . .

HIGHLAND
SECRETS

Chapter One

Edinburgh Castle, February 1752

The guard's keys rattled against the heavy pine cell door, creating a strange echo in the chilly, stone-vaulted corridor of the prison. Before turning the large key he had fitted into the lock, the burly, grizzled man glanced over his shoulder at the plump, silent laundress behind him.

He said gruffly, "Mind ye behave now, lass. If ye don't, I'll leave ye locked up wi' her ladyship, and mayhap give ye a touch o' the cat tae teach ye manners."

"Aye, ye'd like that, ye fousome auld flit," the laundress muttered. Shifting her large bundle to her other shoulder, barely missing the guard's head as she did, she waited with scarcely veiled impatience for him to open the door. The hood of the dingy, dark-gray wool cloak she wore against the winter cold was drawn low, concealing her face, but her tone left no doubt of her irritation when she added, "Yon prisoner be Lady Maclean, and the gentry looks after its ain folk. Ye'll no want her complaining tae your governor aboot a lack o' proper respect."

"Och, an she'll be doing that anyways, won't she? Got a

tongue on her sharp as a needle. Dinna be long now," he added, pulling open the cell door. "I'll be a-locking of this after ye, so raise a shout when ye want tae be let oot again."

She said no more, stepping past him into the cell. There was a squint in the door above her eye level, so she had no assurance that he was not watching. Taking a chance, she pulled her handkerchief from her sleeve and stuffed it into the hole, then watched to see if he would push it back. When it stayed put, she turned to face the cell's occupant. Making a slight curtsy, she said in quiet, much more cultured tones than those she had assumed with the guard, "I bid you good day, madam."

The light in the cell was dim and gray, coming as it did through high, barred vents from an overcast sky. The slender, middle-aged woman sitting on the lone wood bench narrowed her eyes, then stiffened, leaning forward to see her visitor more clearly. With patent disbelief but in a reassuringly firm voice, she said, "Diana?"

Grinning, Diana Maclean dropped the bundle to the floor and stepped nearer, pushing back the wool hood to reveal her glossy dark curls and sparkling hazel eyes. "Aye, it's me," she said ungrammatically with a chuckle of relief, "though you would do better to call me Mab or some such thing, in case that turnkey overhears us. Moreover, we must make haste, Mam. Are you well?"

"Aye, as well as anyone could be in this dreadful place. I've not known whether to wish I had company or be glad they have left me alone. At least they did not stuff me into that odious room above the portcullis where they kept the Duchess of Perth and her daughter for a full year after Culloden. They say the Tolbooth is worse than this, too, but I find that difficult to believe. At least they've let me have a proper chamber pot. Most folks make do with a bucket." She was still looking at Diana as though she could not believe her eyes. "What's that on your teeth?"

"Boot blacking," Diana said, slipping off her cloak. "It tastes terrible, but Neil said the turnkey might try to kiss me, and I thought if he did, black teeth might put him off. As to your being alone," she added, "be glad you are, and that they did not secure you with irons and shackles. I'd never have dared to do this if they had, but thank heaven, Neil was easily able to learn that you had a cell all to yourself.''

"Aye, because they've freed every other woman of rank,'' Lady Maclean said bitterly, "and I've tongue enough still to scorch the ears of any fool trying to house a less suitable female in here. But what do you think you are doing? I am glad they've allowed you to visit, of course, but why the blacking and those dreadful padded clothes? Your rank alone ought to protect you from that detestable turnkey.''

"I hope you don't think the clothes too dreadful, Mam,'' she said, stripping off the faded blue dress she wore and the bulk of her plump figure with it, "because you must put them on. Quick,'' she added, straightening her shift. "We must make haste, for Neil is outside the gate, waiting to take you to Glen Drumin.''

Lady Maclean still had not moved, and now she looked puzzled. "Are you out of your senses, child? You cannot mean to take my place here.''

"That is exactly what I mean to do, Mam. I've got a proper dress for you in that laundry sack, which you will wear under this fat-laundress costume of mine, and I'll put on the clothing you take off. Fortunately that brown stuff frock is not notable enough to make the guard wonder why you are still wearing it instead of a clean one.''

"I doubt he notices much,'' her ladyship agreed, "but surely you and Neil did not come to Edinburgh alone, Diana.''

"No, Dugald and some others are waiting with him,'' she said. "They've got a coach to take you from the city, and once beyond its walls, there are horses to speed you to the MacDrumin. He will keep you safe. After all, he's successfully hidden his business from the English authorities and their Scottish lackeys for years.''

"But dim as that turnkey is, he'll see the difference between us in a blink!''

"No, he won't. He never saw my face, and if you take care, he will not see yours either. He expects a plump woman with a bundle to leave, and that is what he will see. The only attention he paid me was when he tried to put his hand on my backside. I growled at him that all he would get if he forced his attentions upon me was a dose of the French pox, so I doubt he'll attempt to molest you.''

"Diana, you never said such a vulgar thing to him!"

"I did. There was no time to worry about decorum. You've been here nearly a month, and all on a whim. Neither the Duke of Argyll nor the Lord Advocate seems to see aught amiss in ill-treating women when they can no longer lay hands on our menfolk. However, I will *not* allow you to stay here when I can help you escape. We Macleans look after our own. The fact that the only men left to us now are boys and young lads like Neil does not mean our ways must change. Now, pray, do as I bid you. Mary assured me that she sees no insurmountable obstacle to the plan, and in any event, this is no time to argue its merits.''

"I suppose not," Lady Maclean said, standing at last and allowing Diana to help her remove the stuff gown. "It will be good to have fresh clothing on, I can tell you. They would not let me have visitors, but even Argyll is not so lost to his senses as to deny me an occasional clean dress. Oh, Diana, do you really imagine your plan will serve? Even if Mary believes in it, it seems far too rash and daring.''

"Don't think about that," Diana advised, making quick work of the gown's buttons and laces. "Think only about reaching Glen Drumin in safety.''

"But I don't know that I should go to Glen Drumin," Lady Maclean said, frowning thoughtfully. "Really, my dear, do you think that wise? The MacDrumin is our cousin, to be sure, but an Englishman owns his estates now, you know.''

"Yes, of course I know, Mam," Diana said, waiting while she stepped out of the gown before handing her a fresh one from the bag. "The Earl of Rothwell has owned MacDrumin's land since shortly after the defeat at Culloden, but Rothwell and Cousin Maggie spend their winters in London or at his estate in Derbyshire, and will not return until summer. We'll have whisked you away long before then, and mayhap even have arranged for a pardon. After all, you did nothing to harm anyone, only cutting down a few trees.''

''You forget they say that I have refused to submit to the *proper* authorities,'' Lady Maclean said bitterly. ''How they expect any self-respecting Scotswoman to bend a knee to German George is more than I can think.''

''Aye, but we need not discuss that now,'' Diana said hastily, adding once she had fastened up the new gown, ''Here, let me fling this laundress costume on over your head. You'll feel a bit burdened in it, I expect, but you need wear it only till you are safely in the coach. Neil has a bonnet for you, with a widow's veil.''

''You've gone quite daft, Diana. I should not let you do this.'' But Lady Maclean held up her arms obediently so that Diana could slip the costume on over her fresh gown.

''You have no choice, Mam,'' Diana said, smiling as she retrieved the stuff dress, stepped into it, and pulled it up. ''If we waste time arguing about this, I'll undoubtedly be caught and identified. Then they'll clap me in here with you, and much as you might think you would enjoy my company—''

''That will do, Diana. Here, turn round and let me fasten that for you. Did you say you spoke to the guard when you came in? That was foolish. What if he makes it necessary for me to speak and recognizes the difference in our voices?''

''He won't do that if you just mutter at him. Oh, and I used broad dialect, too,'' she added, looking over her shoulder. ''I know you were used to scold whenever we aped speech of the lower orders, but you must admit our skill has proved useful more than once. Your voice is like enough to mine that if you remember not to come the gentlewoman over him, he will not hear any difference.''

Turning, Diana looked critically at the now-plump Lady Maclean, then reached to push curling salt-and-pepper curls back from the older woman's forehead. ''Cover your hair with the hood, Mam. He did not see mine, but he has seen yours, and we must give him no hint that aught is amiss.''

Obeying, Lady Maclean said, ''But what about you? He'll

see you at once. Really, Diana, I cannot simply leave you like this.''

"Yes, you can."

She spoke with more confidence than she felt, but for her mother's sake, she did not betray any fear. Giving Lady Maclean a quick hug, she tousled her own hair a little more, stepped to the door, and pulled her handkerchief from the squint. Then, calling for the guard before she had a chance to lose her nerve, she turned to the bench, raised the handkerchief to her face and sat down.

Trying to imitate her mother's posture, she slumped forward, hoping to look tired and depressed. The handkerchief concealed her face. Her hair remained uncovered, but in the dim gray light, she did not think he would note the difference between her glossy tresses and her ladyship's graying curls.

Hearing the keys rattle against the door, she fought down rising panic and avoided looking at Lady Maclean. It was not the first time circumstances had forced that stately dame to play a role other than her natural one, so Diana did not fear any foolish mistake. Still, she would feel boundless relief if no one raised a hue and cry within the next few minutes.

The cell seemed darker when her mother had gone, leaving her with her thoughts. She felt little of the triumph she had expected to feel. In truth, she felt only surprise that the ruse had succeeded, despite her cousin Mary's assurance that there would be no trouble.

Upon arriving at the Castle, Diana had crossed the drawbridge over the dry ditch without incident, for the two guards were chatting and showed no interest in her or anyone else. Walking between the high stone walls of the inner barrier, she saw three more soldiers, guarding the portcullis gate at the far end. But they showed interest only in an elegant crested carriage that had drawn to a halt there. With no more than a glance at her bundle and costume, one of the men waved her through.

She had visited the Castle only once before, some years ago, but Neil and Dugald had given her excellent directions, and she strode along with as much confidence as if she had really been the laundress who was to visit the following day. Neil had learned about the woman through some means of his own, and they had pieced together the details of their plan accordingly.

The crested carriage rattled by as she passed the powder magazine, but she did not catch even a glimpse of its occupant. It moved on up the hill toward the new governor's house and parade ground. Seeing the house, she knew she was going the right way.

Following the hill up and around, she passed through the old archway known as Foggy Gate and found herself on the hilltop site of the original Castle. To her left were the shot yard and St. Margaret's Chapel. To her right lay the governor's garden and the palace close.

Crossing the garden, she had felt her confidence increase in a surge of energy. She felt no fear. Neil had been the reluctant one, for Diana had only contempt for Argyll's men, knowing they tended to dismiss women as harmless and weak. Not one paid her any heed when she walked briskly into the close.

A soldier at the entrance to the great hall directed her to the prison vaults beneath it, where the turnkey, though he had never seen her before, willingly showed her to Lady Maclean's cell. And there she sat now, waiting tensely.

At least half an hour passed without any alarm before she began to wonder how she would get out. They had talked at length about the possibility that she might not get out at all, and despite the show of confidence she had put on for her mother, she rather feared she might be there for some time. It would no doubt be horrid, but better that she should suffer, she told herself, than Lady Maclean.

The cell was nearly bare. Its only furnishings were the hard bench on which she sat, the chamber pot, and a shelf containing a pitcher and mug. The whole place smelled nasty, and the taste of blacking on her teeth made it worse. Since she had no reason now not to remove it, she got up to look into the pitcher, intending to dampen a corner of the threadbare blanket on the floor by the bench to scrub her teeth. A large cockroach floating in the water banished that thought, however.

Fighting a wave of nausea, she scrubbed her teeth with her

sleeve and, perversely, wondered when they fed the prisoners. Not that she could imagine eating their food if it matched the rest of her dreadful surroundings, but come mealtime, they were sure to discover her.

To one of Diana's active nature, the next hour crept like a century. The bench was hard, there was no pillow, and when she picked up the blanket, it smelled like vomit, making her glad that she did not need the foul thing for warmth yet.

The longer she sat, the more amazed she was to have found Lady Maclean in good health. Getting up again, she began to pace, but in the close confines of the cell, she found the exercise frustrating and tiresome, and sat down again.

A constant low hum of noise assaulted her ears, moans and whining punctuated by occasional crashes or bangs, even a shriek once, though that was not repeated. The solid door muffled the sounds, however, so when she heard men's voices nearby, she jumped up to see if she could hear anything of interest. To her surprise, she had no sooner reached the door than she heard the unmistakable sound of a key in its lock, and barely had time to leap back before the door swung inward.

The turnkey said cheerfully, "I've brung ye visitors, me lady. There she be, me lor— Ay de mi!" The man crossed himself and put out both arms to block the way of the men behind him. "Dinna touch her, me lords! She must be a witch or worse, for by all that's holy, I swear I niver seen that wench afore."

Diana ignored him. Watching the two well-dressed men behind him, she stood straight, squaring her shoulders and giving back look for look.

The older one, a dark-haired, long-faced man, gaped back at her. The younger looked blank. He was taller than the first and more powerful-looking, with broad shoulders and a narrow waist. His hair was also dark, but his eyes were gray, the irises light like pale granite with black rims around them. He looked steadily at her, his chiseled countenance still revealing no particular expression.

Diana shifted her gaze back to the older man, finding it easier to meet his dark frown than the other's steady look. This was not how she had imagined her unveiling. The pair were neither guards nor soldiers. Both wore elegant clothing and carried themselves like men of substance and authority, especially the younger one.

The elder, looking irritated and confused, said, "Where is Lady Maclean?"

Glancing back at the younger man, certain that of the two he was the more dangerous, Diana quickly collected her wits. Making a deep curtsy, she instilled as much awe in her voice as she could when she said, "She be gone, your honor, but dinna be wroth wi' me. I couldna help it. I swear tae ye, I couldna!"

The older man said brusquely, "Turnkey, who the devil is this female?"

"Did I no just tell ye, sir, that I've niver seen the wicked wench afore? This be magic, I warrant, and black magic at that."

"Don't be a fool," the younger man said. "She passed through neither these stone walls nor the iron bars of that grating yonder. There is only one way into this cell and that is through this door. You must have let her in yourself, turnkey."

"Och, but the only one I let in were the laundress, me lord. I swear it on me blood and bones, and I let her oot again me self. Only her ladyship were within."

The older one said, "What have you done with Lady Maclean, wench?"

Diana did not look up or speak. Her courage was fast deserting her, and it was not at all difficult to let her hands shake or to show signs of growing panic.

Before she realized that he had moved, a large hand clasped her shoulder. She felt its warmth through the material of her dress, and its size and strength. Her breath caught in her throat. She could not have spoken then if she had wanted to.

"Tell Governor MacTause what happened, lass. You are the laundress, are you not?" When the governor uttered an exclamation of shock, echoed by the turnkey, the young man said, "It is the only logical explanation, you know. The laundress is the only one who came in, and only one person has left. Therefore, since this is not Lady Maclean, she must be the laundress. Your dangerous Jacobite tree-cutter has escaped, MacTause.''

''But, me lord,'' the turnkey protested, ''this wench don't look at all like the laundress! That one were round as an onion.''

''Padding, I'll wager. Who put you up to this, lassie?''

Feeling tongue-tied for perhaps the first time in her life, Diana bit her lip. She wished fervently that she could weep at will like Mary could. All her cousin had to do was widen her eyes, let her face crumple, and huge tears would spill down her cheeks. But although such a skill might aid her now, she lacked the ability, and when she looked up into the gentleman's face, she knew that if she tried to lie to him, her tongue would betray her. His gaze was too penetrating, his intelligence too plain. She looked quickly down again.

The turnkey said grimly, ''You just leave the wench with me, your lordship. I'll soon have the truth out of her. The claws of me cat will—''

The hand on her shoulder tightened, but his voice remained calm when he said, ''That will not be necessary. She has been frightened enough already, and you can see with half an eye that she is no hardened conspirator.''

Governor MacTause said grimly, ''Just how do you propose to make her tell us what she knows, Calder? I remind you, she has allowed an important prisoner to escape, and the law is quite clear about such a crime.''

''As to the importance of your prisoner,'' Lord Calder said, ''I dispute that, as you know. We have more pressing matters on our plate than making war on women, MacTause, which is why I asked to see this dangerous prisoner of yours. You and his grace have kept her locked up for no good cause that I can see.''

''She broke the law,'' MacTause said, ''and in any event, it is not my business to determine who stays and who leaves.''

''It is your business to see prisoners treated properly, however. To house any woman of quality in a place like this—'' He broke off abruptly, then added in a more even tone, ''But we will not pluck that crow again. As to how I shall learn what this young female knows, why, I shall ask her. Look at me, lass.''

Reluctantly, Diana forced her gaze to meet his. His eyes were like flints. His dark eyebrows were thick, nearly meeting above the bridge of his nose. The bones of his cheeks showed prominently. His chin was strong and well formed. His lips—

He said sternly, ''Tell me the truth now, or you'll find yourself in an abundance of trouble. If you speak truly, I promise no one will harm you.''

''Now, see here, Calder—''

''Do you deny my authority, MacTause?''

''No, of course not, my lord. I merely wish to point out to you—''

''We can discuss your concerns later at length. Just now, I want to hear what this young woman has to say.'' He paused, watching Diana and waiting.

Diana licked her lips, then said in words scarcely above a whisper, ''I dinna ken what ye expect of me, your lordship. Aye, sure, ye canna think they told me aught but what they wanted me tae do. I . . . I were sore affrighted, sir. Deed, and I be affrighted the noo, as weel!''

That last bit, at least, was no lie. Lord Calder, whoever he was, was no one with whom to trifle. Despite his sensible attitude about her mother's imprisonment, every instinct shouted at her to be wary of him. She fell silent again, waiting.

When he did not speak at once, she felt as if he were peering into her soul and seeing the truth written there in flaming letters, but when he spoke, he said only, ''You see, MacTause. Clearly, some damned Jacobites have forced the lass to help free her ladyship. She cannot know more about them or she would tell us. She is poor and uneducated, and practically shaking in her boots with terror. I say we send her about her business. We gain naught by punishing her for this.''

''But she helped a felon escape! We've not had an escape since I came to the Castle, my lord. Surely, you cannot mean to let her off with no punishment at all.''

''I doubt you'd get anything but the labor for your pains,'' Calder said, ''but if you must punish her, simply deny her future access to the prisoners. Hunger teaches a harsh lesson, sir, and the lass doubtless counts on income from doing their laundry to feed herself and perhaps a family as well.''

"But, me lord," the turnkey protested, "this lass—"

"Silence, you," the governor snapped. "Had you done your duty, the Jacobite woman would still be here. I've a good mind to—"

"You would be wise to do nothing in haste," Calder said with a sharp look. "Once people begin casting blame hither and yon, there is no telling whom it will splash, MacTause. Little said is soon amended, you know, so 'tis better, I think, to send the lass on her way with a warning and a fright. I will undertake to explain the whole to his grace in such a way as to show that no one could avoid what occurred. No doubt he will set his men to pursue her ladyship, but that we cannot help."

"She is a dangerous Jacobite traitor," MacTause repeated stubbornly.

Diana's fists clenched. Pressing them into the folds of her gown, she kept her gaze fixed on the stone floor of the cell lest they detect her fury in her eyes.

Calder said calmly, "The widow Maclean is only a woman, MacTause, and even the most dangerous Jacobites were powerless against Argyll and the Crown."

She dared not look at any of the three men. She did not doubt that Calder and MacTause assumed she was the usual laundress for the prison or that the turnkey had tried to inform both gentlemen that he had never laid eyes upon her before that day. The next few seconds increased her tension. Would the governor ignore Lord Calder's advice and order her whipped? MacTause seemed to perceive a threat in the younger man's words, but not knowing where Calder derived his authority, she could not guess how much influence he wielded.

Abruptly MacTause said, "It shall be as you wish, my lord, of course. Turnkey, take her up to the guard in the hall, and have her put outside the castle walls. He will learn her name and inform the guards at the entrance that they must never allow her to step a foot inside these walls again. Do you understand?''

"Aye, your worship," the turnkey said grimly. "Come along o' me, wench."

"Take care, turnkey," Lord Calder said gently. "She is not to be harmed."

Unable to believe her good luck, Diana nevertheless did not breathe easily again until she was outside the main gate, where she found Dugald awaiting her.

"I did not expect anyone still to be here," she said, tucking her hand in the crook of the tall Highlander's arm. "Did Mam get away safe?"

"Aye, they've got her outside the city gates and away," Dugald said. "I stayed 'cause I knew our Kate would have me head if I left afore I learned what had become o' thee. We'd best make haste the noo," he added. "We'll no catch them up, but your Neil did say he'd wait atop Firthin's Hill to see could he spy us a-coming. We didna think to see thee out so soon, Mistress Diana."

"Nor did I," Diana admitted. "A certain Lord Calder is visiting the governor, and it was he who set me free. Do you know aught of him, Dugald?"

"Nay, lass. Did they just turn thee out then?"

"I had to give the soldiers a name," she said, chuckling. "I said I was Mab MacKissock."

"MacKissock?"

"Aye, 'tis one of the Campbell septs. Let them blame some misbegotten Campbell for Mam's escape."

Dugald laughed heartily, and feeling truly free again, Diana laughed with him.

Rory Campbell, Lord Calder, watched the burly turnkey lead the girl away, wondering why he suddenly felt reluctant to let her go. One look into her golden eyes had told him she was no practiced traitor. In any case, she was too young to have been part of the troubles that had ended at the Battle of Culloden six years ago.

She looked no more than seventeen, and since girls of her class aged quickly, she was probably younger. He had not asked her age because he had not wanted to suggest more interest in her than he already had suggested. MacTause was no particular friend of the Duke of Argyll's, but Argyll's temper was uncertain at best, and Rory had no wish to annoy him further.

He had tried his kinsman enough by disagreeing with him about keeping Lady Maclean in prison. As the duke had pointed out, furiously, Rory did not even know the woman. But Rory believed the Highlands would prove easier to rule if the English and his Campbell kinsmen would stop persecuting the few remaining Jacobites for no greater crime than believing a Stewart had more right to the throne than the man they called German George.

As the youngest Baron of the Scottish Court of Exchequer, he was sure he could accomplish his duties more easily if the previous owners of the lands he administered would cooperate with his factors instead of trying to block them at every turn. The best course of action seemed obvious to him, but Argyll disagreed and, as chief of his clan, deserved and demanded respect and obedience. Still, Rory knew no one would be less amazed than Argyll to hear he had come to Edinburgh to meet Lady Maclean and judge for himself just how dangerous she was.

"Will you still be staying the night, my lord?"

MacTause's question pulled him from his reverie. They had been walking silently back toward the governor's house, and lost in his thought as he had been, he had paid little heed to his surroundings and none at all to his companion.

Realizing that to make an unnecessary enemy would be foolish, he smiled and said, "I must get back to Perthshire, sir. My plate is full these days, and much as I'd like to accept your offer, I cannot."

When the older man bit his lip, looking worried, Rory added matter-of-factly, "What comes of today's event is more important than the event itself, you know. I'll tell his grace you took quick action to see that such a thing cannot happen again."

"You may be sure of that, my lord."

Rory took his leave, hoping MacTause would recall his warning. To punish the turnkey would do no good. To show mercy would be much wiser, for the man would take good care never to let a pretty face sway him again.

As he settled back into his comfortable carriage, he felt a twinge of pity for the golden-eyed laundress. Though he had saved her from whipping, or worse, he feared she would find herself left destitute or forced into the stews to survive. She would not starve on her back, for she was attractive, but such a life would be short.

He put her firmly out of mind then but found to his surprise that her image continued to intrude upon his thoughts in the days and weeks that followed. Busy as he was, he could not forget her. Thus, when administrative duties for the Exchequer took him into the western Highlands six weeks later, he was pleasantly surprised, albeit astonished, to discover her employed as a maidservant at Castle Stalker.

His first thought was that her Jacobite friends must have helped her find work after she lost her livelihood, but he rejected that thought when it entered his mind. Not only had MacTause discovered that her name was MacKissock, which was nearly as good as being a Campbell born and bred, but no Jacobite had access to Stalker. Moreover, he doubted that respectable Highlanders of any political persuasion would encourage an innocent young female to work there.

Located as it was on a sea-girt rock, guarding the strategic point where Loch Linnhe met the Lynn of Lorne, Castle Stalker was presently the strongest, most impenetrable of the Campbell strongholds in the Highlands. Its primary occupants were rough Campbell men at arms. Its purpose was strictly military.

Rory decided then, logically, that Mab MacKissock must have grown up in Argyll, which was strongly Campbell country, and was perhaps kin to Stalker's captain. However, he was able to indulge himself in that comfortable conclusion only until his host informed him that a dangerous Jacobite prisoner had escaped the previous night from a tower room previously believed to be impregnable.

DANGEROUS GAMES   (0-7860-0270-0, $4.99)
by Amanda Scott

When Nicholas Barrington, eldest son of the Earl of Ul-
combe, first met Melissa Seacort, the desperation he
sensed beneath her well-bred beauty haunted him. He
didn't realize how desperate Melissa really was . . . until
he found her again at a Newmarket gambling club—being auctioned off by her father to the highest bidder. So,
Nick bought himself a wife. With a villain hot on their
heels, and a fortune and their lives at stake, they would
gamble everything on the most dangerous game of all:
love.

A TOUCH OF PARADISE   (0-7860-0271-9, $4.99)
by Alexa Smart

As a confidence man and scam runner in 1880s America,
Malcolm Northrup has amassed a fortune. Now, posing
as the eminent Sir John Abbot—scholar, and possible
discoverer of the lost continent of Atlantis—he's taking
his act on the road with a lecture tour, seeking funds for
a scientific experiment he has no intention of making.
But scholar Halia Davenport is determined to accompany
Malcolm on his "expedition" . . . even if she must kidnap
him!

YOU WON'T WANT TO READ
JUST ONE—KATHERINE STONE

ROOMMATES (0-8217-5206-5, $6.99/$7.99)
No one could have prepared Carrie for the monumental changes she would face when she met her new circle of friends at Stanford University. Once their lives intertwined and became woven into the tapestry of the times, they would never be the same.

TWINS (0-8217-5207-3, $6.99/$7.99)
Brook and Melanie Chandler were so different, it was hard to believe they were sisters. One was a dark, serious, ambitious New York attorney; the other, a golden, glamourous, sophisticated supermodel. But they were more than sisters—they were twins and more alike than even they knew . . .

THE CARLTON CLUB (0-8217-5204-9, $6.99/$7.99)
It was the place to see and be seen, the only place to be. And for those who frequented the playground of the very rich, it was a way of life. Mark, Kathleen, Leslie and Janet—they worked together, played together, and loved together, all behind exclusive gates of the *Carlton Club*.

Available wherever paperbacks are sold, or order direct from the Publisher. Send cover price plus 50¢ per copy for mailing and handling to Penguin USA, P.O. Box 999, c/o Dept. 17109, Bergenfield, NJ 07621. Residents of New York and Tennessee must include sales tax. DO NOT SEND CASH.

ROMANCE FROM JANELLE TAYLOR

ROMANCE FROM FERN MICHAELS

DEAR EMILY   (0-8217-4952-8, $5.99)

WISH LIST   (0-8217-5228-6, $6.99)

AND IN HARDCOVER:

VEGAS RICH   (1-57566-057-1, $25.00)